Bruce Be

Murder Unseen

A detective novel

LUCiUS

Text copyright 2021 Bruce Beckham

All rights reserved. Bruce Beckham asserts his right always to be identified as the author of this work. No part may be copied or transmitted without written permission from the publisher.

This is a work of fiction. Names, characters, places and incidents either are the product of the author's imagination or are used fictitiously. Any resemblance to actual persons, living or dead, events and locales is entirely coincidental.

Kindle edition first published by Lucius 2021

Paperback edition first published by Lucius 2021

For more details and Rights enquiries contact:
Lucius-ebooks@live.com

Cover design by Moira Kay Nicol
United States editor Janet Colter

EDITOR'S NOTE

Murder Unseen is a stand-alone crime mystery, the sixteenth in the series 'Detective Inspector Skelgill Investigates'. It is set in the vicinity of Carlisle, the county town of Cumbria, and the 're-wilded' valley of Ennerdale, which lies in the far northwest of the English Lake District – a rugged National Park of 885 square miles.

THE DI SKELGILL SERIES

Murder in Adland
Murder in School
Murder on the Edge
Murder on the Lake
Murder by Magic
Murder in the Mind
Murder at the Wake
Murder in the Woods
Murder at the Flood
Murder at Dead Crags
Murder Mystery Weekend
Murder on the Run
Murder at Shake Holes
Murder at the Meet
Murder on the Moor
Murder Unseen

Glossary

Some of the Cumbrian dialect words, British slang and local usage appearing in *Murder Unseen* are as follows:

Abeun – above
Allus – always
Arl – old
Alreet – all right (often a greeting)
Bangers – sausages
Bait – packed lunch/sandwiches/snack
Beck – mountain stream
Bewer – girlfriend
Birl – spin
Blag – cadge/bluff
Boot – trunk (of car)
Bo-Peep – sleep (Cockney)
Bothy – mountain hut
Butcher's – look ('butcher's hook' – Cockney)
Ciggy – cigarette
Cluedo – board game, *Clue* in North America
Cuddy – donkey
Cur dog – hardy fell sheepdog
Deek – look/look at
Donnat – idiot
Fell – hill, mountain
Gan – go
Gill – small ravine
Ginnel – alley
Girt – great
Happen – possibly, maybe
Half-inch – steal ('pinch' – Cockney)
Hause – mountain pass
Heaf – fellside habitually grazed by sheep
Hogg – lamb that has finished weaning
In-bye – walled pasture near the farmstead
Int' – in the

Kaisty – fussy about food
Lonnin – lane
Lowp – jump
Mancunian – from Manchester
Mash – tea/brew tea
Misper – missing person (police slang)
Nowt – nothing
Off pat – rehearsed
Ont' – on the
Owt – anything
Parkin – sticky cake of oatmeal, treacle and ginger
Pike – peak
Pony - £25 cash (Cockney)
Quicks – fast bowlers (cricket)
Reet – right
Reiver – thief (generally of livestock)
Rommel – poor quality
Scran – food
Scrow – mess
Sneck – latch/lock fastener
Tarn – small mountain lake, usually in a corrie
T' – the (often silent)
Tek – take
Thee/thoo – you
Theesen – yourself
Tod – fox
Us – me
Water – lake (Old Norse)
While – until
Wukiton – Workington
Wyke – inlet where a boat may be landed
Yat – gate
Yowe – ewe

1. THE CASE FOR DS JONES

Mid July, Friday – The Partridge Inn

'Sorry I'm late.'

'You're sounding more like me every day, lass.'

Emma Jones, Detective Sergeant, narrows her hazel eyes in a decidedly amused manner. It would be a little disingenuous of Skelgill to suggest that he might similarly apologise; his argument, if pressed, being that timekeeping in his job is out of his hands; external events are the master of a detective's agenda. However, she can appreciate that there is some substance in his assertion, and the inaccuracy is more one of semantics than sentiment; a more apt rejoinder might have been, "Tell me about it". But she knows her colleague well enough by now to understand that what Skelgill says and what Skelgill means often bear only a loose connection; trickier to perceive is whether he intends it or not. But on this minor point of tardiness there is no dubiety.

Conscious of, but not objecting to his gaze she slips out of the jacket of her tailored navy suit and drapes it over the spindle-back chair opposite him. But then she slides nimbly around what was once a sewing machine table to alight beside him on a repurposed church pew. She half-rises to readjust the embroidered cushion, perhaps reflecting upon the fact that pews were not designed with comfort in mind, and certainly not for the enjoyment of alcohol; this old wood must have absorbed many a lesson to the contrary. However, her choice of seat is informed by Skelgill's placement of the beverages; before her are two glasses, one with ice and lemon and the other an inch of colourless liquid, and a bottle of tonic water. Skelgill points to the glass nearest to him.

'That's gin. I didn't know what your plans were.'

DS Jones glances at him, her expression a small kaleidoscope of possibilities, and not easy to read. But she exhales softly and reaches for the indicated glass.

'I need this. That was pretty awful, Guv.'

7

Skelgill starts, pressing back against the oak settle but then jerking forward as though he, too, finds the austerity not quite to his liking. For what must be the cosiest bar in the Lake District, the snug at The Partridge has its flaw in this regard, albeit nothing that a couple of drinks cannot remedy. As discomfort ebbs the ambience takes hold; there are worm-ravaged beams like blackened honeycomb; nicotine stained walls hung with hunting scenes; a good hundred caramelised whiskies illuminated from behind; the low background chatter of local voices, creaking like the handpumps that dispense real ale to traditional straight glasses; the aroma of yeast and hops and wood smoke. These external sensations blend with the growing inner warmth to make it a haven hard to leave, once anchored.

'I've only just got here.'

Skelgill gestures at his brim-full pint of pale Jennings ale. Untouched, it is presented as evidence – perhaps in case she suspects he is already on his second.

DS Jones might be excused for thinking that Skelgill has decided to ignore her entreaty – or, more likely, that he has ignored it but doesn't know it. But in fact for once she would be wrong on either count.

'I was in with the Chief. We've agreed you should lead this Carlisle case – if there's owt to it.'

DS Jones makes an involuntary kind of gasp and, when she was about to mix up her gin, instead she simply drinks neat from the glass, swallows and gasps again – this time the burning alcohol the cause. She stares into the liquid for a moment as if surprised by its potency. Then she downs the rest. Skelgill laughs. DS Jones gives a quick shake of her head, like a cat bothered by a fly.

'Run that by me again, please, Guv.'

But Skelgill begins to rise and with some difficulty untangles his legs from the unforgiving seating arrangement. He crosses to the bar – raising a smile from the girl serving with something he says – and returns promptly with another gin. He sees that the trepidation in his colleague's eyes has been replaced by a glimmer of exhilaration.

'You call the shots. Leyton's tied up with these farm burglaries. I've had next week booked off for months and the Chief's insisting I take it. She reckons I'm spoiling her stats.'

'What will you do?'

'I'll be kicking around here. I've just put the boat in along at Peel Wyke.' Suddenly he seems rather reticent. He indicates loosely their surroundings. 'They've got a guest coming that wants a couple of sessions with a fishing guide. They've given me the use of the staff flat in the old stable block. It's empty at the moment.' Skelgill produces a key with a brass fob labelled "tack room" and lays it on the table surface. 'It doesn't save much of a journey – but –' (he taps his beer glass) 'it takes driving out of the equation for an early start – and the breakfasts are half decent.'

DS Jones is looking vaguely amused – perhaps knowing his longstanding antipathy to the idea of guiding; however, she does not remind him. Now he makes a nod in the direction of the bar.

'They've even set me up with a tab.' There is a note of triumph in his voice. He regards her questioningly; he seems to be seeking some accord. 'Handy place to meet.'

DS Jones combines gin and ice and tonic before taking a more conservative sip than previously. She sits somewhat impassively, before she responds in a considered manner.

'Cool.'

Skelgill picks up his pint and holds it towards her and she reciprocates. He makes up for lost time, inhales and swallows about a third of the ale. He smacks his lips.

'What was so awful?'

Now DS Jones has to gather her wits. She stiffens, as if garnering her lapsed resolve. So he was attuned to her lamentation.

'Well – I met the parents – Mr and Mrs Jackson?' She intones it as a question to confirm this was his understanding of the purpose of her mission. 'They're beside themselves – they're in their late sixties.' She pauses reflectively. 'I don't know why I didn't expect that – after all, Lisa Jackson is thirty-seven.'

'It's not old.'

DS Jones remains unflinching.

'It's not. She's in the prime of her life.' She turns to regard Skelgill earnestly. 'She's just started seeing a new man, whom she apparently really likes.'

Skelgill, mollified, drinks but raises his eyebrows, as if to say, "there's your first line of enquiry".

DS Jones reads this and responds accordingly.

'The Jacksons don't know who he is – just that he's called Gary. But there's been a long-term on-off relationship with a married man, Ray Piper.'

Now Skelgill nods more circumspectly; but the name rings no bells – there is no reason why it should. He looks like he is wondering whether to pursue this conversation. His gaze flicks to the clock behind the bar; usually running about five minutes slow, its hands approach eight p.m.

'It might be a storm in a teacup. These things usually are.'

But DS Jones is shaking her head. She seems to be staring at the girl serving without actually scrutinising her.

'The parents, Guv – they would know.'

'Do yours know – what you get up to?'

'Actually – yes, I keep them informed – because of the risks we face – and the hours.'

'But she's a grown woman, all the same.'

DS Jones makes a sign that she will rewind the narrative.

'She owns a maisonette in a cul-de-sac, Goosehills Close – off Warwick Road?' (Skelgill nods to indicate he knows the location; it is the main route into Carlisle from the east.) 'She texted them twice this morning – initially from home and then during her regular walk to work. She'd asked if they wanted anything from the supermarket. Her mum needed eggs so she'd replied that she'd drop them off later. Her firm shuts at four on a Friday; she'd told them she would be there by half past. They didn't hear from her during the day – which they'd thought was unusual. Then when they'd not heard by five they tried to call her – but her mobile was going straight to voicemail and she didn't respond to texts. She doesn't have a landline but they

10

phoned a neighbour. Lisa Jackson's car was parked in its allocated place but there was no answer at the house. That was when they called us.'

'Maybe a crowd went straight from the office to the pub. Poets day, and all that. They're probably still there – we're not even talking four hours. If her phone's out of charge – or there's no signal.'

But DS Jones is again shaking her head.

'Obviously by the time we were involved the office was closed for the day but I managed to get one of the partners – the fire brigade have a contact number for the emergency keyholder. Lisa Jackson never turned up for work today. Nor phoned in sick. The company director said both aspects were out of character – that she was almost always at her desk before the official start time of eight-thirty.'

Skelgill has a vague sense that he is beginning to do exactly what he discourages in his subordinates – to speculate – but he continues, regardless.

'Happen she's eloped with the new lover boy – thrown caution to the wind.'

'Guv, at risk of repeating myself, I come back to the parents. They're obviously very close. They normally hear from her half a dozen times a day. She's considerate – they say she always thinks about whether they'll worry about her – she's their only child. And she asks them to pop in and feed her cat if she knows she's going to be later than six.' Now she turns to look intently at Skelgill. 'I just know about this, Guv.'

One of a large dysfunctional family of madcap brothers who spent most days scattered to the four winds, anxiety of this domestic nature is alien to Skelgill. From an early age intergenerational communication was neither sought nor provided – although the brood could be relied upon around teatime to home in on the likes of lamb hotpot, drawn by aromatic tentacles to their humble source. But, reflecting upon his colleague's assertion, in mitigation he reminds himself that when he feels some incongruity he does not fight it. So why should he expect her to?

He finishes his beer and, gathering their assorted empties, he rises.

'So what will you do, lass?'

DS Jones seems to delay her answer, as if giving herself the opportunity to change her mind.

'Look – I know I'm the one always quoting the data – ninety percent of mispers are false alarms.' She runs a carefully manicured finger around the rim of her remaining glass. 'But – I don't think I should leave this until Monday. I want them to know I care.'

Skelgill frowns. An onlooker, unacquainted with the nature of their conversation, might think it is across the decade that divides the couple that he stares, and wonder what is their relationship, this out-of-the-way rendezvous, the secluded inn that nestles in woodland beside the old coaching road. But closer to the mark would be the recognition of some value that he shares with his companion, albeit her sentiment is of a more altruistic nature. Skelgill is the cur dog that senses a yowe is lost on the fell, that will relentlessly quarter the ground, deaf to the shepherd's whistles, literally dogged in its mission, driven by some inner determination that it will not be defeated. He relaxes, and his features take on a more pragmatic demeanour.

'Give them a call now.' He gestures to her phone on the table. 'If you've got no signal ask Charlie – he's probably in the office behind reception. Mention my name – he'll let you use the landline.'

DS Jones lays a palm over her handset.

'Actually, I did just ring them from my car. To say I'd circulated Lisa's description and that we're looking out for her. Also to let them know that we've checked with all the local hospitals and that there have been no admissions in her name or matching her description.'

Skelgill, tilting the glasses, hovers.

'So, what?'

'I think I ought to see the ex-boyfriend first thing in the morning.'

He seems to read something into his colleague's manner.

'Want us to come?'

He uses the vernacular 'us' meaning he alone.

'But – there's your fishing. And – if I'm supposed to be leading this.'

Skelgill gives a dismissive toss of the head and turns away.

'You don't have to decide now – sleep on it.'

2. RAY PIPER

Saturday morning – to Carlisle

DS Jones finishes her phone call and waves to Skelgill. He breaks off his conversation with the driver of the fish van that is delivering to the kitchen door of The Partridge. He jumps into the passenger seat and DS Jones pulls away. Her expression is pensive.

'No news.'

He says it more as a statement than a question.

'They've not heard from her and there's no sign that she has been back to her house. Her phone is still not responding. And we've had nothing – no reports or sightings.'

They sit in silence for a few moments; DS Jones steers the car across the junction of the busy A66. As they continue on a narrow winding lane she refers to Skelgill's attempts to glimpse Bassenthwaite Lake through the foliage to their right.

'You really needn't come, Guv. What about fishing?'

'Where did you think I was at five?'

DS Jones ponders his rejoinder. For Skelgill to curtail his angling – on what seems to be a perfect summer morning, clear and calm with promise in the air – raises the question in her mind of whether he may be struggling to delegate. She reflects that in fact he is at once good and bad at this particular managerial skill – typical of him! It is a dichotomy captured in the way that he will peremptorily abandon his subordinates without a word of explanation – and yet rarely commend them when they subsequently use their own initiative and present him with new findings. But 'good' is probably too generous, and 'bad' likewise too harsh – if indeed these adjectives are appropriate at all. Fashioned – assembled – wired-up as he is, he relies almost entirely on intuition – and just how does one delegate instinct?

Such ambiguity aside, he had been swift to volunteer his support when she had mentioned meeting Lisa Jackson's ex-boyfriend. Of course, there may be more to that than poor delegation – but, she has to admit, a chaperone is welcome, if only he does not cramp her style.

'I might need you to direct me. I used the satnav on my phone to get here.'

It seems appropriate that she is driving – and Skelgill appears happy about this, too. For once he gets to look at countryside that so often flashes by.

'Better hang a right here, then.'

'Oops, yes – it's easy to miss.'

'Got to cross the Derwent – unless you want to end up in Workington.'

He cranes to see past her as they turn onto Coal Beck bridge – the view of the outfall from Bassenthwaite Lake. Afloat, Skelgill often imagines the river as a separate entity, a ribbon of colder water hurrying from the Borrowdale fells, that snakes unseen along the bed of the lake, a tangible headstream that leads migratory salmon and sea trout to their mountain spawning grounds. Apart from one rainy day last week the weather has been dry by Lakeland standards, and the reconstituted watercourse is benign, really a shallow trickle between exposed rocks. But the Derwent is to be respected; the fastest river in Europe, it perennially confounds the best brains in Cumbria Water's flood prevention department.

DS Jones responds to his interest in the lake.

'Did you catch anything out there?'

Skelgill makes a rather scornful growl.

'Can thee not tell, lass?' He exaggerates his local accent, holding up splayed fingers as though expecting them to be scale-spangled. But she shakes her head. 'Must be that fancy soap.' For confirmation he puts his hands to his face and inhales. 'Aye – a couple of jack pike – but nowt to write home about.'

DS Jones makes to speak, to offer encouragement – that he has plenty of time – but a junction is approaching and he interjects.

'Left at the pub – then all the way until we meet the A595 at Bothel.'

15

'That's a right turn, I think?'

'Aye.'

DS Jones concentrates on the manoeuvre; Skelgill notes that she takes extra care to make sure the road is clear, and is diligent with her mirrors as she accelerates away. That said, keeping within the limits she drives with efficient purpose; she seems to have the bit between her teeth.

'I was surprised how quickly I got here. I thought I would be ages late.'

'Carlisle's only twenty miles as the crow flies. You're used to coming down the M6. It'd be nearly thrice the distance.'

'Sure.'

Now heading due north, they pass the great roadside boulder that marks the official boundary of the national park, and it strikes Skelgill that here more than in most parts the countryside quickly sheds its wild character. There are a couple of minutes of unkempt pastures, overrun by common rush and marsh thistle and sparsely populated with sheep that eke out a dismal living; but almost in the blink of an eye the landscape is entirely agricultural, and unattractive – a contrast heightened by modern farming methods that discourage small fields, hedgerows or diversity of any kind. Unless one were to turn and view the fells that are gathered like storm clouds on the retreating horizon, the traveller could be excused for thinking he or she were in almost any part of rural England. Even the Anglo-Saxon place names signposted at junctions create ambiguity, the likes of Sunderland, Wigton and Thursby – left behind are the Old Norse suffixes of –*thwaite* and –*keld* and –*beck*, 'clearing' and 'spring' and 'stream' respectively. But this is still Cumbria, indeed this region the old county of Cumberland, of which Carlisle with its imposing near-millennium-old castle has long been the administrative capital. Though modest in size the town accounts for more than a fifth of the population of what is the third biggest county in England by area. As such, Carlisle probably punches above its weight; it has a university, a cathedral that dates from 1122, a football league team founded in 1904, a mainline railway station on Britain's key north-south artery, and no less than three junctions on the M6 motorway. Probably of more interest to Skelgill, however, is that it sits astride a renowned salmon river, the majestic Eden.

That Skelgill and DS Jones have travelled cross-country means they enter the conurbation from the southwest, leaving the trunk route at a junction marked by a sign that incorporates both the tourist attractions and directions to the city crematorium. Perhaps they read this simultaneously – a reminder of the gravitas of their mission – for they both inhale as if to free themselves from the soporific shackles of the car's soundproofed interior and the light Saturday morning traffic, which has lulled them into feeling that this is not a working journey.

DS Jones seems to sense what Skelgill would want to hear.

'Ray Piper lives on the outskirts at this side of town. I got his address from Lisa Jackson's parents. They're obviously quite familiar with him – without being on friendly terms, if you see what I mean. I don't think they approved of Lisa going out with a married man. They told me that last autumn for about three months he moved in with her. But then he went back to his wife just before Christmas – the Pipers have two school-age children.'

'Was that the end of the affair?'

DS Jones narrows her eyes, though it coincides with a curve in the road that brings them momentarily into line with the rising sun.

'Apparently not. They think there has been continued contact – but she doesn't give them a running commentary because she knows it upsets them. Their view is that he's been taking advantage of her.'

'What age is he?'

'Early forties. I haven't had chance to run a check.'

She glances a little guiltily at her colleague – as though this is a significant oversight. But Skelgill just shrugs.

'See as we find, eh?'

DS Jones smiles appreciatively. Skelgill is the last person to reprimand her for a lapse in protocol.

17

'There is one thing, though, Guv.' She pauses, for sufficiently long for Skelgill to look at her. 'They're work colleagues.'

Skelgill does not especially respond. He turns his gaze back to the road ahead, though as they travel forward his eyes seem unfocused. After a few moments he inhales, and then holds the breath before he finally speaks.

'So, the wife and bairns – they might be home.'

It is a bland remark and unrelated to this new revelation, but in a practical context a significant point.

'I imagine so, Guv.' Now DS Jones has a determined look about her. 'But it can hardly be a secret – if he moved in with Lisa Jackson. At least – not from his wife.'

Skelgill nods grimly but does not comment. DS Jones seems to recognise a landmark ahead, and checks her rear-view mirror and indicates to turn right.

'They said it's at the junction with the BP garage – Coniston Drive – number one, actually.'

'It'll be that first house on the left.'

DS Jones completes the turn and draws to a halt across a makeshift driveway that has no dropped kerb. The house is part of a terrace of four, and the austere nature of these, and those others along the street, suggests they are former corporation properties, snapped up by private buyers during Margaret Thatcher's people's home-buying revolution. When they were built in the 1950s, car ownership was minimal, especially on an estate like this, and little provision was made for parking. Now the majority of householders have dismantled their walls and made hardstanding of their front gardens. It is an untidy look, leaving little room for greenery, the most common embellishment a black satellite dish hung beneath the soffit.

All police officers notice cars and their registration plates, and number one Coniston Drive has two vehicles crammed into its frontage. There is a dark blue rust-spotted Ford Fiesta that Skelgill calculates is actually fifteen years old, and a five-year-old white BMW 7 Series with a chequered black go-faster-stripe decal along each side. The latter looks incongruous in its surroundings. A lot can be deduced from a man's choice of car;

they are worn like designer clothing to boost the ego; and here Skelgill reads someone who wishes to impress beyond his means, the flashy marque, the oversized sedan – but a long way from new, a budget second-hand selection that would only fool a certain kind of victim.

'What does he do?'

His question is the natural corollary of his train of thought. DS Jones answers with less bias in mind.

'Again – at the moment I only know from what the Jacksons told me. He's a project manager – that may not be his exact job title. The firm they work for – it's called InnStyle – it undertakes refurbishment for hotels and pub chains. Lisa Jackson is an interior designer. Ray Piper's job is to oversee the actual reconstruction work.'

'Well paid, do you reckon?'

DS Jones looks quizzically at Skelgill; salaries are not something that is normally on his radar.

'I suppose a bit above average – but I don't think he's a director or a partner, or anything like that.'

Skelgill is staring censoriously at the property.

'He's not much of a prospect. Mid forties, lives here – second-hand motor.'

DS Jones might wonder what underlies Skelgill's assessment – but he does not give the impression of self-referencing. Perhaps he simply makes a pertinent observation. And it interests her – now that she is leading the case – to understand what he sees, what he thinks – or feels. And at least he is letting her know.

'I suppose it depends on your perspective – I mean – on Lisa Jackson's perspective.' Now she falls silent as thoughts well up. But she decides to share them. 'I don't know if he's her boss – but probably he's more senior. If she looks up to him – and if she's a little bit vulnerable – single, lonely, maybe. Or he might just be charming, witty and handsome.'

Though DS Jones's tone is even, Skelgill interprets there to be a hint of irony in her rider. He rises to the challenge.

'Let's find out if I've got a twin.'

He thrusts open the passenger door, but he hesitates and turns to his colleague. He sees that despite the flippant exchange she is taking a moment to compose herself. She checks her naturally streaked blonde hair and what minimal make-up she wears in the driver's mirror. She has on the same smart navy suit in which she arrived at The Partridge yesterday evening, but a different blouse in pale cerise that is quite low cut and which hitherto he had not appreciated. For his part, though not exactly scruffy, his casual attire would be more in keeping were they investigating in a rural rather than suburban environment; but appearance is no impediment to Skelgill. He addresses her in an upbeat tone.

'Don't fret – I promise I'll only stick my oar in if you get lost for words.'

DS Jones grins gratefully, but there is the faint suggestion in her eyes that she does not believe for a minute that he will be able to hold his tongue. Now, any reticence she has felt she casts off with a shake of the head and she is quick to lead him briskly between the two parked cars to approach the front door. There is a bell-press, but she uses the letterbox to rap firmly three times. Skelgill seems to approve of this. He can see from the position of the keyhole that the door will open from the left, and he stations himself about a yard behind his colleague, in line with the corresponding jamb.

Almost immediately there is a clatter of footsteps on a staircase, but surely too rapid to be an adult, and indeed a child's voice – a boy it sounds like – cries out a protesting "Mam!" A moment later the door opens – it is not the boy – but a grown man.

Skelgill ignores him. Looking past into the hallway he sees a boy of maybe eleven – barefooted but otherwise clad in a Manchester United football strip – push open what is the kitchen door to reveal another younger boy similarly attired, seated and squashing a slice of bread and jam into an already stuffed mouth; and a smallish slim woman of around forty with long dark uncombed hair and wearing a pink towelling dressing gown, bending over a work surface as though she is making more

20

sandwiches. The older child shrieks vociferously, "Mam – Cole's took my socks!" and he feigns a rabbit punch at his brother – who immediately sets up a fake bawling accompanied by cries of denial. The mother, turning to intervene, glances along the hallway – and, though she cannot presumably perceive all that much, her expression is one that startles Skelgill – for it is surely a look not of embarrassment for her domestic predicament, but of consternation for the presence of the two strangers. She leans past the boy nearest to the door and closes it. The din continues from within, but is damped by the barrier.

All this in the several seconds it has taken DS Jones to establish the householder's identity and introduce the detectives with their full titles. Skelgill turns his attention to the man. A couple of inches above average height and of trim build with short brown hair, he wears smart black jeans, a fresh pink check short-sleeved shirt beneath a lightweight tan leather jacket and polished brown brogues. He looks ready to go out – he even has on a pair of classic driving gloves, the type with perforations across the knuckles and along the fingers, and holds in one hand an insulated travel mug; tucked beneath the same arm he has a copy of the local daily newspaper. He appears detached from the disorderly episode that is unfolding behind him.

'How can I help?'

DS Jones addresses him squarely.

'It's in connection with your colleague, Miss Lisa Jackson. I would understand that you might wish to come outside, sir.'

She ends with an inflection that implies a question, although there is equally an undertone of authority in her delivery. Thus far Ray Piper's expression has remained impassive; now there is a minute but distinct hint of hostility, if only in an involuntary constricting of the pupils.

'Why – what's she been saying?'

Skelgill is watching the man intently, albeit outwardly casually, his own expression an avuncular, rather disinterested concoction that surely suggests boredom with going through the motions, as they must be, whatever they want. But what Skelgill sees might be equally misleading: there could be extreme self-control; or

21

very little feeling – or perhaps it is neither of these. Ray Piper's features – a severe, narrow mouth, sharp nose and almost lashless cold grey eyes – are set amidst hairless skin that seems tightly stretched over the entire skull to produce a mask-like appearance. The ears are unnaturally small and sharp. It is a disconcerting countenance.

DS Jones does not immediately answer the man's question, and in the momentary hiatus it appears he adopts her suggestion, for he steps down and pulls the front door shut behind him. For a moment he stares at DS Jones's car that blocks his exit. Then he takes a couple of paces to where the white BMW is reversed hard up against a high garden fence in which there is a side gate. He places his newspaper on the narrow, near-horizontal section of the boot lid and carefully puts down his mug on top of the folded journal. He turns to face them, his hands on his hips. Still without expression, he waits for DS Jones to respond.

'It's not what she has been saying, sir. We are investigating her disappearance. She hasn't been seen or heard from since yesterday morning.'

'Why would I know? I'm not her keeper.'

The man's underlying accent is local – and Skelgill detects this brogue trying to break through the more carefully modified enunciation. For his part, he maintains a silence, as promised.

'When did you last see her or have contact with her, sir?'

Skelgill is pleased that DS Jones has not been knocked off her stride. Now the man takes a moment to answer, although his plasticised features reveal no sign that he is trying to remember.

'On Thursday. She wasn't in the office yesterday.'

'Did she mention anything that might explain why she has gone missing?'

'I don't see why she would tell me.'

DS Jones keeps her gaze trained on the man.

'That's a no, is it, sir?'

Now he folds his arms. Skelgill wonders if Ray Piper is self-conscious of nervous perspiration, despite that he wears a jacket.

'We passed the time of day once or twice, that's all.'

22

'Yesterday morning she gave her parents the impression that she was on her way to work, and would visit them after the close of business. In other words she intended to go to your firm's office. Was she in the habit of stopping off anywhere on the way?'

Rather indifferently, he shrugs.

'You'd need to ask her line manager. Norma Marston's Creative Director.'

'I was referring to a personal contact. An acquaintance who might have had an emergency – perhaps someone who fell ill or needed a child cared for, or help for some reason?'

'It's nothing that I know about.'

'We understand you were previously in a relationship with Miss Jackson. You might have become familiar with her close friends – who they are, at least.'

The man does not seem fazed by DS Jones's direct manner. Of course, the detectives' knowledge of the affair has been implicit from the outset – and that they have spoken with Lisa Jackson's parents. He makes no attempt to deny the assertion.

'We tended to keep ourselves to ourselves.'

'Where were you from eight a.m. yesterday, sir?'

Now there is a distinct hardening of Ray Piper's expression; although Skelgill suspects that it is indignation affected for their benefit. That aside, his sergeant has certainly raised the ante.

'I got to the office a couple of minutes after eight. I was at work all day. After work I went to pick up my sons from Brunton Park. They're on a Carlisle United soccer school all this week and next. I'm about to take them now.'

The man's intonation is matter of fact, his eyes fixed unblinkingly on DS Jones as he speaks. But now Skelgill realises there is something DS Jones may not know. He shifts forward.

'Mr Piper – the football ground's along Warwick Road – on the way to Miss Jackson's address.'

Skelgill appends no question to his statement. The man stares at him frostily. But Skelgill has no cost in keeping quiet and he returns the compliment. The man involuntarily moves a hand to touch the side of the BMW.

23

'I could hardly have given her a lift home – if that's what you're thinking. Since she didn't come to work.'

'But you have done – recently?'

Ray Piper seems resentful of this revelation. And he appears a little unnerved. He glances at the front door of his house.

'In the past, yes. I lived there at one time. I expect you know that.'

The detectives do not acknowledge his statement, and Skelgill takes half a step back to indicate to DS Jones that he won't continue. Accordingly, she picks up the thread.

'When did your relationship with Lisa Jackson end, sir?'

The man exudes further acrimony; it might almost ooze from the prominent pores of his waxy complexion. When he speaks barely a facial muscle flexes.

'I moved back here last December.'

'And did you continue to see her?'

'We worked together, obviously.'

'Again, I'm talking about on a personal level, sir.'

The man's tone is becoming increasingly irate.

'We've had the odd coffee after work – and I've given her a lift home once or twice in bad weather. That's all.'

'So there was no intimate relationship?'

'No.'

His denial comes without hesitation.

'And were you in mutual agreement about that state of affairs?'

'You'd have to ask her that – but as far as I'm concerned, yes.'

'Would you say she was in a good frame of mind?'

There is now perhaps a shift in Ray Piper's demeanour, just the faintest gleam of light in his eyes.

'What are you suggesting? That she could have committed suicide?'

'It's just a question, sir – not a suggestion.'

For the first time he looks away and gazes abstractedly into the middle distance. He gives a slight shrug of the shoulders.

'I couldn't say. She might have been more bothered than I knew.'

There is a sudden scrabbling at the front door of the house and the two mini Man Utd mascots tumble out, engaged in a desperate tussle. Wrestling to hold one another back, their dispute becomes clear.

'Shotgun the front!'

'You had it last night!'

'I didn't!'

'You did so, you liar, Cole!'

'SHUT IT!'

Without warning Ray Piper lurches forward and violently wrenches the two boys away from the car, gripping each of them by the upper arm – so fiercely that they wince in tandem; the smaller looks like he would cry were it not for the audience. Their father propels them roughly and opens the rear passenger door.

'You're both in the back. And keep your mucky feet off the seats.'

His voice is now lowered but its tone is malevolent. With controlled circumspection, however, he presses shut the door. When he turns to the watching detectives – their expressions registering disapproval – he realises that behind them his wife is waiting on the threshold bearing a black Nike sports bag in each hand. He strides over and takes the bags, but does not address the woman or make any attempt to introduce her – it is only she that speaks as he moves away.

'Their bait's packed but we've no juice left. There's a five-pound note in the zip compartment of Robbie's bag for him to buy them both some.'

Ray Piper glares at his wife but otherwise makes no acknowledgement. As he deposits the holdalls on the front passenger seat of the car she glances worriedly at the detectives, but when her husband is done she simply retreats behind the front door. Ray Piper crosses to the detectives, closer than he has been previously. Perhaps in the proximity of his sons he wants to speak more privately.

'Is that everything? I need to leave for them to be on time.'

DS Jones does not answer directly.

'Do you have a mobile number, sir – that we can reliably contact you on?'

He shows no reaction, but he pulls out a slim wallet from inside his jacket. They see within it are several business cards in some of the slots designed for credit cards. He has difficulty because of his driving gloves but after some effort manages to slide out the uppermost card. He balances it on his palm, not quite yet offering it. Now he looks directly at Skelgill, as though this is some special appeal to him.

'The office – they don't need to know about me and Lisa?'

This is news to the detectives that the affair has been kept secret – though perhaps it should not come as a surprise to them. However, without hesitation, it is DS Jones that answers.

'I'm afraid we can't guarantee anything of that nature, sir.'

Skelgill is waiting to see if she will add some kind of assuaging rider, such as "We understand what you are saying and will not raise it unnecessarily" – but nothing is forthcoming.

Instead she smiles in a businesslike manner.

'Thank you for your time, sir. If you do hear from Miss Jackson – if you could contact the local police immediately. You can imagine – her parents are extremely anxious.'

Ray Piper shows no emotion and watches them as they return to their vehicle.

DS Jones moves the car, but just a matter of yards to clear the driveway. Then she switches off the engine. She reaches into the rear seat and lifts up an A4-size notebook. As she leans close to Skelgill he smells her perfume – or perhaps it is deodorant that has been activated by a hidden tension that she has not revealed. She quickly sets about writing up notes of the interview. While she is doing so, the BMW leaves. Skelgill waits patiently. He cranes around to survey the property. He sees Ray Piper's wife open a pair of curtains in the smaller of the two upstairs windows – perhaps one of the boys' rooms. She has shed the dressing gown to reveal a rather flimsy slip – almost a negligee – and seeing his attention rather than shrink back

26

modestly she stands for a moment and returns his gaze; her expression is pensive if perhaps less apprehensive than before. Then she steps away and Skelgill reverts to his colleague as she closes her notebook.

'You don't pull your punches, lass.'

His says it teasingly – but with a possible hint of reproach – and it is to the latter sentiment that she responds.

'Why do I feel like someone's just walked over my grave, Guv?'

It is an apposite rejoinder – that her uncompromising approach was entirely justified by Ray Piper's disconcerting manner.

'Aye, he's a creepy sort.' Skelgill in fact uses a somewhat more colourful noun.

'Intimidating.'

DS Jones's voice is reflective. Skelgill, his lips compressed, nods grimly in a way that suggests he finds the idea despicable, and that he would be happy to provide a remedy if called upon. Perhaps his colleague is glad of his presence.

'You didn't mention the new boyfriend.'

'I thought we should keep our powder dry on that one, Guv.'

DS Jones here has the opportunity to 'do a Skelgill' – and not explain herself. But, then, she is not Skelgill.

'I have the feeling that's not our last conversation with Ray Piper. I don't want to give him advanced warning of anything we might decide to discuss. You know – the first thing he said – "What's she been saying?" – it felt like a prepared response.' She hesitates for a moment, before pressing on. 'Say he knows something has happened to her.'

Skelgill makes a doubtful face.

'You might be jumping the gun there, lass. Especially until we've got hold of this new bloke.'

DS Jones raises both hands in a gesture of acknowledgement – but then she reinforces her case.

'When I asked him about Lisa stopping off on the way to work, I phrased it in the past tense – as though we're

27

investigating a death. He didn't flinch at that. And he was quick to infer the idea of suicide.'

Skelgill does not reply, though he raises his eyebrows – perhaps in recognition of his colleague's subtlety and attention to detail. It intrigues him that she can put into words aspects that he simply processes as vague impressions. She forms an orderly list on paper; he is more likely to emerge from an interview with something akin to a bag of marbles rattling about in his pocket.

'I'll tell you one thing, lass – he weren't bothered.'

'You mean about Lisa?'

'Aye. It was us that troubled him.'

There ensue a few moments' silence. Then DS Jones pulls on her seatbelt and restarts the engine.

'I was wrong about one thing, Guv.'

'Aye?'

'Charming, witty and handsome.'

Skelgill suppresses a triumphant chuckle.

'Where to next, Jeeves?'

DS Jones smiles witheringly.

'I'd like to see the parents again – and then Lisa Jackson's house – her parents have a key. You okay to come – or I could drop you back if you prefer?'

'Trying to get shot of us already?'

3. THE JACKSONS

Saturday morning

07:50 *"Hi – how are you both?   How's Mum's swollen ankle? Gizmo says hi as well! Anything you want from Tesco? Love you, Lisa."*

07:57 *"Alright, darling. She's not too bad – having breakfast in bed. Can she please have half a dozen eggs for a Victoria sponge she's going to bring on Sunday? Tell Gizmo we've got him a tin of sardines! Love you, lass. Take care. Mum & Dad."*

08:11 *"Just on my way to the office. Will call round with eggs after work – see you about 4:30ish. Lisa xx."*

Skelgill inwardly sighs. He scrolls through the earlier text messages. This is the tail end of an ongoing dialogue along much the same lines; nothing contentious that he can see – merely a picture of the loving, dutiful daughter and doting parents that DS Jones has described to him. He leans forward and carefully places the couple's mobile phone on the coffee table. He sees his colleague's gaze flick briefly to the handset – he knows she will be thinking of its importance as potential evidence – but he somehow doubts that Lisa Jackson's parents will ever want to delete this conversation. But DS Jones has screen-grabbed and forwarded yesterday's messages to her own number, along with a recently taken selfie of Lisa and Gizmo, her black cat. Skelgill helps himself to sugar and a custard cream biscuit and settles back into his comfortable armchair. His colleague has returned her attention to the monologue of Arthur Jackson; he seems to be spokesman for the couple. He has reiterated several times that Lisa would on no account do something like this – borne out by the mobile phone testimony of multiple exchanges every single day – that it is so out of character – that his poor ailing wife is fraught with worry – that she hasn't slept a wink and – now contradicting himself – that she has suffered ghastly nightmares. All through, Mrs Jackson nods continually, her anxious eyes fixed fearfully upon her husband of more than four decades.

The room – the sole front room of the small retirement bungalow in a development about a mile to the southeast of Lisa Jackson's address – is rather cramped with its chunky velveteen three-piece suite set around the gas fire and television set. On the left, behind the door as they had entered, Skelgill had noticed a glass cabinet filled with various collectibles and, on top, an assortment of framed family photographs – all in colour, but some significantly faded – and all except one of them the Jacksons with their daughter – the exception being a professionally taken wedding photograph of the couple, the date indicated as 1970s by Arthur Jackson's extravagant sideburns, hair, lapels and shirt collars. Pride of place above the mantelpiece, however, is given over to a graduation photograph – presumably now some fifteen years out of date – a fresh-faced Lisa in cap and gown with one of those tubes they give them to hold the pose. Skelgill sees a fair-skinned young woman, a brunette, her features quite delicate – certainly pretty – and very distinctive blue eyes that seem to have a light of their own; and he gets that sinking feeling – a notion he commonly experiences, especially when looking at photographs of his own departed relatives: the innocence of life, unknowing of their fate. What steps would folk take today, if they only knew what path lay ahead? He starts, and tunes back in to what Arthur Jackson is saying.

'The lass wants us to meet her new feller on Sunday, for afternoon tea. Margaret's baking a cake today. I'll have to leave her while I get the eggs myself.'

The man seems a little confused, as if he cannot quite take in the reality of what is happening to them, and as if by willing normality they will precipitate their daughter's return. He looks half expectantly, half mournfully at his wife. Skelgill regards them more intently for a moment. Going by the portrait he sees little of Lisa in either. The father is grey and nondescript, the mother, well – the same; it is as though their distinctive looks have crumbled under the shock; they are pale and careworn. But the blue eyes are there, in the mother. Some inner hope burns fiercely, despite the defeated exterior.

30

While Skelgill tunes in and out, like a passenger numbed by bland scenic uniformity and flirting with sleep, DS Jones is asking for a list of friends – what Lisa's interests are – does she go to a health club or yoga – has she mentioned any trips away? He notices that she takes care to speak in the present tense – the here and now – about Lisa as she is – and that Lisa's parents hang on her every word – indeed, more than that – they regard her with a desperate fervour. He reflects that it is not a pleasant part of the job – to have another's happiness invested in oneself, to be believed to possess some special powers of remedy – when the detective can do little more than apply an ordinary person's common sense. It is a near-impossible tightrope to walk, to convey optimism and yet not give false hope. He considers that DS Jones treads the line as well as could be expected. Probably better than he would. She begins to draw the meeting to a close – she asks again about the mystery new man 'Gary'. She explains that clearly he could provide the explanation – and reiterates that perhaps the new couple have acted on a whim, that they may have got themselves into a situation where they are unable to communicate. The parents look a little doubtful at this – it does not fit with the daughter they know. But now DS Jones surprises Skelgill with a request to record a short video on her mobile phone – and rather than give them chance to procrastinate she begins recording and suggests they might have a message for Lisa. This seems to do the trick – to form the words of a public appeal would not come naturally – but both parents know what they want to say to their daughter, and in turn they make short requests for her to get in touch, and that they are looking forward to seeing her tomorrow as arranged, and that Gizmo is fine and she is not to worry.

The practical act of speaking to Lisa in the midst of all the abstractions and hypotheses seems to rejuvenate the couple, and the detectives are able to leave them on a positive note, although as they pull away Skelgill glimpses Arthur Jackson, a spectral form behind the window's reflection, gazing anxiously after them, absently wringing his hands. It is a scene of pathos he has witnessed all too often.

'What's with the video?'

'I want to get something out on the police Twitter feed as soon as possible. The local media will pick it up – they all follow us. I think it's the best way to find Gary. Or, at least, find out who he is. I'll edit it and upload it when we stop – in fact –'

As the traffic lights at which they wait turn green DS Jones swings into the slip road that leads to the Tesco supermarket that Lisa Jackson was presumably intending to visit en route to her parents' house yesterday afternoon.

'There'll be a café – do you want to get something, Guv?'

'You know what they say about bears and woods.'

DS Jones flashes him a sideways glance.

'So does this mean I'm in charge of meal breaks?'

'Aye, well – you'll hear my stomach rumbling soon enough.'

*

Skelgill had been uncharacteristically subdued in the supermarket cafeteria. In the time it took him to consume a bacon roll DS Jones had edited the video of the Jacksons, added the photograph of Lisa Jackson, along with explanatory text, and uploaded it onto the constabulary's social media feed. She had also personally emailed several press and radio contacts to make sure, "belt and braces" as Skelgill had remarked. Now they are parked on the road outside Lisa Jackson's neat-looking maisonette – although there is just about room on the driveway for a second vehicle, behind what is presumably her VW Polo.

'Reckon we can eliminate the Jacksons?'

DS Jones grins ruefully.

'Actually, I did check where they were, although I don't think they realised.'

Skelgill regards his colleague evenly. He had not noticed himself.

'I asked if they could have missed any calls on their landline – but they said they didn't leave the house yesterday – Mrs Jackson's swollen ankle. So unless Lisa actually went there, and is either locked away upstairs or is underneath the patio – I think, yes – we can.'

'Aye – there's no chance they're involved.'

Skelgill screws up his features in a manner that suggests some deeper sentiment has become manifest as a result of their encounter. To bring home the true gravity of a crime – if a crime it is – there is nothing like meeting in the flesh the folk whose problem one is charged to solve. The authorities might wish to beat down the crime statistics, but only an officer on the ground can resolve to right a wrong.

Now he inclines his head towards the property.

'You go in.'

'Pardon?'

'I might intimidate the cat – they're not keen on me.'

'You've got a cat, Guv.'

'I don't see a lot of it.'

DS Jones casts her superior an obviously doubting look – but it dawns on her that – actually, yes – he is delegating, so perhaps she ought to take advantage. She can always call him in if there is something worthy of a second opinion. Though she might suspect his motives less had he not purchased a second tea in a takeaway cup and a copy of Angling Times from the newsstand.

'Okay – leave it with me.'

But his sergeant has barely disappeared through the front door when Skelgill clambers out of the car, stretches, yawns and casually looks around. He immediately recognises at a diagonal across the close the local busybody. Although actually this is an unfair characterisation, for every neighbourhood needs someone of this ilk. The man – in his early sixties Skelgill guesses, though fit-looking with short-cropped hair and the tanned skin of a keen outdoor type – is fiddling with his green recycling bin on his driveway – quite clearly actually doing nothing of practical use, but just creating an excuse to see what is going on. Nonetheless, Skelgill is impressed that he is sufficiently observant that in the short time they have been here he has spotted them and deduced that their presence is out of the ordinary. Skelgill saunters across

33

the smooth tarmac. The man waits, half apprehensively, half pleased that his services are about to be called upon.

'Morning, sir.'

'Alreet?'

The man seems bemused by Skelgill's use of "sir" and his reciprocated greeting contains the semblance of a question. Sufficiently so that Skelgill waves his police warrant card.

'Cumbria CID – we're looking for a Miss Lisa Jackson.'

The man gives a short thrust of the head, as if propelling an invisible football back in the direction from where Skelgill has come.

'That's her house. She's not done owt wrong, has she?'

'Not that we know of. Her folks are worried about her. Have you seen her lately, sir?'

The man frowns.

'I'm trying to think when. She's been about. I mean – I haven't missed her, like. She had someone staying the night before last – I know that.'

'Thursday night?'

'Aye.'

'How do you know, sir?'

'There were another car ont' drive – and it were still there first thing yesterday – covered in condensation – same as hers were.'

'A white 7 Series BMW?'

The man looks at him sharply. He frowns, his eyes narrowed.

'Nay – it were a four-by-four – a Hyundai – metallic brown, beige maybe.'

Skelgill regards him intently.

'You didn't clock the reg by any chance?'

The man shakes his head.

'It were newish – but – that BMW – you're talking about the bloke as used to live with her.'

Skelgill nods. He is about to speak but man continues.

'That were here, too. I mean – not parked.' He indicates with a thumb over his shoulder to the lounge window. 'I were reading the News & Star. I heard a car drive in – big engine –

then it were idlin' for a few seconds and then a girt load of revs –
that's when I looked out. It were gone – except he'd only driven
down t' turning circle. Then he came speeding back past and
away ont' main road towards town.'

'When was this?'

'About five to eight.'

'Yesterday morning?'

'Aye – that were when I noticed the other car – the four-by-
four.'

'The driver of the BMW – did you recognise him as the chap
you mentioned?'

'Oh, aye – Poker Face – that's what the wife used to call him
– looks like a character from a Russian spy film.'

Skelgill inhales pensively.

'The Hyundai – did you notice how long it was there?'

'It were gone by five past eight. I went to make the wife a
mash at eight. I hadn't heard it, but it were away when I came
back.'

'You didn't see the driver?'

The man shakes his head.

'How about Lisa Jackson – did you see her leave?'

'I were probably through int' kitchen – she normally goes at
eight an' all – she's punctual. She walks, though – so I wouldn't
have heard the car, any road.'

Skelgill nods.

'We might need to send a local officer along to get a
statement. Mind if I just take a note of your name, sir?'

The man looks pleased.

'Sidebottom – Frank Sidebottom.'

'Right.'

However he seems a little disconcerted that Skelgill does not
write it down – perhaps that he has not written anything down –
but now Skelgill causes a successful distraction by casting an arm
to indicate the man's front garden. Though small and unfenced
like all those in the suburban close it is a veritable cornucopia of
horticulture, prolific floribunda roses and drooping purple
Buddleia from which drift wafts of sweet perfume, and verdant

35

borders thick with thrusting electric-blue delphiniums and multi-coloured ranks of snapdragons.

'Nice job.'

'Keeps us out of mischief – according to the wife.'

The man grins at Skelgill – but suddenly a little sheepishly – as if he detects the paradox in that he apparently does have his nose in some trouble. However, he offers a redeeming question.

'She's alreet, is she – the young lass?'

Skelgill does not try to hide a genuine doubt, so his reply is perhaps a little unconvincing.

'We've no reason to think otherwise. But thanks for your time, sir.'

Skelgill is back in the passenger seat of DS Jones's car when she emerges from the property. He notices she is wearing blue nitrile gloves as she carefully closes the front door. He looks up from his fishing newspaper as she slides in beside him.

'Any joy?'

DS Jones regards him a little guardedly. He can see that there has been no major revelation – but there is a small light of excitement in her eye.

'It's very clean and tidy – like a holiday let ready to move into. But there were a couple of things. On the draining board two coffee mugs that have been washed and left to dry – and two wine glasses, likewise. Beside the bin an empty bottle of chardonnay and in the fridge a three-quarters empty bottle of the identical brand. That's quite a lot of wine for one night – especially for one person.'

Skelgill – not intending her to see – raises his eyebrows as if he might beg to differ. He is about to assist with a possible explanation when she hurries on.

'The bed hasn't been slept in.'

'How do you know that?'

Skelgill sounds disbelieving – but he is met with an old-fashioned look from his colleague.

'The top sheet and quilt cover and pillow cases are crisp, ironed – fresh smelling.'

Skelgill looks suitably chastised.

36

'Is there another bed?'

'There's only one bedroom – and a tiny box room with a desk and shelves – looks like her home studio.'

Now Skelgill takes the opportunity to fill in a couple more pieces of the emerging jigsaw. He relates what he has gleaned from neighbour Frank Sidebottom. DS Jones listens avidly; she seems a little agog at his clandestine sleuthing – although perhaps Skelgill reads more accurately the sentiment that underlies her reaction.

'Chucks a spanner in the works, eh?'

DS Jones seems to know what he is getting at. She nods ruefully. Skelgill continues.

'Don't be too quick to convict Poker Face, just because you've taken a dislike to him.'

Again she nods – but there is some resistance in her expression.

'Thing is, it's more than that, Guv.'

Skelgill makes a face to show he understands, but does not remark. For her part, DS Jones gazes out through the windscreen, as if she is envisaging the unfolding of some scenario.

'So she might have been a passenger in that SUV when she sent the text.'

Skelgill is looking about more actively.

'I don't see any cameras.'

'We've got public order cameras in the town centre, Guv – quite close to her office.'

'Where is the business, exactly?'

'I think, just this side of the railway station. I'll check.'

DS Jones takes out her mobile phone and begins to consult the maps application. But Skelgill is already getting out of the car.

'Come on – it can't be above a mile. We're talking twelve minutes.'

It might be twelve minutes at the rate Skelgill is accustomed to striding out across the fells, but DS Jones suspects that few people would walk to work at that rate. Indeed, technology bears her out – nineteen minutes is the computerised suggestion. However, rather than gainsay him she opts to provide a more consensual datum.

'Precisely one mile.'

Skelgill grins rather smugly over his shoulder – but he waits for his colleague to catch up. She is still consulting the map as she approaches.

'It's basically Warwick Road all the way to just before the old Citadel, then a right turn into a side street that appears to be a dead end. It's called Lychgate Lane.'

Skelgill seems to hunch his shoulders.

'Don't look now, but we're being neighbourhood watched.'

But he instantly breaks his own rule and gives an ostentatious salute to the house opposite – and, within, Frank Sidebottom moves closer to the window and responds with a thumbs-up sign. He remains in situ observing them as they reach the end of the close and turn left in the direction of the town centre.

'Think she would stay on this side, Guv? It seems the natural thing to do, go with the traffic flow – plus it would be busy on a weekday morning. It'll be easier to cross near the shops, where there are more lights.'

As if choreographed to reinforce her point a small convoy of noisy traffic passes them, paying scant regard to the speed limit; more laboriously, three multi-coloured single-decker buses bring up the rear.

'The buses will all have cameras as well, Guv. If she did walk I don't think it's going to prove difficult to find her.'

But Skelgill has already become distracted. In only a matter of yards Warwick Road crosses the River Petteril – well known to Skelgill, a trout stream that has its confluence with the Eden at Carlisle, and its source on the eastern flank of Blencathra, the striking mountain that guards the northern reaches of the Lake District. It is not often he sees the river in all its glory – though perhaps that would be overegging the pudding – here in the suburbs, somewhat canalised for flood-control purposes, it is not the most spectacular of watercourses.

'Shall I stop timing, Guv?'

38

But Skelgill tears himself away from the parapet. Thoughts of fish bring him back around to the matter in hand, via the sardines mentioned by Arthur Jackson.

'Did you see owt of the cat?'

'Oh – er, no – but I put out some extra food and fresh water. There's a cat flap in the back door.'

Skelgill gives her an intrigued sideways glance. He seems to approve of her actions. However, he has a caveat.

'Mind you, you don't have to worry about cats.'

'You mean – them being kind of wild?'

'Mine's been livid since I brought it from Scotland.'

DS Jones seems to miss his joke – instead she frowns pensively. Perhaps it is the idea of the animal being self-sufficient but less so its owner.

But now there is another landmark that diverts Skelgill.

'There's Brunton Park.'

He indicates to their right. Across the main road the turnstiles of the football stadium are visible just a short distance down a side street and, towering behind the red oxide painted gates, the superstructure of the main stand. Affixed to the railings banners advertise "Young Blues Summer Soccer Camps". DS Jones stares reflectively.

'It's no distance from Lisa Jackson's house, Guv.'

Skelgill is nodding, though it strikes him as mainly coincidence.

DS Jones, however, is thinking of the detail. But there are many permutations of why and whether Ray Piper might have been in the vicinity; although the children's football school certainly provides an excuse, had he needed one. That said, the banner states 9:15 a.m. to 4:15 p.m., which, apart from the company's early finish on a Friday, does not correspond to his likely working hours. Perhaps Mrs Piper is responsible for most of the lifts.

They move on. A first-time tourist heading into town this way might be disappointed. Straddling the route of Hadrian's Wall and just ten miles from the border with Scotland – one might expect a picturesque settlement hewn from local stone, ancient buildings and narrow lanes. But Carlisle is built predominantly of pre-war red brick and quite a bit of modern concrete, and looks more like Leicester or Coventry than a truly northern British city; it is quite out of character with its lofty latitude. Until the centre is reached, therefore – where are found the grander edifices – there is not a lot to distract the eye.

But the detectives are playing a game of I-spy – and DS Jones is noting down numbers and locations of CCTV cameras on private premises. Nearing their destination she is just doing so for a computer and mobile phone repair shop when Skelgill suddenly disappears inside. She decides she ought to follow him. A youngish man, casually but smartly dressed gets up from a workstation behind the counter where he is dissecting some device and greets them with a broad smile.

'Morning, what can I do for you?'

Skelgill is about to speak when he seems to remember that DS Jones is leading the investigation. He stops in his tracks and turns a little self-consciously to his colleague. But DS Jones is quick to grasp the situation and quite seamlessly takes over. She introduces them and explains they are trying to trace a missing person.

'Was your CCTV recording yesterday morning – between eight and eight-thirty?'

'Yes certainly. It's twenty-four hour.'

The man seems keen to help and needs no further instruction. He steps away for a moment and then returns to the counter with a laptop computer. He deftly types in a series of instructions and then swivels it around so they can all view the screen. Initially the camera is filming live – so they see passers-by in real time. The definition is remarkably sharp – DS Jones comments accordingly.

'It's the model we sell – it means I can demonstrate how good it is. I mean – what's the use of these bird's-eye views of a hoodie – they all look the same. This camera gives you high-definition at eye-level. It's filming from inside the shop.' He looks up and grins. 'The one above the door outside is a dummy.'

40

But he understands they want to see yesterday's footage and he does not wait for a response to his admission. He efficiently interrogates the dashboard to search the appropriate date and time. Meanwhile DS Jones locates the picture of Lisa Jackson on her mobile phone.

'We're looking for this woman. You can see she's dark-haired – she is of slim build and medium height.'

'We can fast forward – just tell me to stop.'

Although they are still about a quarter of a mile from the town centre, there is the possibility that Lisa Jackson would already have crossed to the opposite pavement. As they watch intently, pedestrians of various genres speed by: commuters, delivery drivers bearing parcels, dog walkers, travellers dragging trolley cases destined for the railway station. There are a couple of false alarms – when the shopkeeper rewinds briefly on his own initiative before fast-forwarding once again.

'There!'

It is Skelgill who is quickest – a woman who walks swiftly past – and the man has to rewind. Then he plays the sequence again in slow motion and freezes the shot. Lisa Jackson – there can be no doubt it is she – she even gives them the benefit of turning to glance into the shop window. She is dressed in pale blue skinny jeans and a navy sweatshirt with a large white GAP motif on the front, and chunky white trainers that perhaps inform the man's observation that she has "a spring in her step". She carries only a slim shoulder bag, black with a pair of half-closed yellow cat's eyes – nothing larger, and no jacket – in other words nothing to suggest she was planning for an overnight stay.

DS Jones releases the breath she has been inadvertently holding.

'Could you play it again at normal speed?'

Lisa Jackson seems to see something in the window that causes her to smile. Not wishing to have too much of a conversation before the shopkeeper, DS Jones takes a different tack.

'Could you possibly give us a copy of this sequence?'

'No problem.' The man reaches beneath the counter and produces a memory stick. 'These have been scanned by my anti-virus software. But my server stores data for ninety days.'

DS Jones nods – he seems to know something about the protocols that she must observe. Nevertheless, she is keen to preserve her own version of the evidence. More 'belt and braces'.

When the shopkeeper hands over the flash drive a customer enters carrying an electronic tablet with a fractured screen that looks like it has been struck by a sharp object. The proprietor acknowledges the man – a respectable-looking gent in his fifties. DS Jones relays their thanks and asks for a business card. The man points to the memory stick in her hand.

'It's all on there – just ask for me – Sam Patel – it's only me, anyway.' He grins amenably. 'Hope that turns out okay.'

DS Jones bows her head gratefully – she notes that he is sufficiently diplomatic not to give away either their identity or their mission in front of the unknown customer.

As they leave with a buzz of the door chime, they hear the new arrival lament in somewhat rueful tones.

'I was at my desk in my study and a squirrel was wrecking the bird table – I tried to shoot it with a BB pistol.'

Skelgill is unable to suppress a chortle of schadenfreude. DS Jones, however, seems more preoccupied with regaining their bearings, now that they know Lisa Jackson got this far. When she turns she sees that Skelgill is looking back into the shop window. She realises that what attracted him in the first place was a monitor that is displaying the live CCTV images. Quite rightly, it was too good a gift horse to look in the mouth.

'Nice move, Guv. Though I'd like to get as much extra footage as possible – in case she was being followed. But it means there's only realistically the train – or that she went on to meet someone in the centre. I can't see that she would have accepted a lift having got this close.'

Skelgill turns and squints ahead.

'The railway station's bristling with cameras. But I reckon I can see one of our masts at the junction. Around the Crescent can get a bit lively of a Saturday night, especially after a big match.'

Sure enough as they approach the point where Lisa Jackson would cross for work – a convenient pelican crossing – about one hundred yards further on a galvanised steel mast fitted with police CCTV cameras is now clearly visible.

'That ought to have picked her up, Guv – even if she turned off for the office I think her outfit is sufficiently distinctive to identify her at this distance.'

Skelgill spots a gap in the traffic and sets off over the crossing without activating the pedestrian lights; DS Jones has to put on a spurt to catch up with him. Just a little further is the narrow entrance marked as Lychgate Lane. In the low morning sun it is shaded and gloomy, but in any event inauspicious, extending for about a hundred yards and lined on both sides by the unfaced backs of commercial buildings and residential apartments, and ending in a timber merchant's delivery bay, its rusted roller shutter padlocked for the weekend. Skelgill casts about as they move along – there are emergency exits and fire escapes, solid and windowless; and he sees no security cameras.

'What number is it?'

'Thirteen – towards the end on the left, I think.'

They walk in the centre of the lane; there is no pavement, just a narrow cobbled roadway with no provision for parking. Both sides are marked with crumbling double yellow lines. They almost miss the door for number thirteen – it is set in a wide recessed alcove – the sort of place where the smokers would congregate on a rainy day – and indeed underfoot there is evidence to this effect. The door, however, is smartly painted in deep blue and there is a brass plaque bearing the name InnStyle Design & Management Ltd, and an entryphone panel with just a single call button. Skelgill presses it – but they hear nothing and there is no answer.

The detectives seem stymied. They loiter in silence for a moment, before Skelgill steps out into the lane and cranes up at the building. But there is little of note above, other than a couple of feral pigeons peering from a window ledge. DS Jones joins him.

'I think I should head back to base – to the DMU – and check our cameras.' She refers to the centralised CCTV facility for the county, the Designated Monitoring Unit. 'And I'll submit an urgent access request to Network Rail. Also I want to run a check on her bank account – to see if she withdrew money or paid for a train ticket or maybe hotel accommodation. Plus I'm waiting for a report on her phone history.'

Skelgill gives a somewhat flabbergasted shake of his head, as though she has plied him with too much information.

'Do you not want to have some of your Saturday? We're entitled to let nature take its course – and with any luck she'll turn up from some jaunt on Sunday night – maybe even teatime for the Victoria sponge.'

But DS Jones does not seem convinced. They begin to drift back towards the junction with Warwick Road. It takes her a few moments directly to answer his question.

'If I can just resolve this issue, Guv. Where did she go?' She hesitates and puts a hand to the pocket of her jacket in which she has placed the flash drive. 'On the video – she seemed happy – pleased with life. I just feel – well – that we're so near.'

'Yet so far.'

Skelgill does not say this cynically. There is an uncharacteristic note of empathy in his voice – perhaps that his colleague will have to bear a greater share of this frustration than she is accustomed to (although that would be doing her a disservice). For him it has always been a puzzling, tantalising sensation – and, as if he needed reminding, one that he experiences every time he goes fishing. A tug on the line, the float dips into the meniscus – or a rise, the kind that reveals no fin, just an eddy, an unnatural convexity of the surface. His quarry is tantalisingly close, yet is otherwise intangible. It disappears and leaves no trace – and yet the very space at hand was filled with his object. Just like Lisa Jackson has passed through the same void as they have – he understands his colleague's point – it is almost as though they can detect the

44

woman's essence, trailed in her wake. Time and space detached. He has witnessed a scent hound on a training exercise unerringly track a target through a busy town centre an hour later – the dog has some extraordinary ability to bridge the discontinuity – at least, within a short window of opportunity. But they have technology – no wonder DS Jones is so keen to interrogate the cameras.

As they retrace their steps along Warwick Road they move mainly in silence. Skelgill reflects upon his own acceptance of the degree of seriousness that his colleague has ascribed to this case. Understandably, she wants to excel – and he to support her – but, as she had stated during their discussion last evening, people go missing by the thousand, almost all of them turn up, and it is not as though Lisa Jackson were a vulnerable child – or even a vulnerable adult. Yes, it is peculiar – she seems to have disappeared into thin air – and, yes, it is out of character according to her parents and employer – but, taken across the nation as a whole, these aspects are commonplace. And, yet – like his colleague – he has some sense that this might be different. And, though he has cautioned against it, he supposes he puts it down to the cold encounter with a detached Ray Piper.

45

4. GARY SCOTT

Sunday evening

'Is there news of Lisa? They wouldn't tell me anything.'

DS Jones hesitates momentarily as she enters the interview room along with a female colleague, a bespectacled detective constable a little older than her. The man seated at the table has risen with a sharp scrape of his chair. He is of medium height and slim build, with short brown hair and blue eyes and regular features, and smartly dressed in casual clothes. And though it is a fairly nondescript appearance, more striking is the impression of timidity, reticence – that he is almost cringing like a dog accustomed to a whack as the first form of greeting from its cruel master; and that it has taken him all of his courage to ask his question. As such, this informs DS Jones's response, when she might have been inclined to take a stern line, by smartly sending the ball back into his court.

However, she does not answer immediately but motions calmly for him to resume his seat, and she and her colleague settle opposite.

'I'm DS Jones – this is DC Watson – she'll take notes. Thank you for volunteering to come in to speak with us.' The man seems about to ask again and she holds up a palm to silence him. 'We have no new information, sir – but if I could just check the details you gave to the desk sergeant.'

He nods meekly, looking no less anxious for the composed reception. But DS Jones's tactic is to get him to begin with something to which he will agree. She opens a file and refers to the top sheet.

'You are Gary Scott, of 53 Featherston Drive, Carlisle.' She glances up – not especially seeking assent – but he nods obediently. 'Age thirty-five. Employed as a quantity surveyor with Eden Garden Homes. The vehicle registered to you is a metallic gold Hyundai Tucson.'

When she reads out the plate number he seems surprised that she has this detail. He opens his mouth as if to comment, but she pre-empts him.

'Are you married, sir?'

She has a carefully manicured nail touching the page where there is a blank box. She looks up inquiringly. It is phrased as an innocent-sounding question – although in the context of this meeting, it may be far from it. And the man's reaction is noteworthy; he seems to recoil and he mechanically raises a hand to his left temple.

'No – I'm, er – a widower.' His voice is strained. 'My wife was killed in a car accident – nearly six years ago. A tree fell on our car. On holiday – in Ireland.'

He lowers his hand and DS Jones realises there is a scar.

'I'm sorry to hear that, sir.' She regards him sympathetically. 'Do you have children?'

'No – no, we had no children.'

DS Jones nods and allows what might be a respectful pause. Then without warning she raises by a quantum the tenor of her questioning.

'And how would you describe your relationship with Miss Jackson, Mr Scott?'

His gaze flicks nervously to the page before DS Jones, as though he fears this is a trick question and the correct reply has already been determined.

'Well – I've really only just recently met her. But – I suppose we're – sort of – *dating.'*

He sounds far from convincing, and DS Jones probes to this effect.

'You don't seem too sure, sir?'

'Well – you see – we met about two weeks ago – there was an interior design exhibition at the Citadel – and the firm she works for had a stand. They're mainly in the leisure sector – but I'd noticed the use of some marble cladding in one of their displays. Lisa was on the stand – she's not a salesperson – but it's a male-dominated industry and I think they'd – well – frankly – put out their most attractive female staff members – press-

47

ganged – she'd said.' He shifts in his seat, and glances uncomfortably first at the detective constable and then back at DS Jones. But they regard him implacably, and he feels sufficiently encouraged to continue. 'Anyway – she offered to show me more detail of the work – it was a project she'd designed herself – so we went across to the little snack bar where there were fewer distractions and more space so she could demonstrate on her laptop.' Absently he raises his hand again to touch the scar on the side of his forehead. 'There wasn't really any way I could see the firm supplying us – we've got our own interior designers – but she asked if I wanted to have lunch.'

'Was that in the hope of getting a contract?'

He regards DS Jones somewhat worriedly, as if it is just dawning on him what might have been Lisa Jackson's motivation.

'To be honest – I thought she was trying to get away from the place. It looked like her boss had turned up on the stand – and I got the feeling she used me as a potential customer as an excuse to leave. I mean – there were snack lunches in the Citadel – but she suggested we go to the new bistro in the Crescent.'

'Who paid for lunch?'

Gary Scott seems surprised by DS Jones's question.

'Er – well – she tried to pay – she said she could claim it on expenses – and then I tried to pay, because I said I could do the same – and I didn't like the idea that I was taking advantage, because I knew nothing would come of the work. But then she said why don't you pay next time.'

He looks at DS Jones as if he feels she might not believe such a thing could happen to him.

'So, she was suggesting you meet again?'

He nods.

'The exhibition was the Thursday – and she said let's meet here for lunch in a week's time.'

When he pauses overly DS Jones prompts him.

'And did she intend that to be a date – or was she expecting to discuss work with you?'

'Well – I must admit – I wasn't a hundred percent sure – and I didn't really like to ask. But when we met – well – it was more like a date. We didn't talk shop and it was just getting to know one another. We didn't have all that long – just the lunch hour – but we kind of joked about making it a regular thing.'

'So, what – you arranged to meet again on the following Thursday – or did you see one another in between?'

He begins to nod and then shakes his head as she adds the rider.

'It wasn't like we were going steady. We arranged to meet again at the bistro – but then she phoned to say there was a problem at work – and would I like to come round for a meal in the evening, instead?'

DS Jones is listening evenly; she wonders if the small increase in her pulse rate betrays itself in her expression – and she can't help thinking whether Skelgill's heart ever deviates from his claimed unwavering sixty beats per minute.

'So this is last Thursday, yes?'

'Yes.'

She judges he is more embarrassed than intentionally cagey; she smiles encouragingly.

'And how did that go?'

'Fine – I mean – do you – do you want to know the exact details?'

Again he glances at each of the police officers in turn.

'It might be helpful – yes, sir.'

'Well – I went to her address – for eight o'clock. I'd stopped off at Tesco to buy a bottle of wine – and she'd thought it was funny because she'd bought the same one – it was on special offer. She'd made a nice meal. And then she'd said should we watch a film? And what happened was – well, we fell asleep.'

'Watching the film?'

'Yes – I think we were both a bit nervous – I mean I wasn't really sure of what – *what* she wanted – and I suppose we were both drinking faster than normal.'

'Had you not thought about driving home?'

'Yes – I did think about that – that if I wasn't careful I wouldn't be able to drive. I remember I said that to Lisa at one point – and she said it seemed early for me to go and why didn't I get an Uber?'

'So how *did* you get home?'

Now he looks a little perplexed, as though he feels he had sufficiently explained himself.

'Well – what I meant – that we fell asleep – I think we'd both drunk a lot more than we're normally used to – so we slept all night – on the sofa.'

DS Jones looks a fraction amused.

'Was that not uncomfortable?'

'Well – yes, but – it seemed a kind of – nice thing to do. I mean – Lisa could have gone up to bed – but she stayed with me.'

'And did you have sex?'

He is shocked by the young female sergeant's question, posed in a matter-of-fact manner like a doctor might ask about haemorrhoids.

He shakes his head, looking decidedly awkward.

'No – we just slept.'

'So – you are not in a sexual relationship with Miss Jackson?'

'The most we've done is a kiss on the cheek when I arrived – and then we did kind of peck on the lips when I left in the morning.'

'Yes – Friday morning – what happened then?'

'Well – Lisa did eventually get up and leave me, to get ready for work – I think she felt fine – I had a bit of a headache. She brought me a coffee and asked if I wanted a shower. But I just said I'd go – I didn't like to impose on her.'

'What time was that?'

'Well – I left just before eight – that's when Lisa said she goes.'

'Did you give her a lift?'

'I offered her a lift – but she said she always walks – that she likes the exercise – and that it would blow away the cobwebs.'

'Did you see her leave?'

50

Now he appears more worried.

'No – she waved me off at the door and went back inside. I think she wanted to see to the cat before she left.'

DS Jones pauses. Briefly, she consults her notes.

'And where did you go, sir?'

'Well – Old Trafford.'

DS Jones looks up doubtingly.

'Football?'

'No – it's the Test Match – England are playing the West Indies. Well – *were* playing – it finished just after lunch today.'

Now DS Jones nods – she knows enough to recall that Manchester has two famous stadia synonymous with the district in which they stand. And that he refers, of course, to the summer sport of cricket.

'So, what were your timings?'

'I went home and had a quick shower and got changed – then I picked up my friend Alan Knott – and we drove down to Manchester. We met another friend – Geoff Arnold – outside the ground – he lives in Wythenshawe and he'd got the tickets.'

'What time did you leave Carlisle?'

'I got to Alan's just after eight-thirty – he's quite close to junction forty-two. Then we arrived just before the start of play at ten-thirty.'

'And coming back?'

He seems a little sheepish about his reply.

'We had three days' tickets. Alan and I stayed at Geoff's place.'

'Were you together the whole time?'

'Yes.'

'Miss Jackson – she didn't travel down to join you, by any chance?'

'No –'

There is a bewildered intonation in the man's voice.

'Did you hear from her while you were in Manchester?'

'I mean – I'd kind of hoped she might contact me. But I didn't like to pester her. In case it would seem too pushy or she'd changed her mind.'

51

'You didn't even text her?'

'Actually – she'd asked me not to – the second time we met for lunch – she said they were a nosey bunch in the office – and you know how you can see part of a text on the screen even if a phone's locked?'

'And how did she seem when you last saw her?'

He reflects for a moment; there seems to be a flicker of optimism, a brightening in his blue eyes.

'Cheerful. She said she'd slept really well. I don't know how she managed it – I remember the cat kept disturbing me. But I was kind of trapped and I didn't want to wake Lisa.'

He zones out momentarily – but DS Jones reads his expression as more wistful than anything. She, too, is pensive, and it takes her a few moments before she shifts the conversation back into more controversial territory.

'Mr Scott, what do you know about Miss Jackson's previous relationships?'

Again he appears a little unnerved – although not, she feels, in some guilty fashion. He makes an appealing gesture with open palms.

'I mean – I know she's not married – and she's never been married. She told me she'd had a long relationship with a childhood sweetheart who was quite a bit older than her – and that everyone had expected they would get married – but they broke up in their early twenties and she didn't really find anyone after that. And she told me that she's not been seeing anyone seriously since the end of last year.'

'What about casually?'

'Oh – well – I don't know – but she doesn't seem the sort – if you know what I mean? I think she is looking for a permanent relationship.'

He emits a faint sigh, and DS Jones appears to have some sympathy.

'It isn't always easy to get there.'

He looks a little relieved by her comment, though he averts his eyes as though she is expressing solicitude for his predicament. But then he is jolted by her next question.

52

'Mr Scott, how did you find out that we are looking for Miss Jackson?'

'Well – Lisa had asked me if I could come for tea today – and meet her parents – she normally has them round on a Sunday. I'd explained I was going to the cricket for three days – that it had been booked months ahead. Today was the final day – play could have continued until seven this evening. I might not have got home until ten. But I said I'd do my best to get back. As it was, England had another batting collapse and – like I say – the game ended just after lunch. I tried to ring Lisa to let her know – but I couldn't get through on her mobile. I don't have her home number. So I just drove straight there. A neighbour saw me knocking and he came out. He said the police were looking for her – and that you were looking for me. So that was when I phoned 101.'

DS Jones is nodding. And it seems Gary Scott had acted promptly, for his call was timed at less than five minutes after they had received a call from 'neighbourhood watchman' Frank Sidebottom, informing them that the driver of the SUV had returned, and detailing his plate number.

He regards DS Jones rather forlornly.

'What do you think's happened to her, officer?'

It is DS Jones that now falls victim to introspection. Police interview training (and basic protocol) is neither to speculate nor to share speculation – especially with a potential suspect. That said, what Gary Scott has told them fits entirely with the observed facts, and the account of the older Jacksons – and it seems likely his whereabouts will be borne out by his two friends. Moreover, as the CCTV footage that DS Jones has pored over confirms, at eight twenty-four a.m. on Friday – when he would have been en route to pick up his first companion – a person that DS Jones is ninety-nine percent sure was Lisa Jackson crossed Warwick Road and disappeared into Lychgate Lane. The problem is, she did not re-emerge.

'I wish I knew, sir.'

5. ENNERDALE

Monday 7:30 a.m.

DS Leyton is contemplating the pros and cons of investigating without Skelgill. At a professional level, life is certainly less stressful. Skelgill rarely explains what is going on his mind. That said, like fellow sergeant DS Jones, he appreciates it is not always within their superior's gift to put into words exactly what he *is* thinking – if, indeed, he is thinking anything at all. He seems to operate more like a wild animal that assimilates information with its five (or maybe even six) senses, and blends it with instinct ultimately to seek out some resolution. And he rarely fails. But working alongside Skelgill can be likened to having a partner whose native currency is a foreign language. Much has to be inferred from his reluctant and often oblique utterances.

On this linguistic point, however, he grins to himself – at least when Skelgill lapses into broad Cumbrian he has his own dialect with which to counter. And it can be an entertaining aspect of the relationship – a certain banter, which, provided he does not try too hard to win, can foster a positive atmosphere. Most people find Skelgill recalcitrant – and he is – but there is a way of being a bad loser that merits respect, and Skelgill is the kind of bad loser you would want in your team if you desired mainly to win; it might not be top of the list of 'traits of the good manager', but – well – there are more ways than one to skin a cat.

Certainly he is missing Skelgill now – for one thing, he can be relied upon to provide a commentary as they travel about his beloved Lake District. And who would not be proud of hailing from this place – surely the jewel in England's crown. Okay, perhaps a bit too much detail at times about rare species of fish and their habits – and the depths and surface areas of lakes – oh, and the old chestnut of there being only one lake in the Lake District. DS Leyton is pretty sure he spotted his boss as he sped past that very water – Bassenthwaite Lake – hauling away at the oars into what is quite a fresh breeze for such a pleasant-looking day.

And Skelgill would surely have something to say about the lake that DS Leyton now glimpses beyond meadows to starboard, if only to reproach him for doubting their whereabouts (and by implication his navigation skills). For his own part, he is a little relieved – that he has evidently come the right way – having felt a creeping trepidation since he turned off the A5086 at a farm apparently called Hodyoad. Thence, via narrow winding lanes he passed through tiny hamlets, Lamplugh, Felldyke, Croasdale, with a growing sense of 'going off the map', deeper into fell country – and finally a dilapidated signpost, "Ennerdale – No Through Road".

Though he must also admit to a small thrill of excitement as he repeats aloud the name. He will have a tale to tell tonight. *Ennerdale!* The geographical home (when not in the studio) of his wife's favourite soap opera – having displaced Eastenders for primacy shortly after their move north. And now here he is heading down into the very valley itself. At this he realises Skelgill would chastise him – he can hear the gruff lecture: *"Up into the dale, Leyton – unless you're telling me that beck's defying gravity."* True enough, for most practical purposes, visiting a dale involves an ascent into the mountains. Unless, of course, you are at a pass – a point of inflexion from which two dales descend!

Notwithstanding the obscure route, his satnav has just about clung on to the signal, and is telling him he has the luxury of time on his side. Besides, neither is the burglary exactly in progress nor presumably the farmer at a loss for something to do. Taking his foot off the pedal he begins to pay more appreciative attention to the scenery – he might almost be passing through a fantasy world called Chocolate Box Country, more benign here on the northwestern fringes of the national park than the bleak and threatening landscape of the central fells. He could aspire to climb one of these gentle hills! It is a scene of simple colours, demarcated like a diligently completed painting-by-numbers.

55

Sea-blue sky a broad ocean on which billowing white-sailed galleons ply their course; brindled fellsides; the shimmering cobalt strip of the lake; grey-walled green pastures flecked with sheep; occasional – very occasional – farmsteads nestling amongst clusters of rather meagre trees; and the proximate vegetation lush – England at its summer zenith – burgeoning verges and roadside banks daubed with magenta and cream – patches of wildflowers that he supposes Skelgill could name; and in flashing woodland glades lime-green stands of bracken – he knows this plant – straining six or seven feet tall, and great fun for hide and seek for the nippers. Overhead a family of buzzards sit on the wind, the youngsters mewing for food.

But an even higher pleasure awaits him. Rounding a bend he comes upon what at first glance seems to be a travellers' encampment. In a secluded roadside layby – a crescent that cuts off into an area of sparsely planted conifers where logs are stacked – is a static convoy of long white, grey and silver vehicles – indeed some of them are sizeable caravans – and it is only when his mind processes the words "Cumbria Television" liveried on one of the plain-sided trailers that DS Leyton realises what is afoot. This is Ennerdale – *the TV Ennerdale!* They are filming on location. Before he knows it he has slewed up to the five-barred gate that blocks the entrance and is beginning to take souvenir photographs on his mobile phone for his wife.

But he has hardly got going when he spies a burly security guard in a hi-vis jacket lumbering in his direction. He takes pre-emptive action. He tumbles out of his car and – seeing a likely reprimand forming on the man's lips – meets him head on, reaching over the gate and brandishing his police warrant card.

'Morning, squire. Cumbria CID. Everything all right here?'

The man is halted in his tracks. Shaven-headed and muscular, he must be in his mid-thirties. Embroidered on his jacket is his name, "Darren". Being a quasi policeman of sorts, and no doubt accustomed to his own word being obeyed, he immediately defers to the higher authority.

'Aye – alreet. What's up, officer?'

56

The man's manner is considerably less intimidating than his appearance. To DS Leyton's untrained ear his accent seems relatively local.

'I'm on my way to investigate a burglary – a farm further up the dale.' DS Leyton gives himself a small pat on the back for getting this right. 'You've not had any problems yourselves?'

The man looks suddenly a little shaken – as if there is an existential threat of which he is only now being apprised – but then he pulls himself together.

'We provide twenty-four-hour security.'

He indicates a large black torch in his belt. Unnecessary at this time of day, it strikes DS Leyton as a formidable persuader.

'Looks like you're doing a good job.'

Darren appears pleased by such praise coming from a policeman, and seems distracted – perhaps he is thinking there are brownie points to be gained with his bosses if he has successfully deterred a robbery.

'How long have you been here?'

'This is day three. It's a five-day shoot.'

Now it is DS Leyton's turn to become preoccupied by a moment of introspection. He runs a hand through his thick dark hair. Should anything be read into this? The film crew's (and presumably the cast's) presence overlaps with the farm break-in – which is known to have taken place on either Saturday or Sunday. He realises he should have in mind the possibility that the culprit or culprits could just have a connection here – now that would be a story! But he does not want to betray signs of suspicion. He treats the man as a confidante.

'We believe we're looking for a single perpetrator. Almost certainly drives a van, male, reasonably fit and strong, given the nature of the break-ins and the gear that's being stolen. I realise it's a long shot – but have you noticed anyone passing who fits that description?'

That DS Leyton has invented on the spur of the moment this profile in order to sound convincing – and that it could apply to about a quarter of the population – does not seem to faze the security guard. He answers thoughtfully.

'Hard to say. It's a dead end, right? There's no one actually lives down here.'

DS Leyton understands what he means. There are no cottages, no hamlet or village – just a handful of remote farms. Darren continues.

'Besides – cars are not allowed past the picnic area. I've noticed the odd walker. But nowt to catch the eye.' He emits a choked laugh. 'Some sheep got in yesterday and scoffed a load of sandwiches that had been left out for the crew. You taking a photo – they're the most exciting things that's happened since I got here.'

DS Leyton nods amenably.

'The missus is a big fan. She'd murder me if I didn't get a picture.'

The man now regards DS Leyton with a look that blends self-importance with the conspiratorial.

'Want a tour? Most of the cast and crew's filming up on the hill – but they're doing a bit down here this morning. There might be one or two famous faces knocking about – if they're not still kipping. We've got a catering van – come and get a coffee – I'll say you're investigating.'

'Which I am.'

DS Leyton grins. The man regards him with just a hint of uncertainty – but nevertheless unlatches the gate and admits him.

*

'I were beginning to think thoo'd got theesen lost.'

It strikes DS Leyton that he is ignorant of the correct descriptor for a farmer when that person is female. He has heard Skelgill refer to a shepherdess – but to use no such equivalent in the more general agricultural context. He supposes farmer must be gender-neutral.

'I'm afraid a bit of excitement cropped up en route, madam.'

The woman regards DS Leyton a little suspiciously.

'Thoo're not frae Wukiton.'

58

He looks a little disappointed that she has not queried the event to which he refers – but instead that she seems to be plucking a location – Workington, he gathers – out of thin air as a means of highlighting his foreignness.

'That's right, Mrs Gillerthwaite – we're based at Penrith. Makes us pretty central for getting about – beside the motorway and the A66.'

But the busy intersection, a key northern pivot, seems a world away from this remote farmstead, the last house in Ennerdale, crowded by gnarled ashes on the glacial outwash plain above the lake, small pastures surrounded by dark pine forest; and, towering above, the ecclesiastic-sounding pikes of Pillar, Steeple and Kirk Fell.

'Happen thoo'll have a mash and a spot o' scran?'

DS Leyton realises he is being offered refreshments. It is something that Skelgill rarely refuses – indeed his superior seems largely to feed himself on the hoof, even if it means cramming two or three meals into a couple of hours. And it seems to be the done thing, not to decline hospitality. Besides, he – DS Leyton – is in ebullient mood, he has something to celebrate, and a nice little treat is just the ticket. He accepts the chair that the woman has pulled out at the oak kitchen table. She has not troubled to take either yes or no for an answer, and lifts a simmering kettle from a blackened range stove that might have risen out of the ground along with the ancient stone farmhouse. She must be in her late fifties, beneath a tangle of grey ringlets her countenance lined, weathered and craggy. Her pale blue eyes are bright, and she moves without impediment, a wiry figure clad in a holed and frayed boiler suit – though both she and her surroundings exude an ascetic cleanliness. She returns to the table with tin mugs of steaming tea and plate of unfamiliar looking squares of cake, about an inch-and-a-half deep, two dense layers of pastry with baked jam sandwiched between. Skelgill would be in his element.

'Help theesen. If thoo're not kaisty.'

He guesses he is not.

'Much obliged, madam.'

59

He takes a slice of cake – there are no side plates so he finds himself hanging onto it, hovering in mid air – but before he can commence with the subject of his visit, she interjects.

'So why've they sent a top detective from ower yonder?'

DS Leyton cannot help feeling a little flattered. He almost finds himself preening with affected modesty, until he imagines the spectre of Skelgill at his side doing just the very thing. But he does not contest her assertion.

'It's because firearms are involved, madam. This gang – or person, if it's someone acting alone – has now targeted seven isolated farms in the past month. And they're only stealing shotguns.'

Mrs Gillerthwaite, who has picked up a square of cake, makes a rather scornful scoffing growl in her throat. She dunks the corner of the sweetbread into her tea and quickly takes a bite. She speaks while eating.

'They shan't have much joy with mine. It's got a knack to it – otherwise it won't fire.'

DS Leyton nods pensively. She does not seem too concerned – either about the loss of her gun or that she has been burgled, out here in this most isolated of spots. For want of an immediate rejoinder, he takes a bite of his cake.

'Cor blimey – 'scuse my French – that's delicious. My missus would love this – she's got a right old sweet tooth. What's it called?'

'Ennerdale cake.'

The woman looks pleased – but her intonation suggests she is thinking how could he be so stupid as not to know.

'Yeah, of course.'

The crumbly melt-in-the-mouth texture is just perfect with a cup of tea, and DS Leyton finds himself finishing his piece and being offered another before he knows it. Is he, he wonders, subconsciously filling the shoes of his absent colleague? He realises he ought to get the interview back on track.

'Quite likely what they do with shotguns, you see madam, is cut them down and sell them on to criminal gangs. It's a lucrative trade.' He leans back in his seat and makes a gesture with both hands to indicate their surroundings. When he had arrived he had found the farm seemingly deserted and the back door open. Mrs Gillerthwaite he had located in some kind of low stable singing to herself as she worked away with a rusty pitchfork. 'And easy pickings.'

The woman seems to get his drift.

'Nay use in a gun locked away, lad. Tod or crow'll be long gone – and t' lamb – else it'll have its eyes pecked out.'

DS Leyton frowns sympathetically. He understands this. A sportsman who lives in the suburbs he could rightly chastise for not storing their gun under lock and key. But the criminals have latched onto the fact that many farmers keep a loaded shotgun propped up behind the kitchen door, and that in this part of the world small hill farms are often run singlehandedly or by an older couple, on a subsistence basis, any offspring obliged to move away to find employment. There are not many hands about to deter or even notice an intruder. Half of the thefts in this case have taken place with the smallholder actually inside the property. The burglar has simply walked up to an unsecured door and brazenly swiped their weapon. Such a 'clean' crime leaves almost no forensic footprint. If challenged – the criminal could simply claim to be a walker who has lost their way.

'Did you notice anyone passing close to the property – perhaps carrying an above-average sized bag of some kind?'

The woman regards him evenly.

'There's sometimes walkers gannin' along t' lonnin. They come to climb Pillar and Steeple – thanks to that donnat Wainwright. Some camp int' bothy at Black Sail.'

DS Leyton nods. A large rucksack would comfortably conceal a stripped shotgun, lock, stock and barrel.

'No unusual vehicles?'

She shakes her head.

'They're not meant to come abeun Bowness Knott.'

She refers to the same picnic area that the security guard had mentioned. DS Leyton had himself continued past, ignoring the sign: "Forestry Commission – Authorised Vehicles Only".

'The lane doesn't actually go anywhere – I mean you can't drive on through?'

'Nay – just up into t' forest. But there's a padlocked yat about a mile yonder.'

While DS Leyton ponders – half wondering what Skelgill would ask – Mrs Gillerthwaite presses on him another square of cake. It buys him time to think – he contorts his malleable features to demonstrate approval as he eats. The woman also takes another piece, dunking as before. He continues to resist this manoeuvre.

'When I arrived – your dogs were barking.' With hindsight presumably cooped up, to his relief what sounded like a small pack in full flight, fangs bared never materialised. There had been a harsh reprimand and obedient silence. 'You don't recall that happening over the weekend?'

She shakes her head.

'Aye – happen they barked a few times – but not as I can link to owt.'

'The gun – it was definitely here on Friday evening – and you noticed it was gone yesterday afternoon – Sunday?'

'Aye – that's about the length of it.'

She seems disinclined to repeat what she had related to the officer who handled her telephone report of the theft. DS Leyton consults the précis he has transferred to his notebook. The gist of it was that she had spent substantial periods either out on the fells or working in one of the barns; she could easily have overlooked a covert visit by a seasoned burglar.

'And you live here alone – there's no one else who might have borrowed it – a neighbour who would be accustomed to doing that sort of thing?'

'Us nearest neighbour's the Thomsons – t'other side of Bowness Knott – it's a good four mile.'

DS Leyton had the feeling it was going to be a bit of a wild-goose chase when he set out this morning; events since have done little to change this view – although there has been the 'Ennerdale Adventure' – which keeps coming back to him in little flushes of elation, and of which he has not contrived to

62

speak to the farmer, much as he is bursting to tell someone. However, the incident has prompted him to throw caution to the wind as far as his waistline is concerned, and now he avails himself of another square of Ennerdale cake – and Mrs Gillerthwaite seems to approve. Skelgill would be proud of him. However, a moment later, the woman plies him with a rather solicitous expression.

'T'aint looking promising, eh, lad?'

DS Leyton starts – a little alarmed at her supposition. But her tone is neither critical nor despondent – just matter of fact. Skelgill's voice, again: "Another thing to remember, Leyton – fell folk tell it as they see it." With this in mind, and bolstered by a sugar rush, he rallies.

"Thing is, madam – we will solve this crime. It might take some time – but criminals always slip up. He – or they – might already have slipped up – when they robbed you, for instance. We just can't see that right now – but as we gather more information, a piece of the jigsaw that looks like it doesn't belong suddenly fits. Then the whole thing begins to make sense.'

He wonders if he sounds remotely convincing – for in his bones he does not feel this optimism. But again it strikes him that this is one of Skelgill's less obvious strengths – he is invariably phlegmatic in the face of new evidence, whether excruciatingly weak or powerfully suggestive.

'Reckon they'll be robbing a bank? Imagine that – the arl feller's gun in a hold up. He'd be birlin' in his grave.'

The farmer seems quite enamoured of the prospect. DS Leyton is thinking it would be nothing so glamorous – more likely drug dealers exacting bloody revenge upon one another. But he treats her question as rhetorical.

'How will you manage – without your shotgun?'

'Ah've got another – an old Baikal.' She regards him shrewdly. 'There's a gun safe int' cockloft.'

So she does have one. After all, a safe is a legal requirement, and it is hard to see how she would have been granted her licence without it.

63

'It might not be a bad idea to try to store it there. If you're going across the fields.'

But this suggestion she waves aside.

'Lightnin' won't strike twice, lad.'

DS Leyton inhales.

'I wish I could say that, Mrs Gillerthwaite – but thieves are well known to return – once they get the lie of the land.'

The woman does not look persuaded. And, truth be told, although this fact might apply in an urban environment, where opportunistic burglars often do revisit residual low-hanging fruit, out here in the semi-wilderness it seems improbable. Moreover, the anonymous gun thief has never yet returned to any of his victims' properties.

DS Leyton decides he ought to make tracks – and he is itching to share his own piece of opportunism. He thanks her profusely – most notably for the refreshments – and assures her the police will do their best to recover her shotgun and bring the miscreants to justice. The woman remains stoic – indeed she has drifted across to the range and seems to be busying herself with some minor chore. She has her back to him but when she turns she is holding a small parcel of greaseproof paper.

'Here – tek 'em for your wife.' She grins as she offers the package; she seems to be covertly eyeing his midriff. 'If thoo can get 'em as far as that.'

*

'Straight up, girl – cross me heart and hope to die – they filmed me, I tell you – I'm gonna be in an episode of Ennerdale!'

DS Leyton has swerved into the first passing place subsequent to the resurrection of his mobile phone signal. He estimates he must be about a quarter of a mile short of the film crew's base. He has his handset pressed close to his ear and his head cocked on one side as though he is struggling to make out what is being said.

'Nah – nah – I didn't get to speak – not that was recorded, anyway. I was just in the background. There's this incident of a couple that have been caught canoodling by the woman's husband – he's gone and crashed his tractor into the back of other geezer's motor. While the uniforms arrest the husband they wanted a detective to be interviewing the lover boy.'

'I dunno who it was – they didn't tell me his name.'

'What? Well, he was about six foot, thirtyish – curly dark hair.'

'*Good looking?* I suppose – maybe some people might think so. He reeked of booze – I'll tell you that, girl. I reckon they've been partying in their caravans.'

DS Leyton narrows his eyes as he listens for a moment.

'*A selfie?* Do me a favour, darlin' – I wouldn't have the brass neck! A thirty-seven-year-old copper asking some celebrity pin-up? Anyway – most of the cast were up on the hill – filming a scene about the heather being set on fire.'

Once more there is a pause as DS Leyton strains to hear his wife.

'Come again, girl? You keep breaking up. What – ah, well – what happened was, I was questioning the security guard about these farm burglaries – in case he'd seen anyone suspicious – and he invited me for a coffee at the catering van. There was one of the producers in there – she was earwigging – and she just asked me if I'd like to be an extra. She said the cove that was supposed to play the detective was indisposed – reading between the lines I reckon she meant he was still three sheets to the wind. I could hardly refuse, could I? The director reckoned I looked just the part!'

'What's that? You're fading again. *When's it on the telly?* Seems it's twelve weeks before it's broadcast.'

'Say what? *Tell Muriel at the coffee morning?* Nah – you mustn't do that, girl. I'm sworn to secrecy – it could cost them a fortune if the plot leaked out and they had to re-shoot.'

DS Leyton seems to receive a shock to the ear – for he jerks the handset away – but whatever sudden electrical interference it was puts paid to his connection. He listens and enquires fruitlessly several times, before glaring at the screen. Maybe

Skelgill is more honest about erratic service than he has suspected.

He drives circumspectly back past the TV encampment – there are no signs of activity through the trees, but Darren is hanging over the gate smoking a cigarette, staring at the ground. He does not seem to notice DS Leyton's passing, which makes him wonder how useful a witness he might have been in any event. Shortly he reaches Bowness Knott picnic area. He is aware that many of the more popular Lakeland car parks now have automatic cameras that capture the registration numbers of vehicles as they enter, and issue fines if a ticket is not purchased at the machine. It is a far cry from the stone honesty boxes they have replaced – but no doubt lucrative for the county council. Rather than fall foul of Big Brother, he pulls up on a patch of verge and proceeds on foot. Sure enough, despite this dale's isolation, there is such a system in place. He glances about. Just three cars occupy an area that could probably accommodate fifty. But this is a workday morning; the weekend would have been a different matter, no doubt. There is the possibility that the thief parked here in order to blend in. He takes out his mobile to discover that the signal has returned. He types into his browser the name of the car park to see if the administrator's details come up – but immediately finds himself sidetracked by an argument over parking charges on an outdoor discussion forum.

"Total rip-off. So-called 'National' park – why pay for something you already own?"

"National Trust is a private charity – it costs them to maintain the facilities."

"What facilities? Camera salesmen were too convincing!"

"At least people pay now."

"Not me!"

"Can I park in your driveway, then?"

"Woke numbskull."

The final riposte is less publishable and casts doubt on the 'woke' part of the former insult.

It baffles DS Leyton how quickly online debate descends into mudslinging. Shaking his head ruefully he returns to his car. As he settles himself, he notices the greaseproof package on the passenger seat. He sighs. Maybe one last one.

6. INNSTYLE

Monday morning

DS Jones waits for the green figure to appear on the pelican crossing – indeed she suffers from an inexplicable moment of inertia and it takes the insistent bleep of the alarm to prompt her to cross, and she ends up scurrying the last few yards. Certainly the traffic has been much heavier this morning than she experienced with Skelgill on Saturday. Although the time is roughly similar, this is the weekday rush hour. Having telephoned the Jacksons at just after seven a.m. to exchange the dispiriting news that neither police nor parents have received any contact from Lisa, or any information regarding her whereabouts, DS Jones is once again retracing her footsteps. Now it is twenty minutes past eight – more or less when Lisa Jackson had walked to work, apparently getting so near and yet (to repeat the phrase Skelgill had completed) so far.

However, it has not escaped DS Jones that there may be incomplete intelligence in this regard. The understanding that Lisa Jackson did not turn up at the office is based on the brief telephone statement she obtained from company director Don McKenzie. And – while he sounded well informed – it seems unlikely that he interrogated all members of staff – and that Lisa's absence was treated at the time not as a matter for a hue and cry, but more just as an aberration that would be explained when she returned to work this morning. Indeed, with a sudden naïve burst of optimism, DS Jones thinks she might meet her – converge with her at the door – and there will be some simple explanation – and to the relief of all the case will be closed. With an exclamation of frustration, she drives off the notion. More realistic is the possibility that Lisa Jackson entered the offices of InnStyle, perhaps communicating with or at least being seen by another member of staff and then – somehow – she left again. This conundrum she hopes to resolve shortly.

Though Warwick Road is busy, both with vehicles and pedestrians, Lychgate Lane – not being a thoroughfare – is almost as deserted as before. She stops and stares, apprehension etched into her features. If anything it looks more dour and depressing still, for this morning a light drizzle falls from a uniformly grey sky, filtering further what limited natural light makes it to the narrow street. 'Almost as deserted' because the timber merchants at the far end have their shutter three-quarters rolled up, and a van is parked side-on with its back doors open. "Wood's of Carlisle", reads the livery, the possibly erroneous grocer's apostrophe not really clarifying whether the first noun refers to proprietor or product. As she watches – she is about seventy yards off – a whistling youth, incongruous with a trendy pompadour haircut and yet wearing a traditional brown shopkeeper's overall appears with an armful of planks and slides them noisily into the vehicle, before ducking back inside the premises.

While she is standing, a young woman in high heels and a pencil-skirted business suit with long glossy black hair that she is trying to protect beneath an inadequate compact umbrella passes her, picking her way over the wet cobbles. Her appearance jolts DS Jones from her reverie and she starts forward – for here is an opportunity.

'Excuse me?'

The girl – she is plainly still a teenager – stops and turns like a fawn unsure on its legs.

'Do you work here – for InnStyle?'

The girl blinks, her enhanced lashes tangling briefly with one another.

'Er – yes?'

DS Jones displays her warrant card.

'I'm from Cumbria CID. I have an appointment with Mr McKenzie. We're trying to trace Lisa Jackson. Did you see her on Friday?'

The girl has full red lips, excessively coloured. She forms them into a downturned crescent.

69

'Er – I don't think so? Lisa's the one that looks like Kate – she's really nice?' DS Jones is wondering which Kate, when the girl elaborates, in a fashion. 'I'm Kylie – I'm the new receptionist. I only started on Wednesday.'

DS Jones finds the picture of Lisa Jackson on her mobile phone.

'Aah. Cute puss.' Then Kylie remembers she is meant to comment on the human. 'No – I don't think I did see her. See what I mean, though – she looks like Kate?'

DS Jones shifts and begins to walk slowly towards the office entrance, as a means of avoiding the digression. The girl totters along beside her.

'What time did you arrive on Friday, Kylie?'

'The same – as now.' She tries again to look at DS Jones's handset. 'It's twenty past, isn't it? I come on the train – it gets in at a quarter past.'

Something else that is easy to check, should this prove important.

'And did you go straight inside – and up to the office?'

'Well – yes – except I had to buzz – they're having a key cut for me.'

'And you didn't notice Lisa arriving here in the street, just after you?'

The girl shakes her head in an exaggerated fashion, and she inhales as if she is about to ask a question – but her response is interrupted by a wolf whistle that makes the most of the resonant stone and brick canyon and wraps them in its intrusive innuendo. Both women look up to see the youth from the timber merchants resting one arm on top of the open door of the van, grinning salaciously. DS Jones notices that the young girl responds with diffidence, lowering her gaze and smiling coyly – whereas she wants to go across and punch the youth (another moment in which she fleetingly identifies with Skelgill). They have reached the recess that protects the doorway for InnStyle.

'You go ahead, Kylie – I'll catch you up.'

When it dawns on the timber merchant's boy that DS Jones is striding purposefully towards him he takes up a slightly less

70

confident pose, half-retreating behind the van door. There is still something of a grin, but it looks like trepidation is beginning to hold sway. And he looks younger by the inch – he is spotty and can hardly be out of puberty.

'What are you doing?'

He begins to stutter.

'I wo' – I mean – I wo' whistlin' thee, an all!'

DS Jones almost bursts into laughter at the logic implicit in his protest. She literally bites her lip while she composes herself. She holds out her warrant card, at which he stares goggle-eyed.

'No – what I mean is what are you doing now – *here.'*

She indicates to the van.

'Loading t' deliveries.'

'Do you do this every morning at this time?'

'Aye – Bazza has his bait and likes to leave by half past – for t' first run.'

She does not inquire as to the identity of 'Bazza' – presumably the driver. She pauses for a moment, and her voice takes on a note of casual reproach.

'Are you in the habit of eyeing up the talent?'

He looks guilty as charged – and makes an apologetic face, and shrugs – overall, giving the impression that these things can't be helped. Again, DS Jones has to contain her reaction – she would be laughing were the underlying issue not so serious.

'On Friday – did you see the girl that just went in?'

He replies without hesitation.

'Aye – I saw her. She started on Wednesday.'

DS Jones is encouraged by his knowledge. She opens the photograph of Lisa on her mobile.

'How about this woman – did you see her?'

He is regaining his confidence.

'Aye – she looks like that Will's bewer.'

That he uses the vernacular for 'girlfriend', and refers it seems to the royal heir apparent and his spouse, answers DS Jones's unasked question about 'which Kate?' Perhaps they are right about Lisa Jackson's looks – and perhaps this helps to give credence to the boy's evidence.

'Did you whistle at her?'

Now he looks a little more sheepish.

'Aye – I know she's older, like.'

DS Jones regards him evenly.

'Did you see her go into the offices?'

'Aye – she smiled at us. She had a GAP top on.'

'And did you see her come out again?' But now he looks puzzled, and she adds a rider. 'How long were you here?'

'A few minutes – maybe five. I had half a pallet of blockboard to put on. But Bazza were away on time – he were standing over us wi' his watch.'

'So – eight-thirty, and you didn't see her? And then you went back inside?'

'Aye – until Bazza got back at ten for t' next load.'

So Lisa Jackson was seemingly inside InnStyle for at least five minutes. DS Jones again can feel her heart making its presence felt. She tries to put aside the rush of thoughts that crowd upon her.

'Did you see anyone else go in after her?'

Now he has to think harder, and strokes absently with grubby fingers the bumfluff of one immature sideburn.

'Not as I recall, miss.'

DS Jones nods pensively. She is eager to move on. She slips into her shoulder bag her warrant card and mobile phone, as a sign to the boy they are finished.

'What's your name?'

'Martin.'

'And surname?'

'Todd.'

He looks wary – as if thinking he is going to have his details taken – but DS Jones decides he won't be going anywhere in a hurry.

'Have you got a girlfriend, Martin?'

He looks uncertain, but then begins to nod. It might just be bravado.

'Aye – kind of.'

'Martin – she wouldn't appreciate you whistling at other girls, would she?'

He lowers his eyes and shakes his head rather mournfully.

'No, miss.'

'Most women like men who act their age, and not their shoe size – you see?'

He looks up – a sudden light in his eyes – and nods obediently as if reformed.

'Aye. Sorry, miss.'

'Good. Thank you.'

DS Jones turns and walks quickly back to the entrance to InnStyle. Just as she moves out of sight into the recess of the building there comes a whistle and the sound of the van door being hastily slammed. She raises her eyes to the heavens and smiles at such helpless incorrigibility. For some reason an image of Skelgill grinning over a pint glass is brought to mind.

She presses the intercom and recognises the girl's voice.

'Hi Kylie, it's DS Jones.'

She is a little disoriented as she enters what must be a gloomy hallway at the best of times. Diffuse natural light emanates from directly ahead, where the passage leads to the foot of a stone stair that disappears to the right. Closer, on the right, is a door that faces her. It has only a mortise lock and no handle and seems poorly maintained and rather ill fitting. She regards it for a moment before moving on. The stair curves, rises and curves again to a landing. A small grimy window set high in the external wall is revealed as the source of light, a little brighter up here. Immediately at the top of the flight is another door. A polished plaque reads, "Reception – Please Enter" and now the woodwork is smartly painted in the same deep blue as the external entrance.

But the contrast is even greater when she pushes open the door, and perhaps this is the intended effect. The dull and dilapidated Victorian stair gives on to a sleek modern open-plan office, in pastel shades subtly lit by concealed lighting; there are glass partitions, brushed chrome fittings, contemporary furniture and stylish desks with slim silvered computer monitors and matching angle-poise lamps. There are several casual seating areas with inviting low-rise sofas. Just a murmur of modern jazz permeates the pleasantly cool ether, and no sense is spared as DS Jones encounters the dual aroma of fresh coffee and the sweet waft from a huge vase of lilies placed to one side of the reception desk. It is like penthouse-apartment-meets-boutique-hotel, and must surely both impress and inspire visiting clientele from the leisure industry.

'Don's expecting you.' It seems Kylie is already on first-name terms with the senior staff. 'The boardroom and directors' offices are on the next floor – just go up the internal staircase.'

The girl half-turns to indicate to where an audacious unguarded spiral of ash boards wind like vertebrae around a central steel column and disappear into the ceiling. DS Jones nods and walks into the open-plan area. About half of the desks – maybe seven or eight at a glance – are occupied and she senses some attention as she mounts the stair and her own relatively modest heels make a click-clack sound on the hard wood. There are glances of passive interest – and certainly no hostility – but most noticeable to DS Jones is that, seated at a workstation set in front of a window that must overlook Lychgate Lane, is Ray Piper. He is not looking her way, but is leaning forward interrogatively, and has his attention firmly fixed on his computer screen.

DS Jones spirals out of sight, and leaves behind the company's engine room to reach a similarly stylish although more exclusive floor with an expansive carpeted landing off which there are just four doors in pale ash. One of these is wide open and she sees a man rise from behind a broad desk. Well dressed in expensive and new-looking casual clothes, black jeans and a close-fitting black wool turtle-neck sweater and black ankle boots – the 'man in black' – of a little above medium height, he is slim and fit-looking, has a fashionable trimmed beard and haircut, and regular handsome features. She would guess he is mid-to-late thirties in age.

As she enters she is conscious of the steady, penetrating gaze of his brown eyes. She wonders what his shoe size will prove to be.

'Good morning.' He smiles to reveal even white teeth and gestures expansively towards a seating area, two more of the trendy sofas set either side of a minimalistic glass coffee table. 'Please – make yourself comfortable. Is there any news of Lisa? We've still heard nothing.'

Like all police officers in these circumstances, DS Jones is trained to treat everyone she meets with concealed caution – criminals are often the most convincing of people – but there is a note of authentic concern in the man's voice that she finds curiously reassuring.

'I'm afraid not, sir. Although we now have more information concerning her movements on Friday. That's what I would like to ask you about, in particular.'

As they both take their seats – on opposite sofas – the man nods obligingly.

'Sorry – but, first – would you like a coffee – we have a fancy new espresso machine – or a herbal tea – or a chilled mineral water?'

He has his mobile phone in one hand, as though he will use it to summon assistance. And that he works his way through the list of beverages suggests he is sensitive to DS Jones's reaction. He is well spoken, a faint Scots accent – perhaps the Edinburgh private school version, she considers.

'No thank you – I'm fine, sir.'

'Oh, please – call me Don. We try to be entirely informal here.'

DS Jones smiles, but with a certain restraint.

'Thanks – but – these things can get awkward if I need to arrest you.'

He takes the reprimand well – raising his hands slightly and making a facial expression of mea culpa – and he seems to approve that she has blended irony with protocol.

'Sorry – but – look – if you're here for any length of time, just ask the nearest person and they'll get you what you want. They'll also show you where the washrooms are.' He makes an upward gesture with one hand. 'We've got loos and showers and storage areas on the top floor – but you have to use the main staircase – where you came in.'

DS Jones does not instantly reply – she is looking at him as though a thought is occurring to her and she is trying to decide whether to speak of it. In the hiatus, he makes his own inquiry.

'You said – you have something about Lisa on Friday?'

It is not DS Jones's intention for the man to dictate the course of the interview – but this in fact coincides with her agenda.

'Yes. We have CCTV and eyewitness evidence that suggests Miss Jackson walked to work as normal and in fact entered your ground floor office door at eight twenty-five a.m. – maybe a minute earlier.'

Don McKenzie looks impressed. He inhales perplexedly.

'I don't know how to answer that. I didn't arrive myself until after ten – I was visiting a job at Carlisle Golf Club and I went straight from home as I live in Wetheral.' (DS Jones nods; she knows the location, an exclusive dormitory village on the left bank of the Eden.) 'It was Norma – Lisa's line manager – who mentioned Lisa hadn't come in – and then it was only later in the day – probably mid-afternoon when it cropped up – and she told me no one had seen or heard from her and that she'd tried her mobile but had been unable to get any response. As I said when we spoke – it was unusual – but you don't tend to think of sinister explanations as a first reaction.' He regards her apologetically, as though concerned that the firm were not sufficiently on Lisa Jackson's case. 'We're really busy at the moment – everyone pretty much has their nose to the grindstone.'

But DS Jones picks up a finer point.

'What makes you use the word *sinister*, sir?'

He seems caught off guard by the reminder that this attractive female detective has steel to contrast with her appearance. But he does not try to be clever.

76

'Well – I mean – that you're investigating.' His tone is questioning, and sounds reasonably so. 'That would suggest you think something has happened to her.'

DS Jones responds equably.

'We have to keep an open mind, sir – or we can end up going down the wrong track.' The man nods, and she continues. 'Do you have any form of clocking-in system?'

He begins to shake his head – he half raises an eyebrow at the idea that such a primitive method would be employed in a modern company like this. Then an idea strikes him.

'Our server records when each person logs on to our intranet – and logs off, of course.'

'Could you provide that information? It would help us to concentrate on anyone more likely to have had some contact with Miss Jackson.'

Indeed, there is the possibility that Lisa Jackson logged on herself.

'Sure – I'll get Sam our computer person to run off a report as soon as we're finished.'

DS Jones gives a nod of approval. She hands over a calling card.

'Maybe you could email that to me?'

'Sure.'

'Do you have a formal start time?'

Don McKenzie tilts his head from side to side.

'Unofficially, eight-thirty. We make sure there's someone here to answer the phone in case a client rings. But, basically it's flexible between eight and nine. Folk have their own keys to the main door – and their own challenges – trains, traffic, kindergartens.' He gives a half-laugh as though he speaks from present experience. 'Some people like to get in early and escape the domestic chaos.'

DS Jones does not probe this point, though it seems to hold an invitation to do so. She glances at the figureless clock on the wall to one side – just a pair of long slender hands that seem to have time standing still, though they have advanced surreptitiously to almost nine.

'I have arranged for a detective constable to come along at nine-thirty and interview everyone – just to get details of movements – anything they might know about Miss Jackson – something she may have mentioned on Thursday or earlier in the week.'

'Absolutely – I'll send round a message if that would help?'

DS Jones nods approvingly.

'I'd like to get some background information on Miss Jackson. You mentioned her line manager – would she be the best person with whom to speak?'

He makes an ambivalent gesture with one hand.

'Well – certainly I would start with Norma – Norma Marston. She'll be able to tell you whom Lisa was closest to. And she'll have her personnel file.'

DS Jones nods.

'How well do you know Miss Jackson, sir?'

Don McKenzie looks relaxed but DS Jones is sure she detects a reaction. Perhaps just those fine responses when a person suddenly senses that they are under the spotlight. A faint stiffening as if to prevent any inadvertent movement or even to blink. The delaying of a breath. The unconscious narrowing of pupils. Of course, it is a paradox – it is natural to try to act naturally, but not easy to execute.

'Well – she's been here for over three years. There are eighteen of us – no, nineteen, Kylie started last week – so I would say I know Lisa quite well – but largely in a work context. Apart from time to time when we have away-days – we go abseiling or quad-biking or something like that.'

'How would you describe her – her personality?'

'She can be good fun – she's very pleasant – a nice person, you know? And sometimes I would say she seems quite thoughtful – I mean, in the deliberative sense – she's always considerate. She's a talented designer and she does her work very conscientiously.'

'What do you know of her personal life – relationships?'

The man shifts back in his seat and folds his arms.

'I don't really know much – I tend not to ask about that sort of thing – especially of our female staff – I think it can be interpreted the wrong way – and I don't like that idea. But to answer your question in broad terms – I understand she's not married. But I don't know if there's someone else in the frame. Again – it's more likely she's mentioned it to one of the other girls.'

DS Jones is wondering if at this juncture Skelgill would loose off the Exocet that is the evidently clandestine relationship between Lisa Jackson and Ray Piper. But she imagines she hears his voice muttering "keep your powder dry, lass" and she concurs. She changes the subject back to the puzzle that must surely be confounding the director as much as it is she.

'Is there another door to your offices apart from the Lychgate Lane entrance?'

He shakes his head. He raises his hands expansively.

'There wasn't a lot of Health & Safety about when they built this. We're above a restaurant that has its own emergency exit a couple of yards along from our door. We've installed drop-down window ladders on all floors in case the stairwell is inaccessible – that's where our main fire escape is, on the top floor – it takes you onto the flat roof and along to a fixed steel ladder – like you see in American films.' He pauses and seems to reflect for a moment; he must realise what DS Jones is thinking. 'We would know if the fire door had been breached as it's alarmed and it has a security seal – I can show you, if you would like?'

DS Jones is nodding.

'Please. I would also like to see inside the door on the ground floor.'

He looks a little surprised.

'Oh – it doesn't lead anywhere – it's just a cupboard under the stairs.'

DS Jones nods but, if he is suggesting it would be a waste of time, she fails to acquiesce. She regards him patiently and he seems to understand he should elaborate.

'It's where the server is housed – as well as the various services – electricity, water, gas, fire and burglar alarms. It means that contractors and the fire brigade can get at them without disturbing us. We call it the comms cupboard but its function is more of a plant room – although you can't swing a cat in there.'

*

DS Jones wonders if she is trying subconsciously to ape Skelgill. She is standing in Lychgate Lane – pensively, meditatively – and now drifting aimlessly, like a water diviner hoping to absorb some invisible vibrations. Skelgill would then peremptorily up sticks, making no announcement about the conclusion he had reached – if indeed there were one at all. She is reminded – she has long appreciated – that her mind does not work like his. She exists at the opposite end of the spectrum that spans the chasm between logic and insight. Not that she lacks intuition – just that hers is more applicable to human sentiments; Skelgill's – ironically in this instance – to practical outcomes.

So she must play to her strengths. There is a logical conundrum here that has a rational explanation. Lisa Jackson entered this doorway at twenty-four or -five minutes past eight – the time is triple-corroborated and the cocky boy actually saw her go in. But, after that, she left no trace.

Don McKenzie has shown her the third-floor fire escape, its security seal intact. Before descending they checked the washrooms and storeroom. At reception he apologised to Kylie for dipping into her desk drawer – explaining to DS Jones that the plant room was not usually locked but they may as well take the key, just in case. There had been a moment of trepidation when he opened it – it had not been locked. He had leant in and switched on the light – and then stood back, rather like a landlord showing a bedsit to a prospective tenant. It had struck DS Jones that he did want to be the first to look. But, apart from a stack of cardboard boxes, a fairly recent delivery by the look of it, the cupboard was bare – at least, in the context that concerned DS Jones. The main wall on the right-hand side was lined with pipework and cabling, fuse boxes and meters, and a sleek grey plastic unit that was the server. DS Jones had used her mobile phone to illuminate the depths of the low recess beneath the rising stair – but this was just empty space.

One aspect of intuition that DS Jones is obeying is that she has decided not to interview any other members of staff – for the time being. DC Watson will be along shortly to take basic details – but DS Jones does not wish to conflate this with more profound questioning – questioning that she cannot undertake until she knows *why* she is doing it. And there are other avenues that must first be checked and securely taped off. Despite the dead zone that is Lychgate Lane – only InnStyle has an operational entrance, along with the delivery bay of Wood's of Carlisle (presently closed) – as she and Skelgill had noted, there are various emergency exits. Two uniformed constables from the local police station are presently working their way methodically around the corresponding properties and businesses, interviewing owners, concierges, janitors and the like, to establish whether any of these could have been open on Friday morning. The idea that Lisa Jackson went into one of them contradicts both logic and the known facts – but it needs to be eliminated as a possibility. As does the outlandish thought that Lisa planned her own Lord Lucan-like disappearance and smuggled herself aboard Wood's of Carlisle's delivery van. DS Jones intends to deal with this matter herself – when a message arrives on her mobile that causes her to have pause for thought.

*

'How's it going, Emma – enjoying the peace?'

DS Jones looks up, her hazel eyes vacant for a moment.

DS Leyton is standing at her side; she has not noticed his stealthy approach on the carpeted floor, amidst the hum of the busy office. He has two plastic cups that appear small in one large hand, and a small parcel wrapped in what seems like baking parchment in the other.

'There you go, girl – got you a tea – you've had your head down since I came in. You need to try a bit of this cake.'

She reaches and takes the cups and DS Leyton drags over a chair. He places the package on her desk and begins to unwrap the folds.

'I feel like I'm already wearing tyre tracks into the M6.'

There is the suggestion in her tone that she thinks she will be wearing them a lot deeper still. DS Leyton raises his head in a gesture of sympathy.

'I was out in the sticks earlier on. Farmer lady insisted I have this – for the missus. It's energy cake – perk you up.'

There is a broken corner and DS Jones pops it experimentally into her mouth. She nods in agreement – she can taste the calories!

'Is that what she called it?'

'What? *Nah* – *nah* – Ennerdale cake. That's where I was – and have I got a story to tell!'

DS Leyton relates his tale – his modest claim to fame, a little embellished at the edges – while DS Jones listens with a mixture of intrigue and delight.

'Your wife will be doubly pleased.' She gestures to the dwindling parcel. 'If you save her some.'

'Yeah – good point.'

DS Jones has taken just another crumbled morsel; her eyes sparkle with amusement.

'I wouldn't mind the recipe for my Mum – she's a demon baker.'

'Hmm – I never thought of that.' DS Leyton ponders for a moment. 'Still – I might have to go back.'

DS Jones licks a trace of caster sugar from her upper lip.

'How did you get on – otherwise?'

Now DS Leyton makes a face of a more hangdog nature, his ample jowls sagging.

'Stable doors and horses bolted – it's one of those.' He shrugs his broad shoulders. 'Easy pickings, these hill farms – no one for miles around, no witnesses, no CCTV – apart from the tourist car parks. I'm trying to work out what I might learn from that – but it's a needle in a flippin' haystack.'

DS Jones seems to zone out for a moment, and DS Leyton realises that in his excitement to share his good fortune he has been monopolising the agenda. He indicates to the printout spread in about a dozen sheets on her desk. It is the report, news of which has prompted her return from Carlisle.

'Looks like you've got your own haystack there, girl?'

DS Jones tunes back in. She regards her colleague in a way that recognises his seniority, in experience if not in rank.

'Actually – can I just bounce something off you?'

'Fire away – you know me – I'll always come up with the dumb answer. I'm the Guvnor's original daft country copper – minus the country part – which gives me a head start.'

She shoots him a reproachful glance that is intended to gainsay his self-deprecation. Then she lays a hand on the page nearest to her, over which she has been poring. She looks at him again, more purposefully.

'Lisa Jackson is still missing.' DS Leyton nods; he is apprised of the broad outline of the case. 'She was seen to enter the only door of her company's premises at about eight twenty-five on Friday. The CCTV evidence suggests she didn't come out. Yet, so far, they don't think she actually went to work.'

'Right.' DS Leyton makes a wide-eyed expression. 'Rings of my invisible shotgun thief.'

DS Jones nods pensively.

'But there's this.' She reaches and picks up the business card that she accepted from Ray Piper. She hands it to DS Leyton. 'She'd been having an affair with this guy, a married man – who also works there. The relationship was supposed to have ended before Christmas – but I don't think it was as simple as that.' Now she pushes her chair back a little to expose the sheets on the desk. 'These are the records of Lisa Jackson's mobile phone activity.' She jabs a finger, almost angrily, at the card her colleague holds. 'He was texting her – up to *twenty* times a day. He texted her four times on Friday morning – before the last sighting. And then no texts since.'

DS Leyton emits a soft whistle.

'You've not got her phone?'

83

DS Jones shakes her head.

'We just have a list of the numbers, not the content. The phone went out of service shortly after she was last seen and hasn't been switched on since.' She indicates again to the most adjacent page. 'These are the texts that never got through – mainly from her parents – but none from him, Ray Piper.'

'And what does he have to say?'

She inhales gravely.

'I think I have to chose my moment very carefully when I ask that question.'

DS Leyton frowns broodingly.

'And where was he?'

'He told us he was at the office from just after eight. I'm waiting for a report back from DC Watson – everyone's movements – she'll be asking them about their colleagues as well – whom they saw, and when – so we might get some corroboration, or otherwise. I've also been promised a report with computer login times. I've yet to check the CCTV for other employees.'

DS Leyton seems distracted, however. Somewhat absently he helps himself to another square of cake.

'Strange one, that – him suddenly stopping texting her. Almost like he knew there was no point. Did she normally reply to these texts?'

DS Jones shakes her head.

'Mainly not. But there is one actual call from his phone – it's on this list of undelivered contacts. But much later – just after one p.m.'

DS Leyton glances hopefully at his colleague.

'He might have left a voicemail.'

DS Jones nods.

'I've put in a request. They take longer to get.'

DS Leyton's expression becomes speculative.

'Could it have been the geezer's missus – all those texts – harassing her with her husband's phone?'

DS Jones looks interested in the idea but shakes her head.

84

'The overwhelming majority of them are during working hours. It appears he was texting her while they were both in the office. Almost like a secret conversation, albeit one way.'

There is a pause while DS Leyton finishes his cake and washes it down with tea.

'Anyone else in the frame?' He gestures at the pages. 'Someone who's suddenly got in touch with her?'

DS Jones is troubled by this question.

'It's mainly her parents' number. There are one or two others that I need to check out – but nothing in volume or pattern.' She brushes away a strand of hair from her cheek. 'However – there is a new boyfriend, a Gary Scott. He seems to be in the clear, as far as his whereabouts at the time Lisa Jackson disappeared. But he slept over at her place on Thursday night. Just before eight on Friday morning a neighbour – seems to be a reliable witness – saw Ray Piper's car pull up outside the house and then roar away.'

'What – like he was checking her out – seeing if she'd got the new geezer staying?'

DS Jones nods pensively, and her eyes glaze over. DS Leyton can see that he ought to leave her as he found her – in peace. He looks at the cake – he looks tempted. Then, with a sigh, he pushes it away.

'Do me a favour, Emma – keep that for me, until close of play.'

DS Jones laughs.

'I'll wrap it with some scene-of-crime tape.'

*

Fortified by a whole slice of Ennerdale cake pressed upon her by her insistent colleague before his departure, DS Jones is acting on a hunch. She does not quite fully understand what the hunch is – and she wonders if this is the same subliminal irritation that drives Skelgill to some of his odd behaviour. Under normal circumstances, without actually discussing the division of labour, he does this job for them, upending the apple cart while they are left to sift the wheat from the chaff – just the sort of metaphors Skelgill himself would mix! But DS Leyton's words have – if not exactly crystallised her thoughts – at least caused her feelings to coalesce. And it is not so much what he said, but the way he took for granted the motive he ascribed to Ray Piper's presence outside Lisa Jackson's home. It settled her upon an insight she might not have so readily reached.

She has donned a headset and is playing music from her mobile phone – this to block out interference and perhaps also to facilitate some form of mental relaxation. When she left Skelgill on Saturday she spent many hours viewing on fast-forward the police CCTV recording from the Crescent. Since there is only one way to reach InnStyle, she was able to flag the time that every person entered or left Lychgate Lane on Friday. She covered the period from seven-thirty a.m. to four-thirty p.m. Now she has logged back on to the file she has created.

Given that the camera is sited approximately a hundred yards away, and had not been specially assigned to monitor the opening of Lychgate Lane, it recorded only a general perspective down Warwick Road. Human figures, therefore, were quite distant and, if frozen and enlarged, rather fuzzy images. Thus, like Lisa Jackson, to identify them would in most cases require knowledge of what they were wearing, perhaps combined with what time they arrived, and perhaps assisted by someone who knows the individuals well enough to pick them out by their gait. This task, however, she is confident her unit could undertake, should it prove necessary – it is just a matter of time and resources.

She flips her screen; on a second window she has InnStyle's website, open at a tab entitled "Meet the Team". There are photographs of the directors and employees. In the second tier of the company organisation chart she clicks on the small picture of Ray Piper. It comes up in enlarged form, along with a short biography. It details his qualifications (a BSc in Quantity Surveying and an MSc in Industrial Heritage and Archaeology) and length of service (five and a half years), and describes him as "a project manager with first-rate problem-solving skills and

86

attention to detail – exactly the person you want on your job, to navigate quickly and cost-effectively around those unforeseen obstacles that often occur during a complex and sensitive refurbishment, in particular on old properties where historical and preservation issues may unexpectedly arise". It highlights that "Ray prides himself in getting the task done on time and on budget". It moves on to describe him as a family man whose interests include his boys' football, art house films and cartography. She stares at the image. It seems quite recent – he looks just the same as when they met. It is artistically lit, creating highlight and shadow, a professionally taken shot – presumably to achieve consistency in the appearance of the website. But she notes that, where most of the staff smile, Ray Piper has attempted a cool look – however, where there ought to be integrity, there is a ruthlessness in his glazed grey eyes. Or does she imagine it?

She switches the screen back to the video recording. When she went through it on Saturday she had one object – she was watching like a hawk for Lisa Jackson – and, of course, about an hour in, at 08:24 she found her. Thereafter, her focus was single-minded – would Lisa reappear? The long dark hair, the slim figure, the white trainers and spring in her step, the GAP sweatshirt and the distinctive shoulder bag. Thus she did not pay particular attention to the comings and goings of others, merely bookmarking them for future reference. Now is that time.

But she begins at 08:24 and, with a strange sinking feeling watches Lisa Jackson disappear into the lane. Now she waits patiently. Sure enough – it seems that the whistling Martin was right – the next movement is at 08:30 when Wood's of Carlisle's van emerges and makes a cavalier charge at the traffic to join the one-way flow beneath the camera at the Crescent. At this juncture no one else has entered Lychgate Lane on foot – and only now, at 08:34 does an older balding male appear, quickly followed by a younger female, who seems to hurry as though she intends to catch up the former.

DS Jones returns to her earliest flag, 07:52 when two females enter the lane together. At 07:59 there is a lone male whom she

87

does not recognise and then, three minutes later at 08:02, Ray Piper. She is certain it is he. She recalls, outside his house, the casual movements that could not conceal a stiff, erect demeanour, one that seems almost repressed. And he is clothed in what could be the same outfit of black jeans and brown jacket.

Next she begins to click forward using her shortcuts. There ensue some twenty-five sightings, a mixture of (presumably) employees entering the lane, and the likes of couriers and postie both entering and leaving shortly afterwards. And then – at 09:52 – her heart makes a little involuntary leap – for she finds Ray Piper again. This time he is leaving. She rewinds and reviews the clip. He crosses the road – not troubling to revert the twenty yards to the pelican crossing, but jogging diagonally between moving vehicles and heading briskly in the out-of-town direction.

She skips on, only three bookmarks, in fact – and the first two of these a helmeted cycle courier making a fleeting visit. The third – at 10:17 – is the returning Ray Piper, twenty-five minutes after he left. Now he is moving more sedately, and he waits to use the crossing. She freezes the image just as he is about to turn into Lychgate Lane. She stares. She knows there is something – and after a moment it comes to her. On a balmy July morning, *Ray Piper is now wearing gloves.* Yes, quite clearly she can make out what must surely be the same distinctive pale tan driving gloves that he wore on Saturday.

Her pulse is raised, a beat in step with the Rolling Stones track that is blasting in her ears, one that she has noticed Skelgill react to while driving, on the rare occasion that he will tolerate music. Alone on her cloud, she allows her mind to wander.

Presently, she gathers her wits and navigates back to 09:52 when Ray Piper left Lychgate Lane. She starts the tape rolling at normal speed. She reclines in her seat, and waits. It seems like an age – but it is only ten minutes – exactly ten minutes – when, with the timer reading 10:02 she starts. A white BMW heading into town turns right into Lychgate Lane. Emblazoned along the side of the car is a chequered black stripe. About a minute later Wood's of Carlisle's delivery van follows it.

DS Jones feels like her heart has migrated north.

At 10:04 – just two minutes after entering the lane – the white BMW emerges and pulls out into the traffic. Now obliged to follow the one-way system it heads directly towards the camera – just as the van had done earlier. DS Jones freezes the action and enlarges the image. If she was in any doubt, Ray Piper's registration number is plainly legible.

*

Loitering in Lychgate Lane seems to be becoming a habit. DS Jones watches pensively as Wood's van rumbles away over the cobbles and, its driver paying scant attention to either pedestrians or vehicles at the T-junction; he barges out into the traffic and disappears to the right. There goes 'Bazza' – real name Adrian Ibson and no indication of the nickname's origin. She continues to stare for a good twenty seconds after he has gone, reflecting upon what he has told her. But now she makes a conscious effort to break out of this reverie, and she takes up her mobile phone.

DC Watson's report is pleasingly intelligible: a list of employees, when they each arrived, whom they can remember they saw when they entered the office. The promised computer login report has also been delivered. These two data sources confirm that Ray Piper reached the office at just after eight and logged on via the pc at his desk at 08:05. Meanwhile, the uniformed constables have completed their survey of surrounding premises, and there is no indication that a fire escape onto Lychgate Lane was left open or breached, nor was there a sighting of Lisa Jackson passing unauthorised through one of buildings.

But DS Jones is ninety-nine percent certain that Lisa Jackson did not pass into any building other than InnStyle. While these reports were accumulating in her inbox, she visited Wood's of Carlisle. At the front, on the high street there is a retail outlet stocking hardware, and, within, a trade counter for wood, cut to size. "A Great Deal In Timber" bragged a faded window slogan, and she wondered if it were intentionally a pun. The enterprise was founded in Victorian times, and no actual Woods have survived. Instead a rather pompous and stout middle-aged woman by the name of Jacqueline Birch was summoned; she introduced herself as the present owner and general manager. She knew nothing of DS Jones's quest – nor that the apprentice boy Martin had been questioned. But she was able quickly to confirm that Lisa Jackson had certainly not passed through the premises on Friday morning – indeed, could not have done so, because the front door was locked until 9:00 a.m. – normal opening time – and she held the keys. DS Jones had requested an audience with 'Bazza' – and was informed that 'Mr Ibson' was eating his lunch preparatory to the 12:30 p.m. departure; it seems the firm sends out deliveries every two hours, beginning at 8:30 a.m.

She was conducted to a poky room, windowless to the extent that the only glass partition gave on to a workshop from which emanated the irregular whine of a circular saw, and the distinctive aroma of fresh sawdust. Mr Ibson proved to be a man of about thirty-five, and – without digressing into detail she would rather not recall – evidently the role model for young Martin in the female-ogling department. Accordingly, DS Jones had dealt with him with a degree of perfunctory efficiency. But, while his roving eye had engendered a feeling of transient distaste, his rustic narrative has left a more lasting impression. Now she replays the conversation in her mind.

"Mr Ibson, when you left at eight-thirty on Friday, was anyone in the van with you?"

"T'were full t' roof wi' blockboard."

"What about the passenger seat?"

"Why would I have had anyone wi' us?"

DS Jones did not answer. Close scrutiny of the CCTV footage from the public order camera at the Crescent would confirm his denial.

"When you returned – it was three minutes past ten – were there any other vehicles in the lane?"

His attention was drawn from perusal of her figure. He regarded her suspiciously – that she seemed to know both the exact time, and that there was an affirmative answer to the question.

"Aye – there were – a car."

"Can you describe what you saw?"

"It were a white BMW – flash, like. He'd blocked us road."

"What do you mean?"

"He were reversed up t' doorway – t' car were across road, at an angle, like."

He made a 'T' with his two hands, his grubby fingers held rigidly.

"What was he doing?"

"He lowped int' car as I approached. Then he had to reverse down to our bay – where it's wider – so I could get past him."

"And he drove off?"

"Aye."

"And his car was backed up against the entrance to the offices – at number thirteen?"

"Aye, thirteen – happen it is."

She questioned Adrian Ibson in a little more detail – and indeed exited with him via the loading bay to confirm unequivocally the position of the white BMW. And, while he could provide a good enough description to identify the man as Ray Piper, he could not shed more light on why his car was parked perpendicular to the recessed doorway. Prompted – and perhaps given his own vocation – Adrian Ibson made the obvious suggestion that the man in question "must've been loading, like."

Loading what?

91

7. DS JONES'S DILEMMA

Monday afternoon

'So you've no news of Lisa, then?'

DS Jones is a little irked that he has pre-empted her opening remarks – and perhaps more so since this is the question asked by those who have genuine concern for the missing woman – when she suspects he harbours no such sentiment.

She has been given use of the boardroom of InnStyle. A large, high-ceilinged, rectangular room, it has sash windows overlooking the busy high street and admitting the watery afternoon sun in square shafts. There are wall hangings, abstracted photographs of completed projects, and on one side an almost invisible glass shelf on which an extensive row of trophies and awards is spotlighted. She suspects that, as well as for internal purposes, the room must be used for meeting prospective clients and could not fail to impress.

The long but relatively narrow boardroom table puts those seated opposite actually intimately close to one another. DS Jones thinks she can see microscopic beads of perspiration on Ray Piper's brow – although it might just be the waxy texture of his unnaturally mask-like skin. She is reminded of Skelgill's adopted jibe: Poker Face.

The man in question sits bolt upright with his palms pressing upon his thighs – he reminds her of someone posing in a passport photo-booth, stretching their spine to line up their eyes with the guides on the glass in front of the camera. This stilted posture was apparent in his entrance, when he had sidled in through the half-open door with his hands at his sides, backing against it to close it in what she felt was a calculating act, for she might have preferred it to be left ajar.

For her part, she is alone, and she becomes uncomfortably aware of this fact. DC Watson she despatched earlier – there are important issues to resolve, such as the corroboration of Gary Scott's account of his movements, and identification of the miscellaneous numbers that appear on Lisa Jackson's phone record. DS Leyton would have come along as chaperone, if asked – but he has his own case to handle – and, besides, his wife and family to get back to, with his exciting news from Ennerdale (and any surviving cake). Not a big man – at least not vertically – but, as Skelgill has remarked to her, "Leyton can stop a bus" – and he does not mean by sticking out his thumb. Skelgill – no doubt fishing at this very moment – would equally provide a reassuring presence. In situations where many people would be intimidated Skelgill becomes consumed by a righteous indignation, and is liable not to pull his punches.

That she is even having these thoughts sends a chill down her spine – but she steels herself and resists the urge to take comfort in a distracting sip from the glass of mineral water beside her notepad. She sees that Ray Piper's gaze has shifted to the page – in some respects a momentary respite from the pale soulless stare – and it galvanises her and she wonders if he is trying to read the content. She feels cheered – a small victory – for she writes in shorthand and she doubts he can translate her own version, never mind that it is upside down. But how much of her hand *does* she reveal? She forces herself to keep her eyes trained upon him. And now she strives to sound relaxed, matter of fact, even friendly.

'We actually have a good deal of information, sir – but, no – we have not located Miss Jackson.'

DS Jones suddenly experiences a wave of self-doubt. What if she has jumped the gun – put all her eggs in one basket – idioms that Skelgill constantly trots out – and she appreciates more than ever that despite his apparent – no, not even apparent – *actual* disregard for correct police protocol, he does instinctively know when to hold back. She has seen him fish enough times now to understand where he gets it from – or at least where it is seen more obviously – a transferable skill of knowing when to strike – and, perhaps more importantly, when not to.

But her decision to interview Ray Piper when perhaps there is more to glean elsewhere is driven by an instinct of her own – the sense that every second counts – that with each moment that passes that essence of Lisa that they trailed from her house will evaporate into the ether, to become forever untraceable. And the evidence, the momentum that she has gathered thus far has received one more small but salient shove of impetus only moments before this interview was due to commence. Upon her return to InnStyle, signing the visitors' book at the reception desk, she had sensed that Ray Piper was observing her from his workstation. She asked Kylie to show her where to find the mineral water dispenser. This took them out of his sight. There ensued a quick-fire Q&A.

"Kylie – when you arrived on Friday, did anyone pass you, or leave the office shortly after?"

Though DS Jones's tone was casual, Kylie seemed to sense the underlying significance of the question.

"Aye – the one called Ray. I mean – he went to the toilet."

"Could you explain?"

"As I reached the door it opened – and he held it for me. And he said something about watch the ginseng tea, it goes right through you – like as a jokey warning, because I'm new."

"Did you actually see that he went up the staircase to the toilets?"

She had shaken her head.

"No – he closed the door and I got settled at reception."

"When did he come back?"

"Maybe – in ten minutes?"

"That's quite a while."

"Well – I did wonder –"

"What?"

"Well – if he'd been for a ciggy, like. I've been wondering what people do – whether you need permission."

"You smoke?"

She had lowered her gaze self-consciously.

"Just socially, really."

"Did he smell of smoke?"

For a moment she had looked perplexed, as if the notion might divert her.

"I didn't notice." Then she hesitated. "Maybe I smelled soap – we've got that nice pomegranate handwash – but –"

She had stopped because Ray Piper appeared, discreetly, upright, hands behind back; it would have been a polite demeanour were it not for his implacable features.

"You were planning to see me? I have a call that may last a while – I need to know if I should put it off."

DS Jones had lifted her glass from the dispenser and said that it would be fine – she would be ready in just one minute. Ray Piper hovered – and the water-cooler conversation broke up. DS Jones found her way to the boardroom with Kylie's account ringing in her ears: that Ray Piper had left the first floor office shortly before Lisa Jackson arrived below.

What else could she do but interview him?

But she remembers her imagined advice from Skelgill – about keeping her powder dry. She decides to see what he will tell her voluntarily.

'Mr Piper, could you just run over your movements on Friday?'

She sees a hardening in his eyes.

'I've told your DC Watson, this morning – and you asked me that on Saturday.'

DS Jones is prepared for the objection.

'Mr Piper – given the confidential matter that you mentioned,' (she pauses, as if to let her words sink in) 'you'll appreciate that from our perspective you are more likely than other staff members to be able to shed some light on events.'

He reacts with a tightening of his narrow lips. He seems to understand that the matter is still confidential, and that she has leverage in this regard.

'Maybe in general, I could. But on Friday I came to the office, I worked here all day, I picked the boys up directly after. I stayed at home. I didn't see or hear from Lisa.'

DS Jones nods acceptingly.

'Did you take your sons to their football camp on Friday morning?'

'No – it starts at nine-fifteen. My wife does it. I came to the office at eight – my usual time.'

She notes his omission.

'How do you get to work, sir?'

'I drive.'

The reply is economical.

'But – there's no parking here?'

'There's plenty of free on-street parking nearby.'

'Do you have a regular spot?'

He looks irritated, as though it is an intrusion into his privacy – but he must realise it is easily established.

'Aglionby Street.'

'I don't know Carlisle all that well, sir.'

Her tone invites explanation.

'It's five minutes' walk. It branches off Warwick Road towards Botchergate.'

DS Jones is sure he must know where the interview is heading. She consults her notes, in a more prolonged way than is necessary. She faces the dilemma that it is no easy task to question someone in the manner of a witness when you consider them a suspect – indeed, unless there is an overwhelming reason not to put them on guard, it can be counterproductive. And, frankly, if he has any intelligence, he would surely expect to be treated with suspicion – even if he were entirely innocent. She looks up and meets head on the cold gaze, though it is neither easy, nor comfortable.

'The fact is, Mr Piper – we also have to eliminate everybody – in the event that Miss Jackson has been the victim of a criminal act.'

He merely continues to stare. She finds it virtually impossible to gauge his reaction.

'You say you were here all day on Friday. On what occasions did you leave your desk?'

He shifts back slightly – as though to suggest this is an unreasonable question.

'I don't keep a record.'

Mentally, DS Jones takes a deep breath.

96

'What about at twenty-five past eight – did you go out into the stairwell?'

This, of course, is a card being shown. Though it can hardly be unexpected. Now Ray Piper is absolutely immobile.

'Like I say – I don't keep a record. I drink a lot of tea – I probably go the toilet half a dozen times a day.'

'You didn't go out for any other reason?'

'I went out for a sandwich.'

DS Jones is surprised by his swift rejoinder – and she wonders if this is to distract her from what she has learned from Kylie. And, yet, it takes them a step closer to his unexplained movements revealed by the CCTV footage.

'What time was that, sir?'

He gives a slight shrug.

'Mid-morning, I should say.'

DS Jones pauses. She knows what he did mid-morning, alright. She saw no sandwich. He might have been inexplicably gloved, but he appeared empty handed.

'Why not lunchtime?'

She detects a flicker of uncertainty in his eyes – although nothing in the immovable facial muscles – the Poker Face – but, yes, in the eyes – surely there is a moment of alarm as if there is something he has not thought of. Or is she grasping at straws, reading too much into the tiniest of reactions?

'I had something else to do.'

'What was that, sir?'

'I needed to put some samples in my car. To take to a client for approval.'

DS Jones experiences a sinking feeling – almost that she has been led into a trap – a pitfall she should have seen coming, but now it is too late. She does her best not to show it, but she struggles to find the right question, and it must sound choked when she speaks.

'So, what did you do, exactly, sir?'

'I went and fetched the car. Loaded the samples in it. Parked it up again. Bought a sandwich on the walk back.'

While she wrestles with the sudden disorientation, DS Jones can hear herself asking what she knows are bland questions, merely to buy time.

'And this was mid-morning, you say?'

'I'd been in a couple of hours, anyway.'

'Did you have lunch at your desk?'

'Yes.'

Something about Ray Piper's curt reply enables her to collect her wits.

'Why did you take the samples at that time – early, I mean? You didn't need them on Friday – since you were here all day.'

Logical thinking has come to her rescue. But now she really is cross-examining him, overtly so, and she can tell he likes it even less. But it does not take him long to reply – in fact just about long enough to make it seem like a not-too-prepared answer.

'The appointment cropped up – I thought I might forget them, especially if I were tight on time to collect the boys from Brunton Park. I needed to get a sandwich at some point – and it was looking a nice morning – I fancied a breath of fresh air.'

DS Jones's heart rate is still elevated, and it militates against clear thinking. Skelgill, who often appears disinterested, is better at this sort of questioning than she has appreciated.

'What exactly were the samples?'

'Ceramic tiles – floor and wall.'

She opts to reveal another card – if he doesn't believe she is on his case, he will surely now.

'You couldn't have carried them to your car?'

But Ray Piper shows no reaction.

'I probably could. It was a hot day – there was no need.'

While DS Jones has not been expecting him to capitulate, neither has she anticipated that Ray Piper would provide an explanation that fits the actions captured by witnesses and cameras alike. She feels like a baby turtle hatched on a beach, flailing seawards but washed back up the shore by a succession of breakers. Yet she knows – her instinct tells her – that the undercurrent, the tide indeed, pulls the other way. She just has

98

to make it into deeper water. She reminds herself that not everything stacks up. He has not mentioned his visit to Lisa Jackson's house. There is the tsunami of texts, abruptly halted. And the gloves. There is the absolute perfect fit of the timings. And the relationship as she understands it between the unwilling Lisa Jackson and the remorseless, relentless Ray Piper, smug before her.

But she realises she must retreat and regroup. Thus she acts to release the pressure valve. She looks over her notes, in a summarising fashion.

'Okay – and after that, sir – you were inside the office until close of play – four o'clock?'

'That's correct, sergeant.'

She wonders if she detects a hint of relief in his voice – or at least in his more relaxed choice of words, amenable even.

'Okay – well, we can probably leave it there, thank you, sir.'

He rises – again, not too fast, not too slowly.

But as he is passing through the door, DS Jones suddenly finds herself calling him back.

'One thing, sir – when was your appointment?'

He turns. He looks caught off guard.

'I'm sorry?'

'To demonstrate the tiles? It wasn't Friday – but as I understand it, you've been here all day.'

She detects annoyance in the slight narrowing of his eyes.

'It was Saturday. The hotel trade are open twenty-four seven.'

'Ah, of course.'

Now he departs without giving her the opportunity to probe further.

*

As DS Jones is leaving the offices of InnStyle it is after five p.m. and the majority of staff have gone home. Descending the spiral staircase she catches a glimpse of Don McKenzie – he has his stockinged feet up on his desk and is engaged in a subdued telephone conversation – it does not sound like a business call. She, too, wants to make a call – but outside where it is more private. In the far corner of the open plan a couple – perhaps the same balding older man she had noticed on the videotape, and a younger woman – are bending over a computer screen, in quiet discussion; and a rather glum-looking cleaning lady is going about with a green vacuum that has a cheeky cartoon character face; neither can DS Jones share its blind optimism. Ray Piper is at his desk, attentive to the screen, immobile like a posed mannequin in an office equipment catalogue – but she suspects his antennae are tuned to what is going on around him. Is he hanging back to keep track of her activities?

As she steps out from the recess onto the cobbles of Lychgate Lane she glances to her left. To her surprise – and, she must admit, consternation – she spies huddled in close confab against the half-lowered shutter of Wood's of Carlisle and evidently sharing a cigarette the incorrigible whistling Martin and none other than new receptionist Kylie! At the sound of the outer door swinging to behind DS Jones they glance up simultaneously. Martin cannot suppress a triumphant grin; Kylie's reaction is more circumspect – limply she raises her free hand. Additionally disconcerting to DS Jones is that the girl clearly mutters out of the side of her mouth – and her companion appears to respond with something equally conspiratorial. Truth be told, it is a little cameo she has witnessed many times in her relatively short career – teenagers on the street expressing their antipathy to the police – and to sharing information with them. DS Jones manufactures a friendly smile – they are a little too far off, and to say goodnight would require her to raise her voice – but as she turns away the lasting impression is of trepidation in the girl's eyes.

She strides briskly towards the junction with Warwick Road. Inexplicably, she experiences a curious sense of anti-climax when no wolf whistle is forthcoming as she exits the lane. Once out of their sight, she produces her mobile phone. She opens her contacts; Skelgill's number is at the top of the favourites list. She is just about to tap upon it when a competing thought strikes her. She opens the maps application and examines her location. She can see Aglionby Street – it forms part of a triangle with Warwick Road, converging with the latter about half a mile from the town centre. She notes the time and sets off walking. There is no knowing where exactly Ray Piper usually parks, but she follows the direction he took on the video – and sure enough by cutting to her right in just a few minutes she reaches Aglionby Street. Maybe a quarter of a mile long and lined by heavily pruned plane trees, it is dead straight and almost entirely residential; a little run down, red brick terraced villas with hints of past grandeur, their bay windows and porticos picked out in white masonry paint; in front of each house a tiny private area demarcated by a low stone wall that probably had its iron railings taken away during the war. There is plenty of unrestricted parking.

She halts. Straining her eyes she cannot see Ray Piper's white BMW – but it could easily be concealed in the lines of stationary vehicles by one of many tradespersons' vans. But she is not about to go in search of it. While it is Ray Piper who is top of her mind – it is a 'Skelgill thing' that she has done in wandering here – and it is Skelgill that must now take precedence. She places her right forefinger on his number.

'Jones – ahoy!'

'Guv – can you hear me okay?'

'You nabbed that Poker Face, yet?'

To DS Jones's ear there is a curious note in his voice – it might be a kind of bravado – just the suggestion that he is playing to an audience. She proceeds with caution.

'Guv – can you speak about work?'

'I'm on Bass Lake – remember what I said about the guiding.'

'Maybe I should call back?'

But despite her words, her tone is an entreaty to the contrary.

'I'll probably be in The Partridge – you know what the signal's like.'

She finds his manner odd – inexplicably evasive – and yet he has not entirely shied away from the subject of her case, despite

101

the flippancy of his opening remark. She takes a more direct tack.

'Can you spare two minutes? I really need your advice.'

The appeal to his vanity seems to do the trick.

'Aye – but if you hear a splash it means we're hooked up and I've gone overboard.'

She registers the small admission that he is with somebody.

'Look – I'll just run quickly through the facts.'

'Aye.'

She gathers herself – without really paying attention she instinctively turns into a long narrow ginnel – the alley that runs between the walled ends of back-to-back terraces. Walking slowly, head down, she begins to recite almost rhythmically.

'Ray Piper has been incessantly texting Lisa Jackson – for as far back as her phone records show. Between checking out her home on Friday morning and Lisa getting to work at just before eight twenty-five he texted her another four times. After that, nothing – other than he tried to call her once in the afternoon. I have a positive ID from an eyewitness that she entered the external door of InnStyle. Ray Piper was already there – and his desk overlooks Lychgate Lane. A few moments before Lisa came in, he went out into the stairwell, and was unobserved for about ten minutes. The next arrivals after Lisa Jackson were two employees together, also ten minutes later. Lisa Jackson never made it up to the office, where the receptionist was at her desk. But neither did she leave the premises. There's a lockable walk-in cupboard just inside the main door, beneath the staircase that runs up to the entrance on the first floor. At 09:52 Ray Piper left the office on foot and returned ten minutes later with his car. Wood's delivery driver arrived a minute later. Piper's BMW was reversed hard up against the entrance porch, literally blocking the lane. Piper claims he was loading some samples to take to a client for approval – but he never went to a meeting on Friday – or today. It seems he actually went on Saturday.'

Skelgill has been listening in silence; now he sounds agitated.

'What – after we'd seen him?'

102

'I imagine so, Guv. At least – after he dropped off his children at their soccer camp.'

'Why didn't you ask him?'

DS Jones takes a few seconds to consider her answer. Skelgill, of course, was not privy to the interview.

'Guv – you know you've said there comes a time when the talking stops and the fighting starts?'

'Have I?'

'Yes.'

'And?'

'I want to fight. I think something happened between Ray Piper and Lisa Jackson in the stairwell. Something sinister, Guv.'

Skelgill makes an exclamation, it sounds to be somewhere between a strangled oath and an objection. He does not need to say it: he correctly reads that she wants to take Ray Piper into custody.

'The forensic evidence may be vital, Guv.'

It takes Skelgill a moment to respond to the prompt.

'What about the new boyfriend?'

'He has an alibi. He was with two mates – he went straight to Manchester for three days to watch the cricket. Besides, we know Lisa made it to the office.'

She knows Skelgill cannot dispute this point – he was integral to their locating the unofficial CCTV footage. But he can still dig in his heels.

'Co-workers – boss – cleaner – delivery drivers – janitors. Have you eliminated them?'

'Guv – there's no alternative explanation other than spontaneous combustion!'

DS Jones hears Skelgill suppress a laugh – perhaps at her exasperation as much as her turn of phrase.

'Guv – we need the car. We need Piper's clothes – we need to get everything checked out for Lisa Jackson's DNA.'

There is another pause before Skelgill speaks.

'Jones – if she was his ex, her DNA's going to be all over his car. A half-decent defence barrister would rip us to shreds.'

Again DS Jones is forced into silence. But at least she can take one small crumb of comfort in that he has used the collective 'us'. She can hear boat noises – clunks and splashes – and she suspects he is manoeuvring one-handed with an oar. When she finds no immediate rejoinder he fills the void.

'Jones – you need something more conclusive if you want me to go cap in hand to the Chief. You saw the flack she got when Smart jumped the gun on the M6 drugs gang a fortnight ago. She's treading on eggshells with the Commissioner.'

DS Jones gasps resignedly.

'Right.'

'Hey up! There's a take – gotta go! Let us know, lass.'

In the second before he hangs up she hears in quick succession Skelgill yell *"Strike!"* and an answering shriek of excitement.

DS Jones continues somewhat aimlessly along the alley – in the direction that will take her back the way she has come. She might be dispirited but there is determination etched into her features. Then her phone, still in her hand, rings. It is a mobile number that she does not recognise.

'Hello?'

'Sergeant Jones – it's Don McKenzie.' She is about to answer but he continues, confidently, and there is a note of polite expectancy in his voice. 'Would it be possible to meet you for a drink – just now. There's something I'd like to speak about with you. I'm at the Halston, it's on Warwick Road diagonally opposite Lychgate Lane.'

*

The Halston reminds DS Jones more of a London hotel than the poor relation that might be expected in the 'unsophisticated' far north of England. Its immaculate Georgian sandstone exterior would not look out of place in Mayfair, and she enters as directed to find herself in a stylish modern café bar – at this hour transitioning from teas and coffees to drinkers taking harder stuff after a day at work. It is about half full but there is a lively chatter and a buzz that is on the up. It strikes her as the sort of smart place Don McKenzie would frequent. At first she does not see him – but that is because she is looking for a lone male – and it is only when a hand is raised that her attention is drawn to a couple sitting together in a curved alcove. She recognises Don McKenzie, for he is facing her – but not immediately the black-haired female until she turns to look. It is Kylie, the new receptionist. She still wears the same expression of disquiet that DS Jones divined a little earlier in Lychgate Lane.

For her part, DS Jones re-evaluates why she might have been summoned here.

Don McKenzie rises and asks what she would like to drink. After her day – and her disconcerting conversation with Skelgill – she feels the urge to fall in with the crowd; but somehow she manages to request only a tonic water.

'Are you sure you don't want a gin with that?'

He seems to read her thoughts – her mood, indeed – despite her attempts at outward competence – and she hesitates before declining. She takes one of two empty chairs opposite the alcove seat and regards the young girl with a look of concern.

'Are you alright, Kylie?'

The receptionist has in front of her a large glass of rosé – about half drunk – and she takes a gulp before she replies.

'Don said I should tell you – about what I saw.'

Her voice is tentative and she looks to where Don McKenzie stands at the bar – but it seems he might have a tab for he returns almost immediately with DS Jones's drink and settles back into his place in the alcove. DS Jones now addresses him.

'Kylie was saying – that you have encouraged her to speak to me.'

He picks up his own glass and nods – and is about to answer, when he remembers the etiquette.

'Cheers, by the way.'

DS Jones reciprocates.

'Yes, cheers – and thank you.'

She waits for him to elaborate.

105

'As I was leaving the office – I met Kylie in the lane –' He looks at her, a little puzzled – but then evidently decides that why she was there or what she was doing is not significant, and continues. 'She has some information – something she has remembered since you spoke with her.'

He refers benevolently to Kylie and DS Jones gets the impression he is making allowances – excuses almost – that she has not been more forthcoming when perhaps she ought. Regardless, DS Jones does not particularly care that Kylie has withheld something if she is about to reveal it now. Don McKenzie turns to her.

'And then there is also another point – possibly connected – that has come to me. I thought if you heard what Kylie has to say we can let her catch the next train – and I'll bring you up to speed?'

DS Jones regards him searchingly – it could be that she objects to his dictating the terms of the interview. But, there again, the pair of them are here voluntarily.

'Sure.'

She turns to Kylie with an expression that invites her to speak. The girl gathers herself.

'Martin says it's a murder case.'

DS Jones has to repress an ironic smile. While there has been a contained reaction amongst the white-collar staff of InnStyle, evidently the shop floor at Wood's of Carlisle have adopted a more tabloid take on the gossip. But perhaps this has served a purpose. She avoids the temptation to inquire how Martin has managed to charm Kylie with a mere four working days' worth of whistles and catcalls.

'It's what we call a missing person investigation – until we have information to the contrary.'

Kylie seems to falter, as though she interprets this explanation as a setback. Don McKenzie prompts her.

'Kylie – the key?'

DS Jones shoots him a sharp glance – that he should not put words into her mouth. He grimaces apologetically. But it has done the trick, for Kylie now responds.

106

'It was when he asked for the key.'

She looks questioningly at Don McKenzie. Now he indicates with a palm that she should address DS Jones directly. In any event, DS Jones requests clarification.

'Mr Piper, you mean, Kylie?'

The girl nods.

'He came to the desk with a box of something under one arm. He said he needed the key – for the comms cupboard – to put the box safe while he went for his car.'

DS Jones's ears are pricked. A box, under *one* arm? She recalls her question, why didn't he simply carry his samples to his car. She nods encouragingly.

'He were standing a bit strange, like – with the box – and he had the other hand in his jacket pocket.' She takes another mouthful of wine; she seems no stranger to the beverage. She glances nervously at Don McKenzie. 'When I gave him the key – he kind of snatched it and put his hand back in his pocket. That was when I noticed there were cuts on the back of his hand.'

DS Jones can feel the fine blonde hairs on her forearms beginning to prickle.

'Fresh cuts?'

The girl nods.

'What kind of cuts – slashes, for example?'

'No – more like – well – like they'd been done by nails – digging in.'

She makes an involuntary movement of one hand, clawing the air.

'How many, did you notice?'

'Quite a few – five or six.'

'Were they bleeding?'

Kylie shakes her head.

'But definitely fresh-looking?'

She nods again, forcefully.

DS Jones intuitively takes a solicitous tack.

'Did Mr Piper see that you had noticed?'

The girl glances at Don McKenzie, and then fixes her gaze fearfully upon DS Jones.

'I think so.'

DS Jones reaches to touch her sleeve.

'I understand you feel nervous talking about a colleague – especially as you are new – but you have done exactly the right thing and you now have the protection of the police on your side.'

DS Jones feels like she is taking a chance – she realises the gravity of what she has just said – and in front of Don McKenzie, to boot. But clearly she strikes the right note – there is palpable relief in the young receptionist's eyes. She takes another drink, less urgently now, and leans to check the time on her phone.

Don McKenzie interprets her action.

'Your train's in about ten minutes.'

He glances at DS Jones, clearly seeking her approbation. There are more questions she would like to ask, but she decides they can wait; they will merely be clarification of timings and suchlike. She nods and Kylie understands. She gathers her things and makes her exit, smiling gratefully at each of the pair in turn.

'I thought that was considerate – what you just said – to put her mind at rest.'

DS Jones looks questioningly at Don McKenzie. He elaborates.

'I think she's feeling intimidated by Ray.'

DS Jones leans back in her seat. It is tempting to treat the company director as a confidante. He has been entirely cooperative and is plainly both intelligent and sensitive. And now he cranks up the heat a notch more.

'Sure you don't want that gin?'

She is sorely tempted.

'I'm okay at the moment, thanks all the same.' She inhales and sits more upright. 'You said there's something else?'

108

Don McKenzie sips and regards her with a look of intrigue over the rim of his glass. Then he nods more purposefully and puts down the drink.

'Yes – something a bit odd – also concerning Ray Piper. It didn't quite give me cause to contact you until Kylie cornered me in the lane.'

'Go ahead.'

'Well – it must have been while you were interviewing Ray – because a call came through for him – and I took it as I was free and I know the job in question. We're refurbishing fifteen ensuite bedrooms for a hotel at Egremont – south of Whitehaven?' (DS Jones nods. She knows it, a pleasant landlocked small town to the west of the national park, a good hour's drive away.) 'The owner, a Miss Brown, phoned to ask why her deputy manager had been discussing a change of tiles for the new bathrooms – when she had approved the original scheme.'

DS Jones listens carefully. He continues.

'I said I would look into it – but, as I say, Ray was in with you – and before I could check with him the hotelier called back. She had more detail – and it seems that Ray told the deputy manager that the owner had considered a change – and so he had taken the new samples down. She denies that entirely.'

DS Jones understands the explanation, but does not as yet see its significance; Don McKenzie reads this.

'I mean – clients can be capricious and forgetful – and I was thinking, well – it doesn't matter – we've fitted the correct tiles in the bathrooms that we've completed. We can forget all about it. But on the other hand I couldn't help thinking it was strange. Ray is jokingly referred to in the office – er, behind his back, to be honest – as "Mr Spock". It wouldn't be like him to make this kind of slip up. What was also peculiar was that he went all the way down to Egremont on a Saturday.'

'This Saturday past?'

'Yes – why?'

'I know.'

'You do?' He sounds surprised.

109

'Yes.'

'You don't miss much.'

DS Jones brushes at a stray lock of hair, when there is none to straighten.

'I'm not sure my boss would agree. Besides – that's all I know. But that is definitely unusual, is it?'

Don McKenzie nods, his brow furrowed.

'Myself – and the other Directors – they're both away on holiday as you know – school-age kids and all that?' (Again DS Jones nods but allows him to continue.) 'We expect to work round the clock – as and when required. It's our business, for better or worse, and we take the slings and arrows and the outrageous fortune – if you get my meaning?'

'Almost.' DS Jones nods. 'Prince Hamlet.'

He looks at her, a little awed – or perhaps confused. But he understands at least that he should carry on.

'Although Ray's a senior manager – I wouldn't expect him to work weekends unless we had a major crisis in progress – or were trying to get a job done to a tight deadline. There's no such issue in this case – it's been running like clockwork – no small thanks to Ray, frankly.'

DS Jones is plainly mulling over what he has had to say – and she picks up her glass and drinks and in the prolonged silence Don McKenzie resumes his narrative.

'So, as I say – I was kind of half-leaving it. I was going to speak with Ray – but then I got caught up on a phone call. You left. Ray must have gone just after – so when I went out there was just Kylie in the lane with her boyfriend. To be honest – I think the lad put her up to having a word with me – and when she started talking about Ray and the samples, well.' He runs a hand through his neatly styled dark hair. 'I'm no detective – but obviously the two things are connected – if only because he was carrying the tiles. I know it doesn't make sense, but –'

But DS Jones rises and lifts her shoulder bag from the back of her chair.

'Would you excuse me for a couple of minutes – I need to make a call rather urgently?'

He looks shocked that she appears to be acting so promptly upon what she has learned. But he smiles and motions to his own handset on the table.

'Me too, actually.'

DS Jones takes the exit and strolls a few yards down Warwick Road until she is out of sight of the windows of the Halston. The time is after six p.m. and she assumes Skelgill will have finished fishing for the day. While he might continue until all hours were he alone, his 'guest' is likely to have tired, and the drizzle has come and gone in spells. But if Skelgill has taken his charge for a pint in the bar at The Partridge, it is unlikely he will have a signal.

He answers.

'Guv, it's me – are you free?'

Skelgill makes an agonised groan before uttering something more intelligible.

'I'm just back at Peel Wyke – tidying the boat – tackle's in a reet scrow.'

She thinks she should ask him how it went – since it sounds like he must be alone – but she presses ahead.

'You said I needed more.'

'Aye?'

Quickly and succinctly DS Jones relates what more she has learned. How it fits with her already well-formed theory about what happened to Lisa Jackson when she arrived for work on Friday. Why Ray Piper might reverse his car hard up against the doorway, into the recess when it wasn't even raining, just to load a box of tiles he could carry beneath one arm. Why he would wear gloves on a warm day. And how she now believes she knows what Ray Piper did on Saturday – not long after they had stood with him, as he subtly inserted himself between them and the boot of his car.

Although there is an aspect that sounds fantastical – that the two detectives could have been so near yet so far (once again the phrase) – Skelgill is nonetheless silenced by her explanation. She hears the cackle of a mallard in the background, and what sounds like a splash as he absently tosses a stone into the water.

'Guv – that's got to be enough for the Chief, surely?'

Now he inhales between gritted teeth, in the way of a reformed smoker.

'It could go the wrong way – I'm just thinking of you, Jones.'

DS Jones makes an exclamation of frustration, although her rejoinder is more conservative this time around.

'Guv – and you've never taken a flyer?'

On this point, she has him. After what seems like a small eternity, he replies.

'Okay – let me sleep on it.'

She lets loose the breath she has been holding – but it is conditional relief.

'Guv – why don't I come across now – I can lay all this out – type up a report to get the chronology right. You know how the Chief likes order and method?'

But a procrastinating grumble is already rising from Skelgill's chest.

'Thing is, lass – I've got to have dinner with this journo. I'm guiding again tomorrow and it seems it's part of the deal that I signed up for. The article's going to be about the hospitality as well as the fishing. A big feature in the Sunday supplement.'

She knows him well enough to understand that his answer is definitive – but also that the reluctance in his tone is decidedly affected. That he offers no alternative leaves her feeling suddenly despondent.

'Okay – but I'll send you the report. We shouldn't lose a minute, Guv. Especially once Piper thinks we're onto him.'

Walking slowly, she returns in pensive mode towards the Halston. A couple of about her age are standing outside, a little away from the door, smoking. For some reason – perhaps since they both wear business outfits – she judges them to be colleagues. The man puts an arm around the woman's shoulder and, though she seems momentarily surprised, she lifts up her face to accept the kiss that follows. It is prolonged, and continues as DS Jones passes close by and enters.

Don McKenzie is sitting patiently, perusing his mobile phone. When he senses her approach he clicks away whatever it was and

112

puts down the handset. He smiles winningly, and looks suitably urbane in his all-black outfit with its very subtle designer motifs. DS Jones takes the initiative.

'I think I will have that gin. Can I get you something as well?'

He gestures to the table – she realises there are two fresh drinks, one in front of him and the other beside him, where Kylie previously sat.

'I took a chance – but it's just a single, in case you're driving.'

DS Jones grins enigmatically – she leans to loop her bag over the chair that was previously hers, and she becomes conscious of his gaze appraising her form as her clothing tightens around her body. She slips past the chair and settles instead in the alcove. They clink glasses and she thanks him for a second time. She drinks and sinks back into the leather upholstery. Now *she* takes a chance.

'Why would Ray Piper harm Lisa Jackson?'

Don McKenzie turns to regard her with a look of astonishment.

'Does this mean I'm no longer a suspect?'

DS Jones chuckles.

'Oh – I expect I could always find something to suspect you of.'

He laughs. But then he takes seriously her question.

'I've always thought there's something a bit unnerving about Ray – you know, what's he really thinking? Behind the mask.' He takes a gulp of his drink, as though for Dutch courage. 'Norma – Lisa's line manager – we were having a glass of wine after work, a few months ago now – and she said she wondered if there was something going on between them. I thought, *Ray?* No way – what would Lisa see in him? But maybe there was.' He looks at DS Jones inquiringly. 'People get pitched into situations – it's human nature.'

'Tell me about it.'

113

8. DASH FOR EVIDENCE

Tuesday morning

'You're sure you don't mind driving?'

'Nah – you know me, girl – I'm like a cat with the cream. Makes use of my limited talents.' DS Leyton snatches a sideways glance at his colleague to see she is shaking her head in admonishment. 'Besides – you look like you could do with a spot of Bo-Peep. Feel free – I shan't take offence – look – the satnav's saying fifty minutes.'

DS Jones sighs philosophically. She realises now just how much yesterday drained her.

'Actually, I did have a couple of drinks last night. That hasn't helped.'

'But the Guvnor came through, eh?'

She suppresses an ironic laugh.

'If you call throwing stones at my window at a quarter to six coming through!'

'He don't know the meaning of doing things by halves.' DS Leyton makes a double-clicking noise with his tongue against the roof of his mouth, and concentrates for a moment as he manoeuvres through traffic lights just as they change from amber to red. 'But it obviously did the trick with the Chief – doorstepping her like that.'

DS Jones sinks back into the passenger seat and exhales deeply.

'I feel bad – to be honest – shifting the onus upwards.'

DS Leyton makes a sound of dissent.

'Nah – that's why we have different pay grades, girl. Beside – it sounds to me like you've got the Piper geezer bang to rights.'

DS Jones raises her hands and draws her slender fingers down over the smooth if uncharacteristically pallid skin of her face, opening her eyes exaggeratedly wide.

'We're going to need more to charge him – but if we hadn't arrested him we risked losing forensic evidence – the Chief at least bought into that argument.'

DS Leyton, who has been summoned to Carlisle in Skelgill's absence, shrugs phlegmatically.

'Did he go quietly?'

DS Jones, along with Skelgill before he returned to his full English breakfast at The Partridge, supported by a plain-clothes unit from the local Carlisle division earlier staked out Ray Piper's home address, and intercepted him as he left the house for work.

'He said, "Don't be ridiculous" – that's all – no physical resistance.' DS Jones edits out the colourful half of what had been a compound adjective – moreover she skirts the subtext, the real venom in the man's voice and hatred in his cold eyes; a chilling moment when she was glad to have plenty of back up as she recited the caution. 'I suspect he appreciated that making a fuss would attract the attention of neighbours – and his two young boys were probably still sleeping.'

'What did you get him on?'

'Suspicion of murder.'

DS Leyton raises his eyebrows.

'Did you tell his missus?'

'He showed no inclination to speak to her – I wouldn't have minded if he'd asked to go back inside, accompanied. I explained his right to make a phone call – but as yet he hasn't exercised it.'

'Solicitor?'

'That neither. And I don't think he will.'

DS Leyton glances sharply at his colleague.

'Reckon he'll keep his trap shut?'

DS Jones narrows her eyes reflectively.

'You know – I don't expect so. He's supremely self-confident.'

DS Leyton gives a little knowing twitch of the head.

'Arrogance – that's usually their Achilles' heel.'

DS Jones nods slowly but does not respond. DS Leyton detects her reticence – perhaps he even reads it as self-doubt. He adopts an inclusive tone.

'So – what's our theory, Emma?'

She instinctively glances over her shoulder – there is no one in the back but her colleague grins all the same. In the company of their superior such a question is likely to be met with disapproval – despite that Skelgill would admit that any detective worth their salt needs an inquiring mind, it jars with his own method. Free of such constraints, DS Jones presses the tips of her fingers together and gazes ahead.

'If you just stick to the simple circumstantial facts – strip everything away – history, relationships, motive – I think Lisa Jackson died in the ground-floor hallway of InnStyle – her body was concealed in what they call the comms cupboard – and removed shortly afterwards by Ray Piper using his car.'

DS Leyton is nodding.

'And where did he take her?'

'I don't believe there was time on Friday morning for him to do anything other than park his car in Aglionby Street and return to work. He didn't leave the office until just after four p.m. – he went to Brunton Park to collect his sons. He says he stayed at home on Friday evening. I plan to question his wife later – but I think that will prove to be the case. The next time he left the house – '

She hesitates in a way that causes DS Leyton to look across.

'You alright, girl?' There is concern in his voice – for he has sensed the surge of emotion that has gripped her.

She composes herself.

'You're aware that we interviewed him first thing on Saturday – informally – just as he was taking his sons to football?'

'Yeah – I am.'

But DS Jones is struggling again. DS Leyton reaches to pat her upper arm.

'I get your drift, girl – don't worry about it – you had the Guvnor with you.'

116

But while she appreciates that her colleague is trying to assuage what he regards as unreasonable feelings of culpability, she cannot so easily shake them off.

'He didn't realise – about what I already felt. I should have acted.'

'Leave it out, girl – you couldn't possibly have guessed what might have happened. Look at the intelligence you've gathered since – the CCTV and all that malarkey at their office.'

But DS Jones is not happy. She looks at him beseechingly.

'We were six feet from his car.'

DS Leyton shakes his head, but does not answer directly. After a few moments he moves the conversation forward.

'When do you plan to grill Piper?'

'I'm torn. I'm worried that I've already been too hasty on some points.' She hesitates; her hazel eyes have a studious look in them. 'You know – his biography on the company website describes him as a skilled problem-solver – expert at dealing with unforeseen obstacles. I want as much ammunition as I can possibly get.'

DS Leyton nods.

'What wheels have you put into motion?'

'The Chief's given the green light for a full forensic blitz this morning. The car's the main thing – and the stairwell area at the Lychgate Lane office. I've managed to get an urgent call on a specialist dogs unit from the Northumbria force – they're on their way over. A search team is going to his house at ten o'clock – I wanted to make sure the children were out of the picture. But to be honest I don't expect that will produce anything. I think any property of Lisa Jackson's will have been disposed of – along with –'

Again she finds emotion is welling up.

'Sorry.'

'Emma – no need to apologise, girl. You wouldn't be human if you weren't affected.'

She nods, though she still retrenches.

'I keep thinking of her parents. I think they knew what a predator Piper is. I think they've dreaded this for a long time.'

117

DS Leyton does not try to offer comforting platitudes. He adopts a more positive stance.

'The best thing you can do is bring him to justice.'

DS Jones gazes ahead; her eyes are glistening, but her expression is resolute.

'The best thing I can do is to find her.'

*

'Cor blimey – this is where I turned off yesterday for Gillerthwaite farm!'

DS Leyton has noticed that his colleague has woken from her catnap, having lost her little battle with the tiredness that had beset her, and encouraged by the gently winding route and perhaps also his more-than-usually-judicious driving. She blinks several times and leans to consult the satnav; it tells her they are within ten miles of Egremont.

'We could do with a few more coincidences like that.'

'Pity there's no follow-up needed yet – we could have blagged that Ennerdale cake recipe and I could show you where I made my acting debut.'

DS Jones, however, does not respond, and he realises he does not have her attention.

'Penny for your thoughts, girl.'

'Oh, sorry – I was just wondering. Don McKenzie – he's one of the directors of InnStyle – he told me that Ray Piper has eight projects currently in progress. It looks to me like he manufactured the appointment – I'm fairly confident we'll be able to confirm that. So – why this one? Why Egremont?'

DS Leyton purses his malleable lips.

'I remember when I was a DC down in the Met. We had this spate of gangland murders. The mob had their tentacles into the construction industry. We had to dig up the concrete foundations of a half-built flyover.' Now he hesitates, seemingly recalling the episode. 'Found two geezers. It was like flippin' Pompeii.'

He glances at DS Jones to see that she is gazing at the passing countryside – but her expression tells of a more gruesome image in her mind's eye. He makes an attempt to mitigate the effect of his well-meant black humour.

'Don't get me wrong, Emma – I'm not suggesting –'

But when he runs out words she turns to him and regards him with an unexpected look of sincerity.

'Don't worry – I think you're probably absolutely right.' She makes a gesture of frustration, grasping the air before her like she might be catching an invisible netball. 'I'm trying not to jump to too many conclusions – despite that when I close my eyes I see them right in front of me.'

On arrival, however, the detectives realise they need have no concern about concrete foundations. Situated about a mile north of the town and reached by a private metalled driveway between paddocks holding sheep, Egremont Hall is a traditional Cumbrian country house hotel, its smart whitewashed walls and neat grey slate roof belying its antiquity, for its fabric dates from the sixteenth century. And, as Don McKenzie has alluded to, the project involves internal refurbishment, the only sign of which is a small fleet of local trades' vans – carpenter, electrician, plasterer and plumber – occupying a secluded section of the car park.

A thin, angular, tweed-suited woman in her mid-fifties who introduces herself as "Constance Brown, Miss, Hotelier" greets them on the threshold. Her accent and enunciation could be described as very 'pukka'. She has a rather birdlike appearance, dark beady eyes behind horn-rimmed spectacles, and an efficient military manner that does not extend to pleasantries or small talk. She leads them with brisk efficiency to a modest private sitting room where a china tea service is laid out and a nervous-looking man in shirtsleeves but wearing a tie and a pinstriped waistcoat rises from one of four rather Spartan armchairs.

'Dennis Thatcher is my deputy manager.'

There ensue some formalities that see introductions completed and tea dispensed, the latter by Constance Brown herself, in a somewhat authoritarian and proper fashion. DS Leyton is thinking that Skelgill would not approve – and would certainly embarrass himself (unaware of having such an effect) with the lumped sugar and delicate silver tongs. He settles back with his own cup and saucer balanced upon his ample thighs, while his colleague sets about clarifying the purpose of their visit. However, the hotelier promptly interrupts her.

'I trust this will not hinder the work in progress? We are in a permanent state of two bedrooms being unavailable, and in the peak season a delay is not something we can tolerate. And I am certainly not about to be browbeaten into adopting a scheme of décor that I did not approve in the first place.'

DS Leyton, knowing his associate, can see that she has to fight back a smile – that the woman fears that the police might somehow have been enlisted to enforce the unasked-for variation to the contract.

'Madam – I have spoken with Mr McKenzie of InnStyle – he will personally ensure the project is completed to your satisfaction. For our part, we are required to confirm some details in connection with Mr Piper – in particular his trip here on Saturday morning.'

Constance Brown appears a little mollified, having got in her defence by means of a pre-emptive salvo, and now adopts a slightly less affronted manner.

'Anybody ought to know I play golf at weekends – I am club captain at Egremont – ladies, of course.' For some reason she regards DS Leyton severely, and he nods politely. 'Saturday morning is an entirely inappropriate time to come. Unless it were a visit designed to take advantage of Dennis's inexperience.'

The under manager colours, a flush of red appearing on each cheek, and he looks uncomfortable in his formal outfit. He must only be in his late twenties, though with a somewhat plump figure and prematurely balding, the first impression is of an older man. He does not attempt to gainsay his employer's assertion, and merely glances apprehensively at the two detectives. DS Jones takes the opportunity to home in on their objective.

'Perhaps, Mr Thatcher, you would kindly tell us what happened – the details of Mr Piper's unexpected call?'

120

Constance Brown gives a little start – as though she feels it ought to be with her assent that her underling speaks. But DS Jones politely ignores her, and gives a gesture of encouragement to the deputy manager.

'What time did he arrive, sir?'

Being referred to as 'sir' seems sufficiently to embolden Dennis Thatcher, and he sits forward on the edge of his chair.

'It was just before the start of play – the test match.'

'England versus the West Indies, at Old Trafford?'

DS Jones can sense that her colleague is regarding her with some surprise – that she is in possession of this knowledge. She nods to Dennis Thatcher, for him to continue.

'That's right. I normally do the week's accounts on a Saturday morning – entering all the purchase invoices onto the system – it doesn't take a lot of concentration.' He glances contritely at his employer. 'I had the radio on quietly – and I was just listening to the preamble – about the hot weather and that the wicket was breaking up and England were struggling against the quicks and it looked like the West Indies might enforce the follow-on and then –'

DS Jones interjects.

'Start of play was at ten-thirty a.m.'

Again she feels her colleague's scrutiny; the deputy manager, meanwhile, seems to get that he should come to the point.

'Yes – so I would say Mr Piper came at maybe ten twenty-five.'

DS Jones nods and turns to smile briefly at her fellow sergeant. He is now diligently taking notes. Meanwhile Dennis Thatcher continues.

'I was in the back office and I heard someone come to reception and ask for Miss Brown. June was telling him she wasn't here – so I went through and asked how I could help.'

'Did you recognise him?'

'Yes, I've seen him before.' Now he looks timidly at his boss. 'But Miss Brown mainly dealt with him.'

DS Jones directs her next question to the proprietor.

'How often has he been here?'

121

'Approximately every two to three weeks. The last time was on the fifth of this month.'

'Does he just turn up – or make an appointment?'

Constance Brown tuts rather in the manner of an Edwardian governess.

'I work strictly by appointment – I cannot have my schedule determined by contractors and travellers appearing at random.' She uses the traditional term for sales representatives.

'And you think, madam, he would have known you would be unavailable on a Saturday?'

'I make it abundantly clear to all suppliers that weekends are out of the question – not least that we are busiest with our guests.'

It strikes DS Jones that such a burden must fall disproportionately on the shoulders of Dennis Thatcher, and now she reverts to him.

'Coming back to his visit, sir. Could you please describe what took place?'

The under manager appears more eager to speak, perhaps now that the revelation of his guilty pleasure has been put behind him.

'He had a cardboard box.' The man forms a shape with his hands in mid air to indicate it was about a foot in each of its dimensions. 'He said he'd brought the alternative tiles.' He glances apologetically at Constance Brown. 'The ones he said Miss Brown had asked about. I just said, well, that I didn't know anything about it – I thought he would leave them – but then he said he didn't know if they would be suitable – something about adhesion that I didn't really understand – and that he'd need to check them in situ in one of the bathrooms that was being refurbished. The contractors don't work at weekends. I offered to take him up but he said there was no need – and –' (now he looks sheepish once again) 'the cricket was about to start – so I gave him a key – it was for the Ennerdale Suite.'

'And what was the outcome?

'That was it. Obviously he knows his way around. I went back through to the office. I remember I asked June a bit later if he was still here and she said she had no idea. She looked in the key deposit box and it was in there – so he'd left without anyone noticing. June was at reception the whole time but she was probably occupied with checking out a guest.' He pauses, pensively. 'Actually, it must have been before a quarter to eleven – because that's when England were all out – I went through to June when they were between innings. I went up to the Ennerdale Suite and there was no sign of the box of tiles. After that it slipped my mind – until yesterday afternoon, when one of the plumbers came down to ask if he could shut off the stopcock at the mains while they conducted a pressure test.'

He looks rather helplessly at Constance Brown – but she does not appear to be blaming her subordinate for the evident confusion. She addresses DS Jones.

'When Dennis mentioned it I was most perturbed. I knew nothing about this and harboured no desire to change the plans mid-flow. It made no sense to me whatsoever. That was when I telephoned the company to tell them that whatever they were up to, to think again. I rather suspected they had come into a job lot of tiles and were hoping to fob them off upon me and make a killing in the process.'

*

'Reckon he must have gone straight there from Carlisle, don't you?'

DS Jones is nodding – in point of fact she is interrogating times and distances according to her maps app.

'It says exactly an hour from Brunton Park – the same way that we came. If he dropped his boys off at nine-fifteen he would have arrived pretty much when the under manager says.'

'So if he got up to any shenanigans it must have been afterwards.'

DS Jones puts down her mobile phone and reaches behind to extract a map from her shoulder bag on the back seat. She unfolds it tentatively. In the restricted space there is just enough room to reveal the section of the route they have taken between

Cockermouth and Egremont, and on which they now return. It is a quiet sixteen-mile stretch of the A5086 that runs through an expanse of gently rolling country criss-crossed by a myriad of narrow lanes and dotted with isolated farmsteads and hamlets. Thereafter, beyond Cockermouth, it is another twenty-five or so miles to Carlisle, an altogether busier road. Though she is unaware of it, DS Jones must make a sigh of exasperation, for her colleague responds.

'The Guvnor would be in his element.'

DS Jones glances up from her perusal of the intricate and somewhat bafflingly coded patchwork of lines and shades. Certainly as a medium the Ordnance Survey is Skelgill's preferred form of reading. Handed a map his eyes light up; he seems to perceive an extra dimension, like an orchestral conductor consumed by melody and harmony when the ordinary person sees tadpoles strung along fence wire.

'It might have to come to that.'

DS Leyton makes a rueful growl in his throat.

'Rather the Guvnor than me. I was never any good at geography – skipping was my thing.'

DS Jones looks at him, bemused.

'You mean in PE?'

'Nah – skipping lessons.' He grins broadly, only just looking back at the road in time to deal with a fast-approaching bend. 'Whoops-a-daisy!'

DS Jones chuckles; DS Leyton is a good companion, he is endowed with a phlegmatic stoicism that invariably errs on the side of the glass being half full, and generally has the happy knack of seeing humour when it is harmless and uplifting. Skelgill is an altogether more spiky character, far less predictable and – she would venture – intentionally so. Sometimes she thinks his qualities of recalcitrance and capriciousness are borne solely out of bloody mindedness, a refusal to follow the herd. She folds away the map and checks her phone again.

'Actually I've got a good data signal – I'll just see if anything has come in yet.'

She falls silent for a few moments as she scrolls through her messages and emails. Then she gives a sharp intake of breath.

'What is it, Em?'

'Actually – it's an audio file – the voicemail that Ray Piper left on Lisa Jackson's mobile on Friday afternoon. You were right about that, by the way.'

Rather than bask in the small glory DS Leyton purposefully raises the driver-side window that he has had open by an inch for fresh air – an instinctive reaction to reduce the road noise. DS Jones engages the speaker function and holds the handset up between them. There are a couple of introductory bleeps, followed by the sound of a connection made and a person inhaling to speak. Then Ray Piper's distinctive monotonous voice.

"Lisa – it's Ray. You've not been answering. I see you're off today. I was thinking we could meet up for a coffee – to have a chat. Let me know – drop me a text. Take care."

Both police officers stare silently ahead, absorbed, replaying the echoes in their minds, using every ounce of their intuition to read nuances of motive and affectation into the cold, unemotional delivery. DS Leyton, who has not yet met Ray Piper, speaks first.

'Covers all the bases – handy that.' His tone is overtly sceptical, should his colleague be in any doubt. 'It sounds to me like he was reciting a script that he's prepared for our benefit.'

DS Jones is nodding – but she can't help wondering if they are indulging in wishful thinking – the eye (or rather the ear) of the beholder, and all that. Nonetheless, there remains what she regards as the major flaw in Ray Piper's message.

'He recorded this voicemail at ten past one on Friday afternoon. If you recall, it was his first attempted communication with Lisa Jackson for almost five hours, when he'd already harassed her with four texts before eight-thirty – probably a record in restraint. During working hours I doubt there's a gap of more than twenty minutes between texts over the last three months. I can't see past your first reaction when we discussed this yesterday.'

DS Leyton briefly runs a hand through his tousle of dark hair before reaching to change down a gear as they approach a 30mph sign.

'We've got his mobile, right?'

'Yes – but it's clean. Superficially, at least.'

'What – like he's deleted everything?'

'Yes.' DS Jones ponders for a moment. 'I imagine he might not have wanted his wife to find texts to Lisa Jackson. But I'm not sure it's going to make a great difference to us whether we know their content or not.'

'What if he'd threatened the girl?'

'Well – that's true. Good point.' She frowns as she considers the issue. 'But he strikes me as the sort who operates through passive aggression. It's what he doesn't say. His is an intimidating presence.'

DS Leyton emits a scornful hiss of denial.

'You'll run rings round him, girl – far better you handling this. By the sound of it I'd be punching his lights out and getting my cards!'

DS Jones grins half-heartedly.

'I'd definitely rather outwit him with the facts. I'm pinning my hopes on having his phone successfully triangulated. That could save endless searching for sites with CCTV.'

'At risk of sounding like the Guvnor, they'll be like hen's teeth out here. Maybe more chance in one of these villages.'

DS Jones nods. They are passing through the former iron-mining settlement of Frizington and she finds herself scanning for cameras – if only the ubiquitous satellite dishes could do the same job. When the police want to track the movements of a vehicle, they turn in part to commercial premises (and increasingly to domestic locations) that have CCTV cameras monitoring for security, but which inadvertently capture passing traffic. But there is no register, nor a central server that can be interrogated from the comfort of police HQ. It is a matter for boots on the ground and can be a thankless task. Many owners have little clue how to retrieve their recordings, if they have even been switched on in the first place. And, increasingly, a

126

significant proportion of cameras turn out to be dummies, mounted purely for deterrent purposes.

DS Leyton picks up her point.

'When do you expect to hear?'

'It could be any moment – it's being treated as a priority – given that there remains the possibility that Lisa Jackson could be alive.'

DS Leyton flashes a glance at his colleague. It is the first mention she has made of the search in this light.

'Technically speaking?'

DS Jones nods, but does not answer.

'But you don't believe that, Emma?'

Now she shakes her head and turns to her fellow sergeant.

'In theory he could have incapacitated and abducted her. But it doesn't fit the facts – and it doesn't fit my feelings. Right from the very first moment I've carried a premonition of bad news.'

DS Leyton allows a few seconds for the reverberations of this statement to dissipate.

'Reckon Piper's missus will help us out? She can't be happy with him messing about with his co-worker. If she wants to get that off her chest.'

DS Jones stares ahead, pensively. It feels like a big if. That Ray Piper is back with his wife makes her think it will not be so straightforward.

*

'Mrs Piper, you understand why we are here – that a Miss Lisa Jackson is missing and that we have reason to believe that your husband may be connected with her disappearance? We are interviewing you purely as a witness and you are under no obligation to speak to us.'

DS Jones thinks that Irene Piper looks like a plainer, more strained, more careworn version of Lisa Jackson. At thirty-nine, she is only a couple of years older; perhaps motherhood is what has made the difference.

She has long straight hair that looks heat-damaged and might be dyed black. Lacking any make up, her skin is fair and has a blotchy complexion suggestive of inner tension, and from beneath hairless brows small greenish-blue eyes dart about nervously, the narrow lips of her mouth compressed. DS Jones wonders if the dejected expression is her normal default – there is the temptation to read it as the demeanour of one chronically downtrodden, but she cautions herself against undue construal just because of her encounters with the woman's husband.

The three – the two detectives and Irene Piper – are seated at a gate-leg dining table at the back end of a through-lounge; the front section houses a three-piece suite and the television. It is a modest-sized house and the room is tidy; the impression is utilitarian, certainly far from opulent, and lacking in feminine touches. There is a French door through which they can see into a garden – less tidy, a patchy lawn with a set of wonky plastic goalposts, a damaged larch-lap fence starved of creosote and a couple of battered bushes, including a Buddleia against the odds attracting colourful butterflies.

The search team have gone. While their unheralded arrival must have seemed an extreme measure to Irene Piper, it had no doubt been explained to her that there is a basic requirement in a missing person inquiry to eliminate the possibility that the subject is simply hiding somewhere. At a more covert level, however, had they found a personal item such as the bag, phone or purse that Lisa Jackson was known to be carrying it would have been dynamite. But, as DS Jones has foreseen, nothing of this nature was discovered, albeit that the search was conducted at the relatively superficial, non-intrusive level appropriate at this juncture. A laptop of Ray Piper's has been appropriated, along with items of clothing similar to those fitting the description of his known outfits on Friday and Saturday. His distinctive driving gloves have not been located, either at home or in his car.

Irene Piper appears almost shell-shocked – perhaps a combination of the news and having suffered her house to be searched – and plainly it has not entered her thoughts to provide refreshments. DS Jones has to remind herself that there is an

128

outside possibility that she is an accomplice – or, at least, accessory – in Ray Piper's suspected misdemeanour. Accordingly, it would be no surprise if the woman regards them as occupying foes. She looks like she could do with a cup of tea, but the ice is not sufficiently broken that DS Jones feels she could offer to make some.

'He stopped seeing her. That's all over. Since before Christmas.'

The woman's unprompted avowal (*outburst* would be too strong a word, for it is delivered ineffectually) is intriguing to DS Jones, all the more for its tenor. She realises she must be on guard for a prepared cover story – yet there is a forlorn plea in Irene Piper's voice, that the omniscient detectives will confirm her stated belief. DS Jones has decided not to interview Irene Piper under caution – and she feels now this is the right decision – albeit 'in her bones', the kind of sensation she suspects Skelgill of navigating by. For her part, she has in mind a destination, and now she embarks on picking a careful course that might lead her there.

The woman's gaze flicks anxiously between the two officers. If she has registered that she has a choice in the matter she does not seem to be exercising her right to object; she gives the impression of being willing to participate – perhaps because she cannot quite comprehend what is happening, nor that her husband can possibly be at fault.

'That can't have been easy.'

It is something of a platitude, but DS Jones's response to Irene Piper's entreaty seems to strike the right note, and she fixes her gaze upon the young policewoman – surely seeking the empathy that another female might provide. She shakes her head, albeit she does not elaborate. But DS Jones is not seeking details of the status of the marital relationship.

'How are your children?'

Now this is a more pointed question – although DS Jones's meaning might range from how they are this morning to what has been the psychological impact of their father leaving the

129

family home for another woman, and then returning. Nevertheless, it seems to provide a relief valve.

'Oh – they're – they're just obsessed with football. As long as they can do that – and play their FIFA upstairs.'

'Do they do a lot with their Dad?'

For a second Irene Piper looks like she thinks this question is meant to trip her up, but DS Jones's tone and expression are genuine. The woman's doubt seems to shift to the issue raised in the question itself, as if she sees the circumstances in a fresh light.

'Well – not really – but – there's the two of them – that's all they need to play against each other.'

'Seems like they keep you busy – keeping track of their kit.'

DS Jones makes reference to the animated cameo she witnessed on Saturday morning, when the boys were squabbling over socks.

'Aye – they're a handful. And they lose stuff all the time. Even though I've sewed labels into everything.'

Now DS Leyton makes a sound of recognition – and the woman seems to read that he is a fellow parent – she plies him with a weak grin of solidarity.

DS Jones continues, treading carefully.

'So – you're a housewife, Mrs Piper – is that how it has been since the boys were born?'

Irene Piper nods; she does not seem suspicious.

'I could go back part-time – I was a dental technician – but Ray prefers that I – that I can do the school run and the football club – and the shopping and laundry and cooking.'

She recites the list of chores mechanically, without any attempt to demonstrate the scale of the burden. But DS Jones is reminded of an article she read recently, arguing that the true economic value of a housewife (using the term generically, irrespective of gender) had been assessed at the equivalent of a six-figure salary. And, yet, the practical reality of many households is that the non-earner is dependent upon – at the mercy of – their partner. When there are children in the equation, it hands the breadwinner the levers of power.

130

Especially when that person is prepared to employ fear as a means of coercion. But DS Jones steers around this perspective.

'It must be a difficult choice between the family's needs and having some extra independence for yourself.'

Perhaps the woman's sentiments are closer to DS Jones's concerns, for she veers off at a tangent to the question.

'When will Ray be back?'

DS Jones does not press her point. Instead she answers, her manner sympathetic.

'I'm afraid I can't say right now. We need to speak with him later to clarify some points. We'll know more after that – and of course we'll keep you informed as a priority.'

Now Irene Piper becomes suddenly animated.

'What will I tell the boys? Is this going to be on the news – about Ray? I heard it – on the radio – that she'd disappeared.'

DS Jones exchanges a brief glance with her colleague.

'Our appeals for information will remain of the same nature, for the time being. It is not our practice to release the names of those who are assisting the investigation.'

'Are there others?' The woman's tone is plaintive.

'There are other lines of inquiry. Naturally when we are trying to find someone, we have to work our way through the people who know them or who last saw them.'

Irene Piper looks a little bewildered.

'But on Friday – that's when she went missing? That's what it said.' (DS Jones nods.) 'Ray was here. He brought the boys home straight after work – he finishes early on a Friday so he was able to pick them up. Then he stayed home. He couldn't have seen Lisa Jackson on Friday – it said on the radio she didn't turn up for work.'

DS Jones is nodding.

'Yes – that's what he told us – and it corresponds to what his colleagues have said. When did you hear about Miss Jackson?'

'On Saturday morning.'

'Did you discuss it with your husband?'

'He'd taken the boys. He didn't mention it.'

DS Jones seems momentarily perturbed, as though she has to rein in her natural inclination to question the reply.

'When we came along – Inspector Skelgill and I – that's when your husband was leaving with your sons. Did he come straight home?'

'I think so.'

'You're not sure?'

'I went to the retail park up by the motorway. I do the big grocery shop on a Saturday morning – and Asda have got next year's school uniforms. And there's a sale on in Primark.'

'Was your husband here when you got back?'

'Yes – he was outside, washing his car.'

DS Jones feels momentarily light-headed and senses DS Leyton beside her, also trying not to react.

'Is that his usual thing on a Saturday morning?'

Irene Piper looks blank – it is hard to discern (though not difficult to infer) what thought may have gripped her – but when she answers she could not in fact be accused of evasiveness.

'It was just after one – I asked if he wanted some dinner – I'd brought the shopping – and I was later than usual because of buying the boys' clothes. But he said he wasn't hungry – that he'd just carry on and wait for his tea.'

'And what about the rest of Saturday?'

'We were both here after that. Ray – he did some gardening, I think. I was inside – I had mending to do. Ray picked up the boys from the football camp. Then we all stayed in – mainly watched television.'

*

'So, the geezer cleaned his motor when he got back. Just like you would on a Saturday.'

The detectives have hardly settled in their own vehicle before DS Leyton makes this observation, his voice thick with cynicism. DS Jones feels she ought to point out the literal validity of his statement – knowing Skelgill would be quick to damp down such

132

a flicker of suspicion – but instead she finds herself adding a little fuel to the flames.

'His car looked spotless to me when we were here at just before nine.'

DS Leyton, as if to seal the argument, squirts the screen washers, automatically triggering the wipers into a brief dance routine.

'And it was a dry day – not like it would have got covered in road spray. Bit of dust, maybe.'

DS Jones falls silent. If solving a crime can be likened to completing a jigsaw, often the detective has to fit together pieces of evidence without knowing what the image looks like on the front of the box. In this case it is different – in her mind the picture has been clear from an early stage – and it seems every little piece they encounter has its place. But she is becoming increasingly aware that one corner remains stubbornly empty.

'Irene Piper seems neither to know nor to suspect.'

DS Leyton turns abruptly to his colleague.

'Is that what you reckon?'

She regards him searchingly.

'Don't you? If what she says is true, he didn't even mention it to her – despite that she'd seen us at the door.'

'She don't strike me as a wrong 'un – I'll give you that.'

'You know – she made me think of a dog that has been maltreated – I remember an RSPCA advert when I was a child. The poor creature was cowering in its cage – it wouldn't come out – it couldn't process the fact that it was free – and safe. I think she was too scared to tackle him about it.'

'Are you saying she's a battered wife?'

'I think Ray Piper is controlling and manipulative. He holds the purse strings – and with the two boys, she's got nowhere to go. Did you see anything in that house that looked like she'd bought it to make it a nice place for herself? I don't think she allows her mind to go through that door. It's like she's inadvertently protecting him, blindly subservient.'

DS Leyton grimaces doubtfully as he wrestles with the psychological conundrum.

'She don't have the knives out for him, right enough – but I can't say she leapt to his defence, neither. It's more like she thinks there's a big mistake.' Now he chuckles wryly. 'I thought you were going easy on her – but you were well ahead of me, girl. I'd have stomped in with me clodhoppers and she'd have run a mile.'

DS Jones looks embarrassed by the compliment.

'To be honest I felt a bit sneaky. I just wanted to find out what her account would be of Ray Piper's movements. And, to be frank, I don't mind whether we get that as admissible witness evidence or not.' She inhales, prior to adding a caveat. 'It would have been nice to know what time he got back.'

'We can maybe solve that with a spot of door-knocking – especially seeing as he was out front, here on the drive.'

DS Jones leans forward to scan around the area. The Piper house is just off the junction that was described to her by Lisa Jackson's father when she originally asked if they knew the address. The landmark mentioned was a BP garage.

'They'll have cameras over there.'

'What – at the petrol station?'

'Yes – and inside the shop. I think we should have a word with the manager.'

DS Leyton switches on the ignition.

'May as well drive in – I need some fuel while we're at it.'

But before he can engage first gear DS Jones's mobile rings and she looks at the number displayed on the screen.

'DC Watson. I'd better take it.'

DS Leyton turns off the engine. DS Jones answers and after exchanging brief greetings she listens, her eyes becoming alert. She interrupts.

'Hold on, please – I've got a map – wait – I'll put you on speaker.'

She places the handset beside her on the central console and extracts the Ordnance Survey map from where she had slipped it into the door pocket. She draws out the concertina folds to their full extent – almost four feet by five – and it requires DS

134

Leyton's help to pin it in position across the interior of the car. DS Jones hastily grabs a pen from her bag.

'Okay – ready. Start again at Piper leaving Egremont – we're up to speed before that.'

DC Watson's voice – she has a throaty Penrith accent – comes on the line with a little burst of static.

'He was stationary, a little outside the town until 10:35 – when he started moving north along the A5086 – then the phone went out of service entering Cleator Moor, at 10:38. It came back on just south of the Lamplugh roundabout – still on the A5086 – at 12:18 – a distance of thirteen miles. I've checked with the service provider and they had no network outages in that sector on Saturday.'

DS Jones is systematically tracing a finger along the route and marking crosses and times – but when 12:18 is quoted she glances up to exchange a look of alarm with her colleague. DC Watson, meanwhile, continues to relay the information.

'He drove uninterrupted to Carlisle, taking the A595 from Cockermouth and arriving at what would appear to be his home address at 12:53, where the phone, at least, remained for the rest of the day.'

When neither DS Jones nor DS Leyton immediately responds, DC Watson adds a rider.

'There's more fine detail – masses in fact – but I thought you'd want the top line.'

'This is perfect – thanks – and please relay our gratitude for them coming through so quickly.'

DS Jones hangs up the call and refolds the map – they only need half. They are now looking at the stretch of road between Egremont and Cockermouth – a red artery that meanders in a northeasterly direction across the pale flank of the countryside. On the basis of her scrawled times, she performs the mental arithmetic.

'It took him one hour and forty-three minutes to cover thirteen miles.'

DS Leyton clicks his tongue.

'I reckon we just did it in under twenty-five minutes.'

135

DS Jones is silent for a while.

'More than an hour and a quarter unaccounted for.'

'And he switched off his phone.'

'It looks that way. But –'

DS Leyton regards her reprovingly. 'No buts, Emma – surely?'

DS Jones sighs. It is a response that bears the hallmarks of a great trial yet to come. Around them it has perceptibly darkened, and with no other warning a heavy rain-shower abruptly begins to drum upon the windscreen and roof of the car, submerging its occupants in a sea of sound. Its effect is hypnotic, and both stare blankly at the map, their eyes unblinking, unfocused.

Then DS Jones's mobile rings again. It is a couple of moments before she reacts.

'It's the dog handler from Northumbria – I asked her to call me immediately if there was anything urgent.'

DS Leyton shakes his head like he is trying to clear his ears of the unwanted sibilance.

'It's coming thick and fast, Emma.'

Inexpertly he gathers in the map, thinking that he is glad Skelgill is not there to slate him from the rear seat. Then he part-rotates at the waist in what must be an uncomfortable pose in order better to listen to his colleague.

'DS Jones – hello? Yes – go ahead, please.'

She listens intently for a good minute, and being right-handed she holds her mobile to her left ear, so DS Leyton can glean no intelligible leakage, not least that the passing storm is not yet done. He has to make do with the one-sided dialogue.

'And no reaction anywhere else – just the two locations?'

'Were there any physical signs?'

'Lavender?'

DS Jones now gives an abrupt laugh at the correspondent's reply.

'Well – I suppose you're entitled to an opinion, too – especially when the dog can't mention that.'

'Sure.'

'By the way – do you have this on body cam or something similar?'

'Great. Well, look – thanks for your help – and thanks for responding so quickly.'

There is another pause while she listens.

'Look – don't apologise – frankly, it was what I was expecting.'

She ends the call. She seems to brood for a moment and DS Leyton picks up on this.

'Bad news?'

DS Jones starts.

'Oh – no – well.' She exhales a resigned breath. 'Look – the Northumbria dog unit – it was a specially trained cadaver dog.'

'Ah. Gotcha. They do their job and if they succeed they only bring bad news.'

DS Jones is nodding.

'The dog reacted strongly to the boot of Piper's car and the under-stair cupboard at InnStyle. It showed absolutely no reaction anywhere else.'

'Cor blimey, Emma – you're some girl. You know how to go for the jugular, don't you?'

Rather than demur, as would be her nature in response to his praise, for once DS Jones looks as fiery as her colleague suggests.

'I know what I'm up against.'

9. INTERROGATION

Tuesday evening

'Mr Piper, in order for us to progress I would like to establish a clear picture of your movements on Friday and Saturday.'

'You are completely wasting your time. I have had nothing to do with Lisa's so-called disappearance. I have not seen her since Thursday at the office.'

DS Jones notes that Ray Piper's enunciation is more careful than she has been used to – "I have" instead of "I've" and no dropped northern aitches. It strikes her that he is conscious of the interview being filmed – perhaps even thinking ahead to its being shown to a jury – yes, thinking that far ahead; she would not put it past him. She and DS Leyton are seated opposite, and DC Watson upon a chair beside the door of the interview room. The latter plays prop for the Police Ladies Rugby League First XIII, and looks capable of taking down the suspect should he make a break for freedom. But Ray Piper seems to have resigned himself to custody. It has been explained that he may be detained without charge for twenty-four hours – but while he might simply opt to sit out this period in silence, he is also apprised of the fact that the police can apply for an extension up to ninety-six hours. Thus it appears to be his strategy to give them no grounds for the latter. In a controlled manner he has taken regular opportunities to protest his innocence, that they have got it wrong. He has eschewed his right to have present a legal representative – reiterating that why would he need a solicitor when he has committed no offence? His demeanour is one of stern indignation; his pose the now-familiar rigid, immobile upright stance; his hands resting out of sight upon his thighs.

DS Jones regards him evenly.

'There are some details that have come to our attention. We need to clarify these, as I say. And there are other gaps in our knowledge.'

'You have not found Lisa. She has not come back. I would like to know how she is.'

This little volley of remarks, DS Jones is sure, is designed to be disorienting – and, yes, again playing to the invisible gallery: that he harbours concern for his 'missing' acquaintance.

'You didn't express that sentiment when we spoke with you on Saturday morning, sir. You were disparaging, if I may say so.'

That DS Jones has instantly gone off script might alarm her fellow sergeant – but it also catches out Ray Piper and this reaction is revealed in a slight narrowing of his eyes.

'You took me off guard – turning up at my house unannounced. I thought she'd made some complaint about me. It was just a natural reaction to defend myself.'

'Why would she have made a complaint about you, Mr Piper?'

There is a pause before he replies.

'No reason that I could think of.'

He has recovered to an even keel. But it is a warning that she is sharp; she has put a shot across his bow. For her part, she considers that he would have been better to deny her accusation; unless perhaps he prefers to highlight that he had referred to Lisa Jackson in the present tense. Now she picks back up the thread of her questioning.

'I'd like to start on Friday morning. What time did you leave for work?'

'About twenty to eight, I should think.'

'Is that your normal time?'

'Yes.'

'And, as you explained, you park in Aglionby Street and walk the rest of the way – and that gets you into the office at around eight?'

'Correct.'

She resists the urge to lower her gaze under his laser-like scrutiny.

'Mr Piper, at approximately five to eight on Friday you were seen in your car in Goosehills Close outside Miss Jackson's house.'

'I went to see if she wanted a lift to work.'

139

His answer is immediate – not a trace of hesitation, nor a hint that it is contrived on the hoof.

This time, it is DS Jones who, perhaps also for the purposes of a jury watching the tape, decides to press the point.

'You didn't think to mention this to us?'

'Why should I?'

DS Jones declines to be sidetracked into providing a justification; she merely regards him pensively for a moment as if subtly to demonstrate incredulity.

'And what happened?'

'I remembered I had something to do at the office. Lisa would have asked me in for a coffee. I drove away without disturbing her.'

'What was it that you needed to do?'

'A critical path analysis that I'd promised to a client. I was expecting some quotes overnight that would enable me to finish it and send it.'

In the background DC Watson, ostensibly stolid but ears pricked like a catnapping bulldog, makes a note to check this claim with Ray Piper's employer.

'Did you see Miss Jackson – moving about inside her house, for example?'

'The curtains were closed.'

'Did you notice any cars parked on the drive?'

Ray Piper makes a small movement of his mouth.

'Can't say I did. Lisa's was probably there – else I would have noticed it was missing. She walks to work.'

'What made you decide to call for Miss Jackson? It wasn't raining.'

'No reason, it was just a whim.'

'What did you do after that?'

'Drove to where I normally park. It's only two or three minutes by car.'

DS Jones glances at her aide memoire.

'And you arrived at the offices of InnStyle at just after eight a.m.' She looks up, intently. 'Did you attempt to communicate with Miss Jackson?'

140

There is a pause, but no movement of the plasticised features.

'I may have texted her.'

'Miss Jackson's mobile phone records show that you sent her four text messages between five past and twenty past eight.'

Again a short silence. Ray Piper remains unfazed.

'I might have sent more than one if I thought they weren't getting through. I know Lisa's had problems in the past receiving texts.'

'What was the content of your message or messages?'

'I expect it was "Good morning. How are you?" – just the usual.'

Though it is unspoken, DS Jones considers that all present must know that, unless Lisa Jackson's handset is recovered, the content of the text messages will remain unknown. There is a small chance that deleted information may be retrieved from Ray Piper's mobile, but it requires expert analysis and is not guaranteed.

'Did you receive a reply?'

'I imagine you know that I didn't.'

It interests DS Jones that he acknowledges his cognisance of their likely activities; but again she exercises her right to dictate the agenda.

'Did you see Miss Jackson arriving in Lychgate Lane from the window behind your desk?'

'I rarely look out. I face away from the window.'

DS Jones does not press for a definitive response.

'At about the same time that we know Miss Jackson reached the ground floor entrance, you were observed to go out onto the stair. Did you see her?'

'I've already stated several times, I didn't see Lisa on Friday.'

His tenor is flat, as though he is trying to sound bored rather than irritated.

'Can you recall now why you went out of the interior office door?'

'Like I said before, the only reason would be to go upstairs to the toilet.'

'You also previously stated that, around mid-morning, you briefly brought your car to load some samples – a box of tiles – do you still hold by that explanation?'

'Why wouldn't I?'

Even Ray Piper must by now recognise that DS Jones will not allow herself to be sidetracked. And, yet, with her next question, she does appear to head a little off course.

'Mr Piper, when you were brought into custody this morning and you were examined by our medical officer, among the points she highlighted – and indeed we have photographed – was a series of small relatively fresh cuts on the back of both of your hands. How did you come by these injuries?'

He keeps his hands out of sight.

'It was a rose bush that I removed. The lads had burst a football on it.'

He is no more forthcoming.

'When was this?'

'Saturday.'

'Are you sure it was Saturday?'

'I don't have time for gardening during the week.'

DS Jones taps her pad with her pen but does not look away.

'It has been brought to our attention that you had cuts on your hands on Friday morning. And that on occasion thereafter you wore gloves.'

Ray Piper is unblinking – but perhaps just too unflinching, as though he is applying an extra degree of self-control.

'I suffer from bouts of psoriasis. My hands were a mess last week. I wore leather gloves some of the time to stop my skin drying out further.'

'Our medical officer didn't mention psoriasis.'

'The antiseptic cream I used on the cuts must have helped. It can come and go overnight.'

DS Jones is conscious of DS Leyton shifting in his seat beside her. This account – is it clever, or true? The girl Kylie would not know about the psoriasis – she could have been mistaken. But would not Don McKenzie have mentioned it when he encouraged Kylie to come forward?

142

Briskly, and in a businesslike manner, DS Jones moves on. She indicates to her tablet, which is on the table in front of DS Leyton.

'I'd like to play you the voicemail that you left on Miss Jackson's number at ten past one on Friday afternoon.'

DS Leyton does the honours. With thick but deceptively dexterous fingers he taps out the necessary commands.

"Lisa – it's Ray. You've not been answering. I see you're off today. I was thinking we could meet up for a coffee – to have a chat. Let me know – drop me a text. Take care."

He looks at the detectives. If it were in his nature he would relax and say "so what?" – but instead he waits stiffly for whatever they might ask. DS Jones obliges.

'Miss Jackson's mobile phone records show that you were in high frequency contact. Most days you rarely went more than half an hour before sending her another message. What made you leave it so long before trying to reach her again on Friday?'

'There's no rule about this.'

'It seems out of kilter with your normal pattern.'

Now Ray Piper deigns to explain.

'I was busy.' He indicates with a shift of his eyes towards the tablet. 'That would have been when I stopped to eat my lunch.'

'When were you thinking of meeting her?'

'When it suited her – I didn't have a time or day in mind.'

'And what would be the purpose of that?'

He looks at DS Jones as if he thinks this is a superfluous question.

'No purpose. Being sociable. I stated before that we've had the occasional coffee.'

'Yes, you did, sir. How would you describe your present relationship with Miss Jackson?'

'Colleagues. Friends. Platonic.'

DS Jones moves on without acknowledging his answer. She is keeping up a fairly rapid pace, as if she wants to make sure he is not given extra time for his responses, or to add caveats and afterthoughts.

'When we spoke yesterday you began to tell me about the appointment that had cropped up –' (now she feigns to read her notes) '– at Egremont Hall. When was that – I mean, the time that the appointment was made?'

'It was in the morning. Before I put the tiles in my car.'

He does not append the word "obviously", although it is implicit in his tone, which is tinged with sarcasm – as if he fully grasps the young detective's modus operandi, and is beginning to tire of it. DS Jones, however, is undaunted.

'We spoke with the owner at Egremont Hall, Miss Brown, and the assistant manager, Mr Thatcher – they say they don't have a record of making an appointment.'

'They wouldn't. *I* made the appointment.'

DS Jones looks politely perplexed.

'How does that work, Mr Piper?'

The man answers in his flat monotone.

'With an ongoing job I'll often put a site visit in my diary. The client doesn't necessarily have to be part of the process. Generally they just want us to manage the job and leave them in peace. That's our role – my role in particular.'

'So, what prompted you to make this appointment?'

'I was reviewing my action list and I remembered a conversation about the decorative scheme. The owner had queried the texture of the bathroom tiles and I'd said I didn't recommend the alternative type she mentioned – they suffer from mineral build up and reduced adhesion, especially where there's poor ventilation in old properties – but I agreed to look at it. I had some spare from another job so I took the opportunity to go down.'

'When did you originally discuss it with her?'

He hesitates.

'It must have been three months ago. Before the job started. When they were assessing our proposals, the various options and costs.'

DS Jones is reflecting upon the extent to which this explanation is at odds with the account provided by Egremont Hall's management. Three months and nothing in writing is long enough ago to make it one person's word against another's. Although she feels she would trust Constance Brown's memory.

'What made you decide to go on Saturday?'

'It was as good as any other day. I wanted to get it off my action list.'

It would seem to DS Jones that Saturday was plainly a good day on which to avoid the pernickety owner.

'What time did you leave for Egremont?'

'In the morning, after I'd dropped the boys off at football.'

'Did you drive straight there?'

'Yes.'

'And how did the meeting go?'

'It was a site visit, not a meeting. I checked the tiles in situ and they were unsuitable, as I'd anticipated. That was it.'

The box of tiles has been located in the boot of Ray Piper's impounded BMW. DS Jones opts not to explore the detail of his call at this juncture. In her mind it is plainly an artifice designed to justify the excursion.

'What about your journey back – what did you do?'

'I felt ill.'

'I'm sorry?'

'I had to stop.'

DS Jones is becoming accustomed to his meticulous excuses, each just plausible yet in a way collectively increasing in their ludicrousness. But now she experiences a sensation of alarm – a sinking feeling in the pit of her stomach – that here comes another prepared lie, and one that is weightier than any other.

'Would you mind elaborating?'

Ray Piper looks almost pitying of the detectives – if only he were able to express such a sentiment. But his reaction reveals that he might even be enjoying the game of cat and mouse.

'Do you really want to know about me throwing up?'

'As I said at the beginning, Mr Piper, it is important under the circumstances that we gain a comprehensive account.'

'I ate a pizza Napoli the night before – the anchovies must have disagreed with me – maybe they were off. I'd not been feeling well since I got up. After I left Egremont Hall it became

145

much worse and I realised I was going to be sick. So I pulled off the road.'

DS Jones cursorily leafs through several pages of her jottings; it is to buy herself a second or two of breathing space.

'This would be on the A5086?'

'I turned into a lane first. I parked in a farm gateway.'

'Where was this exactly?'

'I can't remember. I was feeling dizzy and disoriented. It was the most I could do to keep the car on the road.'

'What was the last village you passed through?'

'I've no idea.'

DS Jones could press this point. His answer – if he were to yield a location – could be of the utmost significance. But she suspects he will continue to stonewall, and there may be a time when she has a stronger hand.

'How long did you stop for?'

'It might have been an hour.'

'An hour?' DS Jones repeats his words before she can prevent herself – it is just a small slip that reveals her surprise at his admission.

But now his tactic becomes clear.

'I got back in on the passenger side, so I could stretch out – not cramp my stomach. I intended to rest for a few minutes. I fell asleep. When I woke up I felt much better and went home.'

DS Jones is wishing she were in telepathic contact with DS Leyton. She can sense his frustration alongside her own. If they were watching this interview as a training exercise on tape they would pause it and break off to compare notes and devise a strategy. Ray Piper's explanation is intriguing in its simplicity and the near impossibility of verifying it. Perhaps its only real weakness is that it is the perfect lie. She decides to test him with one of their indisputable facts.

'Mr Piper – why did you switch off your mobile phone for the part of your journey between Egremont and Cockermouth?'

'I didn't switch it off.'

He stares coldly.

'Triangulation of your signal – that is as you move from cell to cell – shows that on Saturday morning it was switched off at Cleator Moor and switched back on just south of the Lamplugh roundabout.'

Ray Piper remains impassive. For a moment he is silent – but if anything there is the sense that he is toying with them, rather than scouring his imagination for a rejoinder.

'It had run out of charge. Since I was ill I didn't notice. I realised as I was approaching Cockermouth – I thought I might have missed a call from my wife while I was asleep. I saw the battery was flat. I plugged it in and switched it back on.'

DS Jones is suddenly enveloped by a wave of self-doubt. Has she allowed her emotions to drive her thoughts and actions – to override logic and procedure? Has she too hastily bought into an explanation guided by intuition – if not by personal prejudice, indeed? Has she not appreciated how Skelgill reins in speculation when it may run out of control? It is an unnerving moment – and she senses that DS Leyton is attuned to her predicament; though, like her, he does not want to give the game away. But – *wait*. She conjures up the images that are imprinted in her mind – the CCTV of Lisa Jackson glancing happily into the shop window – jauntily crossing Warwick Road into Lychgate Lane – and, then, the trained cadaver dog's spontaneous and frenetic barking when it is introduced to the under-stair cupboard just inside the door of number thirteen. DS Jones steels herself, and presses on.

'Did you drive directly to your house?'

'It would appear you already know the answer to that.'

Ray Piper's tone is flat, when irony might be anticipated.

'I'm sure you would expect the police to verify any account that is based on one person's word.' And now she allows an openly artful tone to enter her voice. 'Besides, you say you have no reason to mislead us.'

He rises to the bait.

'I went straight home until it was time to pick up the lads. I brought them back and we stayed in for the rest of the evening. I was at home all day Sunday, come to that.'

147

DS Jones has been judicious with the evidence she has gathered. While Ray Piper can be in no doubt of why he is being questioned, she has at no point tried naively to trip him up, albeit she has given him several opportunities to contradict their knowledge before confronting him with it. Now she treads even more carefully – for she does not want at this stage to mention that they have interviewed Irene Piper – as much or to the woman's sake as anything.

'We are having your vehicle inspected for forensic purposes. That examination is continuing. It has been reported to us that the boot compartment in particular appears recently to have been cleaned and smells very strongly of lavender.'

Ray Piper simply returns her gaze with compound interest; the human reflected as the reptilian. He makes no response, other than a slight shrug, which might suggest that he feels neither obligation nor inclination to explain. DS Jones offers a prompt.

'Isn't that rather unusual, Mr Piper?'

'What – to clean your car?'

'When did you clean it?'

'On Saturday.'

'After you arrived back from Egremont?'

'Yes.'

'What's the explanation for the description I just gave of the boot?'

'One of the lad's trainers had dog dirt on it.'

'When did that happen, sir?'

'It must have been when I picked them up on Friday. I thought it were just mud. But I made them take off their trainers and I put them in the boot. I didn't notice any smell until I got the tiles out at Egremont Hall. So I sprayed the car with air freshener when I cleaned it later.'

Ray Piper folds his arms. For the first time he allows himself the hint of a smug grin.

148

10. TO THE PARTRIDGE

Tuesday evening

'Cor blimey, Emma – it's like we're travelling in a parallel universe. There's what we know happened and there's what Piper's made up – completely different, every flamin' step of the way.'

DS Jones, hands on hips, facing away from her colleague, is staring blankly at the photographs and maps and yellow sticky notes spaced along a timeline that stretches across the wall of the vacant office she has set up as an incident room (a protocol alien to Skelgill, but one that suits her logical mind). DS Leyton hits the nail on the head: Ray Piper has treated the process like one of the critical path analyses that he spends his working hours perfecting. Yes, he has anticipated every question he might be asked; what took place, minute by minute, hour by hour. And for each small detail, there is an alternative explanation, one that is both plausible, largely, and – more alarming – difficult if not impossible to disprove. For what she believes quite likely was an unpremeditated murder, the retrospective contingency planning is extraordinary in its thoroughness.

She had terminated the interview with the cleaning of the car. Even the notion of the dog excrement on one of his sons' training shoes was in effect corroborated by his behaviour on Saturday morning. Witnessed by herself and Skelgill, he had cautioned the boys to keep their feet off the backs of the seats. At this point she had concluded – for a second time in interviewing Ray Piper – that she needed some breathing space. Let him feel smug. Though he had asked to be released, and when she had declined a small blood vessel had pulsed at his temple and she was glad she was not alone with him. It made her think of his wife.

In response to her colleague's remark she sweeps an arm along the timeline and turns to face him.

149

'There's only one possible explanation for the disappearance of Lisa Jackson.'

'He's banking on us not finding the body.'

DS Jones regards her fellow sergeant intently, her full lips untypically compressed into a narrow line and her normally smooth brow furrowed. In her hazel eyes worry is in the ascendency over her customary determination. She appreciates a little more what Skelgill must sometimes feel when they hit a roadblock, and understands something of his apparent indifference, when in fact perhaps he is detaching himself in order to feel his way around the impediment. And now DS Leyton has – with his characteristic candid naivety – called it as he sees it.

He is right. Ray Piper *is* relying on them failing to locate Lisa Jackson.

DS Jones is sufficiently well schooled in criminology to know that, in her lifetime, in only a handful of cases have murder convictions been achieved without the victim's corpse. Hitherto it has not entered her mind that they might fail in this respect. But her colleague's simple statement casts a spotlight on Ray Piper's entire strategy. If he can provide a convincing account – an account at least plausible – what jury would send a man down when there is no concrete proof of a killing?

When she does not speak DS Leyton rouses her from her brown study.

'I reckon we need an extension, Emma. To the full four days, if we can get it. We want every last scrap of evidence we can lay our mitts on.'

She appreciates his supportive approach. Her more seasoned colleague seems entirely unconcerned that she has been preferred to him in the hierarchy of the investigation, and content to play second fiddle.

'You gonna have a chinwag with the Guvnor?'

'Pardon? Oh – I don't know. I think he might still be guiding. There's a quid pro quo – he's struck a bargain with The Partridge and it's not so easy to interrupt him. I figured I'd need to see the Chief myself.'

DS Leyton makes a face that suggests it would not be a good idea.

'If I were you I'd let the Guvnor take the flak. He's an old hand at disobeying orders and getting away with it. And he's nailed his colours to your mast.'

DS Leyton refers to Skelgill's intervention in gaining sanction for the arrest of Ray Piper.

DS Jones nods reflectively. Skelgill gets results; that is probably why a blind eye is so often turned to his antics. Far less is it due to an acknowledgement of his disabilities – plain as day to her but apparently unrecognised by the powers that be – they are simply treated as quirks of behaviour, something to do with his upbringing in the fells, half feral, allowances made – an innate, relentless, remorseless determination to scour the county of crime. Break the law in Cumbria; you wouldn't want Skelgill on your case.

Maybe she should call upon him.

*

'You must be gagging for a vodka tonic, Emma.'

Startled, DS Jones turns on her heel – though there is no mistaking the Mancunian drawl of DI Alec Smart. She does not answer immediately – knowing that his solicitude cloaks a proposition that she does not wish to take up. Framed in the doorway and leaning like a vampire awaiting permission to cross the threshold he regards her thirstily.

'You've been looking a million dollars these last few days.' He fingers the lapel of his designer jacket. 'City executive beats studenty sidekick, hands down.' He stifles a salacious laugh as though there is a double entendre in his words.

DS Jones feels her cheeks colouring. True, in her lead role on the case she has taken to tailored business suits, to present to interviewees an aura of professionalism. And, yes, she normally wears more casual garb that is appropriate for trailing incognito about the countryside at Skelgill's coattails. But while Skelgill might be blissfully ignorant of the first impression he makes

151

upon a member of the public – that they wonder why the unshaven, tousle-haired detective is wearing a shirt with fishing flies hooked into the breast pocket – she has been sidestepping DI Smart long enough to know that his designer outfits and not-so-subtle brand labels are less about good taste and more about ego; and she feels a sudden nostalgia for Skelgill's indifference.

'Unfortunately, I have an appointment.'

She has grasped the nettle – she has submitted her excuse before it becomes increasingly difficult to evade his clutches. Conscious of his gaze following her – her skirt is short and tight and her heels higher than her regulation trainers – she moves across to a table and begins to pack into her shoulder bag her laptop, tablet and mobile phone. Alec Smart's weaselly features betray no reaction to the knock-back. He inclines his head in the direction of the display on the wall.

'Nice to see the job being done properly, for a change, Emma.' He plies her with a sickly grin. 'I must put in a word on your behalf – there's a nice little number coming up in my section. Your talents are wasted counting sheep. And you won't find me muscling in and taking the credit when all the hard work's been done.'

DS Jones does not concur with the inference. Much as Skelgill finds it almost impossible to resist basking in the glory of misattributed praise – generally realising too late that he has done so – she has never known him erroneously to claim the credit for solving a case; he has a sportsman's sense of fair play. More likely, DI Smart describes his own modus operandi. She does not know how to answer honestly. Under close surveillance she fastens a button of her jacket and slings the bag over her shoulder.

'I had better go – else I'll be late.'

DI Smart performs a gunslinger's motion.

'I'll ride shotgun, if you like – give you a second opinion – a few tips – in the bar afterwards.'

She approaches him.

'Oh – thanks – but, it's a personal appointment.'

152

She contrives a face of apology that she hopes does not go so far that it reveals the white lie that squirms just beneath the surface.

DI Smart remains blocking the doorway. He brushes one hand over his carefully styled hair.

'Well – you know where I am – come up and see me some time.'

For some reason he affects a French accent. But still he does not move.

'Are you wanting to come in – to see the exhibits?' DS Jones gestures to the wall.

'Nah – you're alright, Emma.' Now he steps half a pace sideways. 'Second thoughts, better not cramp your style, eh?'

It would be undiplomatic to agree with his suggestion – but he does cramp her style and she is obliged to turn sideways to pass him, and obliged to face him, as to turn her back would be too offensive. She simpers as she makes eye contact and ducks through an invisible mist of expensive fragrance that smells of alcohol, thus freshly applied, and she passes through the door otherwise unscathed. She senses his eyes on her back; she turns.

'Well – goodnight.'

She strides briskly away, relieved that Skelgill was not on the scene.

*

DS Jones is still thinking about DI Smart's importunity while she waits at the last set of lights at the crossing above the busy M6 motorway. She has hardly got going but already her mobile rings. She hopes it is not he. But it is a different number – and one she has recently stored. She activates the phone on hands-free.

'Mr McKenzie?'

'Hey – how's it going?'

'Er – okay – thanks?'

Her querying inflection perhaps hints at a slight affront – that he is too familiar. Frankly – and she knows it – he suffers because of the hangover from her last conversation. But he seems straightaway to detect that he has struck the wrong note and in the hesitation that ensues she senses he is rearranging what he has to say.

'I thought you would like to know as soon as possible. Your DC Watson contacted me to ask about a proposal Ray Piper sent off on Friday morning?'

'Oh, yes. Sorry – please go ahead.'

'I've been with Sam our techie person – she stayed back to interrogate the system for me. Ray sent an email with an attached critical path analysis to a client on Friday morning – just before midday. Of the emails he received prior to that – since Thursday night – none of them were related to the project.'

'What about in the post?'

'Hmm, that's possible – though it's more difficult to check – he may not have kept the paperwork. But, to be honest, even one-man-and-his-dog subcontractors are electronic these days.'

The lights change to green and just as automatically DS Jones pulls away. The brief solitary sanctuary of the car has brought home to her just how many themes and memes and emotions are spinning around in her mind; one after the next has arisen during the day, wind devils that will not settle, and now Don McKenzie evokes a couple more – and not merely the small fact that he provides. But she rallies and thanks him and poses a question that might just help her a little.

'The issue with the tiles that you brought to our attention. Would it be a realistic thing for any employee to do – to take them halfway through the project knowing they were unsuitable – when seemingly the client has no interest, anyway? Miss Brown suggested that your firm was trying to fob her off with a job-lot of cheap material.'

Don McKenzie emits a gasp of exasperation.

'It makes no sense whatsoever. Not only is it unrealistic – it's actually entirely uncharacteristic of Ray Piper, as I intimated. He invariably gets everything buttoned down at the outset.'

DS Jones delays before she asks her follow-up question.

'So what is your opinion about this site visit?'

154

'Well – if it were for a work-related reason – and why else would Ray go to one of our jobs if it weren't work-related? – I can only think that there was a problem that he wanted to cover up – or at least deal with, without any fuss.' Now it is Don McKenzie's turn to pause meaningfully. 'But I doubt if that's what you're thinking.'

Once more, DS Jones feels inclined to share her thoughts – there has been the lack of Skelgill as a sounding board – and Don McKenzie would give her a kinder reception. Moreover, he has demonstrated a desire to be nothing but candid – at no point has he put his firm's reputation before assisting her inquiries. And with the non-appearance of Ray Piper at work this morning – the name of the person arrested still unannounced – he is intelligent enough to draw the obvious conclusion and not embarrass her by asking.

Distracted by her latest dilemma DS Jones negotiates the Rheged roundabout at speed, surprising a car shaping to pull out and having to swerve to avoid a glancing blow. Its male driver honks a protest and then sees it is a young woman at the wheel and makes an obscene gesture with his tongue. DS Jones forgets herself and mutters a curse – although "dickhead" might in part apply in self-reproach.

Don McKenzie ventures a polite inquiry.

'You're driving?'

'Not as well as I ought.'

'I wondered if you were heading up here.' A plaintive note has entered his voice. He clears his throat with an *ahem*. 'I believe it's my round.'

DS Jones checks her mirror – the car she almost struck is catching her up and she puts her foot down in no uncertain terms.

'I'm sorry – I have an appointment.' Then her tone softens. 'Besides, haven't you got bedtime stories to read?'

*

'Good girl – here we are. Now where is *that* man?'

DS Jones draws to a halt against the dilapidated picket fence that marks off a little gated wooded garden opposite The Partridge. The ancient inn was once directly adjacent to the old coach road, a staging post between Keswick and Cockermouth on the route to the coastal ports. Twice bypassed by progress, it benefits from a public yet effectively private sweep of residual tarmacadam that curves past its long crouching frontage, and thus ample parking. That DS Jones receives no audible reply is owing to the identity of her passenger. On impulse she has collected from Skelgill's dog-sitting neighbour his endearing but slightly crazy bullboxer. Acquired under somewhat controversial circumstances – when eyebrows were raised at Skelgill's philanthropy – the creature seems to understand there is the prospect of connecting with her absent step-master.

A female voice does however catch DS Jones's attention. As she rounds the car she observes that, smoking a cigarette in a patch of evening sunlight, a stylishly dressed and coiffured dark-haired woman of around thirty is standing outside the rustic porch addressing a mobile phone. Beside her is a smart Gladstone bag and on top of it a handbag, which, if original, should in DS Jones's assessment be kept on a chain. Rather than risk Cleopatra making one of her infamous introductions – or, worse, running off with the handbag – DS Jones reaches into the car and clips on the dog's lead. Rightly so, for the animal makes a break for freedom that almost defeats her. However, it appears that Cleopatra's interest is in a drinking bowl thoughtfully situated at the foot of one of the weathered timber uprights of the porch; DS Jones consents to being dragged her across.

The woman is slim and of similar height and build to DS Jones, though her heels make her seem taller, and as DS Jones passes in front of her she senses the stranger's appraising gaze. It seems to be par for the course this evening. For her part, she has changed out of her formal wear, and now her 'studenty' look (as DI Smart put it) combined with her enviable complexion probably makes her seem younger than her age. There is something of this appreciation in the woman's manner, as if she

156

regards DS Jones to pose no threat to her status – when in fact there might only be three or four years between them.

DS Jones stoops beside the dog while it drinks. Without feeling especially curious, she overhears the woman say she is waiting for an Uber – and make some quip about being stranded out here in the sticks. Certainly with her tanned model looks and striking make-up and tight leather trousers she would seem more at home were she hailing a black cab outside a trendy neon-lit West End nightspot, than in the environs of the seventeenth century inn crowded by shadowy forest with darkening fells above. However, when the woman unexpectedly mentions her superior's name, DS Jones's ears prick up. Pretending to adjust the dog's collar, she tunes in to the one-sided conversation.

'What's that, darling? Oh, no – he's still at the lake – winding in his tackle.'

She emits a throaty chuckle and the suggestion of innuendo is bolstered by her next response.

'You know the form, Camilla – what goes on tour stays on tour.'

Now she tuts reproachfully.

'Oh, I should say something like Indiana Jones meets The Wicker Man. *Seriously!* But I think I got everything I wanted. Not all of it is printable.'

She listens for a moment, drawing on the last of the cigarette and discarding it absently.

'Say again, darling? Camilla – you're breaking up – well, it's probably me – the reception up here is positively antediluvian. *The fishing?* Well – I caught a pike – if that's what you mean. Hugo will probably be livid that he sent me in his stead.'

The woman laughs again at whatever may be the rejoinder. But perhaps now she gets a sense that the dog has emptied the bowl and that the girl may be eavesdropping – but DS Jones is equally attuned and rises and leads Cleopatra away. Having received information as to Skelgill's whereabouts, she sets off along the wooded lane towards Peel Wyke.

It is just a matter of a couple of hundred yards to the tiny harbour, tucked away down a short damp track and surrounded by tall oaks. The air along the lane is still and cool and scented by the occasional pine, and the coo of a woodpigeon resonates about her, disguising its location. In the hedges green nuts like elfin hats are gathering on the coppiced hazels, and spikes of enchanter's nightshade dot the verges like fairy candelabra. She knows she ought to feel relaxed – the greenery supposedly an instant tonic for one's wellbeing. But she is insufficiently attuned to these natural sensations; the case is challenging enough, yet at every turn today a new conundrum has presented itself to her: not clear and capable of rational solution; instead vague and unsettling at the subconscious level.

But Cleopatra's mind operates on a much simpler plane.

As they reach the gateway to the track she must get wind of her master – or perhaps she just recognises where they are. Whichever, she catches DS Jones off guard with a sudden lunge that strips the leash from her hand. DS Jones might be fit and athletic – but all she can do is overtake the dog with the speed of sound.

'Guv! Look out!' There is a note of futility in her warning.

Skelgill, standing in his boat and thus waist high to the bank, is glowering in concentration as he attempts to collapse an uncooperative landing net. He glances up just in time to see the 'canine cannonball' launch itself from the harbour wall. Instinctively he discards the net and, with some aplomb – perhaps practised at the manoeuvre – absorbs the impact of the flying dog in the way of a goalkeeper catching a powerful shot in the midriff and flopping forwards onto the ball. The alternative, had he remained upright, would have probably seen the pair of them follow the net overboard. The wriggling dog licks his face ecstatically before it quickly loses interest and turns its attention to scouring the craft for edible morsels.

Arriving breathless, DS Jones sounds distressed.

'Guv – are you okay? I'm sorry – she was too strong for me.'

Skelgill, looking somewhat dishevelled, pushes himself to his knees. However, he seems phlegmatic and if anything regards Cleopatra rather in the manner of a proud parent.

'Let me get ashore first if you're planning on doing that.'

158

DS Jones reacts awkwardly for a moment – as though she feels chastised. She responds a little stiffly.

'I am pleased to see you.'

She is more pleased to see him than he knows – and he glances up as if he detects an aberration in her tone – but there is the practical expedient of stabilising the boat. Though it is loosely moored the momentum transferred by the dog's dynamic arrival has caused it to drift away from the bank. He flourishes a boathook. The landing net, at least, is designed to float and is easily retrieved. Then he reaches out with the pole towards DS Jones.

'Here – grab hold.'

DS Jones is happy to oblige. She is glad she has changed out of her business outfit. Skelgill makes several more loops of the painter around the depth gauge board that he is using as a mooring post and then begins to pass up various items of fishing tackle and boxes of supplies to his colleague. His shooting brake is parked just twenty feet away with the tailgate raised, and she loads the car while he makes fast the boat and with a heave gets the dog back onto dry land. Skelgill lets the latter into the back seat – and then regards DS Jones with a familiar grimace.

'Hop in – I'm gasping for a pint.'

DS Jones experiences a paradoxical sense of comfort in that, while Skelgill references his own needs, he for one does not try to ply her with drinks. However, as she clambers in, finding gaps for her feet amongst the various items of debris that populate the passenger footwell, she notices a business card lying on the dashboard. It displays the branding of a national Sunday newspaper. Skelgill, as he slides in, sees her looking at it.

'Am I glad that's over. Hairy-arsed journalists have never been my cup of tea.'

Rather ham-fistedly he snatches up the card and stuffs it out of sight. He starts the car, jams it into reverse and then surges forward, too fast for the bumpy track, almost running down a pheasant poult that has not the sense to turn left or right into the undergrowth. Bouncing, DS Jones hangs on by the overheard strap. But, in a day of grasping nettles – or maybe not always

159

doing so and regretting it – she decides to grasp this last one before Skelgill can dig a hole for himself.

'I think I might have just passed her? A dark-haired woman in leather trousers – she was talking on the phone – I heard her say she was waiting for a taxi.'

She utters the words casually, as though it is a matter of little interest, and she affects to look at overhanging branches that scrape the car as they exit the gateway onto the metalled lane. But she senses that Skelgill is editing his narrative.

'At least Charlie's going to be happy – seems the article's mainly about the food and accommodation. I reckon the fishing were just to fill the dead time.'

DS Jones continues to gaze ahead.

'I couldn't help overhearing a snatch of her conversation. I don't know if she was speaking to her editor. She said it wasn't all printable.'

She leaves the suggestion hanging. It has taken barely thirty seconds to drive back to The Partridge and Skelgill slews in, nose-to-nose with DS Jones's yellow Golf. He yanks on the handbrake, the ratchet protesting, and he sits for a second as if he is making up his mind. Then he reaches around with his right arm and pulls back the sleeve of his khaki fishing shirt.

'I had a lapse into Anglo-Saxon.'

Two opposing arcs of raw vertical gashes mark his forearm, oozing slightly.

'*Yow!* Guv – that's awful – it must be agony?'

'Ach – there aren't so many nerve endings there. I got clamped by a pitbull once, hardly felt a thing.'

'Don't you have your first aid kit?'

Skelgill tosses back his head.

'I'd left that crate in the car – to make more room in the boat.'

DS Jones begins to open the passenger door.

'Let me do it now – we should get antiseptic on those cuts.'

Skelgill tuts, but yields.

'Aye. Happen you're right.'

160

They go round to the rear and Skelgill reposes beneath the tailgate while DS Jones bathes the wounds with surgical spirit and applies a sterile dressing pad and fixes it with a bandage. It is an operation mainly conducted in silence, though Skelgill, in spite of his claim about nerve endings, grits his teeth when the alcohol is applied. Already kneeling, DS Jones ducks to split the bandage with a bite, and then tears it to make a tie. She looks up with something of twinkle in her eye.

'At least with lacerations like these you couldn't be accused of trying to strangle someone.'

'There were a couple of times I could have done, I tell you, lass. I thought I was supposed to be fishing with a bloke.'

DS Jones observes him knowingly – but she seems to regard this as an honest answer. She jumps up – perhaps too quickly – and looks momentarily dizzy.

'You can tell me the gory details when I've got a large gin and tonic.'

*

Skelgill's arrival in the snug bar is delayed by a detour to reception for a word with landlord Charlie. He enters the shadowy oasis of browns to see his colleague sipping a drink in the corner of their last conversation and Cleopatra beneath the settle rooting into the silvery wrapper of a bag of sea salt and balsamic vinegar crisps. DS Jones anticipates his expression of reproach.

'They were meant for us to share – but unfortunately I stood up and turned my back to admire the stuffed fish.'

The specimen cabinet that houses an ancient pike, once a record for Bassenthwaite Lake, successfully diverts Skelgill. He dwells on the addendum to the caption, subsequent records; a list that ends with "D. Skelgill." But when he inhales to remark DS Jones inadvertently steals his moment of glory.

'Vicious jaws, Guv. I can see how you got the cuts. Were you dangling your arm in the water?'

Skelgill sinks down and raises his pint in a sign of cheers. He gulps about half of it and sighs with relief.

'Nay – she wanted a selfie with the fish – but she didn't want to hold it. I was trying to position it from below, out of sight – not take too long about it, before I got it back in the lake – and it just flipped and caught me.' He regards DS Jones defensively. 'It weren't trying to bite – just a panic reflex. Thing is, they're all muscle – handling a big pike, it's like trying to wrestle a croc smeared with lard.'

DS Jones does just wonder if Skelgill were rather blasé – if not cocky – and does not want to admit that he received his come-uppance. She grins wryly.

'Probably just as well it bit you, Guv. Your friend Charlie might have had an insurance claim on his hands.'

Skelgill regards her with a self-satisfied grin.

'He's agreed to wipe my slate clean at the end of the week. Compensation for injury in the line of duty.' As if being reminded of this benefit kindles a sense of urgency, he empties his glass. 'I'll get your money back on these. Same again?'

DS Jones smiles.

'You *were* gasping.'

As good as his word, when Skelgill returns, he presents his colleague with a banknote. She tries to decline but when he says it is either that or he'll donate it to the mountain rescue she agrees to the latter – and in the avoidance of doubt she rises and folds the note and slips it into the charity tin at the bar. She resumes her seat. She is wondering where to begin when Skelgill assumes charge of the conversation.

'Poker Face.'

He uses the nickname in a more sober fashion than previously; indeed his inflection suggests he understands she has something to get off her chest.

DS Jones feels a sob of relief coming upon her – and has to choke it back – such that Skelgill interjects.

'I hear you've set up an incident room.'

She looks surprised – and also perhaps a little sheepish. But it puts her back on track.

162

'How do you know that?'

'I've got my spies.'

But it would not be like Skelgill, she thinks, to behave in a clandestine manner – and she only has to wait a moment for him to reveal his source.

'George was tapping me up for a good spot for grayling on the upper Eden. He reckons you're going great guns – the Chief's had visiting top brass in to see it.'

DS Jones shrugs self-effacingly.

'Appearances aren't everything. I wanted to display the timeline – my brain doesn't work like yours, Guv.'

'Jones – if I relied on my brain I'd never solve anything.'

She laughs involuntarily – wondering if he will be offended – but he joins in with her, taking the kudos for his joke. Perhaps he is as keen as she is for some light-hearted relief. He raises his glass to admire the straw-coloured bitter against a wall light.

'In fact, you'd better bring me up to speed while my brain cells can still cope.'

DS Jones nods – it *is* back to work – but at least now she feels more at ease.

'Poker Face. It couldn't be a more apt description. He's playing a long hand and he knows exactly what he's doing. He's highly intelligent. He's over-qualified for the job he does. He's got a bachelor's degree and a master's.'

Skelgill rather turns up his nose. His colleague might be a graduate, but he has been known to carry a small chip on his shoulder where qualifications are concerned. But DS Jones does not dwell on the point. Unhurriedly, she relates all that she has learnt in what seems more like a week than the mere day since she last provided a debrief. She concludes with DS Leyton's prediction: that Ray Piper has set himself up for a defence of the *corpus delicti* variety.

Skelgill is in agreement that the crux is the seventy-eight extra minutes that it took Ray Piper to travel between Egremont and Cockermouth – ostensibly sleeping. He rises to his feet.

'Hold your horses.'

163

He is back within the minute bearing an Ordnance Survey map. Rather dog-eared, it comes from a collection in the residents' lounge provided for the use of adventurous guests.

'This is a bit out of date – but it's an inch to the mile – good scale for an overview.'

Deftly he opens and refolds it to cover the stretch of road and surrounding area in question.

'At best you'd average twenty miles an hour along these lanes. There's a limit to how far he could have gone.'

DS Jones suddenly perks up.

'Oh – I'm having a heat map produced.'

'Come again?'

'Well – it's exactly what you're getting at – but computer generated. It's a project I'd heard about at the University of Cumbria. It will show the most extreme points he could have driven to in the time available – and also, imagine that he parked at any time, how far he could have walked across country.'

Skelgill considers this idea; he concludes it does not rub against the grain, traditionalist that he might be.

'Allowing how long for concealment of the body?'

'Actually, I think it's best if the computer programme allows no time for that – because it could be as little as thirty seconds, when you think about it.'

Skelgill scowls to show his disdain for what would be a callous act.

'Aye, fair enough.'

'Obviously if we pick him up somewhere on CCTV it would narrow down the options and concentrate the area of interest.'

Skelgill is measuring distances on the map with his thumbs, stepping them quickly over one another.

DS Jones understands his method.

'I did a rough estimate myself. Technically it's six hundred square miles.'

The daunting statistic sends them both into silence. But after a moment's rumination Skelgill spreads the fingers of both hands and lays them on the map.

'It's nothing like that much. Think of a spider's web. We're not talking about the whole surface area – we're talking about the fine threads.'

DS Jones seems encouraged.

'I wouldn't expect that he went far on foot.'

'That's why he's driven into the country.'

'And he did have on his good shoes – we found no outdoor footwear.'

'What state were they in?'

'Clean – they looked just like they did on Saturday morning. They're being tested for residues.'

Skelgill jerks his head in frustration.

'What about petrol?'

'What do you mean, Guv?'

'He's the sort that fills his tank when it gets to halfway.' Skelgill says this perhaps a little disparagingly, as if he holds a prejudice against such organised behaviour. His own method is to go by the banknotes in his wallet at the time – and he is not unknown to run out – although in typical Skelgill fashion there is always a jerry can sloshing around in the back of his car; when it doesn't smell of fish it smells of petrol. He maintains it comes in handy for starting the Kelly kettle on a wet day. 'Find out from his bank when he last used his credit card for fuel. Subtract his known movements.'

DS Jones considers this suggestion pensively. She can immediately see there are hurdles – not insurmountable, but tricky. There is establishing how much fuel remains now in the BMW's tank, and what would be its consumption. There is the delay waiting for the bank to come through with information. And – most subjective – there is the determination of any extra journeys Ray Piper may have taken; he could easily lie to eat up fuel unaccounted for. She finds herself voicing a doubt.

'Will that get us any further than the heat map?'

Skelgill takes a sup of his ale and dwells as he savours the hoppy bite. He smacks his lips decisively.

'Maybe not – but his story about sleeping in a layby – that he went nowhere – it would blow that clean out of the water.'

165

DS Jones feels her eyes widening at the prospect. Her voice becomes more animated.

'Actually, first thing tomorrow I'm going to the filling station next to his house. I've arranged to look at their CCTV to see if we can confirm the time he got home on Saturday. There must be a good chance that he buys his petrol there.'

'It could be your silver bullet, lass.'

The word 'lass' rouses Cleopatra from beneath the oak settle, no doubt believing it is her exclusive epithet. She gazes at the pair with mournful eyes that speak of the empty potato crisps packet licked clean of salt. Skelgill looks at DS Jones.

'I don't suppose you brought her food?'

'Oh – er, well – no, I – didn't know –'

Skelgill waves a palm to indicate no matter. He gathers in their empty glasses and gets to his feet.

'She can make do with crisps. Maybe roast chicken, eh?' He regards DS Jones earnestly. 'We'll cadge a doggy bag off Charlie at breakfast.'

11. CARLISLE

Wednesday morning – 7:00 a.m.

DS Jones can hardly believe her good fortune. It might not be a silver bullet, but they have certainly struck oil. Her heart is beating fast, and she is desperate to phone Skelgill to relay the news. But she calms herself – this is not about luck. Ray Piper has miscalculated – he has not allowed for solid, thorough police work. She and DS Leyton had conceived the idea of checking the CCTV at the filling station; Skelgill had contributed the notion of investigating petrol consumption. Perhaps what none of them had banked on was just how comprehensively the garage's modern technology has captured data.

'Here's the printout, Miss.'

DS Jones finds the overly polite youth endearing; there is none of the cocksure insouciance of his contemporary over at Wood's of Carlisle. Johnny Parker, a teenager who is clearly lacking in self-confidence, he is son of the owner and a part-time IT student at a local technical college. He might be a greenhorn when it comes to members of the opposite sex, but he knows his way intimately around the firm's computer system. DS Jones's trepidation at being handed over to him was rapidly assuaged. Following a brief explanation of what she hoped to learn (simply whether the security cameras may have picked up a certain car passing along the adjacent public highway) he had asked her for the registration number – and in a matter of seconds produced two transactions with associated video footage!

The number plate recognition system has caught Ray Piper not merely in passing, but in purchasing petrol from the forecourt on Saturday, at 08:16 and 12:50. She peruses the document for a moment; it is a copy of the purchase receipts, detailing items, quantities, times and credit card number. She indicates with the tip of a clear-varnished nail.

'How accurate is your clock?'

The youth looks momentarily crestfallen, as if she has found an error and he is personally responsible.

'It uses NTP, Miss – network time protocol – it's accurate to within a few milliseconds.'

DS Jones grins inwardly – and nods knowledgeably, at the same time thinking she must not adopt too many of Skelgill's traits.

'Okay, excellent.'

She has explained, without revealing specific details, that she is conducting an investigation into a serious crime; it is so close to home that she does not wish to introduce any bias. And, speaking of the clock, she is working against it: the statutory twenty-four hours of Ray Piper's detention expire shortly. She expresses her thanks and confirms their arrangement for the secure transfer of the video footage.

Once in her car she calls Skelgill, praying that he has a signal.

'Bassenthwaite Lake Fishing Guides, how may I help you?'

DS Jones laughs – partly in relief – but he is obviously in good form.

'You sound like you've caught something already, Guv.'

'Aye – a couple of sunken trees – but mustn't take the gloss off fishing in peace.'

She considers for a moment that he might be over-egging yesterday's excuses; although his tone does not particularly suggest it. Besides, she too is upbeat.

'I've just finished at the garage. Guv – I think you're right about the fuel. Ray Piper filled up before and after his journey – and I mean *filled up*. On the forecourt CCTV you can see him clearly topping up right to the filler cap on both occasions. He used 18.6 litres of petrol.'

'What's that in proper money?'

DS Jones glances at the calculations she has made in anticipation.

'Just over four gallons.'

And what's the round trip from Carlisle?'

'Eighty-six miles.'

'Do the sums, will you?'

168

DS Jones chuckles.

'It's just over twenty mpg.'

'No chance.' Skelgill is vehement. 'Cruising country lanes? That's a three-litre automatic he's got – you'd be talking minimum thirty. He's used an extra gallon.'

DS Jones is silent for a moment.

'So he might have gone about fifteen miles distant from the A5086.'

'That would be impressive in your sleep.'

Now DS Jones is nodding. Skelgill's germ of an idea has come to fruition. Armed with this information they can surely prove that Ray Piper did not drive to the first convenient rural pull-in. Already she is assessing what are the implications for the heat map. Using Skelgill's analogy of the spider's web, it seems they should be concentrating on the intersection of the radial filaments with the outermost capture spirals.

'There's more, Guv. Quite a lot more.' She does not keep him in suspense. 'On his first visit, as well as petrol he bought the News & Star – remember, we saw him with it? The boy who helped me – the owner's son – he serves at the counter on Saturdays and he recognises Ray Piper. He says he doesn't usually buy a paper. Thereafter, on his second visit, he spent time at the motor accessories section – he bought a car interior cleaning spray and air freshener – lavender. These are all itemised on the till receipts. And there's CCTV at the cash desk.'

'Bingo.'

'What was he thinking, Guv?'

Skelgill makes a scoffing exclamation.

'Happen he wasn't thinking well – maybe a false sense of security. Not to put too fine a point on it, he'd done his dirty work.'

'I suppose he might have thought that a full tank would disguise his journey. Or he decided that it would look more natural if he bought petrol as well as cleaning materials.'

'Hmm.'

Skelgill is evidently multitasking – it sounds to DS Jones as if he might be trying to bite through resistant nylon fishing line.

She hears him spit what she deduces is a loose end. It takes him a few seconds to respond.

'Jones – I don't reckon he banked on you rumbling his cover story so quick – getting on the trail while it was still fresh. All this would be a lot harder to untangle in a couple of weeks' time.'

DS Jones reacts modestly to his compliment.

'The fuel was your idea, Guv.'

'Aye – but you would have had it, soon enough.'

DS Jones could argue, but she moves on.

'Like you said, Guv – it doesn't tell us where he went – but I think it's exactly what we're going to need to justify the extension.'

Again it takes Skelgill a moment to respond.

'So, what's the plan?'

'I've sent an urgent request to see the Chief as soon as I get back. Then I want to conduct a press conference.'

'With the Jacksons?'

'I don't know if I can put them through it – given what we suspect.' A troubled sigh escapes her. 'I mean – I'm going to be asking members of the public for sightings of Ray Piper's car in a lonely, out-of-the-way spot. How is that going to read to her parents?'

More muffled sounds reach her down the line, followed by a grunt that she recognises as Skelgill heaving his line across the water.

'Not the best part of the job, Jones.'

'I know, Guv. I think I'll go and see Mr and Mrs Jackson once I've got the Chief's agreement – get a feel for how they're bearing up.'

Skelgill makes what might be a growl of encouragement.

'Chin up, lass. Don't let what he's done bring you down and work to his advantage.'

'You're right. I shan't. I know the best thing we can do now is to see justice done. I can't help –'

She gets no further as Skelgill interjects.

'*Hey up!* I'm in! That's done the trick – Harris strikes again!'

She has some vague recall that 'Harris' is a homemade pike lure fashioned from the handle of a proprietary brand of paintbrush.

'I'll leave you to it, Guv.'

But Skelgill has apparently dropped his phone. There are grunts and splashes and hollow clunks as he shifts about the boat, presumably manoeuvring one-handed while playing the fish with the other.

*

'We are particularly interested in sightings of a white BMW 7 Series on Saturday morning between ten-thirty a.m. and twelve-thirty p.m. We believe the vehicle was in an area between Egremont in the south and Cockermouth in the north, and bordered by the Solway coast in the west and Honister Pass in the east. The car has a distinctive black stripe along each side – known as a racing stripe – broken into chevrons to give the impression of movement. We would like to know if this white BMW was seen parked at the roadside, perhaps in a layby or at a viewpoint or a beauty spot, or a public parking area – or indeed in a more unusual position. In addition if there were any persons inside or near the car. We believe the vehicle is connected to the disappearance of Lisa Jackson, and we urgently request that members of the public report sightings, either by dialling 101 or the dedicated incident line number on the screen behind me. Thank you.'

DS Jones pauses; she has spoken without a script, all the time looking directly into the lens of the BBC Cumbria camera that is trained upon her, and now she holds its unblinking gaze for a last moment, an earnest entreaty to the viewer to take seriously her exhortation. Then she glances briefly at the Chief; the latter's red hair is drawn back severely, she nods curtly but with satisfaction. DS Jones turns to the audience comprised of about a dozen journalists.

'I'll now take questions.'

171

Perhaps predictably, there is something of a blizzard of enquiries. DS Jones immediately gives up the idea of dealing with them in an orderly fashion and instead takes notes in shorthand, making brief eye contact with each of the inquisitors.

'Wasn't Lisa Jackson last seen going to work on Friday?

'Do you have a subsequent sighting?'

'What are you hoping to learn through a report of the BMW?'

'Are you looking for a body?'

'Is this now a murder inquiry?'

'What about the man you've got in custody?'

'Who is he?'

'Is he her boyfriend – a relative?'

'Have you charged him?'

'You must have held him for longer than twenty-four hours?'

'Is it his car – the BMW?'

The Chief is looking agitated; the questions are intrusive but DS Jones remains unflustered. She completes her note taking and pauses to assess the content.

'If I may I will deal with these points in a single answer. As was announced yesterday a forty-three-year-old male is assisting with police inquiries. An extension was granted to hold this person in custody for a maximum of ninety-six hours while investigations continue. This is a standard procedure, as it is to protect the person's identity. In the context of the inquiry, no charges have yet been brought. Naturally we have to remain open-minded until we have evidence to the contrary – but clearly we are very concerned about the safety of Miss Lisa Jackson, since her disappearance is so entirely out of character.'

It appears that DS Jones has ridden out the storm, putting up a shield of harmless facts and authentically sincere platitudes. Then a hand shoots up at the back of the conference room. It is a young man, trendy-looking in a leather jacket and plying them with a disarming boyish smile. A little alarm bell rings for DS Jones; the smile belies a smart brain.

'Can you confirm or deny that the man in custody is a co-worker of Lisa Jackson's, by the name of Ray Piper?'

Heads turn and there are rumbles of discontent from the more seasoned hacks. DS Jones, momentarily unprepared, reveals a small flash of disapproval in her countenance. Why has her erstwhile schoolmate – Kendall Minto of the Westmorland Gazette – decided to toss in this little hand-grenade? Is it an attempt to gain a private audience in due course?

'I refer you to my previous answer. I would reiterate that a woman is missing and that – as I am sure you can imagine – her family are suffering great distress. We ask you the media to play your part in publicising our appeal for sightings of the white BMW on Saturday morning. Time may be of the essence.'

DS Jones's tone is grave and conclusive, and the Chief is already rising; DS Jones follows her lead and they exit via a door behind the twin lecterns. She glimpses Kendall Minto's gaze tracking her movements – but the other hacks are converging upon him like hyenas intent on skinning a carcass.

*

'I was watching on the internal loop, Emma. He's a card, that young Minto geezer.'

'He likes to rock the boat.' But DS Jones does not sound resentful. 'I suppose while most journalists wait to be spoon-fed at least he gets out and about. I can't really blame him. And it's not exactly rocket science to go sleuthing around Lisa Jackson's place of work. But I do wonder how he got Ray Piper's name. I felt her colleagues would be tight-lipped.'

'All it takes is a little sweetener.'

DS Leyton refers to a cash bribe. DS Jones nods.

'There are the hands at Wood's timber yard – they would have fewer reservations.' While she doubts they would know Piper by name, maybe wolf-whistling Martin has winkled it out of receptionist Kylie.

DS Leyton is pondering. He shrugs his broad shoulders.

'It's no great skin off our nose, Emma – if his name gets about. Unless I'm missing something?'

173

'There's his wife and children to think about.' A moment's silence ensues as they consider this aspect. 'And Ray Piper if we release him without charge.'

DS Leyton stares at her in surprise.

'That ain't gonna happen, *is it?'*

*

DS Jones is taking a breath of fresh air. She is in the vicinity of the Pipers' house and the BP filling station. Her planned visit to Lisa Jackson's parents has taken a slightly different course – on telephoning their mobile number she learned that Arthur Jackson was at Goosehills Close to feed his daughter's cat. Now she feels guilty that she saw him alone and left him to bear the burden home to his poorly wife. The couple had of course watched the edited report of the press conference. Thankfully the editor had erred on the side of caution, and had restricted the piece to the public information request. No mention had been made of Ray Piper. Nonetheless, Arthur Jackson's mournful words have stayed with her.

"It's not good news, is it, lass?"

She had wanted to say they should not give up hope – but in her heart of hearts she did not feel this.

"I know you have been preparing yourselves for the worst – and I'm really sorry, but the evidence we are beginning to gather points to Lisa having been a victim of foul play."

The man had made it unfairly easy. But perhaps in his grief there was a small appreciation – for what can be crueller than to give vain hope?

"We'd just like to know. It must be very hard for you, dear."

He had patted her on the shoulder and they had separated each with a tear in their eye.

And then, yet another snippet of evidence had come to her. On leaving Lisa Jackson's property she had gathered her wits and crossed to the home of the vigilant neighbour – ever vigilant, it seemed, for the front door was opened before she was halfway down the path. And her reason to call upon Frank Sidebottom

174

was a hunch that had proved correct. In earlier discussion DS Leyton had shone a light on a possible possessive motive behind Ray Piper's behaviour. It occurred to her that their suspect's pre-work visit – ostensibly to offer Lisa a lift (but in her male colleague's opinion leaving in anger on seeing the new boyfriend's car) – was not a one-off. What if it were a regular thing? That he suspected Lisa of entertaining male friends and was checking up on her. And, sure enough, Frank Sidebottom was able to tell her that he had observed Ray Piper's car the evening before Lisa disappeared – Thursday night. At first he had assumed it was parked and empty. But then he had realised someone was inside. He thought perhaps it was 'Poker Face' dropping off Lisa Jackson – perhaps they were chatting before she went indoors. But, as he watched, the BMW's lights came on and it sped away. The brown Hyundai was on the driveway next to Lisa's car. The time was just after ten p.m.

No doubt Ray Piper will deny that he was ever there.

But he cannot refute the CCTV evidence of his visits to the BP garage. Half an hour ago, DS Jones rendezvoused at the site with a technical officer. The latter is presently obtaining secure downloads of the footage of Ray Piper's movements and purchases.

DS Jones is wondering if she should make an unannounced call on Irene Piper; it is late morning and presumably she will be at home. There is a justification – to convey the news that an extension has been granted to hold her husband in custody. DS Jones is coming full circle on her walk around the housing estate – she has agreed she will sign off with the technical officer at noon. As the Piper home heaves into sight she begins to recall her first impressions – on Saturday morning when Ray Piper answered the door. She shudders involuntarily. *That Lisa Jackson's body was surely in the boot of his car.* For a fleeting moment darkness descends and she raises an arm as if to ward off the black terror that comes flapping at her. She forces herself to think logically – to think about Ray Piper. What was to be learned from that encounter? Already he had been to fill up his car with petrol – no doubt with his journey in mind. And he had bought the local newspaper – uncharacteristically. Why? To see if there were any reports of Lisa Jackson's disappearance? He had on his driving gloves – indoors, in summer! Had he donned them quickly when the doorbell rang, anticipating even then that the police might call? And the manner in which he had walked to the car when they had invited him outside – why not just pull shut the front door and stand on the step, keeping the high ground? And his attire, smart-casual office wear, appropriate for the site visit that he had planned. She had particularly noticed his shoes – they say the way to judge a man (though Skelgill would confound such analysis, known to turn up to meetings in mud-encrusted walking boots, rock-climbing pumps, or even on one occasion chest-high fishing waders). But Ray Piper's polished brown brogues may just provide some evidence of where he went – his two unavoidable points of contact with his surroundings. Again it is a notion that recalls Skelgill. Some parts of her superior's car might be fixed together with wire (there is the makeshift radio aerial, a coat hanger bent into the silhouette of a fish) – but one compromise he will not make is the tyres. As he puts it, a flock of yowes – or, just as treacherous, what they deposit in their wake – awaits around every Lakeland bend. Tyres that hover on the legal limit are an accident waiting to happen.

It is with an image in her mind's eye of a tread pattern cutting through mud that she reaches the Piper property and stops dead in her tracks.

12. THE REDMEN

Monday morning – five days later

'Iron ore.'

Skelgill is holding a small clear glass phial to the light of the window in DS Jones's incident room. It contains a mere pinch of red ochre powder that could be mistaken for chilli or perhaps turmeric. DS Jones steps alongside him, almost as if she were viewing it for the first time.

'The geologist's report states that it is characteristic of the high-grade hematite that used to be mined in West Cumbria. Some of it was good enough for jewellery – but it was also used as a pigment by the cosmetics industry, and you can see why.'

The sun suddenly emerges from behind a cloud, dazzling them both. Skelgill is obliged to lower the sample and they each take half a step away, as if self-conscious of being too close for normal conversation. Skelgill hands over the test tube.

'I had a bunch of uncles used to work at Florence Mine – just to the southeast of Egremont.'

DS Jones points to the Ordnance Survey map that she has spread upon the table beneath the window. It seems she has been undertaking some research, for Skelgill spies a coloured arrow marking the spot to which he refers. And indeed she expounds upon his statement.

'Florence Mine closed in 2007. The site has been repurposed as a local community arts centre, although apparently most of the old buildings are intact. On the Saturday morning there was an exhibition – a couple of hundred people attended – the place would have been busy. And they had a steward on the entrance, charging for parking. But in any event, I'm pretty certain Ray Piper never went there – the triangulation of his mobile phone shows he travelled no further south than Egremont Hall. He drove directly to the hotel, and after the meeting headed back north. Then the phone stopped transmitting just before Cleator Moor.'

DS Jones is tracing the route on the map. It is the more detailed version that she was using with DS Leyton – two-and-a-half miles to the inch.

'So where did he pick up the red dust?'

DS Jones indicates with a circling motion of her hand.

'This area immediately to the east of Cleator Moor and Frizington – it sits above the main subterranean ore body. There was a concentration of iron works – some of the tunnelling even undermined the villages and whole streets subsided.'

Skelgill leans as close as his focal length will permit. He vaguely knows the lie of the land – he has driven through on occasion. But it is outside the national park, there are no hills that produce distressed walkers (besides it is the territory of another rescue team); and there is little fishing of note; the River Ehen winds through the vale, but it is best known for its freshwater pearl mussel population. Thus it is not an area he has oft frequented. As he stares at the map its backstory begins to reveal itself – there are abandoned limestone quarries, and the course of a former railway (though what English OS Map doesn't have that?); here and there is the legend *"shaft (dis)"* or *"level (dis)"* respectively indicating the site of abandoned vertical and horizontal cavities. He pictures a lost landscape, known to his forbears, where once pale-faced miners would have descended for their day's toil, to emerge at the end of their shift wearing masks of the dark red Cumbrian earth, joking and thirsting and punching their way to the local inn. He retains something of this folk memory, this knowledge of a fate that met many country youths, drawn to the work in the iron mines and coalfields, snatched from the healthy air of the fells for a life in squalid accommodation on subsistence wages; when the landowners discovered that sheep were not the most profitable fat of the land and raised dark Victorian plantations of a sort, pitheads, when smoke and red dust wreathed the bloodied landscape; the satanic mills.

His meandering thought process prompts a question.

'Since you've done your homework, how long ago are we talking?'

DS Jones lightly touches the map as if she is feeling for the answer. On the back of her noticing the fine red ochre residue in four patches on Ray Piper's unevenly slabbed driveway, washings from his tyres and wheel arches, scientific endorsement that it is iron ore came only last evening. But she has not spared the midnight oil.

'To all intents and purposes, I would say the best part of a century. Most of this is reclaimed as agricultural land now. Florence Mine was an anachronism. Notwithstanding, there must be a couple of dozen other sites of immediate interest to us.'

Skelgill is nodding. He has clocked most of them already.

DS Jones continues, however.

'I've searched for records of iron mines. The other main area historically was Eskdale – I hadn't realised that's why the light railway is there – it was built originally to transport ore to the junction at Ravenglass on the coast. The mines were around Boot – too far south to have been within Ray Piper's reach.'

Skelgill nods slowly in agreement. He sweeps a hand over what they would regard as the eastern limits of their area of interest.

'Up in the fells it's mainly slate they mined, like at Honister Hause. Copper, above Coniston. And lead and zinc, small scale stuff, often inaccessible – even difficult to reach on foot.'

'And no red soil, Guv.'

Skelgill inhales in a way that makes DS Jones think he is about to voice a caveat – but he never gets there because the explosive appearance of DS Leyton in the doorway wins their attention.

'You gotta see this – come quick!'

He beckons and disappears and they follow without question. He rounds into what is a kitchenette with provision for those who prefer packed lunch and do not want to eat at their desks. On one wall a TV is broadcasting the local channel and DC Watson is glued to the set, rather goggle-eyed it must be said, a teacup held in suspension as if to emphasise her bewilderment.

Unbelievably, a familiar countenance fills the screen.

179

'Poker Face.'

It is Skelgill who utters the words – otherwise they fall silent and listen. The tickertape at the foot of the picture is running the bare bones of the story: "MISSING CARLISLE WOMAN LATEST ... LOCAL MAN CHARGED ... RELEASED ON BAIL ... PROTESTS INNOCENCE."

As they watch they glean that Ray Piper has been doorstepped by a news crew and, rather than retreat back inside, he has stood his ground and is calmly answering questions. He is dressed in his regular smart casual attire and carries a briefcase – as though he is on his way to work. To the degree that his immobile features allow, he affects that he is the victim of a miscarriage of justice – and asserts that the police must be under pressure to secure a conviction following the well-publicised 'M6' drugs gang debacle (DI Smart's recent embarrassment).

There is a collective holding of breath when the interviewer asks Ray Piper directly, "Did you kill Lisa Jackson?"

Ray Piper seems in DS Jones's assessment to be a little more agitated by this question – but it is his reply that grips her:

"I've assisted the police with their inquiries and their investigation will show that I don't have anything to answer to."

It is a response that leaves her thinking how would an innocent person (or a guilty one, come to that) respond in such circumstances – knowing they are playing to an audience that contains likely jurors one day not too far off? Why not take the opportunity of an emotional appeal: "How do you think I feel? This is a waking nightmare – I care for Lisa – I would never harm her – I'm praying she's safe". Instead Ray Piper has chosen to reiterate his defence: *that the police will not be able to prove their case.*

Perhaps her colleagues have noticed this point, too.

DS Leyton is first to react.

'Hadn't we better have a word with the TV station? I'm not sure they should be reporting this – it's bad enough that he's managed to get bail. Now he's rubbing salt in our wounds.'

But the article – which is clearly not live – has been carefully edited, and is probably treading just inside the boundaries of

180

what might be considered acceptable. The focus switches to the voice of the reporter, as Ray Piper is filmed driving off in his wife's old hatchback. DS Leyton adds a parting remark.

'He's got some brass neck.'

They nod in silence. The news item ends and the three return to the incident room, leaving DC Watson to her breakfast. DS Jones is next to speak.

'He looked like he was going to work.'

'Reckon he's left his missus in the lurch.' DS Leyton refers to the vehicle.

DS Jones nods. His own car impounded as evidence, she is not surprised that Ray Piper has taken the remaining family transport. Presumably the boys and the shopping will be left to his wife to sort out. But she is somewhat alarmed by the prospect that he might have been setting off to InnStyle. As DS Leyton has intimated, was he just brazenly intending to turn up as though nothing has happened? His original absence while in custody is one thing – his colleagues would have gained only a limited perception of events – but now there is the TV interview in which he has been directly challenged about Lisa Jackson's murder. She is wondering how Don McKenzie will handle the matter, when a call is put through.

Rather absently she answers on speaker while she is checking some papers that have appeared on her desk.

'Sergeant Jones? Hi – it's Don – Don McKenzie. Have you seen the TV news?'

On reflection, the coincidence is predictable.

'We were just watching it – we knew nothing about it.'

'Sure – I guessed that. I think I'd trust journalists about as far as I could throw them.'

'Are you being harassed?'

'Er, no – not so far. At least, not me personally. But I wanted your advice – about what I should tell the guys in the office – about what to say if they are approached.'

She glances about at her colleagues. DS Leyton is paying attention; Skelgill seems to be engrossed in the map once more.

181

'There's no law to stop a journalist asking questions, or a member of the public answering – but the media are governed by *sub judice* – they could be held in contempt of court if they were to broadcast anything that might prejudice a fair trial. But I would recommend you ask your colleagues not to engage.' She sits down at her desk and takes up a pen and a notepad and begins to write in shorthand. 'In fact I'm going to suggest we bring forward the taking of formal statements from all your staff. They may be required to appear as witnesses. I don't want the media putting words in their mouths.'

Don McKenzie sounds like he might be a little tongue-tied himself.

'Ray turned up for work this morning.'

'We thought it looked like that's where he was heading.'

'I sent him home. I've furloughed him on full pay. I didn't say it was permanent – just that I needed to speak with our lawyers and he seemed to buy into that. To be honest – I couldn't see how we could have a situation where a senior employee charged with murder is sitting amongst the rest of the team as though nothing has happened.'

There is a questioning note in his tone, to which DS Jones responds.

'You're surprised he was granted bail?'

'Well – to be frank, I am. But, then again – I'm new to this kind of thing.'

'The court deemed he poses neither a flight risk nor a threat to another person. It's not unprecedented in these circumstances. There are also custody time limits that may come into play and work to our disadvantage. Naturally he is subject to strict bail conditions, governing his movements and concerning whom he may contact. Obviously your people could fall into the latter category.'

'Sure.' The man seems both relieved and yet still apprehensive. After a pause he comes to a point that he has evidently stumbled over. 'Er – my statement. Could we have an informal chat about that first? Away from the office? I could probably organise parole.'

182

Perhaps he senses his joke falls flat, for he gives a nervous chuckle. DS Jones is half wishing she had the call on the handset and not on speaker.

'I'll see what I can do.'

She ends the exchange in a businesslike manner, and then makes some more notes only intelligible to her. DS Leyton is watching her sympathetically.

'I've had another report of a missing shotgun – owner's not sure if it's mislaid or half-inched – but I have to go and check it out. Farm over towards Appleby.'

DS Jones regards him earnestly.

'I'll catch you later – I'll update you.'

DS Leyton takes his leave. Skelgill is still studying the map on the table. DS Jones observes him for a moment, then she rises and walks across.

'Guv – I know you've got that seminar tomorrow for the rest of the week.' She refers to an Inspectors' refresher course in team-building to be held at Newcastle-upon-Tyne that Skelgill would rather miss but has been unable to concoct a sufficient excuse, having avoided it several times already. 'I just wondered – if today –' (she places a hand on the map) 'this is so much more up your street – could you help me to scope out the search?'

Skelgill regards her somewhat implacably. Then his gaze shifts to where her slim fingers are spread across the shaded contours. He grins rather sardonically.

'I'll see what I can do.'

*

'It calls them the "Redmen" of Egremont.'

Skelgill, preoccupied with an oven-bottom muffin, can only nod. Eventually, with some difficulty, he swallows.

'Aye, real folk.'

He raises the bread roll as if to prove his point. Sandwiched between its two halves a generous coil of Cumberland sausage renders it almost incapable of being bitten; but Skelgill's gape is of pike-like proportions. DS Jones grins – he is rarely happier than when he feels at home. They are parked in Egremont's high street, an opportunistic pre-lunch stop (what else when Skelgill has control of the wheel). Lowering the passenger window by a couple of inches – for it is steaming up as light rain patters on the roof of Skelgill's car – she turns back to the object of her attention. Set in an area of pavement is a heritage sculpture, an ochre-coloured figure bent into heaving an iron-wheeled bogie; just across on the opposite corner a similarly fashioned memorial features a flat-capped worker holding court to two youngsters, looking every inch a scene that might have been witnessed in this very street a century ago, when the lads stopped to listen in deference to their elder – and they have been transformed into the iron they would in their day come to hew.

Despite that the detectives believe Ray Piper ventured no further south than Egremont Hall – a mile to the north of their present location – Skelgill has suggested they begin with Florence Mine. He uttered some cryptic remark about "Ghostbusters" – but somehow, seeing the immortalised iron miners, DS Jones understands; getting her boots on the ground might just give her a feel for what she is looking for.

Skelgill despatches the last of his roll and drains his tea and smacks his lips. For her part, DS Jones has made brave inroads into a slice of quiche that could feed a small family – but a good half remains upon the tin plate that Skelgill has supplied from his kit.

'Might stop again on the way back through.' He eyes her unfinished quiche. 'Want a bait box for that – keep it fresh?'

Ordinarily, in local parlance, DS Jones would assume he means a lunchbox – but, salvaged from amongst Skelgill's angling accessories, a 'bait box' is quite likely to have last hosted some unspeakable squirming content that only fish find palatable.

'It's okay – I've got the greaseproof wrapper. If you're having another, I'll save it for then. I'm keen to get moving.'

Skelgill starts up the engine. He checks over his shoulder and performs a tight one-eighty, the squeal of his tyres turning the heads of passers-by. DS Jones surveys the businesses that trade along the old Georgian thoroughfare. Undoubtedly its heyday is long past; and yet, despite the chronic economic blows that have rocked towns like this, she detects an air of optimism – England's nation of shopkeepers will never surrender – even if it means trying one's hand at a tattoo parlour, a nail bar or a spray-tanning boutique. She smiles to herself – there is an irony in the latter, here in the home of the Redmen. Then suddenly her heart flutters – for from the very door emerges a woman who looks unnervingly like Lisa Jackson. For a fleeting moment they make eye contact, and the woman must wonder at the intensity of the gaze she receives from the girl in the speeding car. Has she never seen someone with a spray tan before?

Almost before DS Jones has realised it – and literally three minutes from the town centre – Skelgill has the shooting brake swinging down a short stretch of tree-lined lane and into an open gateway. Suddenly before them towers the rusting superstructure of Florence Mine.

'Wow – look at that!'

There could be several interpretations of her reaction. The buildings themselves are an extraordinary sight, abandoned perhaps, but superficially intact, an irregular cluster of rusting sheds and hoppers linked by conveyors and ladders and girders, at the apex the massive pony wheel of the winding gear supported by a tiered gantry against the grey sky. The greenery that has encroached provides a second visual incongruity: burgeoning shrubs of willow and elder, and even small trees of gean and rowan throng around the workings, as if Mother Nature is striving to subsume man's angular monstrosity beneath her soft curves. Still there is a third aspect – and it is this to which DS Jones responds. The wet ground everywhere is bright orange-red.

Skelgill's reaction – to the same aspect – is slightly different. He accelerates almost recklessly and slews through a great puddle and performs a handbrake stop upon the damp compacted material of the forecourt. Immediately he jumps out and inspects his tyres – and then the soles of his boots. DS Jones follows suit, wide-eyed, a look of wonderment on her face. The puddle is like a small red volcanic lake; reflected in its settling surface is the winding house and its elevated scaffold, disquietingly symbolic of lives despatched cheaply. And all around them, stretching between the ruined buildings and the collapsed conveyors, the earth – the soil – the spoil – is the colour of iron oxide.

'Guv – no wonder they called them the Redmen.'

She rounds the car and Skelgill briefly gestures at the offside front wheel. The flat surface of the tyre and the mudflap and inside the wheel arch is already coated in a fine film of red ochre. Clearly the substance is all pervasive and persistently adhesive. He exposes the underside of his boot to demonstrate. They seem to need no discussion. While DS Jones begins to take photographs with her phone Skelgill strides towards the base of the pithead tower, a red brick construction. From an entrance runs a section of overgrown narrow-gauge rail track. He disappears from sight. There is a metallic scrape and DS Jones looks up from her camera work to see him – quite bizarrely, it seems – enacting the statue in Egremont town centre – for he is heaving bodily against an iron-wheeled bogie and successfully propelling it along the length of track! He stops and flashes her a grin – but then purposefully he returns to the entrance and begins to rummage about on the ground. He crosses back to her, bearing something in his hand.

'Feel the weight.'

It is a fragment of rock, the size and shape of a hen's egg.

'Wow.' It seems to be her word of the moment. 'This must be the hematite, Guv.'

But Skelgill does not pay particular attention. Instead he turns to stare grim-faced at the buildings.

'That bogie looks like it was abandoned mid-use. Happen they just walked off the job one day.'

DS Jones narrows her eyes, surveying the scene, perhaps trying to picture his narrative.

'You could imagine it looked like this a hundred years ago, Guv.'

186

'Aye – I don't suppose there's much new-fangled when it comes to sinking a shaft and hacking at a seam of iron ore.'

DS Jones nods reflectively.

'It must have been hellish.'

Her metaphor is apposite – how unearthly to descend from here each day into the stifling labyrinth of red ochre, inadequately lit by flickering lamps that aped the flames of the underworld.

But now she gathers her wits, and deals with their predicament.

'The place is deserted, Guv. If he'd arrived now he would have had free rein.'

Skelgill casts about. Sure enough, across at what must have been storage sheds and now where signage indicates the present-day community facility there are no parked vehicles, no doors open; no signs of life. Evidently it is not staffed when not in use for events. Nevertheless, it is good to know the place was buzzing and the entrance manned on Saturday morning – he would have been deterred without even entering. And, despite that they have been undisturbed during their short visit, it is barely half a minute's drive from the nearest habitation ("Scurgill Terrace", he had noted). There is always the likelihood that a local dog walker or jogger or inquisitive kids will turn up – or even a hobbyist, for this remarkable time capsule, this relic of culture past and lost is surely the subject of informal tourism.

DS Jones is still absently weighing the fragment of ore, as if subconsciously intrigued by its unnatural density.

'Guv – Ray Piper's master's degree was in Industrial Heritage and Archaeology.'

Skelgill would be excused for suspecting some unconscious telepathy between them. He regards her pensively. He nods; he gets her gist.

There is a moment's silence. DS Jones transfers the piece of stone from one hand to the other, and then notices the residue it has left behind.

'I wonder if this has a chemical fingerprint that's unique to this mine. I maybe will speak to SOCO about collecting samples from any other sites we investigate.'

Skelgill appears dubious – though she has a reasonable point. If there were a match to the sediment recovered from Ray Piper's driveway it might later corroborate where he went. But first they need to find 'other sites'. He hauls open the driver's door of his car.

'Let's gan and have a deek, eh?'

*

'I think if we go right at a turn marked "Wath Brow", Guv. It looks to me that there's a roughly diamond-shaped section of country that contains the vast majority of the old iron mine workings.'

'Just remind me.'

DS Jones refers to the map.

'From the junction, northeast to Ennerdale Bridge, on to Croasdale, turning back west towards Kirkland and Rowrah – then south to Frizington and Cleator Moor.'

Skelgill keeps his eyes on the road ahead as he processes the route into his mental satnav.

'Here comes Cleator. The turn you're talking about is a mile further on.'

There is little distinction between the villages of Cleator and Cleator Moor, indeed admittance to the latter is announced only by a small street-type sign innocuously planted in the verge and half obscured by an unkempt privet hedge that precedes the first property. And there is a continuation of the austere terraces of harled cottages that front directly onto the narrow pavement and which can only be distinguished one from the next by their jutting black satellite dishes, punctuation marks in a repetitive monologue. These archetypal former mining villages make a stark contrast when in fewer than ten miles the traveller can be subsumed by the splendour of the Lake District national park. Perhaps the prominent technology triggers Skelgill.

'Any joy with CCTV along this stretch?'

DS Jones shakes her head.

'Not so far, Guv. We've found a couple of live cameras further north – but there's nothing on them. It makes me all the more convinced that he turned off straightaway and only rejoined the trunk road close to Cockermouth. When you think about it, the longer the stretch of uncertainty, the bigger the prospective search area.'

'And what about your appeal?'

Now she gives an exasperated sigh.

'You wouldn't believe how many "white BMWs" were out on the road on that Saturday.' She deploys crooked fingers to form the parentheses. 'Of course, half of them weren't even BMWs. Several reports are from people who remember parking next to one at a picnic spot – but nothing really of note – and nothing in this sector.' She taps the map to refer to their present location. 'Working through the sightings – it's a terrible drain on resources.'

Skelgill knows only too well from his travails in the mountain rescue the near futility of a search when there is no peg in the ground – and that is when the search area might be just a single mountain, and the subject wanting to be found, maybe incapacitated but capable of blowing a whistle or flashing a torch. But now they reach the junction to which they have referred.

'Here we go.'

As they turn off he sees DS Jones watching an oval ball kicked high into the air – it is Wath Brow Hornets, and they pass close to the local team's ground. Players in yellow-and-black jerseys are being put through their paces; of course, rugby league is now a summer sport; his own memories from schooldays are of wrestling in half-frozen mud.

'Decent side, by all accounts.'

DS Jones does not answer; it seems her mind is actually elsewhere.

'Penny for your thoughts.'

She exits her momentary daze.

189

'Oh – it just reminded me – of walking past the football stadium in Carlisle – and Lisa Jackson's house – and her parents. I feel the burden – that they must be carrying – and of solving this for them.' She gazes out over the countryside as they transition from mining village to agricultural land with the first hints of Lakeland character. 'Even given what we know – it's such a huge area.'

Skelgill looks less daunted; he swings the car enthusiastically into a bend and over Wath Bridge, crossing the River Ehen – his spirits seemingly lifted by the more familiar landscape.

'Chin up, lass.' He repeats an earlier exhortation. 'She's only in one small spot. Who knows – maybe we'll even strike lucky ourselves.'

DS Jones nods, but broodingly. She cannot help thinking that they are relying on a tenuous piece of evidence – indeed, not strictly *evidence* in this context, but more of a clue – the ferrous oxide that suggests Ray Piper visited an iron mine. Even now, every few hundred yards they pass an indistinct turn off or a farm gateway or there is an overgrown ditch or a small tangled copse, there are sheds and byres and ruins – there are literally hundreds if not thousands of places that a corpse could be hidden when all the roads that Ray Piper might have driven are taken into account. It would require just seconds to stop a car and commit the evil deed. And, while none of these places are 'unsearchable' per se, collectively they represent a task that would be beyond the resources of any police force. Even if they enlisted the British Army and every trained tracker dog in the country it could take months to scour their broad area of interest, and still not do it properly.

For his part, Skelgill seems to know the way well enough, despite his professed unfamiliarity. As they pass through Ennerdale Bridge he name-checks the river as they re-cross the Ehen, and even the innominate beck (unnamed at least on the map she holds) that creates the impression that the hamlet is on a small island; and he seems ready for the unforgiving sleeping policemen that mark its boundaries; though it does not stop him cursing them on behalf of his car's shock absorbers.

However, when they pass first one and then a second minor turn marked "Ennerdale Lake" and on each occasion Skelgill seems to lift off the pedal as though he is having second thoughts about their route, DS Jones is prompted to question him.

'What is it, Guv?'

'The signs are wrong.'

'Oh – how do you mean?'

'It's Ennerdale Water.' He turns to regard her severely. 'There's only one lake in the Lake District.'

She grins; suddenly she understands.

'The signposts must be for the tourists. Maybe the roads department thought "water" would seem a bit confusing.'

Skelgill clucks.

'Wrong kind of tourists, if you have to tell them that. Besides – Wast Water, Ullswater, Coniston Water, Derwentwater, Crummock Water – how many waters does it take?'

DS Jones, amused by his indignation, suppresses a smirk. And now she is reminded of another light-hearted distraction.

'You heard about the Ennerdale film crew – from the TV soap opera?'

'Leyton's starring role? How could I not? According to the jungle drums he's been headhunted by Eastenders. He's already got the accent off pat.'

Now DS Jones laughs.

'I think it's made his year – his wife's a massive fan. Apparently when it's screened in the autumn we're invited to his house for a big cinema night in, with popcorn and pizza.'

Skelgill raises a sceptical eyebrow, but under her reproachful scrutiny he yields.

'Aye, well – pizza, maybe.'

Their trajectory is rising, and now DS Jones seems more relaxed; she gazes past Skelgill as the landscape unfolds.

'Look at the view, Guv.'

Indeed, to their right, to the east, is a magnificent vista of the true Ennerdale, the wild valley that holds the eponymous water, just visible as a grey sliver like mercury that has slid down the

191

fells and settled in the dale bottom, while successive spurs descend to its shores, truncated by long-melted glaciers, their ranks fading into ever paler shapes that finally merge with the distant sky.

'What's that peak – the prominent one directly in line with the lake?'

Skelgill glances cursorily. But then he stops the car – perhaps he, too, wants to admire the view, easily missed when the narrow lanes require concentration.

'Pillar.' He sounds wistful. 'There's a popular round – Pillar and Steeple – plus Scoat Fell and Haycock if you like, Caw Fell, even. Folk do it from Bowness Knott.'

'I think that's where they were filming – along that route. I suppose it really is Ennerdale, after all. It's where the shotgun was stolen – from the last farm, right up in the dale.'

'Aye – Gillerthwaite, it's called.'

DS Jones sighs reflectively. 'You know, that theft could have taken place at the same time that Ray Piper was driving around here?'

Skelgill glances sharply at her, as though he is expecting her to make something more of the connection. But it seems she has nothing to add.

'How many crimes were committed that Saturday morning?' He grins, somewhat roguishly. 'I was fishing without a rod licence.'

She looks at him, amused.

'Don't fret, lass – it'll be backdated.'

DS Jones chuckles. She has no doubt Skelgill would talk his way out of any awkward situation. Besides, she is aware that in angling circles it is considered that for Skelgill to be patrolling the local waters is worth a small army of bailiffs – even if he does omit to renew his various permissions.

But now they fall silent as they gaze upon the scene. And DS Jones's mind returns to their task. The immediate countryside shows no sign of once being an industrial landscape. There are large rolling pastures populated by sheep and bordered by straggling hedgerows supplemented by wire fencing – none of the dry stone walls characteristic of much of the Lake District. She reflects that the stunted hawthorns that line the lane, wind-bent and severely grazed, look like rows of oversized bonsai trees.

'This area isn't what I expected, Guv.'

Skelgill reaches and taps the map spread across her lap.

'We need to get past Croasdale. There's a ridge called Cauda Brow. That's where the workings start. After Kirkland there's left turn at a school building – that'll take us through the rest of it.'

DS Jones follows his indication. She traces the route to which he refers – it is the tiniest representation of a thoroughfare, an unclassified road that eventually dips down into the valley of the Ehen and roughly follows the course of the river on its northern side. She is amazed by how much he has absorbed from his reading of the Ordnance Survey map.

'Guv – it leads right back to Cleator Moor – I hadn't realised that. It joins the A5086 a short distance from where we turned off at the rugby club. Ray Piper could just as easily have taken this road.'

She makes a sound of exasperation, still staring at the map.

'What's up, lass?'

'Surely he switched off his phone before Cleator Moor so that he could leave the road soon after. But this old mining area, it's at best a five-mile detour. We know he covered an excess of thirty miles – you were right, the tests on his car confirm that. Does that mean he drove round and round searching for a suitable spot?'

Skelgill is baring his front teeth, a rather unbecoming shrewish expression that speaks of some inner discontent. Everything he has seen or learned about Ray Piper tells him the man would not have left this most vital part of his plan to chance. Besides, it hardly takes a criminal genius to look at a map and determine where there exists an old mine shaft close to a rarely used lane.

'I reckon more likely he went round the houses to leave the area – afterwards. Like you say, the longer the corridor of uncertainty, the better it suits him.'

They are both pensive as Skelgill guides them to Croasdale, more of a farmstead than a hamlet, and over a narrow bridge of the same name (over a beck of the same name). Thereafter the road climbs steeply to Cauda Brow, and a left turn marked for Kirkland. Sure enough, they have travelled barely four hundred yards further when they crest a rise and gain the first sight of old industry. On the slope to their right a distinctive hillock rises up, too regular in shape to be a natural feature. DS Jones is suddenly animated.

'Look at the red, Guv!'

She refers to the steep side that faces them, where vegetation has not taken a complete grip. The exposed red ochre soil and scree confirms the landform to be a spoil heap. She consults the map.

'It corresponds – it says *"tip (dis)"* – and also *"level (dis)"* – which must be on the other side of the mound.'

Skelgill pontificates.

'If you can see a spoil heap you can bet there's been a mine nearby. They never had any cause to take the waste far. Why pay extra for that?'

DS Jones nods, still scrutinising the map.

'There doesn't seem to be any obvious access from this road.'

Skelgill does not answer; he drives judiciously, as if expecting an oncoming vehicle – but the map is accurate, and soon they find they have passed the first site of interest. DS Jones comments.

'I suppose a shaft is more likely. A *level* is a horizontal tunnel – right?'

Skelgill makes a face that suggests some disagreement.

'A shaft's more likely to have been filled in. Farmers use them for their junk – and carcasses. Or they fill them because of the risk to livestock. A level's generally considered less dangerous. Unless it meets a vertical shaft – especially when it's half under water.'

He leaves the notion hanging – she knows he has tales of mountain rescues in old mines – some that he does not enjoy to recount. As they progress she watches the countryside analytically. What now begins to strike her – something she has suspected, feared, shied away from – is that even this relatively small area – which at a rough estimate is eight or ten square miles – would pose a daunting task to search. The road is bordered by impenetrable walls and hedges and in places small copses, and the surroundings are crisscrossed by more of the same. The land rises and falls unevenly, providing no clear vista – and while they can see what may be other spoil heaps, there is no obvious starting point for a search. The standard method – officers moving line abreast – would be ineffective in this terrain. But there is another aspect that troubles her.

'It wouldn't be very easy to stop along here, Guv.'

The lane is single track in places, elsewhere at best a squash and a squeeze. To park would be asking for trouble – a tractor or even a large van coming along would find its way blocked. But as if in recognition of this phenomenon, Skelgill suddenly swings the car into what is a virtually hidden opening. DS Jones exclaims in surprise.

'What's this?'

'Just following my nose. Runs in the family.'

Skelgill seems quite gung-ho about the manoeuvre. They find themselves on an unmetalled track, mainly grassed over but for the semblance of parallel wheel marks, that rises between tall hedgerows. He veers hard into the bushes on the driver's side to allow space should a farm vehicle need to pass.

'After you, lass.'

He means she should get out and that he will follow through the passenger door. It involves a rather ignominious contortion of his lanky frame. He sets off directly, however, striding up the slope. DS Jones hurries after him, trying to fold the map into a manageable size and scrutinising it at the same time.

'If I'm right this seems to stop soon – maybe at a wall or a gate.'

But in fact the track does not terminate, and after its crest and then a curving descent it both levels and straightens out, and now gives the impression of an abandoned railway. Underfoot is thinly grassed stony earth and there is the impression of a ditch either side. The land immediately adjoining the way is unnaturally irregular and suggestive of spoil heaps, and of other human interference, though it is overgrown with thick patches of shrubs such as willow and hawthorn and in between dense undergrowth of willowherb and brambles. But perhaps what is the most distinctive feature is that, at intervals along the verges, intermingled with rank grass are piles of builder's debris. DS Jones is first to comment.

'Fly tipping.'

Skelgill is nodding, his eyes narrowed.

'None of it's recent, though – look at that lot.'

He is right. Examination of the nearest heap – comprising the likes of which might be seen in a skip outside a house undergoing refurbishment, splintered timber, smashed plasterboard, lumps of concrete – shows it to be weathered and decayed and colonised by the more ancient orders of plants: mosses, liverworts and mildews. Successive heaps bear the same hallmarks. And there are no discernable tyre tracks associated with the dumping. It is as though the illicit practice has fallen into abeyance.

'Maybe the builder that was doing this went bust, Guv.'

'Aye – and it was his little secret spot.'

'You would think the landowner would be onto it.'

But Skelgill shakes his head and indicates with a thumb over to their right.

'There's limestone quarries in that direction. I reckon this is part of the same land. There's probably no cause for the company to trouble with it.'

DS Jones does not respond immediately. She is thinking that this site offers many of the criteria that Ray Piper might seek. They have been here for twenty minutes and no soul has passed; there is no habitation or farm building in sight; it has vehicular access – and the once systematic fly tipping is proof of the

196

anonymity it provides. But there is a fly in the ointment, so to speak; she becomes conscious that her gaze is resting upon a cluster of red clover growing on a shingly bank.

'The ground here, Guv – there's no sign of iron oxide.'

Skelgill glances about.

'Aye – if anything this'll be old limestone spoil.'

'How far do you think this track goes?'

'You get to a little place called Winder – maybe half a mile. There's a tarmacked lane from there up to the A5086.' He does not add that it is called Skelsceugh Road, and that the local street names seem to be trying to tell him something.

DS Jones consults the map. Again she can see that he is correct. It seems his scrutiny in the incident room has transplanted its blueprint into his head with preposterous fidelity.

'Yes – I see where we are. Maybe there's nothing to stop you driving right through here?'

'Might not do your coil springs any good.'

DS Jones falls silent, to the extent that Skelgill questions her.

'What's up?'

'Oh – coming out here – I mean – thanks for doing this – it's really helped me get my head around the challenge.'

'Except you're acting like your head's exploding.'

He regards her intently. She grins ruefully.

'Well – kind of. It makes me realise it will take a lot more planning – to narrow down the task.' She gives a sweep of the arm and her tone becomes a little despondent. 'Even with dogs and a big team – it could take several days to search a small area like this. There must be dozens of similar locations. And that's just within the iron-mining district.'

Skelgill seems to be glaring reproachfully at her; contritely, she holds up her hands, palms outward.

'I know, I know – it could be a complete red herring. Yes – he drove over ground covered in iron ore – but that's all. It could mean nothing.'

Skelgill's stare is relentless.

'I reckon you're on the right track with that one.'

13. FINDINGS

Friday – four days later

'Morning, Guv – I wasn't expecting you back this early.'

DS Jones enters Skelgill's office and carefully deposits a mug of piping hot canteen tea on his desk – they do not have a scheduled meeting so he might interpret the action as an impromptu request for an audience; clearly she knows he is here. And she carries a roll of white paper that is about three feet in length.

'They said I was too clever – no need to stay for the summing up.'

He sounds perfectly serious, but DS Jones assumes he is being ironic – more likely he has been kicked off for his obstinacy or has simply unilaterally decided to come home from Newcastle.

'Was it useful?'

Skelgill pulls open a drawer and produces a mug of his own, in brand new condition. He too places it upon the desk; he rotates it to display the graphics. There is a Venn diagram; three interlocked hoops with the words Task, Team and Individual printed one in each circle and a heart superimposed over the point of intersection.

'That's all you need to know to be a good manager. There you go – you have it. I've just saved you from going on the course.'

He pushes the mug closer to her. She picks it up obediently and considers it for a moment.

'Is the idea that you should give equal priority to each aspect?'

Skelgill grimaces.

'The Chief's got one, I've seen it in her office – hers says Task, Task and Task – and there's a dragon instead of a heart.'

DS Jones emits an involuntary burst of laughter, which seems to please Skelgill and he reciprocates with a grin.

'I shouldn't worry too much, Guv – if anyone tries to change you we'll be the poorer for it.'

Rather more modestly than might be expected he deflects her compliment with a dismissive wave.

'If anyone tries to change me they're wasting their time – me old Ma could tell them that in two seconds and skip all the expense.'

DS Jones regards him with mock reproach – but now he takes the initiative. He inclines his head to indicate the roll of paper.

'Any road – what about your task – the search? I took it that I would have heard if you'd had a breakthrough.'

DS Jones responds with an expression of mild dismay. She moves to sit down in the seat by the window. She raises the tube but then lays it across her lap.

'Can I come back to that? There are some other developments in our favour.'

Skelgill reaches for his tea.

'Aye, fire away.'

'Well, probably the most significant point is that Forensics found a single strand of Lisa Jackson's hair that had adhered to exposed masking tape on the box of tiles that was in the boot of Ray Piper's car. We matched it to samples from a hairbrush from her dressing table.'

Skelgill looks up over his mug, an eyebrow raised. Clearly this sounds promising. However his colleague does not appear so animated as might be expected.

'I re-interviewed Ray Piper – this time he attended with his solicitor. I mean – he answered all my questions – he's sticking to his line – and he's clearly confident. As you anticipated, he said Lisa had been in his car many times.'

'Not in the boot.' Skelgill's tone is indignant.

'He claims he put the box temporarily in the passenger seat when he cleaned the car. He also suggested the hair could have been picked up in the offices of InnStyle – that the box was under his desk for several days.'

Skelgill continues to scowl.

199

'Twenty folk work there and it's her hair on the tape. How many more excuses does he have up his sleeve?'

'One for every eventuality, Guv.'

Skelgill takes another slurp of hot tea and broods for a moment.

'You know what happens to a house of cards.'

DS Jones regards him keenly, as though she pins some hope on such wisdom.

'There is more evasiveness. On the subject of InnStyle, we've interrogated their intranet in detail. We know from the CCTV and witness evidence that Ray Piper put the box of tiles in his car at around ten a.m. But he didn't log the appointment to go to Egremont Hall onto the company diary system until five minutes to four, shortly before he left the office.'

Skelgill obligingly offers a prompt.

'What's his story?'

'That he didn't get around to it until then.' It is plain from her tone of voice that DS Jones considers the explanation unconvincing.

'And what's yours?'

She leans forward, resting her forearms on her knees and raising her feet so that only the tips of her trainers touch the floor. Skelgill is glad to note she has reverted to her more familiar casual attire, although to his eye her outfits always appear extraordinarily well tailored.

'Piper would have known that at any moment a contractor could have arrived and opened the comms cupboard – even just a meter reader, for instance. I think he used the tiles solely as an excuse to fetch his car and remove Lisa Jackson's body at the first possible opportunity. It was a desperate measure – a panic reaction, if you like. Only later did he compose himself and hatch the plan to go to Egremont Hall – which he chose because it provided a reason to head across country – not because of the job itself. That's why the whole tiles fiasco made no sense either to Constance Brown or Don McKenzie. I suspect he left it to the last possible minute to enter the appointment into the company diary system so that nobody would see it. Don

McKenzie says that he would definitely have asked why he was visiting a client on a Saturday.'

Skelgill appears to be in two minds about what she is saying – but after a few moments' hesitation he reaches a conclusion.

'I'll buy that.'

DS Jones gives a brief smile of acknowledgement.

'There's a similar inconsistency concerning what Ray Piper said about going to Lisa Jackson's house before work on the Friday but then driving away because he remembered an urgent email – which he didn't send until late morning.'

Here, however, Skelgill adds a caveat.

'That might be due to a small distraction around the eight-thirty mark.'

His tone is sarcastic – but she understands he means the arrival of Lisa Jackson at the premises and what ensued.

'Related to that, Guv – the injuries on his hands – that he claims were caused by the rose bush. We've conducted a second thorough search of the Pipers' property. Firstly, there's no sign of a shrub having been removed; secondly no indication that he ever does any gardening. There's a small shed crammed with outdoor furniture and kids' toys. An electric lawnmower was the only item of gardening equipment. There were none of the usual tools that you would expect to find, not even a shovel. There were, however, the remnants of a small bonfire. He says he burnt the rose bush. We're testing the ashes, obviously.'

'What does his wife reckon?'

Now DS Jones makes a face of some resignation.

'This will come as no surprise, Guv – but she's basically playing ignorant, forgetful – on all fronts.' DS Jones reacts involuntarily to her own statement; she drops the roll of paper and rises to stare out of the window, her slim form seems to Skelgill to confine uncharacteristic tension – it is clearly an act of frustration. But he waits; he knows the feeling. In due course she resumes her seat. 'I'd say she's terrified of her husband – and naturally of what might happen in relation to the children. When I first spoke to her, she did admit that Ray Piper was

201

gardening on the Saturday afternoon – I think that was a genuine answer.'

Skelgill is glaring, and now the exact nature of his objection becomes apparent.

'What use is a bloke that has no shovel?'

DS Jones looks amused by his turn of phrase; and as an observation it is a classic Skelgillism, at once ridiculous and incisive. But she treats his question as rhetorical and waits for him to elaborate.

'His drive's got a slope on it – what about when it snows?'

She concurs with his scepticism; she has little doubt that had Ray Piper used such an implement he would not have brought it home as evidence. She continues in a similar vein.

'Meanwhile he expects us to believe that he uprooted a rose bush with his bare hands.'

Skelgill makes a disapproving face while he drinks more of his tea.

'Another interesting point, Guv – a brilliant bit of work by DC Watson. She's been going over the CCTV recordings with a fine-toothed comb. When we seized Ray Piper's car, along with the box of tiles the only other item in the boot was a red golf umbrella – nothing suspicious about that as such – many people own them because of their extra size. When the white BMW passes beneath the camera at the Crescent, having turned out of Lychgate Lane, the umbrella is quite clearly visible on the rear parcel shelf.' She sees that Skelgill is watching her closely, seemingly intrigued to hear whatever is coming. 'But when he drove into Lychgate Lane a few minutes earlier – although the image is not quite so sharp – the parcel shelf is clear. The box of tiles was no bigger than a foot in any dimension; if the boot was otherwise empty why would you move an umbrella?'

Skelgill is nodding.

'One excuse he can't use is the weather.'

'That's right, Guv – and besides, he had the back of the car virtually under the cover of the porch.'

There ensues a moment's silence before DS Jones continues.

'I've also been looking into the relationship between Lisa Jackson and Ray Piper. He still maintains that everything was normal between them. I don't see how him bombarding her with text messages and she mainly not replying can be considered normal. But, despite that, it was a situation that they seemed to keep under wraps. Other members of staff had at best vague suspicions, and we've not managed to find a confidante of Lisa's – a close friend – who knew anything about it. In time I think she would have confided more in Gary Scott. But my impression is that Lisa – like Irene Piper – was intimidated by Ray Piper. I re-interviewed Gary Scott and showed him a photograph of Piper. He immediately identified him as the person Lisa had referred to as her boss, the first time they met at the exhibition in Carlisle town centre.'

'I thought her line manager was a woman?'

'Exactly, it's Norma Marston. Or perhaps she would have said it about Don McKenzie. But, when you think about it – Lisa had just met a chap she quite liked – and Piper turned up. It wouldn't be the best thing to say, "There's my ex – he's pursuing me obsessively" – easier to pretend it's the boss and suggest they get out from under his feet. But Piper was on her case, Guv.'

Again Skelgill detects an undercurrent of rising emotion. He flicks a hand at the roll of paper.

'Which brings you to the task.'

He intones this with uncharacteristic solicitude; she rallies.

'Can I spread this on your desk? We might need some paperweights.'

Skelgill contributes his now-empty tea mug and his course memento. DS Jones unfurls the sheet and they each hold down a remaining corner.

'So, this is the famous heat map.'

'It's the latest version – it's being constantly updated as we add in new information.'

Skelgill's interest is genuine. Had she handed him a report of the search, quite likely he would have dropped it into his in-tray and asked her for a verbal précis; the written word is not his friend. But a map is another matter, as DS Jones was most

203

recently reminded during their morning around Egremont and the old iron fields. She watches as first he seems to absorb the general gist of what the imagery represents, and then homes in on specific detail, tracing selected routes with his forensic gaze.

'You've kept in Florence Mine.'

'Ray Piper was here, heading north, away from Egremont, when his phone stopped transmitting.' DS Jones indicates with her free hand. 'But technically he could have doubled back along this route, avoiding the town. I know we feel confident that the activity at Florence Mine would have deterred him – but it's the only location so far where we've found extensive deposits of iron oxide on the ground.'

'Have we searched the place?'

'Yesterday. It felt like a superfluous exercise. But on the other hand I think it was necessary for peace of mind. The access to underground workings is highly secure – and otherwise the search teams found no indications of disturbance, and the dogs picked up no scent.'

Now she points in quick succession to three small flags on the map.

'These are mineshafts that we have checked and eliminated – and their immediate surroundings. None of them had exposed red soil in the vicinity – at least, not where you could reach with a vehicle. This one is the first site that we saw, Guv – the disused shaft that's behind the spoil heap just after Cauda Brow. If you remember, there was no access from the public road – it would have meant the risk of obstructing traffic and the challenge of lifting a body over a five-foot wall and carrying it for a quarter of a mile. On which note I should add that the lab report detected no alien residue on his shoes.'

Skelgill can see the scale of the challenge – it is daunting and must be weighing upon her. The heat map has been designed to show, like blood-red veins, the lanes that radiate from the A5086, to the maximum distance that Ray Piper could have reached, knowing the time and fuel that he expended. In crimson fading into cooler pink is the corresponding countryside across which he might have trekked, spreading out on either side of each road, and narrowing to a point as time and distance expire. Rather than a spider's web, as per his original simile, the broad area of interest has a shape rather like a multi-fronded palm leaf. What is strikingly apparent is that they have been concentrating, for good reason, on the zone of historic iron fields to the east of the trunk road, close to the point Ray Piper switched off his mobile telephone; but if he went west he could have got all the way to the Solway coast. As DS Jones has lamented, they are potentially clinging in desperation to the ferrous oxide from the BMW's tyres as a straw to keep their heads above water.

Skelgill lets go of his corner of the map and it begins to curl up. Without explanation he turns to his computer and navigates to the online maps application. When he has found the location he seeks, he switches into satellite mode. DS Jones waits patiently.

'Look at this, lass.'

He turns the monitor so she can better see it.

'Oh – that's Florence Mine – isn't it?'

'Aye – look at the red ground. It's visible from outer space – once you zoom in.'

DS Jones narrows her eyes, her expression a blend of optimism tinged with concern.

Skelgill reaches to pat the map a couple of times with the flat of his hand.

'Can you get one of your boffins to write a programme to identify this colour – find all the possible sites.'

DS Jones seems a little awkward.

'I hadn't thought of that – although I have tried what you just did on a local basis. But sites could be overgrown with woodland or vegetation and invisible from overhead.'

Skelgill inhales and then sighs ruefully. He seems genuinely invested in her difficulties. He looks at her earnestly – perhaps his training course has made at least a temporary impression.

'Sit down a minute.'

DS Jones removes the mugs and allows the map to roll up. She gathers it in and resumes her seat. Skelgill leans back in his sprung chair.

'Have you talked with the CPS?'

He refers to the Crown Prosecution Service, under whose aegis the decision to prosecute lies. DS Jones understands the nub of his question.

'They think we have a strong enough case already.'

Skelgill throws up his hands in a gesture of vindication.

DS Jones continues.

'Especially since, by the time of the trial, Lisa Jackson will have been missing for something like three months.'

Skelgill nods solemnly. It is a macabre fact to project forward – but nonetheless a powerful one that will work in their favour. To accuse someone of murder when the alleged victim has not been seen for a mere fortnight might lack conviction, so to speak. But for Lisa Jackson to have disappeared off the face of the earth for a quarter of a year will be another matter altogether. Now Skelgill does voice his opinion.

'So, what's there to worry about?'

DS Jones is appreciative of his supportive manner. But she does not give an entirely truthful answer – for the image that haunts her quiet moments features Lisa Jackson's parents, broken and mournful, huddled together on their sofa.

'The jury, I suppose, Guv – if we don't find her. There have been so few convictions without a body.'

14. TRIAL

October – three months later

'Ladies and gentlemen of the jury, as representative of the Crown I wish firstly to thank you for your diligent attention during the nine days of this trial hitherto. There is no greater responsibility placed upon the ordinary citizen than to judge one's fellow – and none more so when the charge is one of murder. Murder presents a particular challenge for the juror, because the victim cannot be here to put their side of the story – they cannot be here in person, to describe what it feels like to have their life taken away. Only the accused, the alleged perpetrator, of those two present at that dreadful moment is able to exercise the privilege of addressing you. Some might say that affords an unfair advantage to the defendant. But that would be to denigrate your ability to put yourselves in the shoes of the victim, to see through the fog of excuses and falsehoods, and to see justice done for the deceased – in this case a woman, Lisa Jackson, struck down in the prime of her life.

'You have heard how Mr Ray Piper, a married man with two children, carried on an affair with Lisa, a single woman six years his junior and co-worker at the Carlisle offices of InnStyle Design & Management Limited. During the autumn of last year Mr Piper moved in to live with Lisa, before moving out again, for reasons that Mr Piper has not satisfactorily explained. The evidence of Mr Arthur Jackson, father of Lisa is that his daughter was uneasy in the relationship, and meant to end it; but Mr Piper's attentions were persistent. Clearly Lisa wished to make a clean break, and indeed in July this year she began to date Mr Gary Scott, and there is evidence, including Mr Scott's testimony, of the beginnings of a good relationship, and Lisa was happy about that. But Mr Piper was not so happy. You have been presented with evidence of behaviour that might be considered stalking – sending multiple text messages daily – largely unreciprocated by Lisa and plainly not encouraged. More sinister is the evidence of Lisa's concerned neighbour, Mr Frank Sidebottom. You have heard how, on the night before Lisa disappeared he saw Mr Piper lurking outside her house in his car, and again, early on the following morning.

'The first stage of a comprehensive investigation led by Detective Sergeant Jones of Cumbria CID established that Lisa set off to work on foot as usual that Friday morning. You have seen several sections of CCTV video recording, including one in which she smiles to herself, and another that unmistakeably shows her crossing Warwick Road into Lychgate Lane, the cul-de-sac where the entrance to the offices of InnStyle is located. The time was 08:24. Moments later she was seen by Mr Martin Todd, an employee of Wood's of Carlisle. It is a firm of timber merchants, and is the only other business that has an operational entrance located in Lychgate Lane – in this case a loading bay. Referring to her resemblance to a member of the Royal family, Mr Todd categorically identified Lisa as she entered the ground-floor door of InnStyle.

'Mr Todd and his co-worker Mr Adrian Ibson were preparing the company delivery van. We learned from their evidence that, after Lisa, they saw no other person enter the lane. Mr Todd pulled down the shutters from the inside, and Mr Ibson's exit onto Warwick Road was recorded at 08:30. A further four minutes elapsed before the CCTV picked up two members of InnStyle staff who arrived together at 08:34. In total, from Lisa's arrival, a gap of ten minutes, ladies and gentlemen.'

Jane Sigmund-Smith QC, Crown prosecutor, interrupts her soliloquy to take a sip of water. While she has spoken without interruption for five minutes now, there can be no doubt it is a choreographed move. Indeed, replacing the glass, she remains silent, and makes a couple of small adjustments to her silk gown and dark court coat. The pause becomes pregnant. She straightens; she is a tall woman, upright and bespectacled, in possession of a strong, clear voice; were it not for the silver lawyer's wig she would look the part of the headmistress of a girls' private school presiding over morning assembly. She glances at her watch.

'My apologies. That was twenty seconds. Ten minutes is a long time.'

She affects a further hesitation, referring briefly to the sheaf of papers that she holds, but which thus far she has not used as a crib sheet. Purposefully, she clears her throat.

'We also know from CCTV and witness evidence – and indeed from his own statement – that Mr Piper, having visited Lisa's address in Goosehills Close before eight a.m., parked his car in his regular spot in Aglionby Street and walked the remaining distance to work, arriving well before Lisa, at 08:02. Mr Piper was observed at his desk by several colleagues. He sits beside a window that overlooks Lychgate Lane – you have seen amongst the exhibits a short police video that demonstrates a clear view of the entrance of the cul-de-sac from that window. You have heard the evidence of Miss Kylie Carr. Miss Carr is receptionist and therefore sits just inside the first-floor entrance, where the company's main open-plan office is situated. You have seen that she was the person to enter Lychgate Lane immediately before Lisa, approximately one minute earlier. Just as she reached the first-floor door she met Mr Piper coming out onto the landing. There was a brief exchange. Mr Piper held open the door for Miss Carr, and closed it after her. Miss Carr settled herself at the reception desk. She states that Mr Piper did not emerge from the stair until ten minutes later. Ten minutes.'

And now another pause to drink.

'I shall return to what happened in those ten minutes. Ten minutes when Lisa would have been alone with Mr Piper, just inside the entrance, in an isolated hallway that was poorly lit, and insulated and soundproofed from the floors above which it serves. But I will remind you at this juncture of two facts. First, that Lisa did not arrive into the first-floor office where Miss Carr sat at reception. And, second, that since the moment the ground-floor door from Lychgate Lane closed behind her, *Lisa has never been seen.*'

Jane Sigmund-Smith QC looks down rather poignantly at her notes, then up over her spectacles at the jury – as if challenging them to understand exactly what remains unspoken, and that it is all the more powerful for being so. She has perfected the art of the pause to a T – for, again, as the defending counsel half-rises, feeling obliged to make some objection, she resumes her closing speech.

'But first we must consider the evidence concerning Mr Piper. For a telling sequence of events now began to unfold. At approximately ten minutes to ten Mr Piper, carrying a modestly sized cardboard box under one arm, asked Miss Carr for the key of what is referred to by the staff of InnStyle as the "comms cupboard" – a storeroom beneath the stone staircase on the ground floor that houses various meters for services, communications equipment, computer hubs and suchlike. You have heard from Mr McKenzie that the comms cupboard is normally left unlocked, for ease of access by suppliers and service personnel, without the requirement for them to ascend to the first floor. The cupboard being unsecured is not a security issue, since the external ground floor door is controlled by an entryphone system.

'Now, Miss Carr at that time was in her first week of employment and did not recognise as unusual either Mr Piper's request for the key, which is kept at reception, or his explanation that he intended to lock away the box while he went to collect his car – an unnecessary precaution for the reasons I have just given. What did strike Miss Carr as unusual, however, was Mr Piper's behaviour. You heard that Mr Piper went to some lengths to keep both of his hands as far as possible out of her sight. This in fact drew her attention, and when he snatched at the key she noticed that there were fresh cuts on the back of that hand.

'The entrance to Lychgate Lane is permanently monitored by the police public order camera sited at the Crescent. At 09:52 Mr Piper is observed hurriedly crossing Warwick Road, and at 10:02 Mr Piper's white BMW with its distinctive black 'go-faster' stripe can be seen entering Lychgate Lane. A minute later, Mr Ibson of Wood's of Carlisle returns to Lychgate Lane in the company van. Out of sight of cameras, but witnessed by Mr Ibson, Mr Piper's car was found to be blocking the lane at right angles, reversed

210

hard up into the recessed doorway of InnStyle. Mr Ibson was obliged to wait until Mr Piper appeared a moment later, leapt into his car, and manoeuvred it to allow the van to pass. At 10:04 Mr Piper's BMW was again captured on camera, leaving Lychgate Lane at some speed.

'It has been pointed out that a red golf umbrella normally kept in the boot was on the rear parcel shelf of the car as it left – but that it was not there when the vehicle arrived. It has been suggested by Mr Piper that he must unconsciously have moved it to make room for the box of tiles. A box sufficiently small that Mr Piper was able to fit it comfortably under one arm.'

Needless to say, there ensues a pause for the jury to reach its own conclusions.

'Yes, the small box of tiles weighing no more than a gallon of petrol. Mr Piper is a fit man, strong and healthy looking. His car was parked a mere five minutes' walk from his office. Yet he chose to lock away the box rather than carry it to the car, entailing all the trouble of driving to and fro around the one-way system in the town centre. I have mentioned that Mr Piper left the offices hurriedly – not waiting for the pelican crossing but jogging through passing traffic. I have mentioned how he arrived in his white BMW and soon after drove away. When he returned again on foot, you have seen it was clearly at a more leisurely pace. That seemed perfectly normal. But less normal on a warm and sunny July day was that Mr Piper was now wearing calf leather driving gloves that were known to belong to him but which he says have subsequently been mislaid. Also slightly peculiar is that Mr Piper has claimed that he was taking the opportunity to buy some lunch while dealing with the tiles – but there is no indication on the CCTV footage that he was in possession of any item whatsoever.

'At the end of the working day Mr Piper left the offices of InnStyle and drove to nearby Brunton Park to collect his sons from a summer football academy. He remained at home that evening. Early the following morning – the police now having been alerted to the disappearance of Lisa – he received a visit from two detectives from Cumbria CID. You have heard in

211

their evidence that he consented to a limited interview on his driveway, and in a rather strange manner insinuated himself between the officers and his car. He exhibited little if any concern for either the whereabouts or the wellbeing of Lisa. He was dressed as though for work, and was carrying a copy of the local newspaper – which you have heard it was not his custom to buy – and had emerged from the house wearing his distinctive driving gloves. The detectives witnessed him leave to take his sons to football. Despite his somewhat eccentric manner the police had no reason to suspect anything at this time. Remember, this was before the evidence that you have heard and seen was gathered, and that they knew only in outline of Mr Piper's relationship with Lisa from her concerned parents. Indeed, the detectives went to some lengths to accommodate Mr Piper, given the possible sensitivity of the subject.

'By his own admission, after dropping off his children, Mr Piper drove some forty or more miles, directly to the premises of a client of InnStyle, a hotel, Egremont Hall, situated about a mile to the north of the village of the same name, arriving at ten twenty-five a.m. The owner of the business, Miss Constance Brown, was not present – you have heard in her evidence that she makes it clear to all contractors that she is not available at weekends due to her extra work in the hotel and local golf commitments. Miss Brown says she was unaware of Mr Piper's intention to visit, and likewise the hotel's deputy manager, Mr Dennis Thatcher. Mr Piper then proceeded unaccompanied to make what could only have been a very cursory inspection. Although he was not seen leaving, evidence from his mobile phone indicated that he departed at ten thirty-five a.m.

'Mr Piper began to return northwards on the A5086, a trunk road that would lead him directly to Cockermouth, en route to Carlisle. You have heard from the evidence of the police IT expert about what is known as 'triangulation' – when three transmitters can be used to identify the location and track the movement of a mobile phone, as it passes from one cell to another. Mr Piper's mobile phone ceased transmitting shortly before he reached the village of Cleator Moor, some three miles

212

north of Egremont, and did not resume transmitting until just before the Lamplugh roundabout, where the A5086 meets the A66 on the outskirts of Cockermouth. You have seen the technical report supplied by the cell phone service provider, that there were no network outages in the area on that day. The distance between the two points is thirteen miles, normally taking about twenty-five minutes on a Saturday morning, when the traffic is light. In fact the journey took Mr Piper one hour and forty-three minutes. *That is one hour and eighteen minutes longer than would be expected.'*

The barrister shakes her head meaningfully, as if to herself – but clearly it is a covert message to the jury. She inhales and moves on, more briskly.

'You have heard the police evidence and the witness statement of Mr Johnny Parker, son of the proprietor of the BP filling station close to the home of Mr Piper. And you have also heard the testimony of the expert police motor technician who road-tested Mr Piper's BMW. Mr Piper used approximately a gallon of unleaded petrol more than would be normal for the direct round trip between Carlisle and Egremont. And therefore he drove between twenty-eight and thirty-two miles further than was necessary.

'When Mr Piper arrived back in Carlisle what was the first thing he did? You have seen the CCTV footage that shows him refuelling at the BP garage. Is that a usual thing to do? He had filled up before leaving and had used only a quarter of a tank. He also purchased a powerful car interior cleaning spray and a strong air freshener. He then proceeded to valet his car inside and out, very thoroughly.'

And now there follows the regulation pause and sip of water.

'But perhaps not thoroughly enough. You have heard the evidence of the dog handler from Northumbria Police. The canine in question is what is rather euphemistically described as a victim-recovery dog. A more common term is cadaver dog – since these highly trained animals are able to detect the smell of death. This sounds melodramatic, yet you have heard from the pathologist that a fresh human corpse soon begins to decay.

213

Decomposition chemicals are produced – volatile organic compounds that contaminate the immediate surroundings. You will recall that the pathologist likened it to heating a fish dish in the microwave oven – the fish is removed but the smell lingers for several days. Such chemicals can be distinguished in minute quantities by the highly developed olfactory system of the dog, a nose that is one thousand times more sensitive than our own. The cadaver dog was taken to search the offices of InnStyle, and the property and possessions of Mr Piper. As you saw from body-cam footage, the dog alerted its handler on only two occasions during that entire search. The first location was what we know as the comms cupboard in the ground floor stairwell of InnStyle. The second was the boot of Mr Piper's white BMW motor car.'

The prosecutor stops to consider the jury. Again there is the headmistress-like demeanour; she might almost be checking that they are each and every one of them adhering to her creed – an imposition of compliance before she is prepared to continue.

'I said that I would return to the ten-minute period that began with Lisa entering the premises of InnStyle. What really happened on that fateful Friday morning back in July – and what events ensued on the Saturday that followed?

'You have heard tell of Mr Piper's personality. His colleagues describe his approach to his projects as possessive and relentless. And these same traits applied in his relationship with Lisa – a relationship that she wanted to leave behind her, but which he refused to allow. You have seen the telephone records that show Mr Piper inundated Lisa with text messages. And although we do not have the content of those messages – Mr Piper says he deleted them because he did not want his wife to find them – you can draw your own conclusions from twenty or thirty texts sent a day and very rarely reciprocated. These are the actions of a spurned lover that does not accept the outcome. On the night before Lisa's disappearance Mr Piper was outside her property in his car. He was back early in the morning, before work – to confirm his suspicion that Lisa's new boyfriend had stayed the night. He drove away in a rage.'

The QC now stands very still in front of the jury. She bows her head and begins to read directly from her notes – her demeanour is preacher-like; she intones the words as though she is reciting a catechism.

'When Lisa arrived at work – happier than she had been for a long time, joyful in her new relationship – Mr Piper was lying in wait. He knew what time she and other members of staff usually arrived. He watched her approach into Lychgate Lane. He left his desk and went out onto the stair. He passed Miss Carr as she entered on the first floor. He made an excuse about the lavatory. He held the door and ensured it was closed after her. When Lisa opened the door on the ground floor Mr Piper was ready for her.

'It was ten minutes before Mr Piper returned to the office – and in those ten minutes no other employee arrived for work. *In those ten minutes Mr Piper killed Lisa and concealed her body beneath the stairs.*'

The prosecutor looks up at the jury but all twelve of them are staring at Ray Piper. In fact everyone in the court – family members, journalists, police, witnesses, even the judge – is looking at the defendant. Ray Piper, seated in the dock, shows not a flicker of emotion; poker-faced, he stares defiantly ahead.

To regain the attention of her audience Jane Sigmund-Smith QC rattles her sheaf of papers – and begins to recite aloud once more.

'*"A project manager with first-rate problem-solving skills and attention to detail – exactly the person you want on your job, to navigate quickly and cost-effectively around those unforeseen obstacles."* So says Mr Piper's biography on his company's website. And indeed now Mr Piper's mind switched into problem-solving mode. He knew that sooner or later Lisa's body would be discovered. A meter reader might arrive. The computer system might fail and a service technician would be called. Or someone might just look in the comms cupboard for an item that had been stored there. So Mr Piper concocted an excuse that would enable him to lock the cupboard and fetch his car. Taking a box of spare tiles from beneath his desk he approached Miss Carr. Knowing the new receptionist would not be suspicious he plied her with the story that he needed to lock the package away. Thus he obtained the key.

'Minutes later he reversed his car into the recessed porch so he would not be seen. We are supposed to believe this was to facilitate the loading of a box of tiles sufficiently small that he was able to carry it under one arm. But of course the burden was a much greater one – one that prompted him to remove the umbrella from the boot and place it upon the parcel shelf. That burden was Lisa's body.

'When Mr Piper returned on foot, you have seen that he was wearing gloves. You have also heard the evidence of the police officers who noticed on subsequent occasions that Mr Piper was either wearing gloves or that he went to some lengths to keep his hands out of sight. Mr Piper tells us that the gloves were worn for a skin condition of which there is neither trace nor medical record. The only 'skin condition' visible to the police physician were extensive cuts characteristic of gouges made by a woman's fingernails. I say to you that the gloves were worn to conceal a message – Lisa's last desperate cry for help – a cry that need not be in vain. *Those cuts spelled out S.O.S.'*

The barrister inhales, and seems to sigh before she is ready to continue.

'Having *safely* – and I use the word reservedly – having safely concealed Lisa's body in his car, Mr Piper now took stock of his situation. Ostensibly, he worked normally – and meticulously he hatched a plan for the disposal of Lisa's body.

'But before we move on to consider that plan – we can see that Mr Piper did not quite act normally. Perhaps distracted *by* his meticulous planning – thinking through every step of his critical path analysis, what he would say to cover up each move – he overlooked one simple thing. His daily quota of text messages. He had already sent four before eight-thirty a.m. Let us remind ourselves from the record – on Monday, twenty-seven – on Tuesday, thirty-one – on Wednesday, just twenty – and, on Thursday, twenty-nine. But, after eight-thirty a.m. on Friday there were none. Not one. Why not? Mr Piper – so possessive, controlling – surely he would have wanted to know what Lisa was doing, whom she was with, her whereabouts? I say again, why not?'

She leaves the question hanging. The courtroom is deadly silent. She approaches more closely to the jury.

'Because he knew she was dead.'

Like the sough of the wind in the leaves there is a ripple of uneasiness that runs around the courtroom, a collective shudder of revulsion. For a moment it seems that the judge might intervene, but the barrister's voice strikes up again, her sermonising tone reinstated.

'Only later in the day, perhaps when his scheme was fully formulated, did the aberration in his behaviour occur to Mr Piper. But he could not now send her a text. He had already erased all of his previous messages – for their content would surely reveal his intentions towards Lisa. He could hardly turn up to the police with just one text message – the others systematically deleted. So, instead, he left a voicemail – something he was not in the habit of doing. You have listened to that voicemail. I leave to your judgment its sincerity. But, surely if Mr Piper had been genuinely concerned for the wellbeing of Lisa, might he not have inquired of a fellow employee if they knew how or where she was, and why she was not at work? But he asked nobody.

'Now, Mr Piper realised the instant he murdered Lisa that he would be the prime suspect. It would quickly become apparent to the police that her disappearance was entirely out of character: a caring, dutiful daughter; a home-loving young woman, so fond of her cat; and her bright new relationship with Mr Scott. The police are in the business of scenting out foul play. And so, from the very earliest time, Mr Piper began to devise a strategy to confound them. That strategy was to make Lisa disappear without trace. Mr Piper believed that success in this regard would protect him from justice.

'He had already removed the box of tiles into his car – an act witnessed by at least one other employee – and now he invented around these tiles a scenario that would enable him to travel to one of his firm's more distant clients. Miss Brown of Egremont

217

Hall – a very competent witness – insists she never had the conversation about alternative tiles that Mr Piper claims. Mr McKenzie of InnStyle has explained it makes no sense that such a change of tiles would be considered halfway through a project. The reason for Mr Piper's visit was fabricated – and indeed he made a token appearance. But that appearance was essential – to provide him with both an alibi and a justification to travel through extensive countryside. We do not know at what point on that Friday Mr Piper cemented his plan – but we do know that he entered the details of his 'appointment' onto the company's electronic diary system only minutes before the end of the day. That way, it was least likely to be noticed by a colleague, and questioned for its unusual nature – for not only was it unnecessary – it was scheduled for a Saturday.

'Mr Piper left work on Friday to pick up his sons from their football academy. Lisa's body was in the boot of his car, where it remained overnight, and into the next morning. It was driven to Egremont, and then – after Mr Piper's cursory visit to the hotel – to a location unknown, where it was disposed of, like fly-tipped rubbish.'

'Objection, Your Lordship!'

In response to the outburst from the defending counsel, the presiding judge, The Honourable Mr Justice Bloggs Kt, asks for a modification. The prosecutor bows her head, seemingly unperturbed.

'I will gladly qualify that statement, Your Lordship. Shortly before reaching the village of Cleator Moor, Mr Piper turned off his mobile phone, knowing that it is possible to track the movements of a person this way. He then left the main route and drove into its hinterland, uninhabited terrain that commingles wilderness with abundant remnant workings of the extractive industries.

'Few residents of Cumbria can have failed to be aware of the appeals made by the police, and the extensive searches that have been undertaken in the hope of locating Lisa's body. But the parameters of the situation are such that an area of six hundred square miles is in play. Despite some promising forensic leads

218

and well-intentioned public sightings, there has been no breakthrough. But, since Lisa disappeared into that doorway in July, her bank account has not been used, her mobile phone has not been switched on, and her loving parents have been left in unbearable limbo. And Mr Piper will not reveal the site of Lisa's lonely grave.'

The defending counsel looks like he is far from satisfied, but the judge waves away his glower of objection. Jane Sigmund-Smith QC continues.

'And so, ladies and gentlemen of the jury, I return to my opening remarks. Lisa and her family await justice to be done. An extraordinarily diligent investigation by Cumbria Police has revealed every single strand of what took place, most notably over those fateful two days. And, while my learned friend for the Defence might argue that these are single circumstantial strands that individually can bear no weight – I invite you to think of a cable. A cable is made up of such strands. Insubstantial alone, woven together into a coherent pattern they acquire a collective strength that can bear almost any weight. And that is what we have here: a coherent pattern, and an unbreakable case.

Her final pause ensues. She bows to the jury in advance of her concluding words.

'Thank you for your attention. I invite you to find Mr Piper guilty of the murder of Miss Lisa Jackson – for there simply is no other plausible explanation.'

*

'There simply is no other plausible explanation.'

Harry Burke QC, Counsel for the Defence looks up from his notes; he has uttered his opening line in a manner as though he were reading to himself and is bemused by the words. He regards the jury, blinking as if a little surprised they are still there. There is some implication that they have been regaled with a bunch of tripe.

'Ladies and gentlemen of the jury, I too – on behalf of my client Mr Ray Piper – commend your application and fortitude.

And I begin by echoing the closing words of my learned friend. However, thereafter we diverge – and with the greatest respect I would point out – on your behalf, as I am sure you are feeling – that these words are more than a little disingenuous. For there is another explanation, which you have heard, not only in the evidence openly given by Mr Piper, exposing himself to vigorous cross-examination – but also in the systematic misinterpretation of many events.

'Now, nobody can blame the police for doing what they are trained to do – to investigate what they believe to be a crime, and to bring the perpetrator to justice. But when there is no crime, there is a problem. As my learned friend pointed out, rather like the hunting pack of hounds that will chase to the point of their own exhaustion a false scent dragged across the fells, the police are programmed to pursue what they perceive as the offending fox – despite that there is no fox, just something that smells like a fox. And perhaps Cumbria Police may be further excused in this case, its timing coming hot on the heels of a spectacular failure – such that it was imperative to secure a conviction in what became in the media a high-profile disappearance.'

The barrister takes a drink, plainly in order to allow his undermining opening salvo to sink in. Jane Sigmund-Smith QC appears ready to object. However, she is on thin ice as far as challenging the drinking tactic is concerned – and she seems to receive a warning glare from the judge should she opt to question the relevance and validity of the slur upon the police. Accordingly she simply plies her adversary with a withering glance – although the onlooker might think she simply disapproves of his appearance. Most senior of practitioners of Burke, Hare and Graves Chambers, by comparison to her he renders a less-than-pristine portrayal of his profession, his attire shabbier and ill-fitting, he unshaven and overweight, a man gone to seed – though he somehow manages to convey that such decline has occurred while he has endured the terrible boredom (and inedible tripe) of the Prosecution's summing up. And, yet, with his flat northern vowels, indeed the hint of a local accent, he

220

carries a certain authenticity about him. It might not be a surprise to the said onlooker to learn there is vodka in the glass.

'So, let us review that other explanation. You have heard from Mr Piper that he and Miss Jackson were once involved in a close personal relationship. So much so that Mr Piper was invited to live with Miss Jackson. But, as is often the case in these complex and difficult situations, things did not quite work out and by mutual agreement Mr Piper moved out and their relationship evolved onto a platonic footing. Since they worked for the same employer, they went for occasional coffees, and Mr Piper sometimes gave Miss Jackson lifts to or from work. Their new relationship was on a perfectly even keel, and no one has come forward to state otherwise. That Mr Piper was perhaps a little more enthusiastic in his text messaging than Miss Jackson – being chatty, being concerned for her wellbeing – does not have to be, indeed *should not be* interpreted as imbued with some hostile intent. As a couple they had been very discreet about their interactions, and it was a means of private communication. And if Miss Jackson were uncomfortable why did she not express this to somebody – or indeed simply block Mr Piper's number on her mobile phone?

'You have heard that Mr Piper was parked outside Miss Jackson's home on the night before she disappeared. Mr Piper denies this. The neighbour, Mr Sidebottom is an elderly man and the street is poorly lit. And why would Mr Piper deny this when he does freely admit he went there the following morning, having set off a little early and having time to offer Miss Jackson a lift – until he remembered there was something he needed to do at the office? He denies any suggestion that he considered a car on Miss Jackson's driveway to belong to some kind of rival for his affections. It was not his business that Miss Jackson allowed someone to park there. Mr Piper went to work as normal.

'Now, you have been presented with evidence that Miss Jackson also went to work as normal. But things were not entirely normal for Miss Jackson – because you have also heard

221

that she had spent the previous night with her new boyfriend – the first time they had slept together – under the same roof.'

'Objection, Your Lordship.'

The judge casts a reproving eye upon the Counsel for the Defence.

'Your Lordship, I use not the euphemism but the literal. Unless I misunderstood Mr Scott's testimony.'

The judge – evidently replaying the pertinent words in his mind – on reflection appears satisfied, and signals for Harry Burke QC to continue.

'So it is perhaps stretching the imagination to suggest that things in Miss Jackson's mind were entirely normal. More likely she was in some state of high excitement or perhaps its negative equivalent.'

Again he employs the tactical pause in order for the jury to process the suggestion – perhaps the provocative notion that Lisa Jackson was in some yet-to-be-revealed way the architect of her own fate – whatever that fate may be. But now the barrister changes tack.

'Before we consider the possibilities, let us recap on what we do know. Mr Piper crossed paths with Miss Carr as she arrived at the office and he was making his way to the gentlemen's washroom on the upper floor – something he like the average person does several times a day and something that he even jokingly commented upon to Miss Carr. No actual evidence has been presented that Mr Piper did otherwise – only mere conjecture in order to fit the police's version of events. Mr Piper is quite clear that he went only to the gents', and categorically that he never saw Miss Jackson on that morning.

'A little later in the morning Mr Piper was working through his action list relating to his various projects and was reminded of an outstanding issue regarding the bathroom tiling at Egremont Hall. Since he happened to have available some relevant samples of tiles, he determined to put these in his car straightaway, lest he forget later, knowing he might need to leave in a hurry at the end of the day in order to pick up his sons from football. Wall tiles, as you will know if you have handled them, are heavy and Mr Piper, rather than risk dropping them, left the office to collect his car, having deposited the tiles safely in the small cupboard beneath the stairs on the ground floor. As you have seen from the evidence presented by the Prosecution, he brought his car to Lychgate Lane – when he loaded the tiles – and drove back to his usual parking spot in Aglionby Street. En route he purchased a sandwich for his lunch. It has been alleged that Mr Piper can be seen on CCTV to be carrying no such thing as he returned, but, as he has stated, the sandwich was in his jacket pocket.

'Attention has been drawn to the fact that Mr Piper at this time and on a later occasion was wearing gloves. But, as he has explained, not only does he often wear gloves to drive – why not, that is precisely what they are designed for – but also that he suffers from irregular bouts of psoriasis, and that he has found from trial and error that thin leather gloves, aerated, such as driving gloves are, help considerably to calm the condition. Indeed it is widely known that most pharmacies sell gloves specifically designed for the inflammation caused by psoriasis and eczema, and that most people treat themselves according to their fluctuating needs. It is a common ailment, and the majority of sufferers do not consult their GPs about the condition.

'Great fanfare has been trumpeted by the Prosecution of some cuts incurred by Mr Piper whilst gardening which, as he explained, took place on the Saturday *after* which Miss Jackson apparently disappeared. You heard from the witness evidence of Miss Carr that she noticed what she thought were cuts on one of Mr Piper's hands on the Friday – but she was clearly mistaken. She admitted that she did not know what psoriasis looked like – or even what it was. What she saw was the inflammation from which Mr Piper was suffering at the time, which can flare up quickly, and disappear just as quickly when treated. You have also heard from the police medical practitioner who examined Mr Piper when he was first taken into custody. Under cross-examination she clearly stated before you that *she could not rule out* the possibility that the cuts had been made by the thorns of a rose bush. And I remind you that there is no *actual* evidence to suggest otherwise – the only *actual* evidence is that Mr Piper has explained what happened.

'I move on. For the remainder of the Friday in question, Mr Piper worked diligently at his desk, dealing with his various projects, sending emails and making telephone calls to his clients and suppliers. None of his colleagues were able to say he acted in a way other than entirely normally. Yet the Prosecution are expecting you to believe that this was the behaviour of a man who has killed a woman – on the premises. I ask you, is that a credible claim?

'It has been suggested that Mr Piper ought to have queried other staff members about Miss Jackson's absence from the office. But Mr Piper has explained that this is not something he would do, as he and Miss Jackson by mutual agreement had kept their former relationship to themselves, and had continued to have contact with one another in a discreet manner by exchanging text messages. Mr Piper had sent a couple of messages to Miss Jackson earlier in the day, and had not received a reply. As he has stated, he felt she would probably respond in her own good time – but when she did not, after lunch, he tried to telephone her – but was only able to leave a voicemail. That voicemail was played to the court. The Prosecution has attempted to suggest this was some kind of fake message, disingenuous – but quite clearly you heard Mr Piper speaking to Lisa entirely as would be expected, wondering where she was, and suggesting that they might meet up for a coffee, as they had done on occasion.

'The Prosecution now expect you to believe that Mr Piper collected his two young sons from their football academy, drove them home, and then spent an evening with his family watching TV and eating pizza – *while all the time the body of Miss Jackson was in the boot of his car.*'

The defending counsel surveys the jury open mouthed, a look of incredulity no doubt intended to convey this is how they ought to be feeling.

'Would a calculating murderer – as the Prosecution would wish to portray Mr Piper – take such risk of discovery? And

224

indeed would any person do such a thing in close proximity to his family? What you are being expected to believe is *beyond* believability.

'Let us return to the facts. The following morning, Mr Piper filled his car with petrol and bought a newspaper. It has been the pattern of the Prosecution case to misattribute motives to many small aspects of Mr Piper's behaviour. Here the Prosecution would have it that Mr Piper bought the paper for news of Miss Jackson's disappearance. Once again it is pure supposition. You have heard from Mr Piper that he bought it to read should he find himself having to wait before his appointment later in the morning at Egremont Hall. As a conscientious employee of InnStyle Design & Management Limited he was sacrificing his own free time to clear up an outstanding issue.

'You have heard how Mr Piper travelled to the hotel, Egremont Hall. The assistant manager, Mr Thatcher, greeted him. The proprietor, Miss Brown, was absent at the time. The Prosecution has made much of the visit by Mr Piper being unnecessary – that Miss Brown denies ever discussing with Mr Piper the possibility of using different tiles. But you have also heard from Miss Brown under cross-examination that she does not take minutes of her meetings with suppliers – and that she conceded, rather grudgingly I may add, that it is possible she may have forgotten the conversation. For his part, Mr Piper has explained how Miss Brown was a demanding and at times unreasonable client – I leave it to you to form your own opinions.' (Herewith knowing grins from several of the jury.) 'Mr Piper took the expedient of addressing an issue that could have reared its head to bite his employer – imagine the cost had Miss Brown insisted that the tiles in all fifteen bathrooms be replaced "as she had earlier requested" after the job was complete.

'Mr Piper performed the inspection to his satisfaction and left Egremont Hall. He does not dispute the timings that the police have presented as evidence of his return to his home in Carlisle. What of course Mr Piper does dispute is their entirely

225

preposterous explanation of what he did on the journey. As you have heard, Mr Piper had not been feeling too well since rising on the Saturday morning, which he attributed to the anchovies in the pizza Napoli which he – and only he – had eaten the night before. I am sure, members of the jury, you can identify with the unpleasant experience of being some distance from home and feeling increasingly like you are about to – not to put too fine a point upon it – that you are about to vomit. Mr Piper initially thought he might be able to make it home, but after setting out from Egremont Hall became increasingly ill, to the extent that he was aware his condition was affecting his driving, and indeed his general perception of his surroundings. In desperation he turned off from the main trunk road and followed a lane until he found a suitable layby where he could safely pull in.

'I shall not venture into graphic detail, since we approach lunch hour – but you heard that Mr Piper, after being ill behind a hedgerow, returned to his vehicle and, in order to recline a little, sat in the passenger seat where there was more room to stretch out. Again I am sure you can empathise with his condition, and it is not surprising that sleep overtook him. When he awoke, around an hour later, he felt well enough to resume his journey.

'As he regained his faculties he realised he had not heard from his wife and at this point noticed that his mobile telephone had run out of charge. It was off. He plugged it into the in-car charger and switched it on. In fact there were no messages, and Mr Piper continued and returned to Carlisle. As you have heard, it had been Mr Piper's intention to valet his car – something he normally did at weekends – and passing the service station near his home he stopped for cleaning materials, and took the opportunity to refuel, since he likes to begin each week with the peace of mind of a full tank. And of course, while he had slept, his engine had been idling, which accounted for the extra petrol that had been burned.'

Another pause for a drink; Harry Burke QC seems to savour the taste of his water.

'We now come to yet further innocent events that the police have misconstrued as damming evidence. You have heard from

Mr Piper that on the Friday – and again I apologise for raising this so soon before luncheon – he realised some dog excrement had been inadvertently smeared into his car from one of his sons' training shoes. He had wiped this away but on Saturday there was still a residual smell. Indeed, the detectives witnessed him chastise his boys not to kick the back of the seats. Accordingly, after his journey to Egremont, he purchased an antibacterial cleansing spray and a strong deodoriser. I think we would all have done much the same. Mr Piper cleaned his car thoroughly for perfectly understandable reasons.

'As to the washing of the exterior of the car, it has been suggested that small patches of fine mud on Mr Piper's driveway merit a sinister explanation – that he visited some clandestine location with a nefarious purpose in mind. But who has not seen a stretch of country lane covered in mud that has been trailed from a farmer's field or a construction site? And, as Mr Piper has pointed out, he noticed no such mud on his car when he washed it. His suggestion – perfectly reasonable, it seems to me, but apparently overlooked by the police – is that the mud may have been transferred to his driveway by another vehicle – a delivery van or a tradesman or meter reader, for instance, on a rainy day – and that the traces of residue that were found on his BMW were picked up from his own driveway.

'I would remind you that no such deposits were found on Mr Piper's shoes. Shoes that he was seen by the police to be wearing that morning and which were forensically examined. If he took his car to some muddy spot – even were it the layby where he stopped when he felt ill – he did not have superhuman powers of levitation. That would be far fetched, would it not?'

Watching with knitted brows, several members of the jury react with what might be uneasy nods.

Far fetched. Two words that seem to me to sum up the Prosecution's case. It is a case that – I am sure you will agree – relies almost entirely upon speculation. Where, indeed, is the real evidence? I put it to you that there is *not one shred* of credible forensic evidence. Think about that – an investigation that has continued for over three months – and no forensics! *Aha* – I

227

hear you say – there was the hair! But what does a single strand of hair prove? Miss Jackson like most women shed her hair freely – you have seen the exhibit of the hairbrush taken from her dressing table. To think she left no such trace at her place of work or in Mr Piper's car in which she on occasion travelled seems highly improbable. I am sure if we brushed sticky packing tape over the seats of our car or the carpet of our office we would find hairs attached. Would we not?'

There is more involuntary nodding of agreement from the jury.

'*Aha* – there was the cadaver dog! It barked near the car – you have seen the video. But I ask you this: at what was it barking? With its nose one thousand times more powerful than ours did it detect something ominous? Or was it simply the odour of excrement that Mr Piper had attempted to mask? In order to translate for us what the dog was telling its handler, did the Prosecution call Dr Doolittle?'

A majority of the jury are smirking.

'Two more words: *reasonable doubt*. This phrase must inform your judgement. I put it to you that there is more than reasonable doubt over the minor forensic aspects of this case. The hair could have been picked up from the passenger seat; the dog could have been barking at something else. Is it not remarkable – in this era of "CSI" – that a supposed murder and the supposed complex disposal of a body can take place without the perpetrator and the victim between them leaving a single significant trace?

'Furthermore I suggest there is reasonable doubt at every little stage of the account put to you by the Prosecution.

'And let us look finally at one 'big' stage in that account. Let us consider the actual moments of the disappearance of Miss Jackson. It is proposed that, since CCTV recorded her entering the dead-end that is Lychgate Lane and she was not seen to re-emerge, there is only one possible explanation – that which has been suggested to you by the Prosecution. It is said she could not have left the offices of InnStyle by the rooftop fire escape because the security seal was unbroken and the alarm not triggered. It is said she could not have somehow passed through the premises of Wood's of Carlisle because she would have been observed – and indeed the front door, the only means of egress, was locked until the retail store opened at nine o'clock.

'Now, I say there is little dispute that she entered Lychgate Lane and indeed entered the premises of InnStyle, as witnessed by young Mr Todd of the timber merchants. There is good foundation for that, which it would seem churlish to dispute. *But thereafter the evidence crumbles away.*

'As you are aware, the lane itself – a short distance from this court – is backed onto by some twenty other properties, commercial and residential, several of which have emergency or fire exits giving onto the lane. Now the police say they checked all of these premises, speaking to the responsible persons in each instance, and they concluded that it was not possible for a door to have been left open, or for a person to pass through a particular building unnoticed. But such a conclusion relies on human infallibility – which we know is an oxymoron. We are all fallible. A door may have been left open by accident – or even by design – and if it were then the police would rely on human honesty to admit, perhaps to a mistake – perhaps to a conspiracy. A door could have been left open, entered, closed – and no one would be any the wiser.

'After Mr Todd secured the loading bay and his colleague Mr Ibson drove away there elapsed at least four minutes before the next person arrived in Lychgate Lane. Miss Jackson would have known the van would shortly leave and could have waited for it to do so. It would take only twenty seconds to cross the lane and enter another doorway. Or, she could have gone first to the ladies' washroom on the top floor of the stair. There she could have waited until after nine a.m. when all of her colleagues had arrived, and could have left at her leisure.

'It seems to me that there are many possibilities in this regard that received only cursory investigation. The police relied entirely on one CCTV camera, combined with the fact that Lychgate Lane is a dead end. Miss Jackson entered the lane but apparently did not come out. But Lychgate Lane is only truly a dead end for vehicles. This is rather like the monster hunter who spends a day camped on the bank of Loch Ness, sees no monster, and returns home to pronounce that Nessie does not exist. In a similar way the police prematurely developed their theory of what took place and thereafter devised explanations to fit that theory.

'That theory is based on the assumption that Miss Jackson became a victim. What if she were not a victim? What if she were a willing actor in her own disappearance?

'We have all heard real-life stories of people who apparently vanish, until it is later discovered that they have simply escaped. They want a new life – they want to leave their pressures and anxieties behind. A new bank account, a new mobile phone, a new hairdo and new clothes – even a new identity – these things are not difficult in this day and age – it simply requires some planning. Then one day – slip quietly and unobtrusively from the old life into the new.

'*Aha* – you say – but Miss Jackson was a home-loving person – she would never have abandoned her parents and her pet cat. But how well does anyone know her? She has lived a very private existence. She kept her relationship with Mr Piper from her colleagues and all friends and family but her parents, and even their knowledge was scant. Does she have savings we do not know about? Has she met someone else we do not know about? Has she won the lottery?'

And now the barrister flashes a rare smile at the jury – they are clearly disoriented by this left-of-field hypothesis; there are some nervous laughs. But now Harry Burke QC's unrefined features become serious once more. He turns to consider Ray Piper in the dock, in a manner that pities him.

'Or perhaps Miss Jackson simply thought it was the best way to end her contact with Mr Piper.'

It may be choreographed, but Ray Piper's impervious mask momentarily slips and there is a look of what appears to be genuine dismay – as if this is the first time he has been confronted with such a notion. Meanwhile the prosecuting counsel is becoming increasingly agitated. She must accept that it is the role of the Defence to sow seeds of doubt – but clearly she sees this as crossing the line – it is the kicking up of dust. She looks somewhere between furious and indignant – but does not seem to have a ready objection. And after a few seconds more the defending counsel resumes.

'Perhaps Miss Jackson's disappearance will not be a permanent state of affairs.'

He surveys the jury; undoubtedly in some of their eyes are expressions of hope. He walks in a circle and it is apparent that he is about to conclude. He faces the jury, and speaks calmly and quietly.

'I began by restating the words of my learned friend. That there is no plausible alternative explanation for the collection of facts that have been gathered. But you have heard Mr Piper's account of his actions – he has taken the stand before you to describe what were two largely uneventful days in his life. By association he has been singled out and an alternative reality has been attributed to those two days. You may judge for yourselves which is more plausible.

'My learned friend used an analogy in her closing speech. That the many strands of information – and I stress *information* and not evidence – wind together to form an unbreakable cable.

'I would suggest to you that the Prosecution case is not a cable, but a chain. The Prosecution have linked together a collection of inferences and assumptions, and – yes – some facts, which are not in dispute. But that chain is flawed. Unlike a cable – which can withstand some of its strands being frayed, a chain is another matter. The Prosecution's chain has many weak links. It is for the Prosecution to prove to you – *beyond reasonable doubt* – that each and every one of those links can bear weight. I say to you, in that regard, there is considerable doubt. Indeed, I would argue that one link is broken entirely.'

He turns away as though he has finished his speech, pulling the arm holding his papers across his chest. There is a frisson of disquiet in the court – although nobody actually speaks – and then he swivels and faces the jury once more.

231

'Miss Jackson was last seen alive. *There is no actual evidence that she is dead.*'

15. VERDICT

Carlisle, Monday afternoon – four days later

'Not proven.'

'What's that you say, Guv?'

'Not proven. It's a third verdict – available in Scotland. Guilty. Not guilty. *Not proven.* We're lucky this case wasn't tried up there – the jury could have gone for that – he'd have walked free for good.'

'What's the point of it, then?'

'Good question, Leyton.' Skelgill runs the fingers of both hands through his hair, which is well overdue for a cut. 'According to my old mucker Cameron Findlay, it's when the jury think the accused is guilty but the Prosecution hasn't managed to prove it beyond reasonable doubt.'

DS Leyton nods pensively as he stirs the foam into his cappuccino. He and his two colleagues are partaking of strong coffees in the café bar of the Halston – although DS Jones looks more like she could do with a strong gin and tonic. And, by what now must seem a rather cruel irony, they are in sight of Lychgate Lane, for the Courts of Justice are located in Earl Street, the adjacent turn off Warwick Road – indeed, also a cul-de-sac, on one side of its cobbles stand properties that formed part of the inquiry, and to which the Defence referred – a predictable if skilfully executed strategy of sowing seeds of doubt. Skelgill is casting about, apparently trying to determine what company they keep – perhaps anyone who was in court in some capacity. DS Leyton seems more sensitive to DS Jones's predicament.

'Come on, girl – any luck, we'll get a second bite at the cherry.'

DS Jones smiles rather wanly. Though appreciative of his backing, for the moment she cannot hide a defeated demeanour. She keeps suffering flashbacks of the confused faces of Lisa Jackson's parents, turning to her in the public gallery. Skelgill

233

now seems to detect her distress; perhaps not surprisingly he misreads her sentiment – he stiffens, bristling, like he is spoiling for a fight – looking for someone upon whom to avenge the injustice inflicted upon his partner – when a possible candidate enters.

DS Leyton is facing the door.

'Look out – here comes trouble.'

His colleagues' heads turn to see framed in the entrance the adolescent features and flamboyant hairdo of local reporter Kendall Minto. It is plain he is looking for them, and has arrived in a hurry, but now he approaches more warily. His brushes with Skelgill have met with mixed reactions, and he circles to DS Jones's side of the table rather as one avoiding an unreadable Doberman. He does not risk nods of acknowledgement; he has his wits about him – he knows such to be an invitation to be told to get lost. He fixes an optimistic, almost fawning gaze upon DS Jones. He is holding out his notebook in a way suggestive of having something to report rather than to glean, like a gunslinger offering his revolver by the barrel. But he begins with a tentative question.

'What does this mean?'

DS Jones is ever polite – and she has a soft spot for her contemporary despite his misplaced affections and his coquettish manner that she knows irritates the hell out of Skelgill.

'We don't know yet. There's a formal process. The case is referred back to the Crown Prosecution Service. If they determine it's in the public interest to reach a verdict they can order a re-trial with a new jury.'

Kendall Minto might be something of a smart Alec, but he is also smart, period. Now he looks apprehensively at Skelgill, in recognition of his rank.

'They must think he's guilty – else why didn't they acquit him? Fours days' deliberation and they still couldn't bring themselves to do that.'

Skelgill makes a disdainful face.

'They probably just wanted their weekend in a hotel at the taxpayer's expense.'

234

DS Jones can see that Skelgill is being churlish – he dislikes that Minto is making the running – and has gatecrashed what is their wake of sorts. But to give the reporter his due, it is a logic that is surely correct. Despite directions from the judge that he would accept a majority 10-2 verdict, the jury had steadfastly refused to give one. The Scots might argue that their 'simple majority' system of fifteen jurors, in which 8-7 is sufficient to secure a conviction or an acquittal, avoids such a deadlock – but then there is Skelgill's original argument about the flawed 'not proven' verdict. Kendall Minto is on the same page, and it cheers her. But where such hope is tainted is that, in order for a re-trial, new evidence may be demanded – and from where on earth would that be hewn?

Now Kendall Minto indicates that he does indeed have news to impart.

'Did you watch Ray Piper's impromptu press conference? Outside the courthouse? It was streamed live.'

The three detectives look at him dumbly. They had left promptly and repaired to the Halston for the very purpose of avoiding journalistic attention.

Kendall Minton continues. 'About him going to China?'

'Struth!' DS Leyton provides a group response.

'One of my fellow hacks had got wind of it somehow – you know – we all have contacts – maybe someone in the consulate. Piper has landed a job in Shanghai and he's made a successful visa application and is rumoured to be leaving in a fortnight. He didn't deny it when the question was put to him.'

Now an awkward silence ensues.

'I thought you should know.' Kendall Minto looks unsure how to deal with the dark reaction he has elicited; perhaps the words 'shoot' and 'messenger' spring to mind. Even DS Jones appears wrathful to his eye. 'Emma – you did a great job – all the press pack think so.'

Now the journalist sees proprietorial disapproval from Skelgill – that it is not his place to commiserate. DS Jones forces a smile – but it does not help that he divides her loyalties. Sensibly, he decides on discretion as the better part of valour.

235

'I shan't drop it. I'll keep you posted – if I hear anything that might help.'

He contrives a strange hand signal that could be a wave or it might be a suggestion that his offer is subject to a quid pro quo. He makes a sharp exit.

Skelgill looks ready to utter a deprecatory Anglo-Saxon farewell – but perhaps he decides it would be cowardly not to do it to his face and refrains. Instead it is left to DS Leyton to remark.

'Jeez – that's put the cat among the pigeons. Yangtze-flippin'-Kiang.'

Skelgill is momentarily distracted by his subordinate's creative expletive.

'No extradition treaty.'

They look at DS Jones.

'The United Kingdom doesn't have an extradition treaty with The People's Republic of China.'

It is another conversation stopper – but an interruption arrives in the form of a text alert from DS Leyton's mobile phone. His reaction to the personalised chime is a somewhat Pavlovian jolt.

'The missus – yikes! I forgot – I'm supposed to get the popcorn and whatnot for tonight. You still up for that?' Then a flash of doubt clouds his features. Already he sounds disappointed. 'I'll understand if you don't want to come – given all this. I'll be recording it. You could drop in another time.'

But DS Jones is suddenly determined. She reaches to touch his forearm.

'No – we'll come – won't we, Guv?'

She glares at Skelgill – like a woman on a mission. He shrugs as if he has no choice.

DS Leyton looks mightily relieved.

'Cheers – the nippers are looking forward to seeing you – I told them there's some *real* detectives coming for tea.'

'Like you're not, Leyton.'

'You know how it goes, Guv – when they see you in your underpants they don't take you seriously.'

'I'll remember to wear mine on the inside.'

DS Jones offers further encouragement to her fellow sergeant.

'Wait until they see you on the TV – they'll think you're Chief of Police.'

DS Leyton makes to leave; his face suggests he doubts it. When he has gone, DS Jones turns to Skelgill; there is again an undercurrent of despondency in her tone.

'I must admit, I don't feel much like a real detective right now.'

Skelgill scoffs scornfully. However his sentiment, rather than one of sympathy, seems to be more of the order of detached resolve.

'The jury's thrown us a lifeline.'

DS Jones does not answer – though she appreciates at least that he seems to be as invested in the difficulty as she is. Her disturbed emotions must settle before her mind can begin to mobilise once more. Again she feels the contrast with her superior, who runs on gut instinct and seems able to find a new gear and pull away smoothly after a reversal; it does not bother him that his thoughts are left to catch up of their own accord. She makes an effort to sideline the nagging distraction. She notices that Skelgill's attention has drifted and he is scrutinising the service counter. Indeed he begins to rise.

'Reckon I'll have another slice of that parkin – keep me going until Leyton's missus cooks up the pizza.'

237

16. SOAP STAR

Monday evening

'Don't fret, lass – we can slope off for a pint once we've seen Leyton play Columbo.'

Having travelled separately Skelgill and DS Jones have parked as close to DS Leyton's modest suburban semi as limited spaces allow. There is a hint of impatience in Skelgill's tone – that he sees his colleague is still apparently under the cloud of the afternoon's setback. He notices with a faint pang of guilt that she carries flowers and a bottle of wine. As they converge at the front gate she hands him the wine but does not speak of it.

'Did you not get my email, Guv?'

There is something in her tone that suggests there is a new reason for her continued dejection. But Skelgill merely grins impudently – as if he would check his inbox!

'On Sunday night Carlisle police were called to a disturbance at a domestic address. The house belonged to Gary Scott – Lisa Jackson's last boyfriend. To cut a long story short, Scott was arrested on suspicion of assault – of a new girlfriend. She's alleging that he tried to strangle her.'

Skelgill shrugs – though it seems to be a belligerent reflex.

'Coincidence. Sod's law.'

'Guv – his wife died in an accident. I didn't look at that in great detail. Once we got the footage of Lisa arriving at Lychgate Lane, and his pal alibied him, it seemed impossible that he could have been involved. But what if there's something in what the Defence suggested?'

Skelgill does not break stride and nor does his expression change – although that in itself is telling. It is plain that he is unnerved by the news but is determined his colleague should not be derailed by it. In his favour is that there is no time to dwell – their presence is obviously eagerly anticipated – they have been spotted by one of the family and the front door is opened by a harassed-looking Mrs Leyton holding a loudly protesting youngest member of the clan.

'Speak about it in the pub.'

Skelgill hisses the words from the side of his mouth but gets no further – just as he nears the front step a loud crash emanates from what might be the direction of the kitchen and a high-pitched commotion breaks out and simultaneously alarms go off. Mrs Leyton thrusts the infant into the unsuspecting Skelgill's arms and turns tail, leaving him on the threshold with the squirming infant. At this moment DS Leyton charges past – also heading for the kitchen, it seems. He grins phlegmatically at Skelgill.

'Cheers, Guvnor.' He reaches to relieve his boss of the bottle and, seeing his discomfort, offers a word of advice. 'Think of her like a large fish.'

He disappears from sight – yanking shut the kitchen door to contain billowing smoke. Skelgill has the baby safely, albeit now held out at arm's length. His nostrils are wrinkling.

'I've smelt better fish.'

DS Jones is roused into action.

'Aw, Guv. She can't help it.' She shoves Skelgill unceremoniously by one shoulder to turn him, and – to his eye with surprising deftness – relieves him of his burden in exchange for the bouquet.

'I'll take her upstairs and change her nappy. Go and sit by the telly, Guv.'

Skelgill needs no encouragement, and discovers a tray of cold beers and a bowl of popcorn have been placed on a coffee table and assumes he is to make himself at home. Judging by the scattering on the carpet it looks like the children have been here first. The television is blaring – and he is reminded of the technological necessities of a young family – the massive widescreen monitor, the slimline hub that brings cable and wireless, the games console and various handsets. His own rudimentary configuration, rarely watched, still features a VCR.

Having settled for a bottle of Jennings Sneck Lifter – and feeling a little uneasy that his lager-drinking colleague must have

239

bought the ale specially – and now glaring at an advertisement for toilet tissue that has a Labrador puppy cavorting with rolls of loo paper – he is surprised by the swift reappearance of DS Jones in possession of a contented baby. Skelgill, if pleased to see her mind has been well and truly taken off the case, finds himself disconcerted by her engagement with the child – so naturally does she speak to the little girl, eliciting both her undivided attention and a succession of coos and giggles.

And now there is a grand entrance. DS Leyton leans in, pushing open the door and making the sound of a trumpet fanfare. Ducking beneath his outstretched arm come his two other children, girl and boy, bearing a large platter, plainly doing their best to behave and not wrestle from one another a disproportionate share of the credit as they present themselves before him.

The fourth in a line of brothers, he needs no lessons in sibling rivalry, and immediately reads the situation. They have made him a pizza. They have made him a huge pizza. They have made him a huge pizza in the shape of a fish!

He is to look amazed, and delighted.

And now, to the surprise of his colleagues, he *does* look pleased. For a man to whom expressing gratitude does not come easily – never mind *feigning* it – he appears genuinely taken aback. DS Jones has been in on the pizza surprise for several days – but she is shocked to see a rare glisten in Skelgill's eyes. And she quickly realises that he is also choked.

'That is a *fantastic* fish – what kind is it, Guv?'

This seems to do the trick, and Skelgill clears his throat. He surveys the creation. It has a black olive for an eye and a fabulous array of scales fashioned from sliced peperoni and jalapenos, and fins of mozzarella and basil. The cooking has been less diligent – and perhaps explains the earlier conflagration – for the whole perimeter of the fish pizza is burnt! Skelgill ponders for a moment longer before pronouncing.

'Char.'

'*Guv!*' It is DS Jones who reproaches him. She thinks he is being facetious.

240

He regards her with raised hands and a face of perfect innocence – he even affects some offence.

'It's a char, I tell you – Arctic char – a speciality of Ennerdale Water, no less. And several other lakes hereabouts.'

He turns to the children, who hover before him – they seem to be trying to read the nuances passing between the adults.

'This is a belter. But who wants to catch a real one? Who wants to come in a boat?'

'Me! Me – it was my idea!'

That both utter simultaneously the same line brings a wry grin to his features.

'Happen there's room for three. One oar each and I'll be cox.'

Now DS Leyton steps forward.

'What an honour, kids – I've been waiting seven years for an invitation!'

Skelgill takes the backhanded compliment in good spirits.

'Leyton – you keep telling me wild horses won't get you to set foot on water.'

DS Leyton has his own twist on this joshing.

'Walk on water? There's only one person we know who can do that, Guv!'

They all laugh – although Skelgill has a faint suspicion his sergeant could mean him – despite that he suffers a recurring hallucination of the Chief striding across the surface of Bass Lake because he won't answer his phone. Before Skelgill can weigh up the two possibilities, DS Leyton notices that the show is starting.

'It's time, ladies and gentlemen!'

It takes just two bars of the Ennerdale theme music to conjure up for Skelgill a vision of his childhood. It is bittersweet, for set against the nostalgia, the warming mug of Ovaltine loaded with sugar, his Ma drawing the coal fire with a sheet of the Westmorland Gazette, the smell of soot, the austere cosiness, and night pressed against the cottage window was the knowledge of impending bedtime, and school tomorrow.

There ensues a scenario that must be played out in millions of homes across England – the adults keenly watching and the kids quickly becoming bored – and in this case wanting to know when their Daddy is going to be on; a living room version of "Are we there yet?" DS Leyton – now that his big moment is nearing – begins to play down expectations, that it will just be a fleeting cameo, and reminding them that he had no lines. Mrs Leyton has supplied a bottle of warm milk, and the baby, replete, soon falls asleep in the arms of DS Jones. Skelgill keeps stealing glances at her; he experiences the same mixture of relief, but also of unease, that he cannot quite fathom. At the interval, during the commercial break, a grateful Mrs Leyton lifts the infant away to bed. The older children finish their pizza and are tiring, becoming fractious, grazing the popcorn like overfed ducks at the park that peck out of habit. DS Leyton announces that there is a cliffhanger (to which he has been sworn to secrecy) that occurs while the police are on the scene, therefore his appearance will be close to the end of the episode.

Skelgill has not watched Ennerdale for years – realistically, he is thinking, it must be twenty-five years, since he was a twelve-year-old. Yet to his amazement some of the same characters – indeed the same *actors* – are present. There is old Albert Gough, still smoking his pipe and hacking sporadically beside his hearth, as cantankerous as ever and a minor miracle that he is still alive – and local tattler Ena Mandrake, still purveying poison gossip from behind the counter of the village inn. Curiously, neither appears to have aged in the quarter century since he last saw them – but perhaps that has something do to with viewing the world through the sharp prism of a child's eyes. But he has no idea of where the various storylines are heading – and misses the laughs enjoyed by DS Leyton and his wife, in particular. But what does interest Skelgill – indeed intrigue him – is the location, and the liberties taken with it. Certainly, some of the filming has occurred in the valley of Ennerdale itself – but every so often he spies a setting that does not ring true – and cannot help himself from whistleblowing.

'That's the church in Buttermere.'

242

'That's Honister Hause.'

'That's Derwentwater – you can see Catbells in the background.'

DS Jones regards him with some amusement, although she suspects his inability to let continuity errors pass might just be spoiling the enjoyment of Mrs Leyton, undermining for her the fidelity of the production.

'I suppose they choose locations for practical reasons, Guv. Like you were saying, Ennerdale itself is pretty isolated – there must be limited sites available, and it must be inconvenient to get the company all the way there.'

Now DS Leyton pipes up.

'Mind you, Emma – when I was there it was the whole shebang – whacking great trailers, caravans, cameras, lighting rigs, electrical cables running all over the gaff.'

But Skelgill is now further distracted by a movie mistake of a slightly different nature. It is the scene that was being filmed roughly contemporaneously with DS Leyton's cameo, when most of the cast and crew were up on the high fellside. There was heather burning taking place.

'When was this again?' Skelgill is frowning.

DS Leyton and DS Jones exchange baffled glances; it would be expected that the timing of events was seared into their superior's memory as much as their own. DS Jones replies.

'Guv – it was the weekend that Lisa Jackson disappeared – remember?'

Skelgill seems preoccupied with his latest objection.

'They wouldn't be burning heather in July – it's still the breeding season. By law they can't start burning while October.'

DS Leyton, however, is well versed in the protocol of the soap opera – never better than now – that filming takes place around three months ahead of screening.

'That'd be why they're showing it now, Guv – so it's right for this time of year.'

Skelgill remains indignant.

'Aye – that's all very well, Leyton – but you can see it's not October. The vegetation – the bracken's bright green and there's

243

willowherb in flower. Look at the actors' shadows – the sun's way too high. And I can hear a skylark.'

DS Leyton folds his arms resignedly, and snatches a surreptitious glance at his wife; clearly she is doing her best to shut out the extraneous distraction. Meanwhile his children, presently sharing an armchair, begin subtly to wrestle for supremacy. He attempts to muster some order.

'I reckon I'll be on any minute. Fasten your seatbelts kids!'

'REWIND! LEYTON! REWIND IT!'

All eyes – including those of Mrs Leyton, who looks slightly terrified – fall upon Skelgill. For he has sprung from his chair and is on his knees before the television set, dementedly groping about as if he is looking for some way of carrying out his own command.

DS Leyton, who has possession of the control for the purposes of his impending appearance, reluctantly presses the pause button. Skelgill jerks back from the set.

'How did you do that?'

'It's a standard feature, Guv – look.' DS Leyton restarts and stops the action. 'It's handy if we're watching something and the littl'un starts screaming blue murder. "Freeze live TV", they call it. You can even fast-forward to catch up.'

'Does it go back?'

'Yeah – but – I'm just about to come on, Guv.' DS Leyton looks around the room pleadingly, as if to enlist support – and that Skelgill is inexplicably stealing his thunder – presumably having found another obscure complaint for the script supervisor.

'You're recording it ahead, aye?'

'Yeah – I am, Guv – but –'

'Leyton – we need to go back.' Skelgill speaks more calmly now, but points decisively at the control. 'Twenty seconds – to where the keeper and the blonde lass start necking.'

He refers to a poor man's 'Cathy-meets-Heathcliff' scene that began with the would-be lovers setting the heather on fire (literally so, for legitimate moorland management purposes). The heat of the moment appeared to ignite their passion – although

244

the ensuing intimacy became swathed in smoke in deference to the nine o'clock watershed, before cutting away to vegetation burning out of control, the metaphor well and truly milked.

DS Leyton simpers at his wife – he looks tempted to mime that his boss has a screw loose. But instead he winks and rewinds the video, as ordered.

'Does it do slow motion?'

'It does, Guv. Super-slow motion, even.'

DS Leyton navigates accordingly.

Skelgill edges closer to the set.

'There!'

His sergeant seems to understand he should freeze the action.

Skelgill now has the index finger of his left hand pressed on the screen.

Beyond the burning heather the fellside falls away into the wooded valley bottom.

The sole lane that winds to its terminus up in the dale is exposed by a gap in the trees.

Small but distinctive, thanks to the many pixels of the Leytons' giant high-definition set, is the object of Skelgill's excitement.

Passing through the gap in a downhill direction is a white BMW with a black stripe down its side.

DS Jones joins Skelgill on the carpet.

DS Leyton crouches beside them.

They are like devotees at a temple.

'Stone the crows!'

'Leyton – run it again.'

His sergeant does as bidden. Indeed he replays the sequence several times – but none of them tire of watching it. The family behind seem to understand that silence is the order of the day. DS Jones is first to speak.

'Guv – is that definitely Ennerdale?'

'Aye – there's Caw Fell.'

DS Leyton speaks excitedly.

'Guv – that must have been the Saturday. When I went to see about the shotgun on the Monday – the security geezer told me that's when they'd filmed the actual heather burning because it was the only day they could get the fire brigade on standby.'

DS Jones is visibly trembling.

'We can find out for sure. I was at uni with a girl who works in TV post-production. They should have what they call the rushes – all the various takes before they're spliced and edited. There'll be the clapperboards – and even better it's likely the original digital files will be timestamped.'

There is a moment of silence as the implications of this sink in. Then DS Leyton remembers something.

'The producer – she gave me her card.' Now he looks a little embarrassed. He glances to his wife. 'We kept it – as a memento – we've got a kind of fan album. It's in the sideboard.'

At this a small wrestling match breaks out as the Leytons' children compete to fetch the item. Their father looks on a little helplessly.

'*Both of you* – if you want to come fishing, mind.'

Skelgill's stern warning does the trick. A truce descends and the pair revert to best behaviour; they present the folder in much the same manner as the pizza. Skelgill hands it on to DS Leyton.

'Just phone her.'

'Hadn't we better wait until tomorrow, Guv – when she's at work?'

'Leyton – she is at work.' Skelgill inclines his head towards the screen. 'She'll be watching this – it's her job.'

'Good point, Guv.'

DS Leyton leafs through the album. It seems mainly to be filled with clippings from celebrity magazines.

'Here it is.'

'I'll do it.' DS Jones springs to her feet. She considers the circumstances – a still bewildered Mrs Leyton, and the inquisitive children, now fidgeting beside their mother on the settee. And then there comes a mournful wail from upstairs, transmitted via a baby monitor. 'I'll phone from my car.'

DS Leyton moves towards the door.

246

'I'll come – we should use my mobile. She's got my number – she texted to tell me the broadcast date – she'll know it's not any old Tom, Dick or Harry.'

Skelgill finds himself left alone with the two children. In his sole company they seem more reserved, as if misbehaving is only worth expending energy upon when there are parents to be annoyed. He begins to tell them about his boat, the infamous Kelly kettle, exploding bangers cooked beside the lake, monster eels, pike that swallow ducklings whole and swarms of deadly midges that eat anglers. He is running low on anecdotes suitable for tender ears when his colleagues reappear – although there is something reassuring about the length of time it has taken them.

DS Leyton sends the kids to the kitchen to help themselves to a special treat of ice cream.

'We got her, Guv – you were right, she was watching it live. She thought I was ringing to complain about the editing – *hah!*'

He turns to DS Jones, who is holding open her notebook.

'To cut to the chase, Guv – she was able to log on to the Cumbria Television server. As I hoped, the files can be interrogated by exact date and time. The BMW was filmed at 11:28 on the Saturday morning.'

DS Leyton triumphantly punches his fist into the opposing palm.

'Slap bang in the middle of when Piper reckoned he was kipping in a layby, Guv!'

Now DS Jones shows Skelgill notes she has made.

'I just did some rough calculations based on timings from my maps app. I assume he couldn't have been driving for more than about five minutes before he was caught on camera.'

Skelgill nods in agreement.

'Aye – five minutes, max. The road goes for a couple of miles at most. Past a track to Gillerthwaite farm – where the gun was taken – and up into the forest. It's gated and locked by the Forestry. Besides, you'd need a tracked vehicle after that – or a Defender, at least.'

DS Jones speaks a little breathlessly.

247

'If he continued on back-roads via Loweswater and Low Lorton, he would have arrived at the Lamplugh roundabout precisely in line with the schedule we established. More critically, from where he turned off his phone at Cleator Moor it would have taken him about twenty-five minutes to reach the limit of the Ennerdale access road. That leaves only twenty minutes at his destination.'

Skelgill turns away and drifts to the window. His colleagues' exhilaration is palpable, which perhaps causes him to retrench. His instincts warn him not to get carried away – that most mountaineers that fall do so in the euphoria of descent – when victory is thought to be secured and caution is thrown to the wind. The mountain is not yet conquered.

Outside it is dark; there is just the inadequate glow of streetlights. What appear to be DS Leyton's children are playing a game of tig-bob-down. A dog walker passes them along the pavement; the young canine looks like it would wish to join in. In windows opposite lights are coming on. Ennerdale has finished and its adherents are getting up to make themselves a mash, or visit the bathroom, or put the kids to bed. The wheels of suburban domesticity slowly turning. But Skelgill is thinking about the wheels of justice. They rotate even more slowly – the standard interval for an arraignment is two months – and in two weeks Ray Piper will board a plane to China.

'We'd better go up in the morning, first thing.'

'Into Ennerdale, Guv?'

The query is from DS Jones. He turns to face her.

'Aye. If it's alright with you.'

'What do you mean, Guv?'

'It's your case, sergeant.'

'It's your back yard, Guv.'

Skelgill grins wryly.

'We'll split the difference.'

Now DS Leyton has a question.

'What time do you reckon it gets light, Guv?'

'Ten to eight – a bit earlier if it's clear.'

It does not surprise Skelgill's colleagues that he gives such a precise answer. But DS Jones raises a caveat.

'Guv – I think I should go first to Cumbria Television. To secure the footage – and to check the outtakes in case they also filmed the BMW heading up into the dale. It would give us an even more accurate fix on how long he stopped for.'

Skelgill nods.

'Why don't I meet you pair at ten-thirty? Bowness Knott car park.'

This seems to gain agreement, though Skelgill notices that DS Leyton appears to be distracted by some thought.

'Haven't you forgotten something, Leyton?'

'What's that, Guv?'

Skelgill reaches for his unfinished beer and casually swings the bottle in the direction of the television set.

'Better get your missus down here for your starring role. Handy, that freeze live TV business.'

17. IRON CRAG

Tuesday, 7:30 a.m.

This morning Skelgill is doubly hungry, perhaps even triply. His surprise appearance at his mother's cottage – she complaining of being given no warning, but he knew secretly chuffed – has seen him furnished with bacon and hot tomato in fried bread, which is burning a hole in his army surplus rucksack. That would be the triply. The doubly is that he has since climbed Red Pike in the dark, clambering swiftly beside the foaming luminescent rush that is Sourmilk Gill; thence ascending from a silent Bleaberry Tarn via the little col known as The Saddle. That he has set out to his rendezvous from what is ostensibly the 'wrong' valley can be understood when it is appreciated that a mere mile as the crow flies separates it from 'right' valley, albeit there is a two-thousand-foot ridge in between. Once dawn breaks he will be able to survey the whole of Ennerdale. Meanwhile there are the bacon butties.

At the cairn he lingers for a moment. Red Pike is known for its view that encompasses five lakes, but these still slumber beneath the autumn twilight, its blanket not yet lifted from the dales. The wind at his back, a moderate northeasterly, four on the Beaufort scale is blowing at a fresh five over the ridge, enough to prompt him to descend thirty feet to a crag; in its lee it is uncannily calm. Sheep have worn the niche clean of vegetation, and he feels for a ledge as a seat.

He pulls down around his neck the bandana he has been wearing as an improvised sweatband. He unpacks his rucksack and puts the empty bag back on as a cushion against the cold stone. For the purposes of navigation he is armed with maps, guide, compass, binoculars, and torch – but first things first. For Skelgill, there is nothing to beat comfort food eaten in uncomfortable conditions. Methodically, he begins to work his way through his slightly soggy feast. The foil-wrapped breakfast has cooled, but he has scalding tea from his flask. Settled in the shadow of the cliff, he sinks into a contemplative mode.

He did not sleep soundly. Sure, they have a potential breakthrough here, but the opportunity is still tenuous – a quality that perhaps informed last night's tangled dream, which revisits him in fragments. He had become separated from DS Jones; it was a world of darkness and inferno, a Dickensian dystopia of black skies and roaring red furnaces and the deafening clang and hiss of steam hammers, and swarming everywhere small mute men, red ochre statues brought to life, if this were an existence.

And now his mind and circumstances seem to merge. Low in the east a pale sliver of sky begins to turn creamy orange; immediately the ribbed underbelly of the cloud becomes defined in pink highlights. Overhead, a mackerel pattern takes form, zigzags of grey with between them sea-blue hints as the sun's rays scatter from the upper atmosphere. Now the sky seems to be catching fire – as if the toothed horizon comprises factories with flaring chimneys and foundries with their kilns blazing out of control – and great tongues of flame radiate westwards to set the firmament alight.

But the fiery dawn is fleeting. The sun shifts above the narrow window of the horizon and the sheet of cloud denies its orange rays; instead the dale becomes filled with monochromatic smoky blue light. Skelgill watches patiently; the vista before him slowly acquires definition and colour. Across to his right lies the pale mercury of Ennerdale Water; flanking the lake the great wild pine forest extends up into the dale out of sight in brushstrokes of deep evergreen. At the head of Ennerdale Water is the glacial outwash plain, fertile pasture and the location of Gillerthwaite farm – or at least its in-bye land where yowes are gathered to lamb and lambs to fatten; on the high fellsides opposite, above the forest stretches the ancient heaf where the hardy Herdwick sheep otherwise roam free. He spies a tiny figure picking its way across a scree; smaller dots, dark cur dogs and paler sheep, move ahead of it.

DS Jones had explored every metaphorical avenue as far as Ray Piper's possible movements were concerned. That he drove

251

only a *short* distance and stopped for a *long* time, possibly trekking overland to find a place of concealment. That he headed westwards to the vast uninhabited Solway coast, to some lonely saltmarsh. That he went east into the old iron fields and circled to throw them off his scent. The latter was the favoured theory, bolstered by the evidence of the red ochre residue, and suspicion that his knowledge had come into play.

Instead, he came here.

Spread before Skelgill, the rewilded valley seems an obvious place now. Motorists are prohibited, trippers are discouraged, and even keen walkers are deterred by the sheer inaccessibility of the dale. But, for the driver prepared to ignore the 'no entry' signs after Bowness Knott, there exists a two-mile stretch of thickly wooded lane before the forest gate; a no-through-road that by definition carries almost no traffic.

Because – and Skelgill finds he is nodding – when you are about to commit a crime, the golden rule is *not to be seen.*

Piper made sure he was not seen when he committed his first crime, of murder in the secluded stairwell – and so he applied that same rule when it came to committing his second and third crimes: perverting the course of justice, and preventing lawful and decent burial. Working in his favour was that it was a Saturday, when foresters and conservationists would be off duty; only the isolated farm might be a source of watchful eyes – but, going by what Skelgill knows of DS Leyton's account, the farmer is not exactly the most vigilant of landowners.

So Piper had used the majority of his available time to travel by obscure back-roads. He left himself only twenty minutes to dispose of the body of Lisa Jackson.

Twenty minutes has been plenty long enough for Skelgill to enjoy his breakfast – but twenty minutes is not long enough to dig a grave; not in fell country, where the shallow peaty earth is riddled with rocks that defy the blade of a shovel from the very first blow.

Another modus operandi is required. Skelgill, if not expressly, has concurred with DS Jones's calculation that Piper drove close to the point of concealment. There is good reason

252

for this logic. Though it is not unknown, few killers carry a body far – not least because it is physically challenging. And it comes back to not being seen. In town the bearer of a large, heavy suitcase, or perhaps a rolled up carpet might not look out of place, but no such anonymity exists in the country.

Skelgill's attention is drawn by the mew of a buzzard. He takes up his binoculars in time to see the raptor dodge the dive of a raven; a minor dogfight ensues, with each bird giving as good as it gets. That said he would back the buzzard in a clinch. It would be like a tiger taking on a grizzly. The bear might be big but it would be outgunned by tooth and claw. The raven veers away across the dale, croaking to a partner that answers from the region of Caw Fell. The buzzard dips lower, below him now, and Skelgill marvels at its ability to quarter the terrain with imperceptible adjustments of its wingtips, the ultimate surveillance drone, manoeuvrable, battery-free, and laser-eyed.

He loses its trajectory against the brindled backdrop but in his line of sight Gillerthwaite farm is suddenly lit by a shaft of sunshine that breaks through the shifting bands of cloud. He notices, rather to his surprise, a car – a small dark hatchback – slowly making its way along the unmade track that leads to the farmstead from the valley road. At this distance the whole scene looks like a child's model. He scans on, beyond the farm, and sees that a spur of the track continues across the flank of Caw Fell. It is not wheel-rutted, but the sun creates a highlight that shows it to be banked on its lower side, an engineered earthwork that has fallen out of use. He follows its line as it traverses, slowly rises, and curves around into the gill that divides Caw Fell from the adjacent Haycock. Half of the ravine is in shadow but its east-facing side is sunlit – and a striking red-brown patch amongst the tumbled rocks and surrounding heather and mat grass attracts Skelgill's eye.

He steadies the binoculars by resting his elbows on his knees. These are inherited 'field glasses' that survived the German shells. Their cloudy lenses and misaligned prisms present challenges in definition, but he persists with them out of a sense duty, like wearing a poppy. The sunlight wanes, but with

253

concerted squinting he discerns that the patch is bracken. As he had pointed out to his colleagues, what proliferates in July as a thrusting green thicket in October becomes a tumbled, collapsing mass of autumn russet.

But as the sun waxes once more, he realises something is not quite as it should be. There is russet, and then there is – well, *red*. It can only be that the earth beneath, showing through the dying vegetation and now illuminated, is unnaturally bright.

Skelgill lowers his binoculars and for a few moments sits motionless, unblinking, unseeing. Earlier, pulling maps from the glove compartment of his shooting brake he had selected alongside the modern Ordnance Survey another precious heirloom, a Victorian Bartholomew cloth map of Cumberland only recently bequeathed by his late great uncle Ernie Graham. Now he unfolds this map; it is diminutive by today's standards; twenty-two inches by twenty-nine, it rests easily across his thighs. But it is a veritable encyclopaedia; in its minutiae there is an untold epic of the bygone county, rich pickings for the inquisitive geographer and historian alike.

Employing the integrated magnifier on his compass he pores over the map, Sherlock Holmes fashion. His focus alights on Frizington and Cleator Moor, the old mining district eight miles to the west of his present position. He is immediately struck by just how intensively the area was worked. The legend *"Iron Mine"* seems to fill every vacant space between other landmarks – a good dozen sites linked by a web of railways unimaginable in this day and age. Of course, he knows this, to the extent they have investigated the residual landscape – but the old map paints the image of an industrial termite field, stained red with the masticated dust of iron ore.

Slowly he shifts his sights in an easterly direction across the canvas. He finds Red Pike, the spot height *2479* (correct). He is reminded that this is the map that exposed the extraordinary conundrum of Haystacks (another story, on which he does not dwell) – but the point being that the names of fells evolve; they are at the mercy of whichever shepherd the surveyor asked at the time, and perhaps what remained in the shepherd's hip flask that day.

And now this little premonition comes to fruition. He cannot find Caw Fell. Instead, the peak opposite is described as Iron Crag. But there is no Iron Crag. Yet it is designated as a summit – it has its own spot height, *2071*.

Skelgill's pulse rate has long recovered from his lung-bursting yomp up from Buttermere; now it quickens. His intuition is kicking into gear.

He scrutinises the map more closely. He sees that the stream that runs down the gill separating so-called Iron Crag and Haycock is labelled as Ironcove Beck.

His heart feels like it is beginning to creep up inside his chest.

He sets aside the Victorian Bartholomew and reaches for the present-day Ordnance Survey. For once in his haste he handles it clumsily, and cusses at the sound of a tear as he draws it out concertina style. Here is the relief of the larger scale, the text that does not require magnification to read.

Caw Fell – yes. Iron Crag – no – but – *wait*. He realises that, printed at right angles next to the markings for exposed rocks above the gill, almost unnoticeable as it blends with the contour lines, is indeed the description *"Iron Crag"* – no longer a designated summit, but an outcrop.

Absent from the old map, but present on the new, tucked into the gill, is the legend, *"Level (dis)"*.

His heart makes its final leap into his mouth.

Skelgill awkwardly reaches around to extract his mobile phone from the side pocket of his backpack. He summons up DS Jones's number. She answers promptly.

'You driving?'

She laughs.

'Morning, Guv – no, I'm being chauffeured.'

'Alright, Guvnor!' DS Leyton's voice booms in the background – DS Jones must have answered on speaker. 'Couldn't miss out on a butcher's behind the scenes.'

DS Jones explains.

255

'We're heading for the studios now – we should be back at Bowness Knott in good time. Where are you, Guv?'

'Ennerdale.' Skelgill suddenly sounds a little defensive – as if he is reminded of the fact that DS Jones is still technically in charge of the investigation. 'Killed two birds with one stone. Had to drop in at me Ma's. I've legged it over the ridge. Got here a bit early. Thought I'd do a bit of a recce – save time.'

Nothing of this nature any longer surprises his colleagues – although there is a short hiatus in which they no doubt exchange knowing glances – that Skelgill cannot help himself. But now he does not hang around.

'Piper, remind me – what was that stuff about him – his CV?'

'Oh – ' DS Jones sounds unprepared. 'You mean his bio on the company website?'

'Aye – whatever.'

'They've deleted it, Guv.' But she quickly continues, knowing this is not the answer Skelgill needs. 'But I took a screenshot. Hold on – I can log on to my case file, signal permitting. Obviously there were the details of his qualifications – the master's degree in Industrial Heritage and Archaeology.'

'There was something else.' Skelgill's voice comes over as harsh.

A silence ensues while DS Jones gets to work. DS Leyton plugs the gap.

'The nippers are over the moon about sailing on your boat, Guv. You were talk of the breakfast table. Knocked me clean off the front page. You'd never have guessed their old man was on telly last night!'

Skelgill grunts, perhaps a vague apology. He is impatient for DS Jones's response. She is ready.

'Here it is, Guv. Ah – did you mean his interests? It says, his boys' football, art house films and – cartography.'

Her delay in uttering the final word suggests that a penny has dropped.

'Did we find any maps when we searched his place?'

'No, Guv. There were a lot of DVDs – the indie films. But no maps that I recall.'

256

'We found a fire in his garden.'

DS Jones hesitates – though she is merely reviewing her memory of the forensic report.

'The ashes suggested papers and possibly some garden clippings. Remember – it was his explanation for what he did with the rose bush.'

Skelgill does not reply immediately.

'Happen you'd own a map or two if you listed cartography among your interests.'

'I suppose so, Guv.' DS Jones sounds tentative. But she steels herself and asserts her nominal authority. 'Is there something I should know?'

'What?' Skelgill, not quite ready to share thoughts that are still undeciphered feelings, reverts to type. 'Look – I'll see you pair at ten-thirty. I'll have half a clue then.'

Abruptly he ends the call and leans back against the rock face. He needs no more confirmation of what he has felt all along – that Ray Piper is too calculating a man to have left this part of his plan to chance. In his 'emergency' he would have fallen back on his skillset. Skelgill has more than half a clue.

Iron Crag. Ironcove Beck. Red earth.

Level (dis).

An iron mine. Close to a track. In Ennerdale.

Skelgill is on his feet and packing his rucksack as fast as the care it takes to fold his precious maps allows.

Bag on, he stands for a moment to assess the terrain. There is a direct path down into Ennerdale from Red Pike, albeit on slightly the wrong bearing. But he considers it will be the fastest route and, unlike cutting through dense forest, offers no risk of a poke in the eye from a bare twig. The path joins the valley road; thence it will be quickest to take the farm track.

This is a run he has done many times, though not so recently, and he is judicious in watching his step, wary of gravity and attuned to his adage of the descent always being more dangerous than the ascent.

About halfway down he hears a text message come in on his mobile; he can check it when he's on the flat – or at least the

257

gentle incline. But by the time he is jogging steadily along the smooth tarmac of the lane he has forgotten about it – and new distractions are coming upon him. Turning onto the track to Gillerthwaite farm he realises the benefit he obtained earlier, viewing the area from Red Pike. Here in the valley bottom his line of sight is largely obscured by high stone walls and uneven hawthorn hedges, and that the track itself is sunken to a degree.

However he gets a glimpse of the habitation when he reaches the point where the walls end at a cattle grid. Here the main track takes a sharp left to the farmstead and the elevated spur continues more or less ahead over open ground. The buildings themselves are partially obscured from this angle by a rather incongruous shelterbelt of Leyland cypress. There is no sign of human activity. No dogs bark at his passing. He speculates as to whom he saw driving the car – of which there is also no sign, but it may be parked between buildings. Equally it could have been driven away; he would not have seen it as his path descended through the trees; perhaps someone delivering a parcel or a neighbour dropping off fresh eggs or milk.

The unused branch of the track now begins to swing around beyond the farm and pick up the rising ground, the lower slopes of Caw Fell. As he noted through his binoculars, it is unworn on its surface but nevertheless distinctive as a manmade roadway. He can think of plenty of similar tracks; they are a common feature around abandoned workings – there had to be a means to shift the mined ore or slate for processing. Nowadays, such green lanes are sought after by off-road enthusiasts in their 4x4s; this one is simply too obscure in its location – and besides it offers no through route of practical interest.

Hogg lambs cavort in the rough pasture around him, occasionally head butting and trying out their strength; then stopping to bleat uneasily for their mothers; but these lambs are weaned, and the yowes have returned to the heaf.

The route leads gently around the northern flank of Caw Fell. As yet there is no real view of the gill, unlike from Skelgill's eyrie on Red Pike. As if it is his winged sentinel, however, the buzzard comes low from that direction, mewing its shepherd's warning.

The wind has dropped; the weather seems to be changing; mist is forming in strands at different levels, some now settling below him as he gains altitude, some strung across the tops, wraiths that reveal layers of cold air as the watery autumn sun breaks through from time to time.

From lower down on his left the gush of running water now reaches him. It is not a stream of any eminence, one of countless innominate watercourses that drain the uplands, over millennia scraping out their gills and thus shaping the post-glacial ridges into processions of distinct peaks. Yet it was once known as Ironcove Beck, and names are for good reason. His view of the little torrent improves now, as the trackway curves into the gill proper, with the terrain rising steeply on both sides. Accordingly, Skelgill's goal heaves into sight.

Abruptly, he ducks down.

But it is not the unexplained red-brown patch that alarms him.

Backed into the fell, perpendicular to him, up to its sills in the decaying bracken is the car – the small dark hatchback he spied from Red Pike.

He drops to his knees and shrugs off his pack. He digs out his binoculars.

And now he recognises it.

Irene Piper's rust-spangled dark blue Ford Fiesta.

Skelgill's first reaction is to take cover – but there is no cover – lying prone would be his only option, and ineffectual. And too little too late – he has already walked into full view – he was contemplating the beck and not looking ahead.

However, the car appears to be empty.

He begins to approach as stealthily as his fieldcraft allows.

He reaches the vehicle and cautiously rounds it.

There is no one.

He pauses to take stock. Beneath the wheels and extending all around, where the earth is exposed it is red and has a tacky quality, reminiscent of the environs of Florence Mine. Immediately it strikes Skelgill that it would be impossible to walk

259

about here without picking up residue on one's footwear. He sees that already the tyres of the car have such a coating.

The site marks the terminus of the mountain roadway – and the explanation for this is cut into the steep rock face: the disused level, the tunnel that enters the hillside. It is the iron mine, the overlooked long-abandoned outlier.

A Stonehenge-like portico – two unevenly hewn jambs topped by a massive lintel – is guarded by a corroded iron gate that has its rack and pinion mechanism on the right-hand side.

Despite that the whole arrangement must surely be ceased up, Skelgill's mind is only briefly diverted by such a question – for it is rendered academic by the fact that the gate is raised like a sluice some two feet from the ground.

His heart is racing again – well above the requirement of the gradient hitherto – his instincts are urging him on. But he reins himself back. Remember – mountain rescue protocol: when you find the casualty, first check for danger.

He can see no recent trace of disturbance around the mouth of the tunnel – although the ground is unforgiving. He casts about more widely. Could someone be watching him? The gill is too steep-sided to afford many hiding places, and the heather and mat grass too short for easy concealment. Higher up there is a clump of gnarled rowans, all but leafless now – nothing there.

Besides – whoever came would surely not suspect they were being followed.

Has the person simply done the more obvious thing – that Skelgill would ordinarily assume in finding a vehicle left like this – that they have driven to this farthest point accessible by car, and continued on foot, up the gill and out of sight over the col between Caw Fell and Haycock? He forces himself to think – the car drove along the track just as he left the summit of Red Pike. Another five minutes and it would have been here. It has taken him the best part of twenty minutes to arrive. If they had gone up the fell, they would surely be out of sight.

There are other permutations – but his gut feel wants no truck with prevarication and he leaps off this growing bandwagon of excuses.

260

He extracts his torch and, while he refastens the straps of his rucksack, grips the milled aluminium tube between his teeth, disliking the sensation. Close to the mine entrance stands a clump of bracken that is still relatively intact. He thrusts the pack into the tumble of fronds and claws up a couple of handfuls of decaying matter from nearby to conceal it completely.

He turns his attention to the iron door. It does look rusted in position – but he takes no chances. He selects from among the boulders that have tumbled down the scree one that is slightly smaller than the opening. It is too weighty to lift but he is able to slide it like a curling stone beneath the base of the corroded gate. It is probably an unnecessary insurance policy, and he flinches at the telltale scrape it produces at his final heave.

He drops to his hands and knees and peers into the tunnel. He is conscious he will be silhouetted in the horizontal band of light. He listens, but there is nothing. Drips are the commonest sound in caves – but the first impression is of dryness. The air lacks the dankness he associates with such places – but neither is there the welcome cool draught that signals natural ventilation. He takes a deep breath; he will have to be his own canary. He crawls beneath the heavy metal plate.

Once clear, he rises cautiously, hands above his head, feeling for the ceiling – it is low – six-and-a-half feet and crumbly in texture – particles fall upon him at his touch.

Now he waits for his eyes to adjust to the darkness; he breathes silently through gritted teeth.

He gives it a good five minutes – but he realises that if he is to explore further – indeed *see* further – he is going to need his torch. The light from the slit of the doorway is diffuse and usefully penetrates only a few yards, absorbed and not reflected it seems by the nature of the rocks. But there has been no sound, and he switches on the flashlight.

The sudden contrast is almost shocking. The chimney blackness is vanquished, instantly to be replaced by the preternatural hue of deep red ochre – all around, floor, ceiling, walls – everywhere – even the iron rails that run away from him and the wooden sleepers upon which they rest are stained by the

261

red dust of hematite; the rock has its characteristic pattern of swirls and bulges and concavities like alveoli of the lungs, where irregular masses of ore have been excavated, *sops* as he heard them called by his Egremont uncles.

The level belies its name, for it rises steadily into the mountainside, penetrating deeper into Iron Crag. This gradient would make sense – gravity employed both to draw the loaded bogies and drain deadly carbon dioxide from the mine. He begins to advance slowly between the rails, stepping from one sleeper to the next, checking the ground immediately ahead before proceeding in stages. He cannot discern how far the tunnel extends – it is not dead straight, and there are bulges in the walls and heaps of debris. As they dug deeper the miners increasingly employed pit props – many are still in place and appear to have stood the test of time – perhaps the dry conditions have preserved them from rot; others lie discarded or sticking out of rubble heaps where small collapses have occurred.

He reaches a distinct side chamber. It is deeper than what thus far have been alcoves. To check it he has to step inside, off the main tunnel. It has a low entrance with a wooden lintel cut into the rock. He ducks and enters. But the space is empty. Though the ceiling rises to about ten feet, and here the ore excels in its artistic whorls and clumps of solidified bubbles and crystalline extrusions that scatter his torch beam in the manner of a disco glitter ball. For a moment he is awed like a visitor to a gallery or museum of natural history.

Then a rude awakening – a sharp noise from the passage.

A pebble – kicked? It skitters before coming to a ringing stop against the iron of a rail.

He freezes.

His impression – though he can't be sure – is that it came from deeper rather than from the mouth of the tunnel.

He listens. He contemplates switching off the torch – but decides against it, and instead adjusts the focus for distance.

He steps out decisively and directs the beam along the passageway.

But there is nothing.

262

He checks the other way, towards the entrance – again, nothing.

All looks the same – the red ochre walls; the uneven heaps; the shadows of the carved niches.

He reflects that the stone could simply have fallen of its own accord.

But he does not want to take that chance.

He has no choice but to use his torch, despite that he feels it puts him at a disadvantage – it reveals his every move.

He switches it into defensive strobe mode, which at least makes the bulb impossible to look at.

He moves forward, checking carefully the alcoves, paying less heed now to covertness.

As he advances deeper the tunnel feels like it is constricting, the hair on top of his head occasionally brushes the ceiling. The walls seem to be closing in.

He stops every few paces to listen – but silence prevails.

Adrenaline has carried him this far – indeed all the way from his putting two and two together perched high on Red Pike – and he has not feared what might lie ahead – at worst it is one man, and he has the measure of him and the guardian angels of vengeance on his side. He has not thought about arming himself in some way. Besides, nothing has come to hand. There are pit props but these are mostly too-massive logs – and there is no room in the tunnel to wield such a weapon. But now, out of habit ingrained in his youth, he stoops and feels for a stone. The fingers of his left hand close upon a rock the size of a cricket ball – though it is many times the heft, and it reminds him of the unnaturally heavy fragment that he gave to DS Jones that she keeps on her desk as a paperweight and cheerleader.

As he is crouched his torch beam reveals a second side-chamber, its entrance even lower than the former. Its mouth is partially blocked by fallen rubble, and the pit prop that holds up the tilted lintel looks unstable. But his torch beam reveals something more.

Something that prompts a sharp intake of breath.

263

Something that is the most significant sight since the disappearance of Lisa Jackson.

Through the opening, against the far wall, is an item he has only previously seen in a couple of fleeting video clips: unmistakably, it has the two blinking yellow eyes of a cat.

It is something he cannot pass by.

Before he knows it, Skelgill, torch between his teeth is slithering through the gap.

He has to go hands first, arms outstretched, like a diver entering the water, driving with his hips and knees and feet.

He tumbles into what is a small cave – and freezes – *for behind him in the passage there is a sudden rush of movement.*

In an instant he realises his miscalculation.

To attempt to exit would be like putting his head on the block.

Still squatting, he rocks back on his heels and directs the beam of his torch into the opening.

There are lower legs clad in black jeans. There are brown brogues with red residue around the edges of their thick leather soles. There is a pair of hands that come down and their long fingers wrap around the precarious pit prop and pull it away.

The lintel collapses; there is a tumultuous crash of debris.

A cloud of ochre dust billows at Skelgill, like the angry ghost of a lost Redman, buried by negligence and now bent on retribution. Skelgill pulls up his bandana to cover his mouth and nose. As the dust settles he sees that the landslide has taken the shape of a conical scree – and where it meets the still-intact curve of the low ceiling there is an aperture, about the size of a fist.

He approaches, wary of further collapse – but need prompts him to scale the heap and direct his torch beam into the cavity. It seems to penetrate through – instinctively he switches it off and puts his face close to the opening. He holds his breath and listens.

Undoubtedly there are footsteps – someone shambling over the sleepers, making off.

There is the very faintest flickering, perhaps torchlight diminishing.

Then sounds reach Skelgill that send a chill down his spine.

First – a rocky scraping. Then – a metallic creaking – *a crash* – and any residual light is snuffed out.

The iron gate has been dropped.

Skelgill clings to the spoil heap. He curses himself for not checking the remainder of the mine – the lure of the side-chamber was too strong, but it could have waited.

He knows he must think clearly under pressure.

He has no water. There may be limited air. And there is the risk of a further rockfall.

His torch is high powered, but at the cost of eating a set of new batteries in an hour.

He stands, gathering his wits

He tries to control his heartbeat, his breathing – but the air feels thin – his vital signs do not seem to want to come to heel. He inhales deeply through his nose – and suddenly he becomes aware of a faint but distinctive odour. Musk.

He turns and switches back on his torch.

He realises he is not alone.

Though he alone is alive.

18. CAKE, AND EATING IT

Tuesday, 9:00 a.m. – Gillerthwaite Farm

'Here we are, girl – Ennerdale cake farm.'

DS Jones chuckles.

Her colleague swings the car off the narrow valley road at a tilted, flaked and faded sign that might once have read "Gillerthwaite Farm" – although now it requires local knowledge to translate what looks to DS Jones rather more like "I'll wait".

'It's certainly the back of beyond.'

DS Leyton makes a grunt of agreement as he negotiates a particularly tricky sequence of potholes.

'One old lady and her dogs in the entire upper valley – no wonder Piper never was seen. He was probably in and out like a rat up and down a drainpipe.'

DS Jones nods pensively but does not reply. Since last evening's soap opera the revelation has preyed on her mind in an unaccountable manner; Skelgill was not the only one of the trio to have endured nightmares. In her case it was a disturbing pursuit of a fleeing Ray Piper through a vast crowded airport, where she continually took wrong turns and found herself in blind alleys, and was frustrated by one unhelpful jobsworth official after another. Finally she had reached a boarding gate that was closed and through the windows she saw the aircraft was taxiing away; in the far corner of the deserted lounge sat an elderly couple, patiently, holding hands; Lisa Jackson's parents in limbo.

She realises she is looking at the contrail of an airliner that crosses a clear patch of blue above the horizon – when her gaze is drawn by a movement on the lower fellside.

'There's a car coming.'

'You what, girl?'

'Look.' She points ahead, a little to the left.

Heading their way, at some speed, pitching and rolling, well beyond the limitations of the surface and the capabilities of the vehicle, a small dark-blue hatchback is crossing an open pasture, scattering sheep before it, following the raised line of a low embankment which will bring it directly to meet them.

'He'll have to wait for us.'

DS Leyton refers to their narrow passage, single-track and walled-in as far as the cattle grid.

DS Jones's voice takes on a strained note.

'I think I recognise the car.'

Her colleague is more matter-of-fact.

'It's a Mark 5 Fiesta.'

But before they can exchange further speculation DS Leyton seems to sense that something about the situation is queer and brings them to an abrupt halt

He would be right. As the Ford approaches the junction – still some fifty yards off – a dishevelled, angular figure darts from around the bend that leads to the farmstead. Wearing a tattered overcoat and with unkempt grey hair flapping, shaking a fist and mouthing what can only be obscenities, is a woman.

'That's her – the landowner.'

DS Jones does not recognise Mrs Gillerthwaite, but she understands. And she is agog – not least because the agitated farmer brandishes a shotgun. The woman plants herself in the path of the oncoming vehicle. Three mottled sheepdogs mill about her.

But the Ford Fiesta keeps coming. The woman levels the gun – but at the last moment in this bizarre game of chicken she jumps with surprising alacrity out of the way.

Now the car accelerates towards the stationary detectives – perhaps the driver has not seen them or assessed the situation – but the impending head-on collision is averted by an even more dramatic moment – the woman takes aim at the car and shoots out a rear tyre and it slews and crashes instead into the wall.

Immediately, a figure leaps from the driver's side and scrambles over the wall.

'Struth – that's Piper!'

267

DS Jones is transfixed by the unfolding spectacle – but now her colleague's words break the spell. She rips off her seatbelt and tumbles from the car.

'Emma – what're you doing, girl?'

But she pays no heed. She vaults the wall, barely touching the coping stones. She lands on all fours on the soft turf of the paddock and springs up like a sprinter exploding from the blocks.

From behind, now she hears her colleague's exhortation.

'Mrs Gillerthwaite – police! Remember me – DS Leyton? Don't shoot! Leave it to us!'

Ray Piper has a lead of some thirty yards. A reasonably fit man and in decent shape – but he runs stiffly and is no match for the athleticism of the young female detective. She skims the cropped grass with the grace of a gazelle.

That said, the dogs canter past her – they seem to have some idea of what might be their role. But while a trained police dog would bring its human quarry down – their method is to interfere by snapping at the fugitive's heels in the way they would discipline a miscreant yowe.

It takes maybe thirty seconds for DS Jones to catch up.

She does not command him to stop – she is using every ounce of her oxygen to run.

He may be unaware of her presence – but he knows it when she brings him crashing to earth with a perfect rugby tackle, hitting the back of his thighs with her shoulder and sliding down to wrap his ankles.

Ray Piper is stunned by his fall. His torpor gives DS Jones a false sense of ascendency.

She scrambles to hold him down and prise an arm around his back.

But while she holds the advantage in fleetness of foot he has seventy pounds on her.

He makes a violent heave and flips her over.

The tables are turned.

Suddenly he is above her and his powerful hands are pushing her down, closing upon her throat.

268

She tries to throw him off with her hips but he is too heavy.

She tries to prise away the hands but he is too strong.

She tries to yell but nothing comes out.

Her throat is being compressed and she cannot breathe.

She is reliving Lisa's last moments.

What Lisa felt and saw.

Ray Piper's wax mask is implacable.

His cold grey eyes convey pure evil.

And then comes a sudden blur.

It is accompanied by a sharp thwack.

She feels no pain.

Her eyes refocus.

Ray Piper's nose has changed shape.

It is spread across his face and spouting blood.

His eyes are still unblinking but now unseeing.

His grip slackens.

He falls away from her sight.

She breathes, in and out in great sobs – but the urge for self-preservation is strong – she rolls over and struggles to her feet, raising her fists, prepared to fight for her life.

But Ray Piper is lying on his back, motionless.

Standing over him, DS Leyton is casually inspecting the knuckles of his right hand.

She sees a trickle of fresh blood.

He steps across and takes hold of her by the shoulders.

'You alright, girl?'

She raises spread fingers to her throat. Gingerly she feels for damage. She nods.

'I'll be fine – thanks. *Thanks.*'

Her heartfelt tone brings a flush of pink to her colleague's cheeks.

'You were a bit too quick off the mark – I never was much of a sprinter.'

She sighs heavily.

'You got here when I needed you.'

'Teamwork, eh, girl?'

She nods, swallowing her tears.

DS Leyton indicates the prone figure.

'While he's still spark out – why don't you nip and get some cuffs from the car? Call for back up.'

DS Jones hesitates, unsure if she should leave her colleague. But she sees his attention is drawn by something behind her. Hobbling across the field and being circled by her dogs is Mrs Gillerthwaite and her shotgun. DS Leyton grins.

'Don't worry – he ain't going nowhere.'

DS Jones nods.

'I'll be one minute.'

*

'It's ringing out, okay – as though he's got a signal – but he's still not answering.'

DS Jones glares in exasperation at the display.

DS Leyton, too, has just ended a call.

'The PC stationed at Bowness Knott says he's still a no-show.' He reads the time from his screen. 'That's it past eleven – it's not like the Guvnor.'

They both stand and gaze about them, a little helplessly, unseeing of the natural beauty of what is the remotest, wildest and least inhabited valley in the Lakes – in which surely somewhere Skelgill is at large.

After a while DS Jones speaks.

'We could try Ray Piper again. If only we knew what he had been up to.'

But her tone is not hopeful. Ray Piper is under guard in an ambulance parked just short of where the crashed Ford Fiesta blocks the track. Having recovered consciousness – but probably not from the concussion – he has refused to speak from beneath the dressings that swathe his head.

DS Leyton glances at his own bandaged hand.

'Pity we didn't have a bit longer before the cavalry arrived.'

DS Jones raises her eyebrows – but there is a part of her that concurs – Piper may be withholding something that concerns their superior.

270

DS Leyton surveys the rising fells; but it is not a landscape he can read.

'I reckon the Guvnor was onto something.'

'I don't doubt it.'

DS Jones is deeply preoccupied. As if she needed reminding, her shocking experience has highlighted what a dangerous man Ray Piper is – a concern now transferred to the wellbeing of Skelgill. But her mind is clearing. She raises her mobile phone and searches for a number.

'I'm going to call Irene Piper.'

DS Leyton gives a kind of nod-come-shrug, as if it is not the worst thing she can do – though perhaps it will be futile. He takes a polite step back and observes. The call is answered promptly.

'Mrs Piper – good morning, it's DS Jones, Cumbria CID.'

There is a pause before DS Jones responds.

'Well – not exactly alright. I have to inform you that your husband has been rearrested in connection with the disappearance of Lisa Jackson.' There may be a further reaction but DS Jones continues quickly. 'I don't have much time right now. I need to ask you – where did Mr Piper say he was going this morning?'

Now DS Jones listens intently, a perplexed crease wrinkling her brow. After a few moments she interrupts.

'I thought he had a new job – in – '

She checks herself and waits while the other party speaks.

'Okay – I understand. Thank you for your cooperation. Someone will be in touch to give you more information in due course.'

DS Jones ends the call and stares reflectively at the handset. Then she looks up sharply at her colleague.

'She sounded relieved.'

'About the arrest?'

'Aha.'

DS Leyton again shrugs, this time with less ambiguity.

'I don't reckon you're surprised by that, Emma.'

She regards him earnestly.

'She said this morning he told her he was going for a job interview at Sellafield – at the nuclear plant. You heard – I didn't ask her directly – but I don't think she knows about the job in China.'

'Maybe he's been planning a flit without her?'

DS Jones nods, but it is plain her thoughts are beginning to gather pace.

'It sounds to me like an excuse to travel in this direction – the coast road south from Egremont passes Sellafield.'

DS Leyton offers a more pragmatic contribution.

'Let's have a butcher's at the motor before SOCO seal it off.'

They pass the two squad cars that have arrived and squeeze past the ambulance with a nod to the male and female constables who stand sentry; the uniformed PCs nod admiringly – but DS Jones is not yet feeling worthy of any accolade. Not least that Skelgill is unaccounted for – but also that Ray Piper's close presence reminds her he has already once trumped justice.

They pull on nitrile gloves as they approach the Ford Fiesta. It is a two-door hatchback. DS Jones takes the passenger side and checks the glove compartment. Her colleague tries the tailgate, but it has no external catch.

DS Jones can see the ignition switch.

'There are no keys – perhaps he took them and dropped them when he ran.'

DS Leyton rounds to the driver side and hauls open the door. With a groan he bends double to locate the boot release catch.

'Emma – look at this!'

She quickly joins him. He steps away and indicates with his bandaged hand.

'*Ah.*'

The monosyllable is not merely an expression of surprise, but evocative of a long-held belief vindicated.

The black rubber floor mat in the driver's footwell is heavily marked with fresh smears of soil – red-ochre soil. DS Jones cannot resist touching one of the streaks. She rubs the residue between the tips of her forefinger and thumb, and nods as if the sensation offers further confirmation.

'He's been there.'

'But where's *there?*'

DS Jones suddenly stiffens. Indeed, for a moment she is unmoving, as if unwilling to admit into their conversation the thought that has occurred to her. Then she relents.

'We'd better look in the back.'

Again her tone is revealing – and DS Leyton seems to understand her meaning. He shoots her a glance of foreboding. Now he reaches in and feels around beneath the steering wheel. He pulls at something and they hear the clunk of the rear door as it springs free of its catch.

They approach the rear of the car in a resolute manner. Purposefully, DS Leyton raises the tailgate.

But the luggage compartment is empty – that is, empty at least of the worst they feared to find. But there are four items: a roll of grey dustbin liners – unused – the label still wrapped around, it states "extra large"; a reel of black Duck tape; a can of WD40; and a galvanised steel L-shaped bar that looks to DS Jones like some kind of starting handle.

'That's a lock keeper's key handle windlass.'

DS Jones looks at her colleague with astonishment – that he seems so sure of his description.

'Last Easter – I took the family for a week on the Lancaster canal – one of those longboats. Nightmare it was – the kids were running riot and I couldn't steer to save me life. But we had one of these on the boat – for operating the locks – raise the sluice to let the water in or out – then you heave the gates open. The reason I know what it's called is I had to buy a new one from a chandler's.' He makes a face of resignation. 'One of the flippin' nippers decided to see what kind of splash the first one made.'

DS Jones is listening, but she is not diverted by his anecdote. She stares at the four items as if they comprise a bizarre game of Cluedo and she must solve the conundrum. She speaks quietly.

'Don't you think – he was intending to move the body?'

DS Leyton inhales. After a while he responds.

'What's the betting he watched Ennerdale last night?'

DS Jones looks at her colleague with alarm. The realisation strikes her that they have treated their finding – due to Skelgill's eagle-eyed scepticism – as a coded secret that only they could have unlocked. But one other person may also have been watching Ennerdale like a hawk. She leans two-handed on the rim of the luggage compartment and breathes heavily, a precursor to an action not yet quite determined – but she senses that her colleague is willing her to come to a decision – to take the lead. She reaches and lifts the heavy handle with one gloved hand.

'Let's show this to Mrs Gillerthwaite.'

'Good call, girl.'

They find the farmer banging about in her kitchen. The door is ajar and DS Leyton announces their arrival with a jovial hallo. However the woman backs away, regarding them suspiciously, staring at their blue-gloved hands as though they are aliens with a mission to perform some experiment upon her.

'There's bin above fifty hoggs reived in the dale this last week – I thought that were his game.' Her blurted defence delivered (a pre-emptive retort to an imagined accusation), now a hint of remorse enters her tone. 'How were I to know thee were staking out t' shotgun thief – come back just like thoo said he would.'

DS Jones – better versed in the local vernacular than her Cockney counterpart – understands the more obscure phraseology.

'Sheep stealing?'

'Aye – that's what I reckoned. What am I supposed to do – just stand by like a daft cuddy?'

The detectives do not exactly exchange glances, but they manage to convey to one another through subtle body language that they should not disavow the farmer of her misapprehension. And DS Leyton, for what he lacks in being countrywise is more than amply streetwise. He glances around to make it obvious he has noted the shotgun propped behind the door.

'Mrs Gillerthwaite – you're entitled to fire your own gun on your own land. That the trespasser in question had a puncture just as he passed you – well, seems a coincidence to me.'

274

He looks inquiringly at DS Jones – she nods hurriedly.

A sly expression crosses the farmer's features. Visibly, the tension drains from her wiry frame. DS Jones cashes in upon the credit they have banked. She holds out the windlass.

'Mrs Gillerthwaite – we have an urgent problem to solve. Can you shed any light on why he had this in his car?'

The woman steps closer, grimacing as if they were presenting her with some obscure species of vermin they have found dead on her land. And, accordingly, there are no signs of immediate recognition. But she carries on staring at the tool.

'He wo' coming down t' Iron Road like a bat out o' hell.'

DS Jones pounces upon her words.

'The *Iron Road?*'

'Aye – there's an arl mine up int' gill – Ironcove, me grandfather used to call it. It's fastened, like – wi' an iron gate.'

'Could this be the handle for the mechanism?'

'I'd be surprised if it weren't ceased up.' But now the sly look returns to her eyes. 'What if yon laddo's got a stash of stolen guns up there?'

The detectives look at one another; they are thinking otherwise. DS Leyton tries to sound casual.

'Mrs Gillerthwaite, could you point us in the right direction?'

'I'll take thee up ont' tractor.'

DS Leyton declines on the grounds that one accident they can explain away – any more could become problematic.

'Reet, then – I'll have a mash on for when the pair of thee come back.'

DS Jones is hoping an extra mug will be needed.

*

'This has gotta be it, Emma – see – the red colouring in the soil.'

'And the iron gate.'

They stand now in silence for a few moments as they contemplate the scene. The dawn wind has dropped completely to leave a calm autumn morning; there is an easterly chill in the air, and the mist has distributed itself evenly to create an all-pervasive ambience of smoky sunshine. DS Jones seems untroubled by the uphill hike; at her side DS Leyton is panting and perspiring. However, it is he that speaks.

'We ought to call a special unit if we intend to search an old mine. Even if we could get it open. These places are death traps.'

Yet they have come this far, and without consulting they pick their way through the tangled bracken to stand before the door. DS Leyton glares doubtfully at the rack and pinion mechanism.

'The Guvnor would know all about this – him and his mountain rescue malarkey. Where the heck's he got to?'

'I'll try him again.'

DS Jones is carrying the windlass. She hands it to her colleague and pulls out her phone. The signal is weak but present – one small benefit of gaining altitude in the fells; the higher one goes the greater the odds of connectivity. Deep in the dale, hard up against the hillside is always the worst position. As she calls and waits the pair turn and gaze out across Ennerdale – they neither of them know the fells like Skelgill, and could not put names to the ridge of summits: Haystacks, High Crag, High Stile and Red Pike, whence he last communicated.

Then both literally jump.

Close behind, a yard or two, invisible and seemingly emanating from a hidden loudspeaker in the iron door, is a melodic tune.

'That's your ringtone, girl!'

'Pardon?' But DS Jones is already moving to locate the source of the sound.

'That's the Guvnor's phone – the ringtone he uses for you. He must have dropped it.'

But DS Jones is on her knees and pulling at the loose bracken. Triumphantly she heaves away Skelgill's rucksack – rising and staggering a little backwards.

'Lor! He must have hidden it.'

DS Jones eyes her colleague questioningly.

'*Someone* must have hidden it – but I agree, it's the sort of thing he would do.'

She stares pensively at the bag, biting her bottom lip. She casts about, up the hillside – she can't think why Skelgill (who at times carries packs she can hardly raise off the ground) would leave this modest load behind. She looks at the gate. She notices the big rock – the ground is freshly scored where it has been shifted. She inspects the rust-encrusted mechanism more closely – it might superficially be corroded, but there is dark staining and the pungent odour of easing oil.

'He must have gone in. Piper must have lowered the metal plate.'

Pennies are dropping, too, for DS Leyton – and now he hesitates no longer. Brandishing the windlass he steps in beside her.

'This is just like a lock gate.'

He fits the larger of two square drive seats onto the shaft that protrudes from the toothed pinion. He gives it a trial push but nothing moves.

He takes a couple of paces backwards.

'It would be a sight easier to lower. Come down under its own weight.'

He spits on his hands and gathers himself and then suddenly charges with a rush of momentum and a bloodcurdling war cry – and the gate begins to rise. He keeps at it, heaving and grunting, his face becoming puce with the effort – and now he shouts to his colleague.

'Shove that rock under it, girl!'

DS Jones gets low and drives with her legs – and the stone slides into place.

DS Leyton winds back a fraction to rest the gate upon the boulder and test the stability of the arrangement.

They step away to survey their handiwork; DS Leyton is breathing heavily. He gives a shake of his head, of the sort acknowledging some kind of feat.

'Take a strong geezer to shift that.'

DS Jones looks at him, her eyes flashing admiration.

277

'You are!'

He waves away her words.

'Nah – what I mean to say – I was thinking of you trying to fight Piper – slip of a girl – fearless – stupid.' But before DS Jones can protest, her colleague sinks to all fours. 'Now it's my turn.'

She realises what he intends – and that he is about to exhibit bravery that would not be appreciated by those ignorant of his history, of heroism in a smoke-filled tunnel of the London Underground. He ducks his head beneath the iron door.

'Right – you give me a shove in the backside, girl.'

'No!'

She grabs hold of his belt and hauls him back. Still on his knees he puts his hands on his hips and is about to complain. She silences him.

'One of us needs to stay outside – to call for assistance if necessary. And for safety – you said it – I'm not strong enough to raise the gate.'

Now she switches her phone into torch mode – she directs it at him and grins wryly.

'Besides – it's my case, remember.'

But before DS Leyton can argue further they both freeze.

Faint, but distinct, there comes a voice – distant – but not from across the fell. *It emanates from inside the mine.*

They look at one another in consternation – as if for mutual confirmation that their imaginations are not at play.

DS Jones drops down to hands and knees and cries into the opening.

'Guv! It's us – hold on!'

And without further ado she crabs beneath the door and is on her feet.

Unlike the beam of Skelgill's tactical torch the light from her mobile phone is more diffuse and has an effective range of only five or six yards. She begins to step tentatively along the sleepers between the rails.

'Guv?'

278

Her questioning call is answered by a cry of "Here!" – and she realises that Skelgill is not far ahead. There is the sound of stones scattering and as she approaches she sees the explanation for his muffled voice. At a height of about five feet, above a rockfall, hands are pushing through a hole and clawing at the rubble. She closes in and directs her light on the spot.

'Guv!'

The hands are withdrawn and in the opening a head appears – hardly recognisable, with its dishevelled hair and its face coated in earth the colour of red ochre.

Then there is a flash of white teeth, which may be a grin – but looks more like a grimace.

'What kept you?'

DS Jones involuntarily emits a short hysterical laugh.

'Guv – are you hurt?'

'Piper – he was here. He could be about. You're not safe.'

That Skelgill does not answer directly, but instead gives this urgent warning tells DS Jones that he must be in one piece.

'Guv – we got him – we intercepted him driving down the mountain track. He's in custody.'

She sees the whites of Skelgill's eyes.

Then abruptly he disappears for a couple of seconds.

'Here – grab this – then you can pull us through. I'll take the rap from Forensics for handling it. It's small beer, now.'

He hands an item through the gap – she takes it and holds it at arm's length in the light from her phone.

She is still – and in the darkness a tear escapes and trickles down her cheek. Skelgill has recovered Lisa Jackson's shoulder bag.

She looks back at him; she sees he is watching her reaction in the eerie gloom.

She swallows as if the dust of the mine has parched her mouth.

'This is not all that's in there, is it, Guv?'

*

'What were you pair doing here?'

Skelgill might have prefaced his demand with, "At the risk of sounding ungrateful" – but it would not be his style.

'Did you not see my text, Guv?'

The three detectives are seated, left in privacy in the spacious kitchen of Gillerthwaite farm; the landowner, still not entirely apprised of what is afoot, has furnished them with a large pot of tea and a tin filled with generous squares of Ennerdale cake.

Skelgill shakes his head. DS Jones elaborates.

'The producer rang just after we'd spoken to you. She'd been called to a location shoot to approve something on the set. She asked if we could come this afternoon instead.'

But Skelgill is not so easily fobbed off. He swallows a gulp of tea.

'Aye – but this farm, I'm talking about. Not why you were early.'

Now his two sergeants exchange somewhat sheepish glances, and DS Leyton clears his throat.

'Blame me, Guv. Since we had time to kill I talked Emma into coming here – so's I could ask Mrs Gillerthwaite for her cake recipe – for the missus, like.'

Skelgill's clothing still bears evidence of his ordeal – although he has rinsed his hair under the cold tap of the Belfast sink, and his hands are clean and the tips of all but one of his fingers are wrapped in fresh sticking plaster, applied by DS Jones. This impediment is not hindering his consumption of cake. He cocks his head on one side to acknowledge the explanation.

DS Leyton takes advantage of his superior's acquiescence.

'More to the point, Guv – how come you ended up in the cave?'

Skelgill takes time over his mouthful – he seems to be making up his mind how much to tell; his manner has been rather subdued since their return.

'When I rang – when I was up Red Pike – I'd spotted the mine and cross-referenced it with my old map and the current OS. I've always thought Piper would play to his strengths.' He

280

looks at DS Jones. 'And you always thought he would drive to the spot.'

She is nodding.

'I think you're right about him burning his maps, Guv.'

'Aye. I reckon he knew exactly where he was coming.'

DS Jones is quick to develop the hypothesis.

'The handle – the windlass. It seems it's easy enough to get hold of such a thing.' She looks at DS Leyton for corroboration. He nods. 'But it's not a regular tool. That Ray Piper possessed it in the very first place – it suggests he had some plan beforehand. It suggests premeditation.' She takes a deep breath. 'You know, we never were in a position to save Lisa Jackson – but I can't help feeling that Lisa Jackson might have saved Irene Piper.'

This is a construction beyond both Skelgill and DS Leyton – and they look at their colleague with bewilderment. But only she has properly encountered Ray Piper's downtrodden wife and formed some kind of tenuous bond with her, of empathy, of understanding, of something deeper, even. Now she offers a forthright explanation.

'Piper wanted to be with Lisa, didn't he? That's why he killed her – consumed by possessive jealousy.'

No one seems to wish to contest this assertion; despite its paradoxical nature, it sits with the chilling notion that Ray Piper intended such a fate for his wife. There ensue a few moments' brooding silence before DS Leyton taps the table with the flat of his hand.

'It does look like he was spooked by watching Ennerdale.'

DS Jones seems relieved that the pressure is relieved; she explains to Skelgill.

'I spoke to Irene Piper earlier – until last night Ray Piper hadn't mentioned his supposed job interview at Sellafield this morning. She said he was agitated – but he told her he was nervous about the meeting. I think there is no doubt that he was panicked into moving Lisa's remains.'

Skelgill is looking discontented, and perhaps she senses something of his chagrin – that his impetuous solo effort contained potentially catastrophic procedural holes. She regards him consolingly.

'If you hadn't tracked him down, Guv – he might have got away with that.'

But Skelgill is still troubled by the affront – that he was caught out and left for dead – or, worse, it seems to him, left to perish in the tomb, like an Egyptian slave condemned with his goddess queen. He would like to know how personally he should take it – was Ray Piper aware of his identity, or did he just think it was an inquisitive fellwalker, or a potholer doing a recce? All the more chilling, in its own way.

'I reckon I'd have got out of there.'

His response confirms to his colleague that his pride is bruised; again she highlights the positive.

'It was a smart move to hide your rucksack with your phone.'

But DS Leyton cannot resist a friendly jibe.

'*Hah* – lucky you had a signal for once, Guv!'

There is sufficient irony in his tone that even Skelgill laughs, a tacit admission of his foible. After all, this is not an inquest into a failure, but a celebration of success. While his guard is down, DS Jones takes the opportunity to raise a related query.

'Is that Hot Chocolate, Guv?'

Skelgill regards her with bafflement.

'It's tea – you poured it.'

'No – I mean the ringtone when I called your number. Hot Chocolate, the soul band.'

It is Skelgill's turn to look sheepish, and a flush appears on his prominent cheekbones.

But before this awkward silence can become a pregnant pause, DS Leyton begins fiddling with his own mobile phone. Then Skelgill's, which is lying upon the table, suddenly bursts into sound: it is the Lambeth Walk.

'Aha!' DS Leyton points at Skelgill accusingly. 'We never phone you when we're with you – but it's all coming out now!'

And without further ado the amply proportioned sergeant slips out of his chair and circles the table, strutting in remarkably good step with the music.

282

'Leyton, you donnat!'

'Can't help it, Guv – it's like standing for the national anthem.'

Their collective mood is lightening. The traumas they have each endured are turning through relief to exhilaration. Of course, the final confirmation of the fate of Lisa Jackson, and thoughts of her parents mean their mission is tinged with sadness – for DS Jones perhaps more so than her work-hardened colleagues – but this is mitigated by their professional training and the knowledge that Ray Piper will now spend the rest of his life behind bars, despite that there can be no equivalence for the harm he has caused. Unnecessary now, but one small missing piece of the jigsaw came to light a little earlier, when DC Watson appeared with evidence bags containing red-mud-encrusted wellingtons and calf leather driving gloves, found by the search team hidden beneath rocks near the gateway to Gillerthwaite farm.

DS Leyton, his routine complete, resumes his seat.

'As a matter of interest, Guv – what tune do you have programmed in for the Chief?'

'Rolling Stones.'

'I Can't Get No Satisfaction?'

'Very funny, Leyton.' Skelgill shrugs resignedly; he realises he must come clean. 'Get Off Of My Cloud.'

His colleagues chuckle – but for DS Jones, especially, these revelations offer a peep beneath his veneer of taciturnity. And she is touched by his choice of the track that bears her name. Spontaneously she reaches towards him and brushes away an unwashed smudge of earth from beneath his hairline.

'You looked like one of the Redmen, Guv.'

She plies him with an engaging smile.

Skelgill does not flinch – but there is a sudden vulnerability in his grey-green eyes that perhaps only DS Jones detects.

He stretches with a groan, pushing his hands out in front of him and spreading his fingers – displaying the plasters that protect his damaged nails and fingertips. Then he casts his gaze upon DS Leyton's bandaged fist.

'I envy you your punch, Leyton.'

DS Leyton reacts rather implacably.

'The paramedic told me to get a tetanus injection – I'm allergic to flippin' needles.'

Again, they all three laugh – DS Leyton is infamous for his 'allergies' – here is a new addition to the list.

Skelgill jerks his thumb to indicate towards the farmhouse kitchen door, where the Baikal 12-bore is propped up.

'Pity you never solved those shotgun thefts, Leyton. That would be the icing on the cake.'

DS Leyton nods; his expression perhaps tends towards that of the good loser, but his tone reveals a certain determination.

'It ain't over until the fat lady sings, Guv.' Then he pats his shirt pocket, where he has placed a precious scribbled note. 'But at least in the meantime I got the secret recipe.'

At this DS Jones passes round the tin, and both of her colleagues take another square. She tops up their teas and then helps herself to a slice. DS Leyton raises an eyebrow.

'That's some appetite you've built up, Emma. Though I can't say I'm surprised.'

DS Jones grins.

'Actually, on that note – I, er – thought it should fall to me – ' She hesitates for a moment. She winks surreptitiously at DS Leyton and then turns to Skelgill. 'You know – Team, Task and Individual? I've booked us a table at the Taj Mahal tonight. My treat to the team, a task well done.'

That she skirts around the 'Individual' aspect is of no matter, for Skelgill seems positively interested – but DS Leyton cannot hide a face of disappointment.

'Thing is, Emma – after last night's interruptions – I promised the missus I'd bring back a Chinese takeaway and we'd watch the recording properly – before tonight's episode comes on.'

DS Jones is sympathetic to her colleague's plight – what with his wife being such a big fan – they did totally disrupt his five minutes of fame.

'Why don't you just come for a drink in the bar while you're waiting for your order – it's right next door?'

DS Leyton nods enthusiastically.

'Good call – I can fill up on that there Bombay mix – you know how one Chinese meal is never enough!'

Skelgill's expression has become somewhat introspective. Now he interjects.

'It's been your case, lass – and you've come through with flying colours – but I'm pulling rank. I'll pick up the tab. Indian and Chinese. Chuck in some ice cream for the bairns, Leyton – keep them quiet while you watch the telly. Tell them I said you're to report back on their behaviour, if they want to come fishing.'

'Wilco, Guv.'

Skelgill, somewhat blithely, turns to DS Jones.

'Sure you don't want to invite your pal Minto along – now there's a spare seat?'

She regards him reprovingly.

'Guv – there are times when three's a crowd.'

Postscript

Excerpt from an article in the Westmorland Gazette, by Kendall Minto

COPS NAIL GUN GANG

In a fascinating corollary to the solving of the disappearance and murder of Carlisle resident Lisa Jackson, Cumbria CID have scored a second coup by smashing an organised crime ring that preyed upon isolated farmsteads.

Regular readers of this column will recall that murder suspect Ray Piper was finally unmasked when detectives identified his distinctive white BMW car in location footage of the popular TV soap opera, Ennerdale (who would have guessed that our police are such ardent fans!).

And when officers analysed the hours of unused footage – known in the film business as the 'rushes' – they discovered a vital piece of evidence in relation to an unrelated case.

Stated Detective Sergeant Leyton, who handled this aspect of the investigation:

"The white BMW wasn't the only vehicle in Ennerdale that Saturday morning. A van clearly marked in the livery of Cumbria Water was also caught on camera. We were able to read the rooftop ID number. We wished to speak with the driver as a possible witness – in fact we wondered why he had not come forward, given the publicity at the time. But when we contacted Cumbria Water they had no record of one of their employees being in the vicinity."

Thus it emerged that Pipeline Inspection Engineer Stephen Flood, 39, ran a profitable and sinister sideline. His job took him to obscure rural locations with access to remote farms. Under the guise of a Cumbria Water inspector his presence did not attract undue attention. Flood has admitted to more than a dozen counts of theft – he specialised in stealing shotguns, which he sold to a well-known Workington fence, career criminal,

George Pickett. Pickett, 56, was arrested and charged and, having entered a plea of not guilty, is due to appear at Carlisle Crown Court next month.

Following a high-profile setback for the Cumbria force earlier in the year, such sleuthing wins have restored faith in our 'boys in blue' – if the outmoded idiom will be forgiven by your humble correspondent's former schoolmate – that is to say local Detective Sergeant Emma Jones, whose incisive and painstaking work underpinned the case against killer Ray Piper. We at the Gazette look forward to reporting on more of her and her colleagues' crime-busting successes.

***

Next in the series ...

Murder at the Falls is scheduled for publication in July 2021. In the meantime, books 1-15 in the Inspector Skelgill series can be found on Amazon. Each comprises a stand-alone mystery, and may be read out of sequence. All DI Skelgill books can be borrowed free with Kindle Unlimited, and also by Amazon Prime members on a Kindle device.

Printed in Great Britain
by Amazon